Dear Mellic & Tom

HOUSE OF
TWENTY-TWO
BUFFALOS

HOUSE OF TWENTY-TWO BUFFALOS

JAHED RAHMAN

To order additional copies of this book, contact:
Xlibris
1-888-795-4274
www.Xlibris.com
Orders@Xlibris.com
766235

Contents

Confession.. ix

Canvas..1

Commotion 36

Confluence 58

Concordance 70

Conjure...80

Convulsion 104

Conversion 141

Conjunction...159

Catastrophe 173

Challenge 191

Complications 206

Circumspection 223

Conciliation..242

Compendium...279

Culmination 325

To my dear parents,

Jahan Ara Begum and Sayedur Rahman

Confession

Life palpably is a journey with unforeseen turns and an unknown end point. While the latter is absolutely beyond maneuvering by earthly forces, the former bears all the attributes of yearnings, potentials, competitiveness, contrasts, and diversions resulting in frustrations and happiness based on outcomes. The customary reflex finds space for frustration to bad augury, while happiness basks in an individual sense of competence. But some outcomes may remain neutral to either of these instincts. They may not be relevant to larger social environment but still may stimulate immeasurable glee in oneself. I presently find myself in this phase of experience in almost a spherical round of life.

My childhood and the initial growing-up phase of my life had penchants for stagy activities besides the norm for academic pursuits. In my early youth, the focus remained mostly the same with a veiled yearning for excellence in cultural and entertainment activities. That was gradually changed with exposure and experience. In the larger gamut of prevailing social setting and limited opportunities, a predominant urge to establish self in tandem with security and recognition engulfed me. That made me land in the most coveted inner casing of social and professional life of the time. I, in my youth, thus joyfully became a member of the most structured fraternity, otherwise known as civil service.

Pounding needs and other compulsions propelled a major change in life passage, mooring me with hedonism and exhilaration in international financial institutions. Social issues having direct bearings on development objectives and challenges of developing countries increasingly became the center of my professional thinking and engagements. I thought of no other interest in life.

Leading a lonely retired life in the unknown setting of Chicago after hectic social interactions and having features of involved rapports with the Bangladeshi community of Vancouver, I ventured on documenting my life. The simple objective was to ensure that my multicultural generations following me have a reference point as to their root—if one is so interested. The other reason was to remain engaged in life.

That eventually took the shape of a book titled *Bends and Shades*.

The publication of that book had premised itself as an outcome of one's effort—though not a writer. Many of my limited readers group had kind words about my first publication. That encouraged me to write a second book of fiction titled *Indu* the following year. The emphasis continued to be the product of someone who is not a writer.

The completion of the second publication made me elated about writing. It soon became an integral part of my life and my living a retired life in Chicago, even though my social contacts, both with younger generations of Bangladesh origin and those of black and white communities, propelled.

In tandem with the turns and events that I experienced, I started scanning the social settings around me so far. The one I noted most was the unwritten penchant in Bangladesh for a family good name, traditions, and related values in combination with the determination to resist changes in any of those elements. That was and has partly been in vogue until now.

My third publication, titled *House of Twenty-Two Buffalo*s, is an outcome of that experience. It highlights the up-front common tendency of negation with anything new or noble by so-called aristocratic families and highlights the larger fear of social vulnerability. The reality, however, is that with the passage of time, some of those are unknowingly integrated as part of family values with unnoticed lapses of time and an unlamented loss of warmth in relationships. Society also mutely accepts many changes eventually. My third publication portrays such phenomena.

I still maintain that I am not a writer. I write for my own pleasure and happiness. It helps me remain intellectually active and enjoy the fragrance of the wee years of my remaining life. I seek the understanding of my readers.

Jahed Rahman

Canvas

Apurba Neer is an upscale habitation in Northwestern Bangladesh. No one around has any clue as to when, how, or by whom this place had been adorned with such a distinguished and refined Bangla name. Normally, the naming of villages or neighborhoods in and around Bangladesh is sporadically done without much attention to meaning or sophistication. Some places have their names without any root or relevance. With names of surrounding habitations like Ghutuma, Shoylla, Hua Danga, Bancharampur, Bhanga, Hulia, etc., Apurba Neer means "unique abode." Transparent as a name of a habitation, it is sufficient to provoke inquisitiveness in one who is prone. That has not been the case with either the inhabitants or neighbors. The exceptionality of the name gradually lost its importance with the passage of time and became one among many.

Various homes in Apurba Neer, like many others in the area, are identified by the title the original homeowners had and are so known for generations. Houses are known as Mia Bari, Kazi Bari, Chowdhury Bari, Mojundar Bari, Master Bari, Thakur Bari, Pondit Bari, and so on. The first part of the title reflects the original owner's occupation or profession, and the second part means "home." The identity of these houses is so continued for generations.

There was a prominent exception: a house with the identity of Biesh Moisher Bari (House of Twenty-Two Buffalos). The great-grandfather of the current resident, Kazi Azmat Ali Shoudagar, had owned twenty-two buffalos which was a symbolic possession at the time, reflecting wealth and influence. The present resident has no connection with buffalo, but the identity of the family's abode continues as Biesh Moisher Bari. Even the impressive title of *kazi*—or the success in business of the current owner (as evident by the much-revered local title of *shoudagar,* meaning a wholesaler of standing) has had no bearing in identifying the house.

Though Islam, as a religion, is primarily premised on an egalitarian social structure, some discernible attributes of class concepts gradually penetrated in the determination of the communal standing of Muslim families in pre-1947 India. Certain elements of this had roots in a land administration system beginning with the reign of Mogul Emperor Akbar and subsequently became more prominent during British colonial rule. The land administration policy, based on a feudal *zamindari* (landlord) arrangement, systematically divided the society into lords (owners of land) and commoners (users of land). People having control of land were, thus, venerated. They enjoyed higher social standings than others, irrespective of success otherwise. Apurba Neer and its surroundings were no exceptions.

The continued identification of his homestead as Biesh Moisher Bari, in spite of a rather successful and rewarding life, was a sore point for Kazi Azmat Ali Shoudagar. He maneuvered in every possible way to shun this disadvantage on a path to social progression. Kazi Azmat Ali Shoudagar especially tried to achieve this while finalizing the marriage propositions of his three elder daughters. He had success in every case, but the outcome was modest compared with the lavish money he spent having relationships with the relatively higher echelons in society.

A very welcome opening happened when the eldest son of Kazi Azmat Ali Shoudagar passed his secondary school certificate examination with distinction. Every one of the residents of Biesh Moisher Bari was happy—sweets were distributed among neighbors and friends; feasts were arranged for relations; and extensive preparation was being made through a consultation process for sending the successful young man, Kazi Tanveer Ali, to the college located at the district headquarters.

There were two exceptions. One was Hashi Banu, Tanveer's mother. Her exception was partly because of frequent pregnancies (numbering ten from an early age), experiencing two miscarriages and three infants' deaths, a lack of understanding about the dietary needs of a mother (both during pregnancy and after delivery), and deficiencies in post-delivery care, as well as the apathetic attitude of Kazi Azmat Ali Shoudagar—like most husbands of the time—about the health status of his wife. Hashi Banu gradually fell prey to a childbirth-related illness locally called *shutika*. Current references suggest that there is no biomedical equivalent of this disease. The disease *shutika* locally derived its name from the Bangla word *shuta* (thread) as patients steadily become thin like thread.

As a chronic patient, Hashi Banu was mostly confined in her bedroom and developed a syndrome of obsessive cleaning disorder, known locally as *chu chi baiu*. To the staggered astonishment of Kazi Azmat Ali Shoudagar and expressed surprise of others, however, she exercised full control on matters related to inner courtyard chores and responsibilities. It was her domain to decide on the minutest matters pertaining to running a large family. Included were decisions on specific daily responsibilities of the household help, principal items to be served each day during lunch and dinner, the making of *moushumi pitah*s (seasonal rice powder–based cakes), medleys of snack and food items to be served to guests, and so on. With all these responsibilities, she had the most loyal and effectual support of her personal household help, Pori. As per tradition, Pori accompanied Hashi Banu when she first arrived as the new daughter-in-law of Biesh Moisher Bari. Thirteen-year-old Pori was the obvious choice of Hashi Banu's parents to accompany her on her maiden journey to her new home—to help Hashi Banu in getting inducted in a totally new setting and among unknown faces. Pori grew up in the family setting of Hashi Banu as the offspring of one of the household staff. Besides being smart with avowed practical sense, Pori had the innate proven ability to assess individuals. She was slightly younger than Hashi Banu, and though the offspring of household help, they had a very friendly relationship.

As marriages of earlier times were usually arranged between two unknown families and two unfamiliar individuals, tradition dictated that daughter be sent to her in-laws' place for the first time in the company of one who could usher her in the new locale without encountering any hitch or embarrassment. It was also a status symbol to have personal help at the time. The practice was also premised on the culture of some relatively less friendly exchanges, initially between newlywed couples. Grooms usually stayed outside, among relatives with daytime visits of shorter durations to his assigned accommodation. The new bride, dressed formally, would slowly be introduced to female family members and community friends, with an incessant showering of advice from seniors, like the mother-in-law, or elder sisters of the groom and others deserving that sort of status. Escorts like Pori had a delicate role in discharging the unspecified but imperative responsibilities. Besides having the implicit burden of representing the decency and honor of the bride's family, such escorts had the onerous job of winning over the heart and confidence of female members of the groom's family to ensure a smooth transition of the new bride. Coyness in communication, acquiescence in attitude, and reticence in contacts were some of the values that new bride was supposed to have. In a simple expression, the bride was supposed to be decorous in social interactions. In that sort of social setting and those expectations, such escorts play an imperative role in privately briefing the new bride about female members of the family, the relationships, and personal traits so the bride can interact with the new faces and avoid any gaffe. The escort also acted as the initial guide to help the new bride in identifying physical facilities like the latrine—generally located quite far away from the main house, the kitchen, the pond, and the washing place. For the sake of comfort and a feeling of ease, the new bride was to be escorted to all such places. Tradition dictated that such an escort should accompany the new bride during her return trip to her parental home. This is called *firani* (return of the daughter with her husband) and generally is scheduled within the first few days of the wedding, following the completion of *walima* (*bou bhat*), the reception in honor of the new bride at her in-laws'. Besides the sharing of good news concerning the congeniality of the bride's new home and conjugal bliss, *firani* is also used as opportunity for better familiarization of the groom with his in-laws.

Pori returned home along with Hashi Banu as *firani* entourage. Her job as escort was successfully accomplished. The family was relieved to know from the son-in-law, Kazi Azmat Ali, that Pori, despite her youth, was of significant help to Hashi Banu in getting used to the new surroundings. More importantly, sheer wit and fulfilling behavior attributes made Pori a very likeable individual in the family. Besides assisting Hashi Banu, she also took over a lot of daily chores from his family members. That made all happy.

Kazi Azmat Ali took everyone by surprise with his follow-up statement during a family gathering. He said, "All my sisters are married, and they are scheduled to leave for their respective homes soon after we return. My mother is relatively old. I will remain busy with business. We do not have anyone in our home to give Hashi Banu much-needed camaraderie. Moreover, our home has an isolated location encompassing a sizeable area with no immediate habitation. As you are aware, our homestead has a generations-old explicit arrangement of inheritance, clearly and unalterably stipulated by my great-grandfather. The home he so dearly built with a big pond and numerous trees is not to be divided among offspring of the succeeding family, according to the Muslim law of inheritance. The eldest will stay, and the others will move out to separate homes with a stipulated share of the family assets. Thus, there is no other family in our Biesh Moisher Bari. The life for Hashi in that setting will be droning on and uninspiring, especially coming from a large family such as of yours. So I have both a suggestion and a request. In observing the bond between Hashi and Pori and noting her sense of propriety in social communication and behavior, I suggest you consider sending Pori to our home for an initial period. If she likes and Hashi agrees, Pori can stay in our place permanently, and both Hashi and I will take full responsibility of Pori's future life."

Everyone present was taken aback by a most unexpected proposition from the new son-in-law. They were unsure about a proper response to such a proposition and were exchanging looks. Hashi remained nonchalant. Based on the last few nights' exchanges and experience, she had total trust in whatever her husband had in mind.

Son-in-law Azmat Ali was definitely better endowed, intelligent, and smarter than most of the assembled gentries. He quietly glanced and noted the expressions of his new relatives and politely said, "I understand related anxieties that might agitate your thoughts and mind against the backdrop of my proposition. I would,

therefore, like to clarify some of them, from my perspective, and
then you can decide as you consider appropriate, and that will be
acceptable to me. First, I am not proposing to take Pori as a *bandi*
[maid]. She will be in our home as help and a companion to Hashi, a
trusted person, ensuring compliance with the desires and directives
of Hashi. That will enable Hashi to maintain a space in contacts
with other household helps. All of us have observed Pori during her
short stay in our home, and the general consensus was that it would
be a good idea. Even my mother specifically advised me to discuss
the proposition with you all, so rest assured that it has the approval
of my family. Second, Hashi will have total jurisdiction on matters
concerning Pori. I will have no involvement except one. That concerns
the on-time settlement of Pori in life in a befitting manner. That
responsibility, I plan to discharge with the full concurrence of Hashi.
Third, there may be the issue of Pori's separation from her family
and parents. Whenever Hashi visits, Pori will accompany her. Pori's
parents can visit her in our home. We have good accommodations
to keep such guests. And fourth, you can, if so preferred, ask Hashi
about her comfort zone with my proposition. I did not intentionally
discuss this with Hashi before. So this is a surprise to her too. To
ensure optimum flexibility in decision making, I am going out, and
you can let me know later."

There was no need for much thought. Most of the apparent
anxieties had already been addressed by this son-in-law. Everyone
was impressed with the sense of propriety demonstrated, and the
bride's parents were happy to note that their daughter was slated to
have a solid life partner. Hashi's concurrence was evident from her
body language. The decision patently was in the affirmative. It was
easy to get the consent of Pori's parents as they were tenant farmers
of Hashi's parents, dependent on them for most things of their life.
Her bond with the new family life of Hashi was sealed as they left
for their new home after *firani*.

Subsequent events of Pori's life progressed as stipulated,
including her marriage with the trustworthy staff of Azmat Ali's
business, Badsha, with the full presence of Pori's family and with
no effort spared for a blissful wedding. Fulfilling his promise and in

consultation with Hashi, the family of Azmat Ali presented the new couple a small piece of land adjacent to their home and built a modest home as a wedding gift. Though she moved out after the wedding, Pori continued to be part and parcel of Hashi's home between sunrise and sunset, fulfilling obligations per her earlier practice. Because of this and the slowly deteriorating health status of Hashi, caused by frequent pregnancies and stress, it became the inevitable routine duty of Pori to take care of raising the children in the family. In spite of having two children of her own, Pori carried out that responsibility. With their father busy in expanding his business and their mother handicapped because of recurrent indisposition, it was Pori who was the contact of reference for everything in life, either needed or aspired to by the children: three daughters and two sons. Pori built up a caring and deep-rooted emotional bond with Hashi's children, more particularly her two younger sons. To all of them, Pori was their Pori Khala (aunt), without any jealousy of other compatriots. As an offshoot of that, Badsha, Pori's husband, soon became Badsha Chacha (uncle) to all the children. This spoke of the position and reflected the esteem that Pori and Badsha enjoyed in the family of Kazi Azmat Ali Shoudagar and Hashi Banu.

Tanveer's impending departure for higher-level education in the district headquarters–based college was a matter of common concern and intense stress for both Hashi Banu and Pori. That disquiet engulfed all hands-on matters and hypothetical issues related to independent living, with specific focus on type and taste of food, the fixing of the bed in the morning and mosquito net at night, security matters, and the like. Both mother and aunt suffered equally. In a family setting, like most families of the time, where decisions of the husband only mattered and were final, the lingering wretchedness of both Hashi and Pori were confined to periodical long and expressive deep breathing and occasional howling. That did not escape Kazi Azmat Ali's notice. To divert Hashi Banu's attention from matters concerning the imminent departure of Tanveer, and in his typical way, Kazi Azmat Ali Shoudagar suddenly decided to have a *jayafat* (mass feeding involving neighbors, relations, and socially relevant others in which people are usually invited as groups, and whoever comes is welcome to have food). This was astutely arranged just before the day Tanveer was slated to leave.

It had been the habit of Kazi Azmat Ali Shoudagar to chew *paan* during states of happiness and stress in his life. *Paan*, both as a whole betel leaf or carved, is prepared with sliced betel nuts, the white lime paste of the shells, and other accessories to release the aroma when chewed.

Kazi Azmat Ali was very happy with all arrangements pertaining to the organization and service of the *jayafat*. As he was about to put a *paan*, meticulously prepared by Hashi Banu to his liking, in his mouth, the familiar face of *ghattak* (traditional matchmaker) Bakshi Mia showed up unexpectedly with his trademark full-mouth smile. Bakshi Mia, wearing a traditional outfit known as a *punjabi* (long-flowing shirt), a white cotton *tupi* (headgear) covering his bald head, and a longish flowing modest white beard from around the area of jaw only gracing his face, with a folded umbrella under his armpit, bent the upper portion of his fragile body to show respect in a traditional manner and politely said, "Salaam alaikum" (local Muslim way of greeting, meaning "peace be upon you").

Bakshi Mia was known to Kazi Azmat Ali for many years, and that association benefitted him enormously in arranging all three marriages of his daughters to a relatively upper stratum of the society. That was a priority of Kazi Azmat Ali as he was not always comfortable with the only evidence of his business success being the tacit title of *shoudagar*. He continually missed a dynastic link with respect to his roots, as those enjoyed by revered local Muslim families generally known as Khans, Chowdhurys, and Mojundars. The identity of his house, known as Biesh Moisher Bari, despite his own business success, bothered him as it was a living testimony of his forefathers' farming background.

Hashi Banu tried to change this attitude of Kazi Azmat Ali but failed, even though most of the time he agreed with his spouse and showed respect to her wishes. He perceptibly acted to make her happy. With such a psyche, Kazi Azmat Ali always maintained a strict sense of propriety, distancing himself in social interactions with ordinary folks. This was the reason why instead of personally getting involved, he oversaw the conduct of *jayafat* from a distance, reclining in an easy chair. This was also the reason why Kazi Azmat Ali refrained from unreservedly welcoming Bakshi Mia despite his unexpected presence making him happy. Against such a backdrop, Kazi Azmat Ali's response to a most revered "Salaam alaikum" from Bakshi Mia was the noncommunicative expression of "Hmmm."

Bakshi Mia was not thwarted by such a cold response. Through the process of arranging the marriages of three daughters, Bakshi Mia knew Kazi Azmat Ali very well and was quite familiar with his gesticulations. Bakshi Mia did not give up and continued looking at Kazi Azmat Ali with all reverence for an affirmative signal to continue typical conversation. Coolness to ordinary folks was definitely an attribute of Kazi Azmat Ali's outside bearing, but he was certainly not a rude person.

After a hiatus manifesting reclusiveness, he looked back at Bakshi Mia and affectionately asked, "Ki khobor [What's up], BM?"—an abbreviation Kazi Azmat Ali always used in addressing Bakshi Mia while in a good mood.

BM was happy and relieved. In his own roundabout way of conducting discourse, BM initiated the conversation, saying, "Hujur [Sir], ai odhomer ar ki kobhor thakbey [what news this wretched fellow would have]. My whole life has been spent traveling from village to village, from house to house, in facilitating matrimonial relationships and guarding the sensitivities of various unknown families. Most of the outcomes, as you know, Hujur, from your own experience, are very positive. Ma sha Allah [By the grace of God], all three of your daughters are so happily placed in their respective lives. The resultant enhanced demand as a *ghattak* has precluded my occasional yearning to get out of this profession."

BM paused for a while and looked at Kazi Azmat Ali to ascertain his attention and reaction. Surprised by the momentary break in BM's rambling, Kazi Azmat Ali slowly opened his closed eyes, held the sides of his easy chair, looked at BM, and reacted with another "Hmmm."

BM took that as a positive sign to continue. He was familiar with the swinging mood of Kazi Azmat Ali, knowing that anything could prompt him to snap off any time, especially family-related discussions or other deliberations not of his liking. BM thought of the strategy of directly communicating the agenda he had in mind and to be explicit, but he just could not do so. It had always been his style and penchant to put forward propositions in a roundabout manner. He continued, saying, "Oh, I heard the astounding news of Shoudagarjada [sons of Muslim rulers were addressed as *shahjada*, so to show respect to the son of a *shoudagar* and following that practice, BM coined the address of *shoudagarjada*] Tanveer's success in his board-conducted examination. I just could not stop but to come here to congratulate him and you. However, on my way to Apurba Neer, something came to my mind. If Hujur permits me, I would like to place that for gracious consideration."

With those words, BM stopped, waiting for a much-desired affirmative signal. Kazi Azmat Ali closed his eyes and put both his palms behind his head and took a reclined position on the backrest of his easy chair. More as innate inquisitiveness, he was trying to guess the mind of BM, but he did not get that much time.

Without waiting for the affirmative indication from Kazi Azmat Ali, BM continued his polite submission, saying, "Shoudagarjada is now about eighteen years old. At this age, young people, as Hujur is aware, are emotionally very unstable. That is aggravated both in terms of impact and consequences if such a person resides far away from family and in a setting like a town with open options. There is, thus, a need for forward-looking prudent decisions to ensure that the honor and dignity of traditional Biesh Moisher Bari, so painstakingly and conscientiously upheld by your predecessors and bloated by you, be preserved and passed on to succeeding generations."

That was a unique indication by a person whom Kazi Azmat Ali had always considered a half-lettered bizarre village personality with, however, special acumen in piloting marriage propositions. He was startled by the implication BM had hinted and felt embarrassed that it did not occur to him earlier.

While Kazi Azmat Ali was momentarily engrossed with related thoughts, BM continued the succulent part of his statement, stating, "As I was coming to your place, a thought engulfed my mind. I came to the conclusion that a marriage proposition may merit your consideration. I have a very pleasing proposition in mind."

As a maneuvering strategy that he had mastered during the long process of pursuing his career and the resultant experience of being a successful *ghattak*, BM deliberately provided some space to Kazi Azmat Ali to internally deliberate his suggestion. He always ensured that his benefactors take the decision he wanted but with the feeling that they had made it. In this case, he pursued the same strategy. And he was not wrong.

Kazi Azmat Ali leisurely opened his eyes, looked at BM, and commented, "Tanveer is still young. Is it not too early?"

That was exactly the type of opening BM was hoping for. As if he had a dress rehearsal, he very promptly responded with due diligence and diction, "Hujur, this particular age is the real problem. Had Shoudagarjada been three to four years older, I would not have proposed this. Young people in this age bracket are very unstable mentally and, for no fault of theirs, remain vulnerable to unspecified allurements in the absence of kith and kin and real friends around. This setting of towns has plenty of such unwelcome options. It has often been noted that the feeling of attachment to family of some young person is significantly impacted upon when left on their own.

"Moreover, you have worked so hard to expand your business. Even though you still carry the title of *shoudagar*, your reputation as a decent man of prudence travels far beyond as a construction pioneer and the owner of the most reputable brickfield in the area. These are to be preserved and further expanded. Because of all these reasons, I thought of a marriage proposition for Shoudagarjada. If you give some thought to my suggestion, you would definitely be assured of inherent positivity. Once he is married, the scope of diversion in an independent setting will be minimal. The face of a new bride at home will keep him close to family locale, values, and associated responsibilities. Begum Shaheeba [Mrs.] will also feel relaxed and happy."

It was time for Kazi Azmat Ali to be dazed by BM's reasoning, whom he thought to be a talkative village guy. He gave serious thought to what was eluded to and concluded that perhaps it was prudent to consider the suggestion, but he was not inclined to agree immediately with BM, which could cause an inflated ego. Kazi Azmat Ali had always been extra conscious of his prestige and sense of self-esteem, a trait of character perhaps inherited. He preferred to play with the present proposition as he did during the marriage proposals earlier of his three daughters. His strategy was to have a designed gap between BM's propositions and his decisions, demonstrating to all concerned that his decision predicated the final arrangement.

To create a perceived obstacle in moving forward with the suggestion, Kazi Azmat Ali told BM, "What you suggested is in my mind too. That has had been a thought within, and so I did not tell anyone. But the issue is that there is no good proposition to my knowledge."

That was precisely the type of aperture BM was looking for. Based on experiences of dealing with Kazi Azmat Ali, he concluded that the *shoudagar* had fallen in line. Instead of losing any time, BM laid out his ultimate proposition, "Hujur, Shoudagarjada is your son. We have seen him growing up. People like me, who grew up under your shadow and care, have special feelings for your family, particularly for your offspring. I have always wished them well. I will do everything to ensure that he has a successful and happy married life. Because of such feelings, I rushed to your place with a specific proposal. If you would permit, I can tell you."

By moving his head, Kazi Azmat Ali conveyed his acquiescence.

BM continued. "Few days back, Janab [a respectful Muslim salutation] Mansoor Shafiul Alam Khan, great grandson of Khan Bahadur Abdur Raheem Khan of Nobi Nagar, sent a messenger to me, asking an immediate visit to his abode. I was taken by surprise. I would never think that such a request would ever be made by the *monzeel* [semi-palatial house] of Khanbahadur. Normally, their message to people like us, as you are aware, carries all the elements of a command."

The identity of a house as Khanbahadur Monzeel carried a special significance in the prevailing social scenery. *Khanbahadur* is a derivative of two different words: *khan* and *bahadur*, having relative commonality as to their roots. The word *khan*'s root is in Persian and Sanskrit and was the revered title of a landlord or town chief. It also is purported to be closely related to Sogdian (Eastern Iranian) words *khana* and *khanva*, meaning "chief." *Khan* was also used as a surname in many parts of Central Asia and Mongolia. The word *bahadur* symbolizes valor and authority. Like the word *khan*, it has roots in Hindi and Persian, with some similarity with the Mongolian word *bayatur*. The conjunctive word *khanbahadur* was used by the British government to recognize loyalty and as a title conveying respect to influential Muslim Indian subjects.

As was his style of communication, BM resumed his narration by saying, "The implicit premonition emanating from this message was bewildering for me. The messenger, however, was very helpful in lessening my apprehensions. Straightaway, I went to the Khanbahadur Monzeel, which is a living testament of past power and glory. What impressed me most was that notwithstanding current tumbledown conditions, the house excelled in decency, hospitality, and manners. For a person of my stratum, both the initial reception and hospitality were unthinkable. I enjoyed it, but a sense of predicament shrouded my thought and mental ease."

Kazi Azmat Ali continued to maintain his ascetic outward stance but kept his eyes closed.

BM took that as a positive sign and indication of interest in matters he was detailing. He continued, stating, "I was called in the *kachari khana* [formal meeting place] soon after the *magreeb* [Muslim prayer at sunset]. I saw for the first time Janab Mansoor Shafiul Alam Khan from a distance as I was shown a chair to take seat. There were a number of other people. Through physical gesture, I conveyed my *salaam* [greeting] to respected Mansoor Shafiul Alam Khan Shaheeb, the response to which was the soft movement of the front end of the flexible tube of his aristocratic hookah [a water pipe to facilitate the vaporizing and smoking aromatic tobacco called *shisha*]. I kept sitting in my position. The assembled gentries were busy talking to Khan Shaheeb, mostly matters that seemed to me to be humdrum. They gradually vacated the *kachari khana*."

Khan Shaheeb apparently was in a relaxed mood, took off his ironed, starched white cotton *tupi* (headgear), put his *kol balish* (side pillow) under his right armpit, dangled the flexible tube of his hookah, and conveyed something to attending household help by nodding. BM, as the new person in the setting, observed with curiosity the particular communication style of Khan Shaheeb in which physical signals and eye movements were the principle conduit of command rather than words.

The *kachari khana* was empty within a few moments. There were only two souls—those of Khan Shaheeb and BM—sitting apart quietly. This was disquieting for BM, with divergent thoughts traveling untidily. He could not make any sense of his own presence in that unruffled ambiance. A household staff member reappeared on the scene with a *mora* (a modest and locally made backless cane stool of round shapes both at the top and lower ends with a clinched midsection) and placed it in front of Khan Shaheeb. BM was escorted by a staff member to be close to Khan Shaheeb on the *mora*. As he took his seat, Khan Shaheeb, in his typical style of parsimonious oral communication, gestured for the staff to leave. There were only two totally divergent souls occupying the aristocratically furnished and elegant *kachari khana*. One was seated on a smooth couch and in total command of the surrounding manifesting aroma of the title his great grandfather had, while the other, a simple *ghattak* (matchmaker), whose thoughts were overpowered by uncertainty and agony, was seated on a cane *mora*.

Total tranquility prevailed for few moments when Khan Shaheeb, after a few short and quick puffs of his hookah, had a rather long draw, gaining the attention of BM.

After exhaling the puff totally, he looked at BM and softly said, "You must be wondering why I sent a messenger to fetch you all of a sudden. Perhaps you have heard about me. At the least you are likely to be aware of our family background, especially my great grandfather Khan Bahadur Abdur Raheem Khan."

Ever vigilant and dexterous in social interactions, BM did not like the space that Khan Shaheeb unwittingly provided to go unutilized. Being conscious of the vulnerability of the offspring of traditional families who derive pleasure in recalling their past glory and avowal citations pertaining to acts and deeds of the family and forefathers, BM quickly responded, fully putting the elegance of the family and respect for Khan Shaheeb in the forefront of his statement to ensure that the ego and intuit of the former were taken care of. So he proceeded with a salutation, leaving nothing to uncertainty, "Khan Bahadur Hujur [meaning both the official title his great-grandfather had and the salutation *hujur*, meaning "sir"], your illustrious great-grandfather and his offspring are very much part of local folklore. Everyone of this and adjacent habitations are fully aware of you. We still get inspiration from you. Your distinguishable persona, enviable sway, and irrefutable reputation travel much beyond Nobi Nagar. It is an honor for me to be in your presence. This poor self is at your service, whatever may be your wish."

Such a spontaneous response undeniably impressed Khan Shaheeb. Still then, he had some internal prickliness that continued to bother him. The subject matter to be shared was the root cause. But more important was the issue of how to tell BM about keeping the family legacy and honor in view. To Khan Shaheeb, the issue was of trust and confidence. He had only heard about BM but did not know him at all. He once again resorted to a long puff of his hookah. Engrossed with thoughts in finding a way out, Khan Shaheeb, without any premonition, opened up to BM as if he was someone whom he had known for a long time and could trust. That was quite a rare happening; the mind was saying something, but the tongue reacted differently. Could it be that it was the outcome of acute internalized stress with sudden disconnect experienced by his body organs?

BM was taken aback when Khan Shaheeb stated, "There is a part of my life that is not that well-known. My late father enforced a seal of absolute confidentiality on that, and it was not to be discussed at any venue within his jurisdiction. The decision was carried out strictly. By the time he died, the issue became irrelevant for my life because of nature's intervention. It gradually went out of importance for all purposes. But one of the outcomes of that segment is permeating the sphere of my current life. Your reputation as a trustworthy *ghattak* encouraged me to reconnoiter about you. Being convinced about your honesty and trustworthiness, I decided to contact you. That is why I called you."

Overwhelmed by the trust granted and the unexpected openness inherent in those few words—and for an ordinary *ghattak* like him—BM became emotionally jaded. That experience was beyond his continuum.

He instantly cupped his hands, put both elbows on his knees, looked down, and softly said, "Hujur, this poor soul is a nonentity before a person of your status. It is unthinkable that I will be sitting alone in your proximity and that too to be a recipient of something very personal. You can trust me with anything. I am a poor and very humble person, but professional exigencies have made me privy to copious sensitivities of varied families. I have in my repository confidential information about many of them. But I have never shared with anyone. I have never ever betrayed the trust instilled in me."

Khan Shaheeb smiled with a feeling of satiated calmness. Looking outside through the wide-open windows of his aristocratic *kachari khana*, he said, "I was very happy with the outcome of my first marriage. But the fact that I had two daughters and my wife was not conceiving caused concerns within the family. My late father could not accept the fact that Khanbahadur Monzeel would not have a male successor. So even against my expressed preference, at the insistence of my family elders, as well the persuasion of my wife, I married a second time in a very low-key manner. I was blessed with two sons. Everyone was very happy. My two marriages are known to all, and I have lived gleefully as heir apparent of Khanbahadur Monzeel with both *begum*s [as wives are referred in higher-echelon Muslim families]. At the height of my youth, quite some time after my second marriage, I went for an extended tour of our estate, which took me to a far-flung and almost inaccessible place known as Harinarayanpur. There were two reasons for me to be there. First, there was the need for someone respectable from the estate to arbitrate in the dispute between two influential brothers of the same family, which was affecting farming in the area. And second—and more importantly for the estate—was to address matters concerning the visible decline in revenue.

"My arrival in Harinarayanpur was on time, with the date earlier communicated through messenger. Members of my staff had accompanied me but were sent back as they were not relevant. It was agreed that the manager of the estate's *tehsil kachari* [revenue collection and accounting house] would ensure my escort on my return journey back to Nobi Nagar. Normally, tradition dictated that anyone like me, out on a visit to the estate as an esteemed guest, stayed with the most notable of the local gentry. But that would not be the case with my visit to Harinarayanpur. Either of the feuding brothers would have been a natural choice, but that was not to be as I was there as an arbitrator. So I decided, as an exception, to be the guest of the manager. The *tehsil kachari* manager was both privileged and embarrassed to have me as his guest. Being the host of the *zamindar*'s son automatically elevated his local social standing. He was conscious of that. The privilege was the cause of his exhilaration. The feeling of embarrassment was rooted in his not having amenities to befit my perceived status. Neither had any immediate bearing on my thoughts and actions. Upon arrival and soon after finishing preliminary pleasantries in the office room of the *tehsil kachari*, I became engrossed initially in working out the details of *salish* [arbitration] hearings on the following day.

"As a neutral place, *tehsil kachari* was considered to be most appropriate venue for *salish* meetings. It was also agreed that the portico of the *tehsil kachari* would be the place for my sitting as the arbitrator. Two chairs for two brothers and *patties* [spread made of local vegetation] would be laid out in the front courtyard for members of the families and interested people to be present. All concerned were informed about the arrangement and the time set for arbitration the following day. I went to the manager's abode nearby. The modest guesthouse [*kachari*] at the homestead of the manager was to be my place for stay. Befitting arrangements were made hurriedly within perceptible constraints. The manager, Hurmut Akhand, was apologetic for not being able to make arrangements for someone of my status. I ignored those statements and opted to take some rest after a long day of travel and delicate conversations pertaining to arbitration. In the process, I fell asleep.

"My short sleep was interrupted by the soft call of 'Hujur' by Hurmut Akhand just before the *magreeb*. Hurmut, in a meekly tone, advised that after the *magreeb*, he would escort me to the main house for dinner, and I was to be ready by that time.

"My reactions and responses were always guardedly limited since I had stepped into his *kachari*. I was conscious of my status and vigilant in upholding my family's standing. Most of my interactions with Hurmut were by sign or symbol, with the designed objective of keeping a proper distance from an employee. I kept quiet while accompanying him to his main house, modest with three rooms. One of the rooms was partitioned to carve out a sitting space. As I was ushered in, I had the feeling that the setting of the room underwent changes to make it convenient for my eating there. Two chairs were placed side by side with an easy chair at the other end. A small table was placed in the middle with a hurricane lantern in the corner. An armed chair was on one side of the table, close to the lantern. A long slim low table was positioned on the left side of the armed chair. The long table was most easily accessible from the kitchen. I had no doubt that instead of crowding the modest table with food items, the long side table was placed as a service one. My initial impression was strengthened further when I noticed an aluminum water jug and glass at the far end of that table. As Hurmut was busy supervising things inside, I had nothing to do but indulge in stray thoughts.

"In a translucent display of allegiance and as a manifestation of due respect, Hurmut decided to serve his venerated guest himself. While placing the dinner plate on the table, he lamented that the current poor health of his wife precluded the preparation of delicate food items that I deserved so much. He casually said that their daughter hurriedly prepared the food to the best of her ability, so I had to bear with that.

"During the process, I always kept my eyes down, listened to what Hurmut Akhand had to say, and responded occasionally by nodding. I was not feeling comfortable at all as there was never an occasion when anyone from Khanbahadur Monzeel ever stayed in the employees' house. My effort to keep eyes down was a deliberate stab not to transcend our current informality or to impact the traditional relationship based on master and employee. Consequently, I never noticed when Hurmut Akhand left the room after placing freshly boiled rice and some vegetables on the table. The momentary absence was very relaxing for me. More so, it gave me some relief from the sustained listening to the reprise of praises about our family and about the competence I demonstrated during the initial meeting on arrival. In that mental setting, I slowly placed some freshly cooked rice on my dinner plate with vegetable items.

"During the process of relishing the vapors emitting rice [my most favorite rice service] and vegetables, I was astounded to see a beautiful hand approaching my plate, holding a big serving of sweet water *ruhu* [fish]. I raised my eyes. Momentarily, I was baffled. I had never seen anyone so attractive. She was just beyond any description. Whether it was her physical beauty or dress-up or demeanor, I just could not think that such a beauty could be in a far-flung place like Harinarayanpur. I even started having a sense of nervousness.

"The young lady, devoid of the persistent nervousness Hurmut Akhand had incessantly demonstrated since afternoon, politely and confidently said, 'I am Rulie, the manager's only daughter. By this time, my father must have told you many times about my mother's illness and my inability to cook. But whatever it is, you will have to sustain the food prepared by me. Rest assured that the next lunch or dinner will also be like this as I can't prepare *polao* [a delicate preparation of rice similar to fried rice with a lot of herbs, spices, and ghee] and roasted meats. Father had to step out to talk to someone who came from the local Chowdhurys' house, so I came to serve you.'

"She left the room. Hurmut reappeared as I was finishing my last bite. He apologized for his temporary absence and explained the reason. Both the Chowdhurys were having a difference of opinion about witness presentation. The matter was minor, but usually, family prestige was tagged, hence they had come here to sort out the problem. Since I was having food, he resolved the issue without bothering me.

"My enjoyment of the supposedly modest dinner was overwhelming in terms of taste and ambiance. Both were enhanced by the unexpected presence and spontaneous discourse of Rulie, without any inhibition because of my position. Besides her inherent grace and spontaneity of behavior, I really enjoyed the way the food was prepared and the way it was served. I specifically liked her last comment of 'Bhalo korey kan jodio ranna bhalo hoy nai. Sara din to obukhta chillen [Eat to your heart's content, even though the food preparation is not good. You were hungry the whole day].'

"With this feeling, I returned to the *kachari* and was very pleased to see some grilled *paan*s placed on the low bedside table and a bundle of clothes on the chair where I initially sat. I instantly started feeling warmhearted hospitality. Those silent but small gestures were very special to me. They were significantly unique as I grew up having the things of life and daily needs as per the preference of elders and practices of the family. I sat on the bed nicely redone during my brief absence and had a *paan*. I chewed rather excitedly and finally swallowed in totality, deviating from the practice of spitting occasionally. I enjoyed the first paan so much that I felt an urge to have the second one. I had that one lying on the bed, looking at the slightly shaded bamboo ceiling and unwittingly immersed in noncohesive thoughts. Very obviously, those thoughts had focus on what I did not get in my family and personal life in Nobi Nagar compared with what I had just experienced in Harinarayanpur.

"My relationship with my first wife had been a typical connubial one with full obedience and dedication. We seldom interacted as equals or as partners. She had been preoccupied establishing herself as the *begum* of Khanbahadur Monzeel and caring for our two daughters. My second wife had been busy all through to create a niche for herself within the domain of the first *begum*. Being blessed with two sons soon after our wedding, and with the recurring indisposition of the first wife, she created the necessary space. She has been very intelligent in fortifying her position, remaining submissive in her daily dealings to the senior wife. She was happy with whatever she got and never had issues rooted in feelings of status and position. I have had a docile second wife whose focus has been to comply with things that I said or desired. Two wives in my life subsisted as a fait accompli. Rulie, on the contrary, in our short first encounter, besides my being the employer of her father, was elegant, spontaneous, assertive, and excelled in communication. She had no space in her thought to be encumbered by the omnipresent position-related complex that was perceptively pronounced in every interaction of her father. Demonstratively, she was much above and independent of the inherent sensitivity of an employer–employee relationship. The confidence demonstrated by her in putting the piece of fish on my plate with frank assertion about her cooking ability was most impressive. I never had that type of service from my wives. Like most upscale families of the time, our daily taking of food [lunch and dinner] had a set protocol. When Abba Hujur [Revered Father], having the inherited title of *khan*, was alive, it was his presence and participation that mattered most. Male adult family members and important visiting male family guests would sit around, and the seniormost lady of the house would supervise the service. Though some elements of the set protocol were relaxed by me after the death of Father, eating still continued to be a males-first event, under the supervision of my first wife, sitting at a distance. Thus, Rulie's gesture of serving took me by surprise and made me happy.

"As I was somewhat bemused by such feelings with my eyes closed, she unexpectedly entered the *kachari* and politely asked me to get up as she was to affix the mosquito net, kept on the chair which I had mistakenly thought to be a bundle of clothes.

"While delicately tying the ends of the mosquito nets on the bamboo frame posts, Rulie mentioned, 'We have a small radio, and I enjoy radio plays very much, but more importantly, I enjoy the play enacted in our home every day. I do not recall a single day when my parents had food at night separately. If they could not make it together, they would prefer to skip the meal. Each dinnertime, my parents sit facing each other and serve food to each other, often sharing the small pieces of fish or chicken from the plates of one another. My mother has intense interest in reading Bangla magazines like *Begum*, *Shaugat*, and *Mahe Nao* and will share stories with my father. Even in the rural setting of Harinarayanpur, this is unique but also the most adoring demonstration of a conjugal relationship. It was always amusing to witness. Initially, I used to eat with them. As I grew up, I realized that the time of eating dinner is the most cherished time for these two people, and I gradually withdrew. They readily accepted that. Their eating time has always been very long because of their riveted eating interactions.'

"Rulie took a step to go out and then returned, saying, 'My father is supposed to fix the mosquito net for you in the absence of household help, but that would be delayed because of their protracted eating style, so I volunteered, and that is the reason I came. After all, you are our *mehman* [guest]. I hope it is okay with you.'

"In spite of having disjointed thoughts since dinner, I slept very well that night. Invigorated by the previous evening's experience and relaxation, I went to the *salish* [arbitration] with full vigor. I had ideas from my previous encounters about the complicated mind-set of some people in rural settings, but what I had encountered that morning was simply absurd. Progress was thwarted by incredible logic grounded on precedence. As the process started, the main issue of the *salish* became tangential, and the process became the center of focus. The issue was the proposition of the younger brother to present a witness whose source of information was what he had heard from a witness. The elder brother objected to the hearsay, and the snag created an obdurate attitude when someone from other side insisted that Muslim jurisprudence allows witnesses who have heard about an incident from a reliable source.

"As the issue was being debated, an elderly person observed, 'If Sahih Muslim Hadith [*hadith* is the collected reports of what the Prophet Muhammad—peace be upon him—said and did during his lifetime] could be compiled over a span of three hundred years, based on written scripts, recollections of Prophet Mohammad's [peace be upon him] *sahaba*s [close associates], sayings of *tabiun* [disciples of *sahaba*s], and *taba tabiun* [disciples of the disciples] could be an important constituent of Muslim jurisprudence, then why a person who heard the incident directly from the person who witnessed that it could not be allowed?'

"For the most part of that day, I was the witness to the intricacies of village politics and continual discourses with no sign of moving toward a consensus. I experienced similar discourses in Apurba Neer, but nothing compared to this. The oblique reference to the *hadith* as a justification to admit a witness sort of elevated the reasoning, making reaching a common position even more challenging. As the time passed, I started having a bad stomach feeling, with occasional growling. In my honest desire to scout for a quick and acceptable resolution of the impasse, I deferred the lunch and thought that the apparent bad stomach feeling was because of that. With the passage of further time, I started experiencing a gradual gush of stomach pain.

"I adjourned the *salish*, asking both parties firmly to resolve the difference by tomorrow, and then the *salish* would be resumed the day after. I publicly said that I was not feeling well and would like to take some rest. I also said that Hurmut Akhand would be available tomorrow to assist in the negotiation. I clearly told all present that the extreme patience exhibited so far had one objective—to have a diaphanous process, with both parties having a fair feeling about the outcome. It was also made clear that I would definitely like to finish the proceedings by the day after tomorrow.

"Returning to Hurmut's *kachari*, I straightaway went to bed, sustaining increasing discomfort. Seeing me returning, the houseboy went inside and informed Rulie and her mother and came back to advise me of the service of lunch in the main house. I did not respond. After some time, Rulie appeared in the doorway and softly drew my attention to the lunch, which had already been delayed. As I turned toward the entrance, she was surprised to notice my face with all perceived symptoms of discomfort and pain. She rushed toward me and blamed me for not informing her earlier.

"She said, 'You can't take normal food, but you can't have an empty stomach. I am going to get some mild and less spicy food for you and will come back soon. You, please try to have some rest.'

"My continuous effort to get rest was in vain, with increasing pain. Rulie came back with a small quantity of carefully chosen food and urged my eating. There was no remission of pain. I just could not swallow anything. On being advised of the situation, Hurmut Akhand returned promptly and positioned himself by the side of my bed in a flustered state of mind. He was in a standing position as he was not supposed to, by tradition, be seated in front of an employer. I signaled him to sit on the chair, which he reluctantly complied with but did not fail to express his gratitude.

"As the time passed, the pain accentuated and was much above tolerance level. My stomach growling was supplemented by occasional loud burps, and discomfort multiplied. Hurmut Akhand promptly left for the bazaar (marketplace) to bring the local pseudo-physician. My body was almost curled up from the intensity of pain. I suddenly felt like vomiting. Rulie sent the houseboy to fetch a bucket. Seeing me bending along the side of the bed, she rushed in and positioned herself just behind me, placed her right hand under my forehead as a support, and held my body to keep me steady. Unknowingly, her body frame was an instantaneous direct support for my aching body. Even in that agonizing situation, I felt the firm touch of her bulging breasts.

"After the bouts of vomiting, I started feeling relative calm and at ease with myself. Hurmut reappeared with the physician, but by that time, my vomiting stints were over. The physician's diagnosis started with possible food poisoning, and his treatment ended with my vomiting. His wise inference was 'no treatment needed' since the harmful granule had exited, but caution must be exercised with respect to future intake for at least for four to five days. Oil and spices were ruled out. He recommended *chirar pani* [water-melted pressed rice] to begin with, followed by mashed food as my stomach stabilized. Side by side, plenty of rest was recommended.

"Since the recommended rest conflicted with the schedule of *salish*, I started feeling gawky. Sensing the nature of my discomfort, Hurmut suggested that he would go immediately to both Chowdhury brothers and invite them to his home to meet with the ailing Khan Shaheeb on the following morning. During such a meeting, a rescheduling of the *salish* would be possible. He also opined that considering the nature of village politics, it would perhaps be advisable to have the *salish* even before full recovery as some sympathy emanating from illness may result in a quicker resolution.

"Coinciding with the departure of the physician, Rulie went to the kitchen to help her mother with the preparation of the recommended diet for the night. As her mother was preparing, she sat by her side and intensely observed the process. She had a poignant feeling about what I would be experiencing throughout the night after recalling her own experience a few years back. Without consulting anyone, Rulie concentrated on preparing a small quantity of ginger juice with globules of honey in it. Her intuitive conclusion was that the element of ginger would give comfort by minimizing burps. The drops of honey in the ginger juice would minimize mouth dryness.

Together, they would serve the purpose of a good antidote, at least during the night when I would be alone.

"As she was pressing the ginger, she recalled pressing the dorsal of Khan Shaheeb to her breast while trying to keep him steady. That unintended act caused shame within her. As a response to that feeling of shame, she placed the *anchal* [tail end of a sari] on her head, forming a *ghomta* [traditional head cover]. Her mother was taken aback, seeing her wear a *ghomta* voluntarily, which she had resisted doing all her life. On her query, Rulie responded by just shrugging it off. A strange mixed feeling usurped her subsequent thought. Holding Khan Shaheeb was the first time that Rulie ever came into close contact with a male body. Notwithstanding the scenery of the said contact and the consequential engrossing anxieties, Rulie's physiology had an approving response. It made her cheery to realize that Khan Shaheeb's body and muscles were remarkably stout for his age of mid-thirty, an age profile related to decay by local standard.

"As Hurmut left to contact the Chowdhury brothers, the responsibility devolved to Rulie to serve *chirar pani*. She acquiescently picked up the serving bowl and started for the *kachari* with the houseboy as escort, as per an earlier directive by her father.

"With confident and stable steps, Rulie experienced a feeling of lassitude as she was reaching the entry door of the *kachari*. By sign language, she told the houseboy to take the bowl and offer *chirar pani* to Khan Shaheeb. That was a most unexpected responsibility for which the innocent houseboy was not prepared. He wondered how his Rulie-bu [respected Rulie sister] could think that. Khan Shaheeb is the boss of his employer. So it ought not be appropriate for him to serve the *chirar pani* to Boro Hujur [Big Sir].

"The resultant low mayhem was sufficient to draw the attention of Khan Shaheeb. Repositioning himself on the bed, he looked out, saw the houseboy, and inquired about the commotion. On being advised, Khan Shaheeb told houseboy to tell his Rulie-bu that he would not take the *chirar pani* unless she served him. Rulie diffidently stepped in and offered the bowl of *chirar pani* mutely. She was standing by his side but hid her face totally with her *ghomta*. On specific query as to why she was suddenly wearing such a *ghomta*, Rulie freely admitted that she was feeling shy for having held him with both arms. A *ghomta* was a convenient escape from any direct eye contact, which Rulie wanted to avoid.

"Holding the bowl of *chirar pani*, I gently requested she take a seat in the armchair and shorten her *ghomta* if she wanted to. Rulie complied without any dithering. As the houseboy was standing by her side, I concentrated on finishing the *chirar pani*. I told the houseboy to take back the empty bowl and also requested for a *paan* without *chun* [lime made by burning shell]. The request for *paan* was deliberate as the houseboy's presence was discomforting for me.

"After the houseboy left, I told Rulie, 'You should and need not have any feeling of disgrace. Rather, you should feel proud that you have made the right decision at the right time. Things could have been worse for me, causing agony to you all for all time to come.'

"I had an unfettered impulse to let her know my surreptitious feelings, to open up myself and the real sensitivities that had been smoldering in my mind since our embrace. My rambled subsequent statements fell far short of a well-tuned symphony expected from a person of my age and status. It was difficult for me to restrain my tongue with my mind in a discombobulated state.

"I looked straight at Rulie and was taken aback by the grace and attractiveness of her eyes, enhanced by the application of simple *kajol* [indigenous eyeliner]. I just could not restrain myself. I continued, saying, 'Your embrace helped me, and I also had the feeling of comfort despite the suddenness of the act. That encounter triggered within me an ardent yearning to experience life differently, even though I have two wives and four children. This sort of feeling is very exceptional as I have never encountered it before. I have had a very happy life and was content with my family environment until I came into contact with you accidentally. What I realized in your touch is the reality of my conjugal life—getting all attention from both my wives but never their love. None ever served food to me, made *paan* for me, asked me to do something [similar to getting up from the bed], or embraced me. They just complied, considering me as one high in esteem. On all those counts, you are exceptional. Your naturalness in social behavior, your confidence in interacting, your promptness in responses—all and that too in the rural setting of Harinarayanpur—impressed me enormously. It has given me a new sense of direction with respect to life and living. In a short time, I found in you someone who, besides being a wife, could as well be a friend, a support, and a guide in life. I am conscious of the fact that this is my selfish conclusion. I have opened up before you to give you time and to know your preference. I will talk directly to Hurmut Akhand only when I get clearance from you. But I need your decision soon as there is not much time for me. I am to go back soon.'

"Rulie's face turned a bright cerise. She was speechless as I was haranguing unabatedly to finish what I wanted to say. As soon as I paused, she quietly left without a word. I was unsure about her reaction. Nevertheless, I had a nice following night as I felt relieved by communicating what I had in my subtle mind. In that happy mood, I thought about a maneuver that was never practiced by me before. Following family tradition, I was taught to be upright and honest in all endeavors and not to cut corners to attain something. With desire and emotion concerning Rulie overtaking my carefully nurtured sense of discretion, I concluded the imperative need to prolong the *salish* proceedings, taking excuse of my weak and weary health status. That was the only way out for me to have the needed time to reach a final position in my impetuous but genuine empathy centering on Rulie.

"I acted accordingly the following day. I coughed occasionally and breathed long frequently to exhibit my continued feebleness. The *salish* was continued. In conducting the proceedings, I consciously tried to be extra nice and polite to both Chowdhury brothers, with the set objective of winning their support and help for the future. As the deliberations reached a common position pertaining to the broad framework of options to redress the problem, it coincided with the *azaan* for *johor namaz* [call for noontime prayers of Muslims]. The *salish* was adjourned until the next day at the behest of the elder

Chowdhury. It was agreed to give me needed respite. That made me happy. I was happier when the Chowdhury brothers requested for the continued presence of Hurmut Akhand to work out the related details.

"I cheerily returned to find Rulie grooming the *kachari* with the assistance of the omnipresent houseboy. Seeing me unexpectedly, she lengthened her *ghomta* significantly to cover not only her full head but also a part of her upper body. Without taking note of Rulie directly but with all intent to communicate with her, I started chitchatting with the houseboy. Most of the few words I directed toward Rulie through the houseboy were beyond his comprehension. He was in a state of confusion but got definite direction when I asked him to bring a lukewarm glass of water for drinking. He promptly went out.

"The traffic outside was nonexistent because of *johor* prayer time. Both of us in that solitary locale were in a state of total silence for a while. Then I pointedly asked her about her response to what I had indicated last night. She took a step backward, and the broom fell from her hand. She pointedly increased the length of her long *ghomta* and stayed put in a frozen posture. I could not wait anymore as I had the worries of the houseboy's return. So I asked her a second time, requesting a response. Rulie shortened her *ghomta*, looked briefly with a subtle expression, and then was on her way out, bypassing me. I could not allow that golden opportunity to go in vain. I held her dangling hand, pulled her to myself, and lowered my face to touch her neckline. I passionately requested a response from her. She did not utter a single word but conveyed thousands of them by snuggling me with her arms. Though that was quite intense, she got herself disengaged and hurriedly went to the main house.

"After a while, the houseboy showed up with the glass of lukewarm water as well as some mashed food for my lunch. I was told by him to have that now, and Rulie-bu would be preparing a curry item of *shingi* fish [stinging catfish] with a very light gravy along with cooked refined rice for dinner. That was to be my gradual transition to normal diet. My internalized impulses were

pronouncedly effervescent. I could not delay the startling transition
of my life itself centering on Rulie. The vibration that I experienced
during the afternoon embrace and my own strong desire to have
a life with love and care propelled the follow-up actions in quick
succession.

"When I proposed to him about marrying Rulie during our
one-on-one meeting following dinner that night, Hurmut Akhand
was flabbergasted. He was speechless, nervous, uncertain, and
logically disoriented. He was familiar with the common practice of
Muslim gentries to have more than one wife but never expected that
from visiting Khan Shaheeb Hujur and involving his own daughter.
He was sure of his wife's reservation but was totally unsure how
to respond to Khan Shaheeb Hujur. His mind-set was embroiled
momentarily because of his sense of dedication, commitment, loyalty,
and obedience, nurtured for generations. He stopped his loud mincing
of *paan*, kept his head down, and set his eyes focused on the floor.

"Sensing his predicament, I broke the silence and said,
'Perhaps you are concerned about the reaction of Abba Hujur
[my respected father]. You need not worry about that. I take full
responsibility and would handle that in a way so that Rulie enters
Khan Bahadur's abode with full honor and dignity. Please remember
that I am his only son, and he can't disregard my wish.'

"Though Hurmut Akhand was partially reassured about my
sincerity, he still had concerns. I continued, saying, 'I am proposing
this marriage with all sincerity and commitment, keeping in view my
enthused love for Rulie. However, it has a stipulation. Because of the
sensitivity that you have in your mind, I request total confidentiality
at this moment. It will be made public only when I have time to travel
back to Nobi Nagar and have the opportunity to talk to Abba Hujur
to get his consent. It may take a little time, but I assure you, it will
be done.'

"Hurmut quietly left the *kachari* without any *kurnish* [the
Muslim traditional way of bowing and saying *salaam* while leaving
an audience] and went inside the home. Perhaps he needed space for

himself or discussions with his wife who, as was told by Rulie earlier, was more attuned to handle delicate family matters. I could not care less. The very fact that I made the proposition was, to me, my most poignant satisfaction. I also realized that it would be too arduous for Hurmut to say no to my proposition in view of generations-old contacts and rapport based on absolutely unequal premises. That feeling of ego made me happy that night. I gleefully retired to bed after mincing two more *paan*s.

"I got up early the following morning with my mind preoccupied by similar thoughts. To me, the rising sun of that morning suddenly appeared to be especially unique with a joyful glow emitting from it. Within my thinking, I embraced that feeling as a positive one. Thus, I concentrated on matters pertaining to the pending *salish* and emotionally prepared myself to ardently conduct the upcoming proceedings as the authoritative representative of the Khanbahadur dynasty. In my mind, I considered it imperative to enable myself to undertake the unhindered persuasion of Hurmut Akhand. In view of my family background and status, any negative pronouncement would be excruciating and dishonorable not only for me but for the prestige, honor, and standing of Khanbahadur Monzeel. Within the amalgam of such obsession, I did not forget to have a visible strategy to communicate with bestowed sympathy from my subjects, especially the two Chowdhury brothers. The *salish* was successfully completed, as planned under my guidance. I consciously did not allow the proceedings to change direction. I remained long on gravitas and short on charm during the entire proceeding. Both the Chowdhury brothers were happy with the outcome, and so were others present.

"During the proceedings, I often acted to demonstrate my continuous weakness because of recent illness. The subjects present were impressed that I decided to have the *salish* even though I was weak and weary. Various kind comments washed over me, but the most relevant one came from the senior Chowdhury. He suggested that I should stay back for some more days to recover fully before returning to Nobi Nagar. That made me happy. I was looking for that sort of pronouncement from local gentries to avoid embarrassment for staying in Harinarayanpur even after the *salish* was over. However, outwardly, I expressed a sense of hesitation and then reluctantly agreed.

"Hurmut was present at the *salish,* but it was a passive presence. This was contrary to his role and personality, so well established and familiar in the locality. But few took note as the proceedings were intense and the outcome was liked by all. I knew what kept him so quiet. I was looking for the opportunity to have a discussion with him when we would be alone, but he was not to be seen anywhere near the *kachari.* I inquired from the houseboy and was repeatedly told that he was talking to his wife.

"It was after *magreeb* [Muslim daily prayer at sunset] that Hurmut Akhand showed up, but he kept quiet for some time. That was very piercing as my high expectation was susceptible to startling frustration. It was both fretting and galling for me. I had no choice but to wait for his gesticulation. He coughed a little, looked around to be sure of continued solitude of the setting, and set his eyes on me. He slowly started talking without his usual salutation of *hujur.*

"He said, 'I have considered carefully what you told me last night. I also had a long discussion with my wife. Our common position is that we trust you and agree with your proposition not because it is your command but because we feel that Rulie also is agreeable. The rest depends on you, but we are looking forward to the early formalization of this decision—after a discussion with Boro Hujur [elder respected sir].'

"Uttering those few words, Hurmut Akhand hastily left the *kachari,* only to return with his wife. Dressed in a light-printed sari, she epitomized a person of culture, decency, and sophistication, contrary to my exposure. That was amazing for a rural setting like Harinarayanpur. She stepped in, embodying both politeness and confidence.

"I stood up and said, 'Salaam alaikum [Peace be upon you].'

"She sat on the chair, while Hurmut Akhand stood by her side. Observing that congenial stance, I recalled what Rulie had told me about her mother's reading of Bangla magazines and her parents' dining rituals. She was sober, soft, and sweet in her outward gestures and prompt, direct, and clear in her subsequent exchanges, which were brief and undeviating.

"She stated, 'Your proposition last night and our concurrence tonight will turn upside down the generational contact and relationship between our two families. It is bound to cause confrontation and face resistance. We both are conscious of that. Still, having trust in you, we give our blessings, will keep it confidential, and will wait for the day when Rulie will accompany you to her home with full stateliness.'

"She left the *kachari* without giving me an opportunity to respond or to reassure her of both spoken and silent concerns. I discussed with Hurmut about the upcoming budget of timing of our private marriage and arrangement. It was agreed to commission the imam [priest] of the *tehsil kachari* mosque to administer the rituals of marriage on the following night. Also, the involvement of the said imam was considered prudent from the perspective of confidentiality as he was an employee of the *kachari*. The discussion following was short and straight, but the night appeared to be too long.

"The feeling of loneliness the following day was more grueling as I was alone the whole day in the *kachari* except an occasional showing by the houseboy. My breakfast and lunch were served in the *kachari*. Hurmut never came to meet me, and even I did not get a wink of Rulie. As I was finishing my lone dinner, he stepped in and told me that the imam [priest] of the *tehsil kachari* mosque would come soon to escort me inside and would administer the wedding ritual, so I should get prepared.

"Everything that needed to be done that night was done with the utmost privacy. The only outsider was the imam. He was the priest to solemnize the marriage and also be the witness. I voluntarily complied with the cultural requirement of publicly showing respect to and seeking blessings from father- and mother-in-law by touching their feet [a traditional way of performing *salaam* and showing respect to seniors] and thereby put a firm seal on our new relationship. I intentionally included the imam in the process. That made him enormously happy. But his happiness burgeoned as he witnessed a bundle of currency notes that I quietly passed in his hand while thanking him.

"The only light moment of that night was when my father-in-law Hurmut went to see off the imam, and the houseboy appeared from nowhere. He came by my side and whispered, 'Boro Hujur, apni to amar dula bhai hoy galen [Big Sir, you have become my brother-in-law].'

"I passed that night and the following three nights enjoying the warm company and assertive embrace of Rulie. To the outward social setting of Harinarayanpur, I was recuperating. Hence, there were not many visitors. My need-based presence in the *kachari* was ensured through its backdoor. Otherwise, I joyously spent most of the time with Rulie. The only sad moment of that blissful time was when Rulie expressed concerns pertaining to Abba Hujur's consent and related consequences. My repeated assurances were helpful but not enough to redress that fully.

"Based on discussions with Hurmut and not to cause any suspicion within the community, I decided to leave Harinarayanpur on the morning of the fourth day. I dressed up and performed *salaam* by touching the feet of my new in-laws. I then entered our room, seeing Rulie seated on the farthest corner of our modest conjugal bed. I slowly went near her and continued standing in silence. I had my own intimidating pressure and avowed sadness but prepared myself not to succumb before her. During the last few nights, I had unencumbered opportunities to be familiar with and assess the depth and nature of her emotions. Her outward confident posture had a hidden soft mind vulnerable to trivial incident, so I did not want to give her any opportunity to break down.

"As longer-than-usual time was being taken by me in coming out and as Hurmut was cognizant of the poignant trauma I was experiencing in taking leave from Rulie, before he uttered any word, he coughed from the adjacent room, rather gawkily, to draw our attention. Getting that signal and without any advance from my side, Rulie slowly stood up and looked at me with all intensity as if she would not see me again. Then she lost all control and surrendered herself on my chest. After a while, and on her own volition, Rulie slowly disengaged herself, keeping her eyes focused on the floor. She placed the *anchal* of her sari halfway on her head and bowed fully to perform *salaam* without a word. In the process of unbending from the stance, she held my two palms and gently tried to lift them up to her chest, perhaps as a prelude to making an emotional avowal, but she could not hold herself steady up to that point. Halfway through, a big teardrop fell on my right palm. Surprisingly, it neither did slide nor was followed by a second one. I kept my palm in a steady position to hold it there.

"I placed my left hand on her head and told Rulie, 'This on my palm is not your tear. It is and will always be valued as a *mukhta moti* [pearl]. This symbolic *moti* will always be with me until we are reunited. That is my pledge to you.'

"I hurriedly left the room without giving any option. As an heir apparent of Khanbahadur Monzeel, I was trained well and learnt quickly on the road of life that while emotions are important, they must not influence the nature and timing of proper decisions. My leaving Harinarayanpur at that point in time was important from associated perspectives. I proceeded without dillydallying.

"In spite of that, as I was leaving their property, I just could not help but look back—to find Rulie standing outside the *kachari*. She slightly leaned herself against the outward doorway with tears in her eyes that glazed under the shimmer of the bright morning sun. I continued my journey for Nobi Nagar, trying futilely, many times, to have the feeling of that teardrop.

Commotion

"It was customary for us to debrief Abba Hujur on returning from any visit or any important engagement. I did that and explained the reason that impacted my scheduled return: the complicated nature of disputes between two influential brothers, which, if not mitigated promptly, could impair our *taluk* [sizeable landholding consisting of many *tehsil*s]. I also mentioned my stay in the house of our manager and about my sudden illness.

"As I entered the inner court of the main house, I was greeted by my first wife, who was standing on the veranda. She had her usual *hath pakha* [round embroidered hand fan] that she almost always had with her because of feelings of uneasiness but was nice enough to gently fan me always upon return. She escorted me to my easy chair placed near the bed. The *chotto* [younger] wife followed quickly with a glass of water, exchanged a suggestive look with me, and slowly stepped out.

"The two wives developed a unique protocol between them for interacting with me. Whoever is physically near to me has the advantage, and the other gladly creates the space. That made my dual married life under the same roof very pleasant. As my *chotto* wife was on her way out, I called her back and asked both to take a seat on the *palong* [traditional bed]. Both were momentarily taken aback but took their seats.

"I took a sip of water and straightway told them what was pressing within me. As I finished my brief detailing about the third marriage, there was a momentary but all-embracing silence. Though I was relieved within myself, my uneasiness accentuated. I looked outside.

"Like on many other occasions, my first wife took the initiative to break that silence. She looked at me and quietly smiled as if communicating the comic improbabilities of her life path. Based on her experience of being a part of Khanbahadur Monzeel for a long period, she internally concluded that no amount of revile would undo what was done. She opted for a reconciliatory reaction, saying, 'I do not have any problem. I am presently sharing my husband with another *begum*. It will now be the addition of the new one.'

"My younger wife adhered to her style of martyr and maintained total silence. She left the room, following my first wife, without a word. Her simple and straight strategy was that no one would ever be able to dislodge her from the position of being the mother of future Khan Shaheeb. That always gave her immense happiness, and nothing in the periphery could unnerve her. I left my easy chair and went to bed both to relax and to think through the appropriate time and strategy for divulging the marriage episode to my father.

"My first wife stepped in and sat at the other end corner of the *palong*. She said, 'I do not have any problem with your third marriage. Chotti [younger wife] promised not to make an issue out of this. Our shared worry relates to reaction and response of your father. It was our common position that you should tell him soonest and get the problem resolved at the earliest. I commit to you, on behalf of both of us, that we will do everything and support you in every way to ensure your continued happiness in future life. We will take the new bride as our sister. You had better meet Abba Hujur tonight after dinner. The setting of *kachari khana* [dedicated meeting venue for family elders and guests], where Abba Hujur generally enjoys his after dinner hookah, mostly in isolation, would be an ideal place and serene situation.'

"I was buoyant from the tone and type of support that was explicit in my wife's words. I was grateful for the consideration both *begum*s had articulated. That took care of one of the two significant obstacles on my way to the pristine happiness I had been dreaming of. There are many sleepwalkers but very few sleeplovers. I felt immense glee in being one of those latter few, recalling Rulie's touch.

"My unexpected entry into *kachari khana* took my father by surprise. This was normally the time he preferred to stay alone, enjoying his hookah, and occasionally some soothing conversation with his faithful assistant, Kalimullah. That particular conversation had more elements of listening by my father with occasional nodding and repeated but soft assertion by Kalimullah of good name and good will that Abba Hujur had both in the nearby and faraway places. As I took my seat by his side, he glanced at me sweetly. With his vocal timbre devoid of any inflection, consistent with his early evening mood, he focused on the brightness and intensity of the glow of the *shisha* [flavored small round tobacco cake] on the top basin of his hookah. He gave an insouciant look with inquisitiveness about my impetuous presence, transmitted in silence. Observing the situation, Kalimullah quietly left the *kachari khana*.

"Suddenly, I moved ahead tremulously. My poised outward physical posture was a camouflage for intense fear and utmost uncertainty, and heightened by internal trepidation about Abba Hujur's possible reaction to what I was going to say. While in Harinarayanpur, I temporarily became oblivious of that. Being physically away from my father and mesmerized by the luminosity and persona of Rulie, his concerns about my new relationship just withered away from my thought process. Now in his presence and in the setting of *kachari khana*, I was facing the reality. I grew up fathoming many of his unfathomable views and responses about sensitive social and family matters. I knew very well that both low tone and slow talking were lethal so far as his position on any issue was concerned. That amply meant that come what may, Abba Hujur will not change his post. Against that backdrop, I positioned myself to remain unfazed. Despite my cerebral preparation, I had murkiness in opening up. I started mumbling.

"While inhaling the smoke of his hookah, Abba Hujur casually observed, 'Do you want to say something? Do you have a problem?'

"After mastering the needed gumption and availing the much-required opening, I straightaway said what was on my mind. I was conscious of the fact that what I did was not right, but it was not very uncommon for Muslim gentries of the time. In following fleeting exchanges, I tried best to remain polite and submissive, even though some of the references were quite provocative. I was always cognizant of the need for upholding family mores and values. I made a desperate attempt not to pronounce any sacrilegious references to some episodes related to Abba Hujur's own youth that I was privy to.

"After a few long successive puffs of his hookah, he slowly and calmly responded with a noticeable granular articulation. That perhaps was so as he tried to suppress his utter anger and disapproval of my unanticipated action. His words were uttered with pervasive coldness and firmness. 'You know me very well. You being the only son, I tried best to be a good father and friend to you, trying to understand your feelings from proximity. I had never succumbed to lust for wealth. I have never premised my relationships based on affluence. I totally distaste the mental setting oriented to treating cash as a cushion. I was never arrogant or impolite in social interactions.'

"In his communication, that sort of rendition was evidently ominous, more so when the staid words were slow and cold. He spoke without looking at me. It was like he was talking in vacuity. Repeated references to 'I' in each of the last few statements were causing concern within me. Observing that, I had a clear vision of the end part of his soliloquy. It was arduous to inhibit my ascendant edginess. Still then, unrelenting efforts were made within to master the necessary gumption, hoping for the best. Anything negative to my love and feeling for Rulie would be disastrous. My left palm placidly touched the backside of my right palm to have the feel of her teardrop.

"A stance of insouciant calm was all pervasive. The silence, to my downright discomfort, persisted for some time. Each loud thrust of sniffing hookah by my father was thrashing my sensitive inner organs. I silently implored an early and affirmative outcome, even if as a miracle. That positive thought was predicated on my being his only son. Against all odds, I honed on what I saw as the best bet for arousing empathy and referred to my two *begum*s' readiness to accept the third wife. By averring that, I tried to bring him back to the discourse.

"He resumed his soliloquy. 'Your sudden decision to marry a third time—even without informing me, your father—is execrable but could be excused. Your marrying in a modest family much below the status and dignity of our family is repugnant but could as well be pardoned. Your obtaining the consent of my daughters-in-law is utilitarian but could rationally be treated as an accommodating posture.'

"After saying those words, he suddenly lost himself apparently in an isolated state of mind. It was difficult to weigh exactly what he had in his thinking, but the stances articulated were redolent enough to generate a sense of positive outcome. I had an inkling. For a moment, I was on the crossroad, with my other pervasive concerns being momentarily tangential to impulsive positivity.

"Abba Hujur coughed a little, more to draw my attention. He then guardedly parked the long hookah pipe in its place, looked at me straight for the first time that evening, and stated without any angry swipes, 'But I can't accept that you married in the family that has been in our employment for generations. It is below the status and eminence of the Khanbahadur Monzeel to accept the manager of one of its *tehsil*s as the father-in-law of our son. If I do so, I would be betraying the trust of my noble forefathers and all the traditions I inherited. So neither the daughter nor her father of Harinarayanpur has entry into the Khanbahadur Monzeel.'

"He then warily lifted the hookah pipe, just short of stating the whole incident was despicable. No window was kept open for possible supplication. A mix of emotions, highlighted by my being his most obedient son all through, and the consequences of the denial came up, but he was evidently in no mood to accede to any further discourse. I was certain that Abba Hujur framed his position without giving me a chance to beseech my viewpoint.

"As I was about to open my mouth, he waggled the hookah pipe to shut me down. His action shook me and rubbed me against the reality I was confronted with. My instantaneous disenchantment fringed around being sacrilegious. Both experience and wisdom prevented me from trying to continue. I knew him very well. Being the only son, I grew up under his shadow. Opportunities were plenty in my life, enabling prudent assessment of his words, actions, and tone.

"Within his outward self of politeness and dignified etiquette, Abba Hujur very circumspectly hid his ability to display irritation in the case of disagreement. I evidenced that while attending a few *salish*es while growing up. My understanding of situations and events that could steer him to display irritation was explicit. That was indubitable when family tradition, family prestige, and the good names of the ancestors were involved. In such situations, he would easily succumb to displaying unseemly thrust. No amount of goading worked in that sort of a situation. From a family status perspective, Abba Hujur positioned himself rigidly. There was no room for being pliable. He was in no mood for stepping down from the pulpit of the high ground premised on kudos for the family. My denouement was that expressing pout would be inept, while any elegiac initiative was bound to be disastrous. I fully and for the first time understood that my father, a genial personality in most of his social and family interactions, is very rigidly tied to the family values that he inherited. For him, one must live and replicate life within the bounds of family traditions and practices. One needs to be the clone of his father and forefathers. Social changes have no relevance in the lives of offspring of traditional renowned families, and they should act within the bounds already demarcated. Abba Hujur was such a product. Nothing else mattered to him. The love and happiness of his only son are trivial matters. In upholding family traditions, he refused to recognize the evolving and natural social changes dictated by time.

"Helpless and distraught, I slowly walked out of *kachari khana* without saying *salaam* to him as was customary. Approaching the home, I encountered my two wives gracing the opposite horizontal frames of the main entry door. Their forlorn hypochondriac expressions were enough to demonstrate full awareness of the outcome of my dialogue with Abba Hujur. I kept quiet, focusing my eyes on the floor. When I walked inside, I was accosted. They escorted me from both sides, each holding one of my hands near the elbow. Apparently they were concerned about my emotional stability and physical balance. They did not ask, and neither did I volunteer anything. There was no doubt about their understanding of it not going well.

"My first wife started muttering all positivity, in spite of a most frustrating negative outcome. 'You have done very well by talking to Abba Hujur candidly. He likes direct communication. It is natural for him to be distraught, but he will eventually accept the reality. You will continue to have our full and complete support.'

"I thanked her by nodding but did not fail to observe that I also know him. Saying those few words, Boro Begum slightly moved away, creating some space for Chotto Begum to serve me a delicately prepared *paan*. The silent premise was while Boro Begum had taken care of emotional stress suffered by me, Chotto Begum was to take care of my physical impel. That was evident, even in that situation, in the noticeable impish smile that adorned the lips of my first wife while saying 'Khoda hafiz [good night]' to her loving Chotti.

"Time passed. On the surface, everything moved routinely in and around Khanbahadur Monzeel. Constraints were noticeable only to those who had the knowledge of the disquieting elements that predicated the family relationship. My contact with Abba Hujur slowly became more formal and basically only related social welfare. I had the edgy feeling of being under the surveillance of his trusted associates. Besides, visits to various *taluk*s were put on hold, commitments were limited to day trips, and assignments were focused on social matters. No festivity or event was organized within the periphery of our homestead.

"I left our property on the way to a school management committee meeting. Suddenly, I faced Imam Shaheeb of the *tehsil* mosque of Harinarayanpur. He was hiding partially under the cover of a huge banyan tree around the corner of our homestead entrance and horizontal to the district board road. Imam Shaheeb told me, after exchanging *salaam*, that he ventured to Nobi Nagar only to meet me in private. As he did not like to expose himself, he was awaiting under the shade of the tree, hoping for an opportunity either to meet or send a message to me. That was his way to conceal his identity from strangers as community folks have the habit of asking all sorts of questions without regard for privacy. With a somber facial expression, Imam Shaheeb started talking. As I understood later, his objective was to communicate quickly what he wanted to say and withdraw rapidly before anyone found him having a conversation with me.

His posture and words had no similarity with the imam I faced while getting married to Rulie. On that early night in Harinarayanpur, he was the submissive staff of our *tehsil* employee, Hurmut Akhand. He conducted our wedding while being always polite with his eyes down. But that was not the person I encountered under the banyan tree, fortunately without any bystanders.

"Imam Shaheeb, without hesitation and with all the candidness he could master, told me from a high pedestal, 'Your wife in Harinarayanpur is about three months pregnant. It is difficult for Hurmut Akhand to keep the marriage of his daughter a secret anymore.'

"I was taken aback initially. I was befuddled but happy. Involuntarily, I sat down on one of the trunks of the banyan tree, holding my walking stick. The limited time and few nights we passed together in absolute happiness gleamed impetuously. I got lost in my thoughts.

"Imam Shaheeb continued, saying, 'Coming here was my decision. None of Hurmut's family know about it. My periodical short leave to visit home was due, availing that I made a detour to visit Nobi Nagar. All reasoning, especially being the lone witness of your marriage, compelled me to act. I thought it to be my religious duty to inform you about Chotto Begum Shaheeba's pregnancy. Under duress, Hurmut had to take me into confidence a second time, the first one being your wedding. Since it would be difficult to keep the marriage a secret anymore and since the family did not hear anything from you, he called me into his house and confided, seeking advice, as I am the only witness to your wedding. Hurmut's wife, known in the community as a lettered and dignified lady, flouted the traditions of *parda* [modesty], came out to meet me, broke down in tears, and addressed me as a brother seeking help. I was honored by that address. The immediate feeling was consistent and very common for anyone of my position and status, especially in the surroundings and the circumstances. The associated onerous challenge and responsibility that guilelessly landed on my shoulder made me edgy. That chore, from all perspective of social affability and moral standard, became an obligation that precluded any maneuver for pliability. My solemn concentration was trying to identify a positive way out. I kept focus on our daughter to assess her reaction. Chotto Begum Shaheeba wore a poised stance with a startlingly staid physical expression. Sitting at a nominal distance from us, she was immersed in stitching something. There were no tears in her eyes. She was neither in a state of rage or frustration. All she manifested was absolute mental preparation to face the likely eventuality. Observing her and assessing reality that the family is to face soon, I told Hurmut and his wife that I need time to put forward specific suggestion, particularly respecting the address of *bhai* [brother] of my sister present. At the same time, I also indicated my decision to avail due periodical leave.'

"I listened to Imam Shaheeb assiduously and asked him to stay overnight, and meet me tomorrow in our family mosque after *johor* [midday prayer of Muslims]. Simultaneously, I alerted him to the requisite secrecy both related to his visit and our short bump into each other. I also told him frankly my inability to arrange his overnight stay because of entailed secrecy.

"Imam Shaheeb sounded more conscious about that need and said, 'Do not worry about it. I have already developed an unexpected contact with one Subhan Bepari residing about a mile north from this location. As I was sitting on one of the banisters of concreted platform with brick steps leading to the pond in front of a mosque, suddenly, Subhan Bepari showed up and sat on the opposite banister. We exchanged *salaam*, and he started asking me all personal questions—name, place of origin, place I am heading to, purpose of my presence there, and so on. I carefully and briefly responded to his queries and then pretended saying, "I am feeling a bit tired and feel like needing some rest, but the problem is I do not know anyone with whom I can stay. So I sat in front of the house of Allah [as a mosque is often referred to], seeking his divine help." I also told him that I am the imam of a mosque in Harinarayanpur and thought that there can't be a more preferred place than this one to take rest in an unfamiliar setting.

"'Surprisingly, Subhan Bepari responded positively. He said, "My own abode is nearby, and it has a modest *kachari* too. So I would be happy to have you as a guest for a night."'

"I was both relieved and happy. We agreed to meet at the same place after *asar namaz* [late afternoon Muslim prayer]. That was both relieving and reassuring to me against the backdrop of associated anxieties. I was happy to know the arrangement that a simple imam of rural setting of Harinarayanpur could work out, even in an outlying setting around Nobi Nagar. With the objective of shortening the meeting, in view confidentiality, I used the excuse of a school meeting to hasten my disengagement with the imam. He would not allow me to do so.

"The imam started, 'I am going home to have discussions with my wife about relocating Chotto Begum Shaheeba. We do not have any offspring. My wife would be very happy. Chotto Begum Shaheeba will be in our house as the daughter of my cousin. That is the only way out as clearance to make your marriage public is being awaited. It is the only recourse to uphold the dignity of our dear Rulie and the social standing of the family. I am just informing you about that. I do not need your consent as I am doing it for the family that bestowed honor on an ordinary soul like me by giving the status of a brother.'

"He then left, assuring a meeting on the following day in the mosque of Khanbahadur Monzeel. I saw him sitting alone in a corner of the mosque with a bundle of cloth. Both his isolation and that bundle of cloth were definite attributes of his *mussafir* [tourist] status. I went out of the mosque with local gentries and then excused myself to return to retrieve my umbrella, left out intentionally. The mosque was empty except the *mussafir* imam. I hurriedly handed over three envelopes to Imam Shaheeb, telling him that the first of the envelopes addressed to Rulie contained a letter from me and that the second one had some money for her. The third one had some money for him.

"Imam Shaheeb initially was dumbfounded and kept quiet. To my surprise, he had direct eye contact with me, the second time in our exchanges during the last two occasions. He paused and then bluntly said with marked absence of his usual tone, 'I am thankful for the money given to me. You have honored me. I may be an insignificant imam of your *tehsil* mosque, but Allah, in his mercy, has given me enough to live my life. My family's financial position has always been a stable one. It was the wish of my late father that I would be an imam to serve communities. My class-eight formal education was abruptly discontinued, and I was enrolled in a *madrassa* [Muslim religious school]. I successfully completed my *madrassa* education and got married but faced inexorable dismay caused by the sudden demise of my father. To obviate the unexpected disarray, I started to wander around, and destiny unwittingly brought me to the far-flung area of Harinarayanpur, where I met Hurmut Akhand. Though he is just slightly older than me, I discovered a father figure in him who incidentally was looking for an imam. I gladly accepted the job of an underpaid imam out of emotional impulse, notwithstanding the distance from my roots. My family's wherewithal came to my rescue so far as poor pay was concerned. My wife's ready positive response, keeping in view my happiness, helped me a lot. The distance factor was mitigated by Hurmut's readiness to give me a week's leave of absence every month, which, though was availed regularly in initial years, has now become more infrequent. Inadvertently, I gradually became part and parcel of the Harinarayanpur community. So with all reverence, I am returning the envelope meant for me but assure you that the other two envelopes will be handed over to dear Rulie by me personally."

"After hurriedly saying those words, Imam Shaheeb collected his bundle of cloth, put his umbrella under left armpit, and obdurately took steps out of the mosque, not giving me a chance to react. Unthinkable gumption demonstrated by him surprised and shocked me. As I slowly meandered out of the mosque with a forlorn mind-set, a brusque thought engulfed my agonizing self. This ordinary imam of our remote *tehsil* had not only unmatched intellect but was gifted by unsurpassed humane qualities—unfettered diligence in serving a totally alien community, irrevocable trust in maintaining the confidentiality of our marriage, and unparalleled commitment in taking care of Rulie. Though heir apparent of notable Khanbahadur dynasty, I, for the first time in life, felt small before that insignificant and insouciant imam of a mosque. His staid words and firmness besieged me internally.

"Time passed. My relationship with Abba Hujur remained inwardly strained and outwardly congenial. My two *begum*s continued to console me, emphasizing patience and prudence. In the midst of such a staid setting and after a few dreary months, Abba Hujur suddenly died. Both sadness and contrition overtook my initial feelings and thoughts. Even the concerns regarding the whereabouts and well-being of Rulie evaporated. I intentionally discouraged any public display of sympathy and had no activity within our *taluk* [land ownership] until *chollisha* [mass community meal on any uneven date prior to the fortieth day of death, as practiced by local Muslims].

"But the aphorism 'Life must move on' prevailed. Slowly and steadily, my shock and sadness muffled. I became involved in preparations for my formal induction as the new Khan Shaheeb, displaying decorous participation. Among many others, all the *tehsildar*s [managers of *tehsil*s] were also present. So was Hurmut Akhand. But I did not have eye contact with him during the induction ceremony. Subsequent inquisition revealed that he left immediately after the event on the pretext of urgent family need.

"My preoccupations in handling my new responsibility and managing the *taluk* trounced initially other feelings of daily life and living. In a mini magnitude, I realized the difference between being a prince and having the burden of a crown. Ensuring and upholding the prestige and good name of a respected traditional family overwhelmed me. I slowly started treasuring the family values and traditions, which perhaps made my father react in a way that I could not accept. I argued with myself to take time to divulge to the extended family about my third sudden marriage with Rulie. It was not that I swerved from my promise and commitment made at the time of that wedding but just that I wanted to be prudent and respectful of the decision of late Abba Hujur.

"After a few months, Imam Shaheeb resurfaced. He did not play the previous game. He came straight to the *kachari khana* of Khanbahadur Monzeel and sought an immediate meeting with me. We had a private meeting in the *kachari khana* that afternoon. Imam Shaheeb initially kept quiet as if he were scouting my mind-set in view of my new identity and position. As palpable from his subsequent and subtle but to-the-point utterances, it was apparent that neither new position nor identity had any bearing on his thoughts and words.

"He looked at me dourly and said, 'A few months after our last meeting, Ma [Mother, as a daughter is so often affectionately addressed in local culture] Rulie gave birth to a beautiful daughter. Notwithstanding the agony lingering by a still secret marriage with you, there was espousal exhilaration everywhere, supplemented by the visit of Ma Rulie's parents. Rulie's mother lovingly named her Aleena. That happiness was, however, a very ephemeral one. Rulie's health soon started deteriorating. In spite of available medical help, she succumbed to the dictate of nature and left all of us permanently, leaving behind dear Aleena. That was a disaster of unimaginable magnitude for all of us. I visited soon after coming to know about her failing health. She handed over to me two envelopes. One of them had money that you sent for her. The other is a brief letter from her. She wrote it three days prior to her death. On hearing the news of her death, Rulie's parents came to our place, stayed for a few days, and decided to take Aleena along with them. It was very appalling for my wife, but we eventually agreed that Harinarayanpur should be the place for Aleena to grow up. We also thought that the grief unexpectedly suffered by them will, to some extent, be minimized by the presence of Aleena.'

"Saying those words, Imam Shaheeb handed the envelopes to me and left without any salutation. I opened the envelope containing Rulie's letter. Unmistakably, she wrote in a quivering hand because of the serious nature of her sudden illness. She wrote,

Please accept my *salaam* at the outset. I am in a very weak and deteriorating health situation. This may be my only communication to you. I am writing this to make two points clear. One, I did not consent to marry you for money or position. In the serene setting of Harinarayanpur, I grew up merrily under the unbounded love of my father and vigilant, supportive, intellectual guidance of my mother. Nothing mattered to us and me particularly. We lived in our own world, oblivious of what was happening outside . . . and then you appeared in my life like a radiant star. Initially, I thought of you as a quaint individual. So I did not hesitate to talk to you in a routine manner without any spurned undertone. Soon, I started admiring your lack of grandiosity in communication in spite of your age and status. Your demeanor impressed me, and I talked about that with my mother too. The unfeigned nudge of unfettered feeling overtook me unexpectedly when I spontaneously held your head at the time of your sickness. The entire upper portion of my physique was holding your wobbly body. I lost all senses of probity and just wanted to assure your safety. That was the first close physical contact I had with any man.

Something thereafter happened to me. I started feeling vivacious despite your age and status. I tried to wheedle myself and conjured all social implications to keep me on track with life. I desperately tried to park that feeling as a callow and instant reaction. The oddity nevertheless persisted. The strange feeling within was ubiquitous. The more I looked at your eyes, the more intense became my internal feeling. Without knowing you at all, a sense of sincerity, commitment, and trust engulfed me. Your subsequent forceful and direct proposition made me exultant. Neither your age, your status, your having two wives, nor your four children bothered me. It was, however, very difficult for my parents. Considering a generations-old employer–employee relationship and out of a sheer sense of loyalty, they hesitantly agreed. All three of us were nevertheless clear in one respect—the ordeal you would face in having me in your abode as a third wife. We decided to repose our trust in your sense of propriety and decided to give you needed time. Unexpectedly, I became pregnant.

The rest is known to you, as Imam Shaheeb told me later on. My unreserved consent to your marriage proposition was premised on unconditional love that goaded me. I still find happiness in that. So I did not open your envelope containing money, though I always kept it under my pillow every night I went to bed. I am sending that back through Imam Shaheeb, and he promised to act on that at a suitable time. Please do not take this as an angry swipe on my part. This is no way a demonstration of sacrilegious reaction. I just do not want my love for you to be embellished by anything material. Rest assured, I am safe and secure in Imam Shaheeb's place. Mami [maternal aunt] has always been precautious in looking after me and our offspring, beautiful Aleena. This is the name my mother very fondly had chosen. All of us liked it. If Aleena is lucky to be at her home any time in future, do not discard this name. It is too dear to me.

I am glad to know from your letter about the "open arms" endorsement of our marriage by your two *begums* [my two sisters]. I am unsure whether I would ever have a chance to meet them. Please convey to them my gratitude and *salaam*.

With all my love,

Rulie

"Staring outside with a staid mind-set for a few minutes, I had a surreal and equally elegiac feeling. In a rambling mood, I walked home and called both my *begum*s. On being apprised, they kept quiet. There was no indication of either relief or happiness. As always, Boro Begum unmoored that depressing situation with a unique proposition that partially unburdened my feeling of guilt.

"She said, 'Since your father is no more with us, all three of us should visit some places of our *taluk*, including Harinarayanpur. We could come back with Aleena as our adopted daughter. This will take care of trepidations you are possibly having. First, we will take full care and responsibility of Aleena as our offspring to put Rulie's soul at peace. It will also make Hurmut Akhand and his wife relatively happy in seeing Aleena in her father's place. Second, adoption conveniently bypasses Abba Hujur's expressed decision as Aleena—or any offspring—were not mentioned. You can, if you so choose, decide later about revealing the truth.'

"That was agreed. We planned our visit aligning with the family's rest and recreation. Hurmut and his wife were taken aback, seeing us in their house without notice. Both were edgy seeing my wives and were taken aback when told that we would be staying in their house. In our known travel plan, Harinarayanpur was deliberately kept out. It was intended to have the appearance of on-the-spot decision. That was a premeditated position as advance information would entail our landing in the senior Chowdhury's abode as per tradition and sense of decency. Moreover, it would have been difficult to bring Aleena with us as we had planned to do.

"That was discussed and decided based on the wise suggestion of my wives. I, of course, made it a point to visit the Chowdhury brothers, telling them ostensibly that we just dropped in Harinarayanpur as my wives would like to thank Hurmut Akhand's wife for the care she took of me when I was sick last time. I also promised that when I come next, I will fully avail their hospitality. Happiness and anguish pervaded equally.

"But anxiety about the potential reaction by Hurmut and his wife to our proposition swallowed me up incessantly. As in many past occasions, my first wife came to the rescue. Before any move by me, she raised the issue informally with Rulie's mother and then became emotional. I had no doubt that ladies are gifted with incredible ability to handle delicate emotional matters. However, in our inclusive conversation, I explicitly indicated our positions. Aleena would be in our place for the time being as our adopted daughter. It was too soon after Abba Hujur's death to announce my third marriage. Aleena's true identity would be revealed at an appropriate time soon. Harinarayanpur would no more be relevant in her life and upbringing, while we too—like the name of Aleena, and we would retain that—would add another name, consistent with our family values and traditions. That is Qulsum. Aleena would henceforth be known as Qulsum Aleena Khan.

"Our return journey was planned in a low-key manner, except for the companionship of Imam Shaheeb at the beginning, so the adjacent community had the impression that Imam Shaheeb was taking Aleena to his home.

"We joyously returned to Nobi Nagar. Qulsum soon became the center point of attraction in our surroundings and family. Everyone started fondly addressing her as Qulsum Bibi, but my first wife insisted that she would call her Aleena. She grew up in the family with twin names of Aleena and Qulsum, based on the preferences of individual family members.

"Qulsum's real identity was carefully made known to her and her siblings at a later time when she was about nine years old. It did not cause any irritation, and our growing sons were happy to have a real sister in her. Time and years passed. She is now sixteen, excelling in didactic pursuits. I am seriously thinking about her marriage for two reasons. I want Qulsum to have a complete family life, which I could not give to her mother. Also, my first wife, of late, is not keeping well. It is her earnest desire to have a grand wedding for Qulsum, fulfilling the silent commitment she made to herself when accepting Qulsum from her grandmother. I have also decided to inform all my dear and near ones in the family and community about her real identity. I am just waiting for a suitable occasion.

"It is against this background that I desired your presence. Your help in finding a suitable groom is what I am looking for. There are no criteria for finding a proposition. Family aristocracy and wealth are immaterial to me. I want a good family and an enlightened young person, and that is what propelled me to open up before you so candidly. This is first time in life I have done so."

BM slowly and softly detailed all that he considered apposite in the circumstances to introduce and present Khan Shaheeb of Nobi Nagar before Kazi Azmat Ali of Apurba Neer. BM thought that he was waiting for some sort of signal on Kazi Azmat Ali's end. But it appeared that in his meticulous detailing of related information, he forgot something. BM civilly looked at Kazi Azmat Ali to continue. The latter nodded.

He said, "In that very private session with Khan Shaheeb, I was a listener. So I kept quiet digesting each word and simultaneously giving him the opportunity to unburden. To my best assessment, Mansoor Shafiul Alam Khan Shaheeb is a genuinely respectable man of rare distinction. I promptly concluded that besides the patrician lineage of the family, it would definitely be wonderful for anyone to have a relationship with him. I, however, have one issue on which neither Khan Shaheeb alluded nor had I any impression. So the only query I made was about the whereabouts of Hurmut Akhand and his family.

"Khan Shaheeb responded, manifesting all the decency that he personified, saying, 'Hurmut Akhand was just a manager of one of our many *tehsil*s. But he was blessed with a sharp sense of wisdom and understanding. He literally absorbed and understood the implication of my saying that Harinarayanpur will no more be relevant in Qulsum's life and upbringing. Within a few months of our visit, Hurmut Akhand disassociated himself from the *tehsil* job, sold his ancestral property, and left Harinarayanpur for resettlement in Imam Shaheeb's place. After that, he did not make any attempt to contact us. I regrettably also did not make any effort. Later on, I came to know that both husband and wife passed away years back in quick succession. I have no idea about what happened to Imam Shaheeb.'"

At Khan Shaheeb's proposition, BM stayed one more day in Khanbahadur Monzeel and was returning home. While tired of the long walk and sipping *gorom chai* [hot tea] at a wayside tea stall, he overheard people talking about the very good performance of Kazi Azmat Ali Shoudagar's eldest son, Tanveer, in his school certificate examination. The news of and talk about the grand *jayafat* being planned for Friday next was the luscious part of that discussion. The *ghattak* intuition of BM became activated. In discussions with his wife that night, he became convinced that a possible wedding between Tanveer and Qulsum will be a win-win proposition for both parties: one looking for a good family and groom and the other having a penchant for climbing the social ladder.

BM continued, saying to his prospect, "Hujur, I would have normally come to convey *mubarakbad* [congratulations] to you and Shoudagarjada on the outstanding achievement in the examination. On my way, the possibility of a matrimonial proposition between Tanveer and Qulsum dawned on me. Thus, I am here today with both objectives in mind. It is now up to your gracious consideration. It is your decision. Based on my earlier involvement in matters of the marriages of your three daughters, I can only say that you can rely on my judgment. Further, having Khan Shaheeb of Nobi Nagar as the father-in-law of your son will be of laudable social significance, about which you know best."

There was a fleeting lull in that discourse. Kazi Azmat Ali, maintaining communication probity, broke that short-lived quietness, stating, "I see merit in your thinking, and if it could be worked out, it may be blissful for both the families. But let me think a bit more and discuss with my wife, and I would have further discussion with you on this matter once Tanveer leaves for the town tomorrow. Meanwhile, you may stay as our guest."

In the midst of attending copious other errands, including exchanges of greetings with socially prominent guests attending *jayafat*, monitoring the service of food, and planning minute details for Tanveer's departure the following day, his internal self was preoccupied with what BM alluded to in the earlier conversation with him. The more he thought, the more Kazi Azmat Ali was convinced about the propriety of the proposition, but the unpublicized third marriage, and in a very nominal family, continued to bother him.

Hashi was ostensibly exhausted and sad, both because of the spillover pressure pertaining to *the jayafat* and the imminent departure of her dear son Tanveer, whom she fondly addressed as Manik (gem). She was preparing to go to sleep after serving her dear husband post-dinner *paan*.

Kazi Azmat Ali, with a very broad smile, drew her attention and said, "You will have plenty of time to sleep once Tanveer leaves but not now. I have something to talk to you about."

He then recalled all that BM had said and the specific proposition that he had concerning Tanveer's probable marriage with justifications why that should be in the near future. Those justifications were recapitulated for the benefit of Hashi. But Kazi Azmat Ali did not fail to convey a sense of dithering because of the unpublicized marriage of Qulsum's parents. Both were quiet briefly. Kazi Azmat Ali did not take much time to notice a shimmer of joy in Hashi's otherwise sad face, a physical sign evident since the day it was decided that Tanveer would go to a district headquarters college for higher studies. He affably looked at her straight and inquired with mixed feelings.

But the response took him by surprise. His moments of despair soon turned to be sustenance of prodigious delight. Hashi, without reservations and demonstrating a straightforward approach, told Kazi

Azmat Ali that she totally aligned herself with the proposition of BM, based on his convincing justifications.

As to Kazi Azmat Ali's predicament surrounding the third marriage and the ordinary background of Qulsum's maternal family, Hashi joyfully stated, "You should not be worried about that. She has the acknowledged blood of Khan Shaheeb. The third marriage, though unpublicized, is of no consequence as he has already told his immediate family about this and will tell others. The nominal background of Qulsum's mother's family is an asset for us. In Qulsum, we will have the combination of aristocracy and minimalism, strengthened by the senses of reality and self-esteem displayed by her mother and the literary attributes of her grandmother." Hashi Banu insisted, "The proposition should not be handled in a dillydally way. If it works out, our social status will receive an implausible push with the pleasure of having a daughter in this home since all our three daughters are married. Pori will be delighted to know about this, and I just can't wait."

It was agreed that Kazi Azmat Ali would have follow-up discussions with BM after Tanveer left. The onus was on Hashi to tell Tanveer about the family's desire to get him married soon.

The following morning, Pori, being distraught by the impending departure of her dear Tanveer, reluctantly took the usual walk to Hashi's abode for routine errands. Contrary to expectation and to her utter shock, Pori noticed a very exultant and relaxed Hashi-bu (sister with respect). She had the immediate feeling of being stumbled upon. Smiling, Hashi asked Pori to meet her in the bedroom. Hashi then detailed all that she and her Kazi Bhai (brother) discussed last night. Pori was overtaken by joy and happiness.

Prior to departure, Hashi hinted to Tanveer about the desire that the family was harboring. The immediate reaction of Tanveer was wishy-washy, with the only comment "Is it not too early?"

It was past noon. All arrangements and logistics were completed for Tanveer's imminent departure. Two rickshaws were parked in front of the *kachari khana*—one to take Tanveer and the other to carry his luggage. Trustworthy Badsha Chacha was to accompany him, ensuring full settlement in the college hostel. Tanveer performed his last two *salaam* by touching the feet of Kazi Azmat Ali, who was in a very somber mood. On the contrary, Hashi Banu was apparently a happy mother. But her real feeling exhibited itself in the form of uncontrollable teardrops when Tanveer bent to touch the feet of his mother. A few of those graced the open neckline of Tanveer's *punjabi* (long-flowing shirt). Tanveer respectfully put his right palm on his open neck, wiped the teardrops, and walked toward the rickshaw with a closed fist, as if he was carrying with him Mother's love and prayers.

Confluence

In the setting of Biesh Moisher Bari, Tanveer was the focus of all attention and visible care, especially after the weddings of all his elder sisters. He also partly acquired that stance. Tanveer was societal in attitude, polite in nature, expressive in communication, and respectful in interactions with all. He had easy access to all in the community and more than his share of involvement in family matters. Everyone in the family was happy and reassured by his keen interest in Father's business.

Tanveer's absence from home initially created relatable emptiness. In that situation, his three-years-younger brother, Tauseef, slowly and progressively came to relevance—not that Tauseef was ignored or lacked attention in the past. As a nascent growing individual, he had his distinct personal focus, preference, and aptitude contrary to those of Tanveer. Tauseef had no visible interest in earthly matters, more so business. His focus and priority of life centered on study. But he equally had the discerning ability to develop very warm, personal, and supportive relationships with people of his choice and liking. Tauseef had a very close bond with his dear Pori Khala. He would emphasize to her, "Khala, the world is much bigger, more challenging, and very fascinating beyond the surroundings of Apurba Neer. There is much more to know, learn about, and strive for than the burden of having the Biesh Moisher Bari identity and the business of my father."

Tauseef never bothered himself about how much of what he discussed with Pori Khala could penetrate her mind or register in her thought. He was happy that she always intently listened to what he had to say and agreed with him. Not only that, but also, Pori Khala always encouraged him to study and learn more so that in life, Tauseef could establish himself in larger society as a distinguished person. All their brief interactions ended with the expression of profound *doa* (blessings) from Pori Khala. Tauseef's genial relationship with her was in no way a manifestation of lack of love or attachment to his mother. Neither did Hashi Banu have any disconcerted feeling. Tauseef, by conscious design, never liked to bother Mother. Most of the time, Hashi Banu suffered from health-related problems. His preferred option was to love her without causing stress. He parked most of his stresses on the stable shoulder of Pori Khala.

Tauseef could not reconcile on two issues. One was his mother's frequent pregnancies dominated by miscarriages and infant deaths. On that issue, he had an acidic position about his father's attitude and approach to life. Even at that young age, he thought a lot about the meaning and priority of conjugal living. He continuously questioned himself about the veracity that dominates a married life. He had no answer to that philosophical inquisition but was certain that had his father opted, he could easily follow some preventive measures as commonly dealt with in print media and governmental publicity materials. Tauseef had a very starched feeling about this, more specifically concerning his father. The other cause of annoyance related to the stipulation made by his great-great-grandfather envisaging that only the successive eldest male would have the right to live in Biesh Moisher Bari and that others would have to have new abodes as they grow up. Tauseef, thus, could never take it as his own home, though it was the place where he was born and grew up. He raised this issue with his Pori Khala many times but had no satisfactory answer. Thus, he developed a mind-set of not treating it as his home and consequently harbored a sense of dispassion with everything associated.

The departure of Tanveer opened up the window for a more cordial bond with his parents, but Tauseef's total devotion to study and lack of interest in business matters were dominant impediments. The family had no time to be bothered by this and accepted without any whine. The common conclusion was that things would work out once Tauseef matured and came of age.

In the meantime, Kazi Azmat Ali became pensive about the marriage proposition that BM had in mind. In giving his consent to proceed, Kazi Azmat Ali specifically told BM to follow the prescribed ways articulated during the discussion on the day after Tanveer left for college.

In a post-dinner conversation, Kazi Azmat Ali reiterated, "You should proceed very cautiously. Our identity should not be disclosed at the preliminary phase as any negation at that point will be a slur on our house, the social status of which generations have very cautiously nurtured. You should first provide full details of the groom-to-be and your full knowledge about him. At only getting positive signals, you should allude to the genial family details, and only thereafter will our full identity be disclosed. In your planned interactions with Khan Shaheeb of Nobi Nagar, you should indicate that Kazi Shaheeb alluded to his desire to find a suitable bride for his son during a brief chat at the *jayafat*. This should be the premise and desired line of action in piloting the proposition." Kazi Azmat Ali then paused but, as an abundant precaution, continued, saying, "You should also elucidate adequately that the proposition is what you have in mind and that you are yet to discuss that with me. The inkling of a probable marriage proposition between these two families hit your *ghattak* mind educing on your previous private conversation with him and desultory discussions with me during the *jayafat* arranged to celebrate the success of my son."

BM was pleasantly surprised. All of Kazi Azmat Ali's stipulations and approach were what he had in mind anyway. In conveying his total identity with the suggested line of action, BM also indicated that he would highlight his association and the trust he enjoyed in the family of Biesh Moisher Bari with a solidly grounded base, having successfully handled delicate marriage relationships in the past. He said that he would emphasize, as the *ghattak* of the weddings of three daughters from that family, that he had earned such trust beyond any doubt and could prudently provide facts in a way that the family can't say no.

BM left Biesh Moisher Bari with zealous feelings. If he could steer this, it will be one of the most esteemed ones in his professional life as a *ghattak*. That thought was enamored by recalling what Kazi Azmat Ali had stipulated during last night's discussion. It convinced BM that Kazi Shaheeb is not only a prudent and successful businessman but also blessed with intelligence and foresight that could as well make him a successful *ghattak*. Had that been so, perhaps BM would not have been relevant in this profession at all. He revisited all that Kazi Shaheeb told him, concluding precisely that the suggested lines have the ones that he would have followed in any case, based on his experience in arranging marriages in all the years passed. He had a laugh at himself. Based on the professional expertise mustered during the process of arranging and finalizing marriage propositions, he concluded that the real challenge is to ensure a passable amalgam between the need of Khan Shaheeb Mansoor Shafiul Alam Khan and the desire of Kazi Azmat Ali Shoudagar. He decided to take a little time and careful steps to obviate any impression of haste.

Bakshi Mia showed up at Khanbahadur Monzeel after about two weeks. He cautiously placed his proposition before Khan Shaheeb, following the directives of Kazi Azmat Ali and the strategy he had in mind. In doing so, he emphasized, "I know the family very intimately and earlier arranged three marriages of the daughters of the family. They are financially well-off for generations. Their present business is flourishing. The family is very small one, with all the sisters happily married and a younger brother in high school. The proposed groom has a name as being amiable, smart, and intelligent with full interest in his father's business. As per tradition of the family, he would inherit the present home without any division, with the younger brother to be relocated nearby in a new home in due course."

There was lull in the discussion. Obviously, Khan Shaheeb was engrossed in internal thoughts about the pros and cons of the proposition. Instead of asking the full identity of the other family, he expressed concern about the relative youth of the groom-to-be.

Bakshi Mia reacted courteously, saying, "Hujur, you have a very genuine concern. I also thought about this before, but my considered impression is the answer lies in how one sees it. To my assessment, a positive inclination will lead us to a positive conclusion, and a negative one will lead us to a gloomy conclusion. The proximity of their age profile and the relative youth of the proposed groom could be a win-win situation. Young girls have tremendous ability to adjust with their spouses, irrespective of age. Despite their age or perhaps because of it, Qulsum Bibi, with her nuanced intelligence, as you mentioned earlier, will certainly be capable to mold the young groom to her liking. The groom-to-be is well-known in the local setting as a responsible and responsive young person. I have no doubt about the outcome. I only came to you being convinced myself first."

After finishing his robust reasoning, he waited for a much-desired response from Khan Shaheeb, but his long silence caused a sense of oddity. Khan Shaheeb's reticent demeanor, centering on the end of the flexible tube of his aristocratic hookah, without any eye contact, aggravated this. BM's apprehensive thinking was premised on the variables, the reflection, or was it an obfuscation of Khan Shaheeb's stance? He had no clarity about the possible conclusion.

Khan Shaheeb eventually looked at *ghattak* Bakshi with an elfin smile, saying, "You have a point. I have analyzed your reasoning in the backdrop of possible ramifications and concluded it to be worth consideration before making a final decision. I would like to discuss with my wives and will let you know tomorrow."

Those few words were of significant assurance to Bakshi Mia and sufficient to obliterate his trepidation. Based on experience, he parked all his hope in a probable positive upshot.

Khan Shaheeb called his household staff and directed them to escort BM to the *mehman khana* (guesthouse of the *monzeel*). As usual, Khan Shaheeb had post-dinner discussions with his two wives, advised them about the presence of *ghattak* BM, and apprised them of the discussions they had earlier.

Boro Begum readily agreed as her focus was on an immediate wedding for her dear Aleena Qulsum. Chotto Begum also consented but had annotations about the lack of specificity of who the family was.

Khan Shaheeb responded with a prelude and opined, "Some ordinary individuals very often display a rare sense of intelligence and wisdom. Hurmut Akhand and *ghattak* BM appear to be gifted by such qualities. In discussions with me, he guided himself with due diligence. He first shared with me unspecified elements about the family and then detailed all he could about the groom-to-be. His obvious strategy is to move step by step. If we generally concur with the status of the groom-to-be, then plausibly, he would share full details. He has shared with me the related background of the family without indicating specifically the name of the housemaster and the location. The family is very well-known in their locale and financially well-off, and all daughters are married with one younger brother. What makes me happy is that probably, *ghattak* Bakshi will follow a similar approach in talking to the other family, preserving and protecting our social standing and the good name of the family. He appears to be an excellent professional *ghattak*, and the good name he has earned is well deserved."

As Khan Shaheeb was mincing his last *paan* of the night, the wives exchanged looks of tacit query as to whether to consent or not. On getting the nod, Boro Begum looked at Khan Shaheeb, saying, "We have always trusted your judgment. There is no reason to deviate from that. If you are satisfied, we are fully on board with you."

The following midday discussions between Khan Shaheeb and Bakshi Mia were unwittingly undertaken in a most germane fashion, signaling positive indication for the groom-to-be by Khan Shaheeb, followed by disclosure of the full identity of the family by the *ghattak* and then the go-ahead signal to proceed. Exultant, Bakshi Mia wanted to leave that evening but had to stay back at the covet of Khan Shaheeb. That expression of desire was indicative of definite interest in the family marriage proposition he was pursuing. That made him very happy, and Bakshi Mia had a nice sleep.

Instead of going to Apurba Neer directly, Bakshi Mia decided to go home and relax for two days. His lifelong experience as a *ghattak* made him comprehend the imperative value of being steady in every stage of negotiations. He was particularly conscious of two fundamentals: never fully open up with respect to the interests of each of the two parties involved, and the varied nature and different shades of issues cropping up during negotiations should not be taken negatively always. Both these keep a *ghattak* relevant in the negotiation process.

With positive developments, Bakshi Mia's shuttles between Apurba Neer and Nobi Nagar increased significantly, handling issues of relevance—the *den mohar* (dowry); the venue of the marriage (usually the bride's home in a rural setting, but this time, having it in a neutral location seemed like a good idea); the date of marriage; the number in the *bor jatri* (bridal party); the *walima* (wedding reception for the bride in the groom's place); the type, nature, and ballpark indication of gifts to be exchanged between the two families; etc.— undeniably very mundane matters. As per cultural norms and social setting of the time, some of such insignificant matters can become serious issues, invoking family prestige and impacting on an amiable understanding. In some cases, such ordinary issues can wreck the negotiation process. A *ghattak* plays a crucial role in this process, extenuating possible misapprehension and mistrust and bringing the whole process to a happy ending. That precisely is the position that *ghattak* Bakshi Mia was in. Thus, he was visiting both Apurba Neer and Nobi Nagar frequently. It was an excruciating journey sometimes, but the by-product of this made him very happy. None of the different positions on the issues were of any magnitude that could impact the proposition per se. In many cases, they subsequently strengthened the interests of both parties to pursue the process. More interestingly, Bakshi Mia noticed that with each of his visits, both the warmth of welcome and the quality and type of food enhanced markedly. Each of the families took him as their front man. To each of them, he became a family man cum well-wisher.

Each of Bakshi Mia's visits enhanced the joy and happiness in both abodes of Nobi Nagar and Apurba Neer. Hashi Banu spared no time in informing Tanveer about the proposition and the progress as soon as he came home for his first holiday. Tanveer had all along been an obsequious son. He kept quiet, but his mother was very content in observing his shy but happy smile.

That was not unexpected. Tanveer was known as an obedient son and had all along exhibited respect and admiration for the opinions and decisions of his parents. He grew up with the personality trait of treating his parents' desires as commands. Because of that and prevalent cultural norms of the time, Tanveer's opinion was immaterial. It was the decision of Father that mattered most. So Tanveer behaved as the acquiescent son of a traditional family.

But that was not Tauseef's reaction. Seeing happiness everywhere and sensing preparatory activities, Tauseef inquired from his dear Pori Khala the reason for that. Listening to her detailing everything, he observed, saying, "What is the hurry? Is it not too early for Bhaiya [Brother] to get married?"

As Pori did not specifically comment on that observation, Tauseef continued, saying, "Had it been my case, I would have never consented, least being happy. What an unwise step in the life of a young man who barely has an idea about the objectives and path of his life."

Based on what she knew, Pori, with the related justifications she could articulate, put forth all supportive arguments. But Tauseef was not to be influenced. He tried to keep the exchanges within the frame of discussions but not argumentation. So he smiled a little and said, "Pori Khala, keep this in mind. I have reservations about marriage, seeing the condition of my *amma* [mother]. Even if I decide to marry, that will be at the time of my choosing and with the bride of my choice."

Pori knew Tauseef very well. She also valued frank access to the loving relationship she had developed with him. Pori responded, saying, "Baba [lovingly for son], I have noted your views and will keep your words in mind. I will always do all that is needed to ensure that you can conduct your life as you think appropriate. But you must not deviate from your focus on studies. You must become someone known all over the country. Apurba Neer and its surroundings are not to be your world. You will always have my *doa* [blessings]."

Tauseef closed that discussion and took an atypical step. He straightway went to his *amma*'s room and sat by her side on the *palong.* Hashi was both surprised and happy. As they exchanged a rare exultant glance, Tauseef observed, "You are blissful as matters related to Bhaiya's marriage are making steady progress."

Hashi Banu affirmed by nodding and saying yes. She also highlighted the happiness of his father and the patrician linkage of the bride-to-be. Tauseef kept quiet with a happy face. It was the turn of Mother to take an unusual step. She bent down and embraced Tauseef, kissing his forehead. It was a rather sporadic experience for both the mother and the son. He left his mother's room nonchalantly.

Hashi Banu could not control herself. She called Pori immediately to share the good news. Pori listened and smiled with observation. "Hashi-bu, you should tell this to Kazi Bhai soonest, and he too will be ecstatic as this signifies total agreement within the family."

With most of the issues pertaining to the proposition being tackled through the skilled handling by Bakshi Mia, it was time for the formalization of the proposal. That involved face-to-face interactions between the two fathers in the presence of close relations and distinguished community elders. This is called the event of *paka kottah* (final word) or *paan chinni* (ceremony presenting betel leaf and sweets as a symbolic warmhearted meeting), similar to a modern engagement event.

Kazi Azmat Ali, with happiness brimming everywhere, charmingly stepped into Khan Monzeel, accompanied by male members of his extended family and selected community gentries. Bakshi Mia was there beforehand, but he assiduously maintained a posture of neutrality, unwearyingly hoping and praying for a booming outcome.

Janab Mansoor Shafiul Alam Khan positioned himself in front of his family's *kachari khana* soon after being advised about the imminent arrival of Kazi Azmat Ali Shoudagar and his entourage. As they faced each other and exchanged *salaam*, both of them embraced each other warmly with their flowing beards caressing each other's neck. The other noticeable commonality was the way both fathers dressed up for the important event with surprising similarity. Both dressed in *sherwani*s (prince coat–type knee-length outfits worn by Muslim gentries during important events), *rumi tupi*s (Turkish-style long caps of maroon color, each with a black tassel on the side and identified with a famous Persian poet named Rumi), and elegant walking sticks. The only distinguishable element was that while Janab Mansoor Shafiul Alam Khan was wearing a black *sherwani*, Kazi Azmat Ali Shoudagar's one was cream colored.

As the party was seated in the *kachari khana* with the demureness of the Khanbahadur Monzeel, *paan*, sweets, and gifts for the bride-to-be were taken inside, and the guests were served sherbet. The local customs ordained that though such an event takes place in the house of the bride-to-be, the onus is on the father/guardian of the family of the groom-to-be to lay the proposition, premised on earnest keenness, requesting the hand of the girl of the house for their son.

After rituals and activities related to the sherbet and *paan* services were over, Kazi Azmat Ali Shoudagar, without wasting any time, politely said, "Khan Shaheeb, it is a privilege for me, my relations, and community elders to be in your *monzeel*, and I would like to convey our sincere thanks for the warmth and cordiality with which we were welcomed. We are here with the fondest desire to request the hand of Betty [daughter] Qulsum for my son, Tanveer. Betty Qulsum will be in our home not as a daughter-in-law but as our daughter, enjoying all the respect and dignity she deserves. We will be delighted to have your affirmation."

Khan Shaheeb, repositioning himself on his cushioned chair, gracefully responded, "Kazi Shaheeb, it is true that our abode has traditions linked with nobility, but we are just carrying on the legacy. Your family has enviable background. More so, yours, as it stands now, is the outcome of personal prudence, competence, and commitment of generations. Your individual good name already has traveled much beyond Apurba Neer. We are honored to have you all as our esteemed guests."

Having said those words, Khan Shaheeb exchanged affirmatory looks with Bakshi Mia, who nodded. After a pause, Khan Shaheeb continued, saying, "Since you addressed Qulsum Bibi twice as Betty, I do not think you left any room for me to be negative with respect to your proposition. I say, with an open mind and all my blessings for the proposition, Alhamdulillah [all praise is due to Allah alone]."

Kazi Azmat Ali stood up in the twinkling of an eye and embraced Khan Shaheeb with the salutation *bhai* and said, "By consenting happily, you have honored me, my entourage, and my family. We are thankful to you. We will do everything befitting the honor and dignity of your family. *Inshallah* [God willing], the wedding will be a grand one."

All present in that gathering were relaxed and jubilant. So was Bakshi Mia as this signified the most noteworthy marriage proposition in his long *ghattak* profession. Some of the gentries congratulated Bakshi Mia for piloting the proposition successfully. He felt elevated.

Happy social exchanges preponderated the post-feast setting. Kazi Azmat Ali and a few of his selected siblings were taken inside the house to bless the bride. Qulsum Bibi was escorted by her two mothers (Boro and Chotto Begums). She was looking very gorgeous, clad in the maroon silk sari with gold bangles, necklace, and earrings that were brought by her new in-laws. Kazi Azmat Ali was very pleased having his first look at his daughter-in-law to be. He brought out a nicely packed ring and handed over it to Boro Begum, saying, "This is from Hashi Banu, my wife, as her blessing. This ring was passed on for generations to the eldest new bride of the family. My late mother blessed Hashi Banu with this. She is now passing on this to Betty Qulsum."

Both wives, as well as others present, were overwhelmed. Chotto Begum held the right hand of Qulsum, and Boro Begum put the ring on her engagement finger.

On being advised and helped by Chotto Begum, Qulsum took shy, small steps approaching the gentries seated on the opposite side and performed *kodom buchi* (performing *salaam* by touching feet), starting with Kazi Azmat Ali and ending with Khan Shaheeb. In approaching him, Qulsum could not check her emotions and collapsed on the chest of her father.

Khan Shaheeb held her steady and said, "Daughters are *amanat* [precious to its possessor as temporary custodian] in their parents' home. One day she leaves her parents' home for her new one. That happens with all grown-up girls. That happened with your mother too."

He could not finish what he wanted to say, recalling Rulie could never step in her home. Sudden allay overtook his speech.

Boro Begum quietly stepped in, saying, "Your real home is where you are going. But wherever you are, our love and affection will always be with and for you."

To obviate further emotional zen, Kazi Azmat Ali interjected, "Betty, we have not blessed you as our daughter-in-law to be. We have blessed you as our daughter. You will not be separated from your parents. Whenever you feel bad or would like to see them, just tell me or your Hashi Amma, and we will make all arrangements without any rider. You should take us as your second set of parents."

That made all present very happy. Khan Shaheeb, accompanied by Kazi Azmat Ali and associated individuals, returned to the *kachari khana*. All the guests left in due course, except Bakshi Mia, who stayed back at the behest of Khan Shaheeb. That was sort of a cultural norm and a way for Khan Shaheeb to convey his appreciation to him for arranging a good marriage. In that moment of quiet happiness, Khan Shaheeb recounted teardrops that fell on the opposite side of his palm as Qulsum rested her head on his chest, and he was trying to console her. He quietly reconnaissanced and unwittingly kissed the relevant side of his palm.

Concordance

With meticulous preparations on the parts of both families, the marriage of Tanveer and Qulsum took place in a befitting manner after six months. The bearing of that event in the respective local settings of Apurba Neer and Nobi Nagar was so swarming that all who were invited and those who were not were equally exultant. It was a rare phenomenon and spoke of the respective social standings of the two families. Despite their age or because of it, both Qulsum and Tanveer bonded sturdily from their first union. Mother and Pori Khala were delighted seeing them interacting as a couple. Badsha Chacha used to get an update from Pori at night and was happy too. Kazi Azmat Ali continued mincing more *paan*s as his way of expressing elation.

What surprised all was the close relationship Qulsum bonded in a short time with less talkative, sort of introverted, and ardently studious Tauseef. Qulsum's affinity was premised on Tauseef's eagerness toward broad-based study focus, including newspapers and journals. It spontaneously reminded her of her mother and grandmother's penchant for books and magazines as she had heard from Boro Amma and Chotto Amma (referring to the two wives of Khan Shaheeb). In Qulsum—and mostly because of her easy and warm gestures—Tauseef had someone almost of the same age to be friendly and open besides being his *bhabi* (wife of elder brother). That relationship had a supporting boost when Tauseef suggested—and Qulsum agreed with the stipulation—that they together could use the greeting of *tumi* (a more friendly informal salutation) instead of *apni* (address testifying respect and seniority) as per cultural requirements in addressing the wife of an elder brother, irrespective of age differences. He was even more delighted with the prompt consent by Qulsum when he indicated his preference to call her by her middle name, Aleena. He quickly formulated a very light justification in support of his preference.

Tauseef said, "You see, to me, Qulsum is a very outdated name compared with Aleena, which is smart and soothing to hear. When I address you as Qulsum Bhabi, the picture of a middle-aged woman with a number of children flashes in my thought. When I call Aleena Bhabi, I can literally figure you out as you are."

Both laughed. Qulsum confessed that when she and Tanveer are alone, he also addresses her as Aleena. That bond between *bhabi* and *devar* (younger brother of husband) was entwined further because of the needs and actions of both. Qulsum started writing frequent letters to Tanveer, and Tauseef was the most genial person to mail them. After a few times, Tauseef suggested that she could request Badsha Chacha to mail them.

Qulsum looked at him with all helplessness and said, "If I do that, Badsha Chacha would invariably tell Pori Khala about the frequency of letters. It will then travel to all, including Abba, and that will be a matter of embarrassment for me. This is the reason I am to request you every time. You are not only my *devar* but a friend too. Will you not help me?"

Tauseef nodded. He always observed that family discourses in their house had focus on business, property, and social standings of people around. He never saw anyone, including Bhaiya (elder brother), read anything or have deliberations related to music, art, or social issues. Tauseef had ideas about such family discourses from reading stories in journals and periodicals. His repeated efforts to engage Bhaiya in discussing other matters of life were futile. For Tanveer, the whole gamut of study and tangential matters end with stepping out of study room in the main structure of *kachari khana*. Tauseef was, thus, surprised to notice Aleena occasionally in his room, reading magazines and newspapers with complete fidelity. Instead of commenting, he started borrowing books and magazines from the school library and friends and quietly passed that on to his Aleena Bhabi. That was a sweet gesture on the part of Tauseef that allowed her to pass some of her lonely time with relative joy and happiness.

She spared no time in informing Tanveer about the friendly support she was getting from Tauseef and how that helped her sustain with a lonely life so soon after marriage. She did not fail, however, to impress upon him the need to concentrate in studies as their complete reunion hinged on the timely finishing of his studies.

A few days after exchanging such communications, Qulsum was overtaken by a surprise beyond expectation when Tauseef handed over the popular Bangla weekly magazine *Bichitra*, lovingly subscribed to by Tanveer without any prior indication. In a separate note to him, Tanveer indicated that he subscribed for full one year and that Tauseef should monitor its receipt. Qulsum became all the more euphoric when Tauseef told him about that.

As she was growing up, Qulsum was frankly apprised of oddities that shrouded her parents' wedding, unexpected constraints that stood on the way of her mother stepping into her home-to-be, her temporary relocation in the abode of Imam Shaheeb, and her sudden death. These were mostly communicated by Boro Begum, who did not fail to restate the wives' unreserved willingness to have Rulie as the third wife of Khan Shaheeb and all that she and Chotto Begum did to bring Aleena to her real but third home in a life span of about one year. During such exchanges, Qulsum hardly had any emotional outburst. That was evident for good reasons in spite of apparent sanities of backlash. Khan Shaheeb broke family traditions in conveying his love for Qulsum, facilitating easy access to him, unlike other children of the family. Boro Begum prudently exercised care and caution and gradually detailed events, with focus on avoiding adverse impact on Qulsum's growing thoughts and future actions. Also, it was so proven later on that though Qulsum grew up in her paternal home under the guidance of two wives, her thinking and personality traits were blessed by all the positive attributes of her mother and grandmother. Qulsum easily adapted herself to the surroundings of her final fourth home in Apurba Neer. A very genial welcome from all helped the process, as well as the youthful and spontaneous embraces and understanding shown by Tanveer.

Pori observed something, and she was not happy. Qulsum's spending most of her time inside the home and a sense of disquiet she exhibited in front of Hashi-bu and Kazi Bhai bothered her. In Pori's assessment, Qulsum personified all the separate and connected elements of being reticent and tepid in her new home. That should not be so after so many months, and she shared her anxiety with Hashi-bu, whose reaction was slow. She took her time observing Qulsum.

One day both of them were in the courtyard at the same time. As Qulsum was taking steps for her usual hurried retreat inside the house, Hashi Banu affectionately called her, hugged her tenderly, and held her in embrace for quite a while without uttering a single word. That perhaps was her chosen way to convey inner feelings.

Hashi Banu took hold of both Qulsum's hands and very compellingly said, "Qulsum Betty, you are not our daughter-in-law. You are a daughter of this house. Move, act, and talk in a way that makes you happy. There is no need to be shy with a soreness feeling. Be as is and be yourself. That will make both Tanveer and all of us happy. We understand that you miss him, but all of us are here to look after you. Tanveer will be back soon."

After saying those words, Hashi had a happy smile and returned to her room. Those spartan few words did an unexpected miracle in shaping the subsequent life and activities of Qulsum in Biesh Moisher Bari. Perhaps this outcome was from the pulsation emanating from the warm and intense embrace Qulsum experienced with her mother-in-law. She was carefree in moving out, and she was forthright in interacting and in putting on a sari informally, the way she used to in Nobi Nagar.

Pori observed the change with delight. Tauseef cheerfully related it as full assimilation of his dear Aleena Bhabi with Biesh Moisher Bari. More than even Hashi-Banu, Kazi Azmat Ali was happy in noting the change and congratulated Hashi for being able to win the confidence of their daughter-in-law. All of them were happy to see stress-free Qulsum at ease but did not communicate anything to her.

It was Tanveer, who, during one of the brief visits prior to his twelfth grade intermediate final examination, conveyed to Qulsum the positive reaction of all. He also did not fail to tease her, saying, "Perhaps your liking of all in our family and the surroundings is so pervasive that my absence does not affect your emotions."

For a fleeting moment, Qulsum was taken aback. That particular comment was certainly in contrast with what Qulsum had experienced in the immediate past, coinciding with the arrival of Tanveer for a short unannounced visit. He was very happy to be at home, and so was she and everyone in the family.

Tanveer withdrew to his room with clear indication to Qulsum to follow him and soon was in a state of lolling on his bed. Qulsum slowly stepped in the room and coyly sat by his side. She was adoring his face and all-inclusive physical expressions. He brought out a small packet from under his pillow. Qulsum was astounded. As she opened the packet at his behest, she found a bright orange-colored Rajshahi silk sari (the best silk sari of Bangladesh) with a sophisticated light green embossed print. Qulsum was surprised and happy. It was the first gift from Tanveer to her.

The startling presence of Tanveer and the most unexpected but equally affable gift made her very exultant. She was enjoying every moment of the unanticipated experience in the warm embrace of Tanveer. Qulsum was in a totally different world of thoughts and feelings. Thus, the sudden comment by Tanveer about "his absence without emotional impact on Qulsum," though it joggled her beyond expectancy, was put to a permanent rest. The backdrop of her birth— growing up in a house where she would not have been welcomed at all but for oversight of her grandfather in articulating positions soon after knowing about the marriage of her parents and the dithering mind-set of her father, laden with family values and good name—was always embedded in her thoughts and actions, and her growing-up persona epitomized that very much. Qulsum grew up under the careful watch of her *boro* and *chotto amma*s but never forgot her real identity, having the blood of the Khan dynasty. She somehow developed a feeling that love loses its spontaneity when subsumed by empathy. Unwavering attributes embedded in the personal traits of her maternal grandmother and positivity inherent in her mother's character enthused Qulsum to exercise exhortation to any indication of insinuated negativity and remain reticent.

This happened, the first such discussion, in their married life of few months. The bubbly Qulsum was inert for a few moments, raised upward her emotion-laden soaked eyes, held Tanveer's hands, and slowly positioned him on their bed. She said with a pidgin expression, "My birth and upbringing are quite uncommon compared with your family, and this is known to all. As a newborn, I obviously did not have any memory of my first two homes. I grew up in my third home under some constraint, the nature and relevance of which could only be assessed by me. Initially, Father was hesitant in showing his love for me. It so appeared, as I grew up, that my grandfather's reaction to my father's sudden covert marriage and the responsibility of upholding the family's so-called good name were palpable hindrances. He was burdened by the thought of assumed obligation and the unspoken contract with my late mother. Boro and Chotto Ammas devoted all their effort and energy in shaping me as a good girl, befitting the image and reputation of Khanbahadur Monzeel. Since they married much earlier and of their only occasional presence in Nobi Nagar, I could not bond with my sisters. My two brothers behaved with me as revered seniors and always maintained a distance, although both of them loved me a lot, especially after the disclosure of my real identity. I grew up as an isolated individual with no one around to interact, to confide, or to be gregarious with. This, for no fault of anyone, was a totally different setting than what I have now in my fourth and hopefully last home. The uninhibited and pleasant vibes enamored in the facial expressions of your parents, the ever-congenial connection with Pori Khala, and the very supporting and understanding relationship with Tauseef have made me at ease in this home. I am unclear about my feelings and relationship with your three married sisters, but for the first time in my life, I have started feeling me—my relevance, my preferences, my choices—with respect to life and living."

Saying those words without any inhibition or hiatus, in a voice full of tremulous emotion, Qulsum continued with her inner feelings, "My sort of depressed identity, notwithstanding the love and care of Boro and Chotto Ammas, had its unqualified safe and fulfilling anchor in the embrace of your arms. So you are never far away from me in spite of our physical separation. Since I set foot on this property, I have had the feeling of being a part of it. As I move around this home, I find and feel you in the words and actions of everyone and everything around me. The question of missing you does not arise. No one can separate you from me."

Tanveer was taken aback by the unexpected emotional backlash shown by Qulsum, so apparent in the cadence of her rather detailed and poignant response. He paused momentarily to balance his reactions and recoup his thoughts. He instantaneously revisited and appreciated the potency and value of reengagement in building a solid conjugal relationship. There was neither the need nor the luxury for awaiting a moment of specific relevance or opportunity to do that. As he observed his father practicing, Tanveer recognized the importance and value of enhancing the spectacle of a connubial relationship in a sustainable way to prevent possible curdling. He committed himself to that.

It was his turn to react. He slowly got both his palms disengaged from the steady clasp of Qulsum's hands. He very affectionately took possession of Qulsum's hand and drew her closer, still remaining seated on the bed. He looked at his loving wife with all the vista of reinvention. He remained speechless for a few moments. Instead of responding to her with loaded words of feeling, Tanveer alluded to his vision of their relationship. Lovingly drawing her attention by pressing her palms, Tanveer observed, "My dear Aleena, whatever you said about your feeling for me is replicable with respect to my feeling for you. I will make every effort to demonstrate this in all my words and actions to follow. My love for you is a very private feeling and will remain so in my entire life. But I have a challenge for you."

Qulsum was confounded by the last remark. She wanted to conjecture the innate implication but was at a loss. So she applied her decisive weaponry of having a focused, prying look but devoid of any glint.

Tanveer put the challenge directly, in simple words. "I have had observed the relationship between my parents since the time I was growing up. That always overwhelmed me, being quite different from those cultivated by our relations and neighbors. My father has always been very respectful to my mother and consulted her in most matters. While decisions, particularly for business-related and social matters, have always been made by him, he used to keep Mother informed or explained the rationale. Showing respect to each other, they created an ambiance of friendliness, helping significantly our growing up as good individuals. It is my cherished dream to have that sort of understanding and ambiance in my family life. I need you, your help, and your support in that endeavor. You belong to a new generation. Social focus and values are radically changing. I need a good friend by my side in all matters of life, especially in upholding the honor and prestige of Biesh Moisher Bari. I would like to have you not just as a wife but as a treasured friend in my journey of life. You will have to shape accordingly."

There was an unintended long silence, not so much because of the nature of the challenge but more because of the embedded nuance of the proposition. Tanveer realized that the objective of having his wife as a friend was not a matter of specific statement but an approach, needed to be orchestrated and pursued systematically by both in every bend of conjugal living.

To deviate from that for the moment, he spoke of Qulsum's earlier reference of the ordeal surrounding her birth and early childhood and said, "There is no gain in referring to that. That was past, and you had no involvement. On the contrary, you are a product of that torment. It did not stand in the way of our union, and that will never have any bearing on our future life. This matter should never be raised or discussed. While my previous suggestion for a nurturing relationship premised on our wedding and friendship is a matter of unforeseen decisions and actions of the future, you can easily adhere to this yearning of mine relating to your birth."

Qulsum was both surprised and overwhelmed with unbounded happiness, and promised to adhere to what Tanveer articulated but could not control her involuntary, unabated teardrops. Her spontaneous agreement did not make him happy, and that took her by total surprise.

To clarify his reaction, Tanveer stated, "Precisely that sort of an approach in life I want to avoid. It is because of this that I envisaged a life based on friendship, where you will always ask me questions to get things clarified before you agree or have alternative viewpoints. That is healthy. That is our journey together. I just do not want you to agree with whatever I stipulate."

Tanveer went on clarifying his position not to ever raise or discuss the issues related to Qulsum's birth and childhood. He said, "Both your father and my father belong to a generation transitioning from an old and known value system to something unfamiliar and unknown. The war of Bangladesh liberation was not just a war for independence. It ushered an era of unnoticed and undocumented rebellion against a known value system. That gradually is impacting the paradigm of societal and family relationships. The acceptable standard of manners and respect; the conviviality of approach, aptitude, and attitude; the sanity and decency of civility in social interaction; and the responsibility and accountability for our decisions and actions have changed. Sheer demographic pressure, causing economic stress and frustration; the misplaced use of technological advances; and misguided entertainment exposure have accentuated the process. All facilitated the sudden dominance of the third hand in our real life setting—people proudly having the third hand of 'excuse' in addition to natural right and left hands."

In Bangla *vasha* (language), the right hand is known as *dan haath*, and the left hand is called *bam haath*. The translated Bangla word for *excuse* is *oju haath*. So often it is jokingly said that Bangladeshis have three hands or *haath*: *bam haath*, *dan haath*, and *oju haath*. If something was not done or could not be done on time, then most Bangladeshis have the ingenuity to use a convincing excuse. For every personal failure or noncompliance, individuals have mustered the art of excuse. For similar experiences at the national level, they always have the excuse of foul play and conspiracy.

Aleena listened intently to every word and more significantly took note of his related body language, tonal variations, and emotional lexis. She quickly decided that neither being reticent nor being tepid would be a discreet option. Either of the actions would reflect negatively on her persona and would be a slur to her intelligence. Though the foregoing loaded statements were uttered by Tanveer in a somber mood from a perceptible high pedestal, Aleena was quite well aware of some of this through her constant exposure to print media and publications. She was thinking of plausible formulations to constitute a partisan response against the backdrop of the need of caution and questioning before agreeing, as emphasized by Tanveer earlier. Keeping the enunciation and desire of Tanveer on their friendship to bond and strengthen and sustain their nascent conjugal relation, Aleena was clear in her thoughts: the need to harbor a frame of level playing field in the inner cell of her heart. To be a friend of her spouse in real terms, she likewise would always make efforts not to commit needless gaffes and avoid situations that would require her to inveterate submissions before Tanveer.

That particular inkling was premised on specific nature and type of understanding and assurances inbuilt in the utterances of Tanveer concerning her birth. They, by connotation, put her mother and grand parents at the high pedestal of respect and love by the son-in-law of Khanbhadur Monzeel. Her eyes soaked. Allena exercised control to arrest falling teardrops.

All that Tanveer stipulated pertaining to be both friend and wife were formidable challenges for her, and she indubitably needed more time to consolidate her thoughts, words and actions. She took the excuse of knowing the background of exposure to and the priorities of the issues highlighted by him, including that of social changes. However, she was upright in expressing her reservations about teaching such matters in colleges. She thus made a specifc query before aligning herself with the stipulations.

Conjure

Tanveer was pleased in noting the prying approach of Aleena and was prompt and frank in responding. He was candid in telling her that what he said earlier were neither his words nor the result of his college education per se. He further stated that the opportunity for a college education had definitely ushered within him the confidence and the ability to think out of the box. His own intellectual prowess was sharpened significantly because of college exposure and independent living, compared with the guarded and closely monitored life pattern of Apurba Neer. It was accentuated and more so enlivened by the unexpected close and genial association with his professor of philosophy, who was commonly known as Logic Sir to most students as the intermediate level pre-philosophy course was called Logic, hence the title Logic Sir.

Tanveer, during his brief stay on the following few nights, progressively narrated the related backdrop of his exposure to and ability to think about broader issues that mattered in the greater frame of life. He said, "Providence perhaps had its larger share and influence in shaping up my close association with our otherwise standoffish Logic Sir. During an initial class deliberation, I differed with a proposition that Logic Sir was explaining and emphasizing. We had exchanges in the presence of hundreds of fellow students. Later on, I received a note from him delivered by the teachers' room office bearer asking me to see him. I was nervous as my earlier exchanges with him in the presence of other students were supposedly contrary to prevalent norm of social/academic behavior.

"I met Logic Sir at the appointed time. The person I faced outside classroom milieu is totally a different one. He instantly made me feel easy and relaxed by his unqualified friendly gesticulation. Logic Sir appreciated the point I made in the class and suggested that I keep focus on keeping my mind open always and in every situation. His very congenial remark was 'Issues pertaining to life, societal behavior and compulsions, and philosophical domains normally have no ready-made and eternal answers. One's search for truth should always be premised on sustained assessment of possibilities to the contrary.'

"He then suggested that if I feel like, I could come to his modest rented accommodation for discussions on any matter of my preference. That was a very exceptional gesture, and my probing mind did not like to miss that opportunity. Gradually, I became a frequent visitor and enjoyed discussions on varied matters. Until I had the opportunity of knowing him adequately and intimately, all my perceptions about knowledge, perspicacity, and judgment were framed within the sphere of pages and lines of mostly hard-covered textbooks. Gradually evolving warm relationship with Logic Sir has opened up my vision to the enormous opportunity that exists to learn additionally from surroundings. I fully capitalized on that. Slowly, I became privy to very emotional details of his personal life. Whenever I recall Logic Sir, emotions within me overflow, and it becomes difficult to check impulsive tears."

Tanveer decided to open up about his emotional stress concerning Logic Sir and opted to narrate that in pieces during his stay. He also insisted that Aleena be very mindful to what he would say both to understand Logic Sir as a person and his views about surroundings beyond the college and Biesh Moisher Bari. He said, "The formal name of Logic Sir was Dewan Tasleem Ahmed. His standoffish personal traits were always a barrier to the development of easy and genial relationships with most. Besides the common identity to students as Logic Sir, he was addressed in a varied manner by different people based on the warmth of the relationship. Some used to call him Dewan Shaheeb [*shaheeb* meaning a salutation with respect]. Others would address him as either Tasleem Shaheeb or Ahmed Shaheeb. That was quite unusual but was the norm in his case.

"During one of many conversations, Logic Sir opened up unexpectedly and shared his life story with me, saying, 'I was about fourteen years old in 1971 during the Bangladesh War of Independence and experienced emotional trauma both during the war and subsequently. Honestly, I did not have much clarity about what was going on prior to and during the war. I definitely was a sort of confused teenager in the evolving syndrome of conflicting political positions. Under the influence of emerging social awakenings predicated by the brutal and abusive use of force by the army, I steadily became an ardent supporter of the war of independence. It was, however, the happenings of the subsequent period that had its harsh mark on my later life. I was anguished, observing the rapid and systematic post-1971 erosion of values at every sphere of public and private life, with nepotism, mayhem, and corruption overtaking related virtues. This was more painful for me as those actions mostly had sanctions of the authorities concerned. Life became vulnerable to whims of the powerful, and young suspects having dissenting views were lifted from homes and started disappearing. In those sort of evolving social constraints and because of the age I was in or despite that, my sensitivity congealed adversely, and unknowingly, I opted for a fracas to counter that. I abandoned my cherished preparation for the competitive civil service examination, to the dismay of my parents and family, and joined the Purba Bangla Bonchito-der Party [Party of Deprived People, East Bengal or PBBP].

'Because of my educational background, youth, and innate leadership quality, I soon attained a position of eminence within the party hierarchy and rose to a mid-level leadership. The hostile attitudes of political benefactors with ruthless decisions and the actions of authorities wielding power started constraining the activities of the political oppositions. Some compromised with reality under the threat and pressure, and some withdrew from the field. PBBP was pushed to the wall as an opposition political organization, and its own survival became an imminent issue for the leadership. Against that backdrop, banking on the commitment of its hardcore leaders and the dedication of remaining field workers, PBBP decided to confront them with a fight against political manipulations and social injustice. As a party of active resistance, PBBP went underground, even though it maintained its clandestine existence and political presence in Dhaka. For field-level operational purposes, PBBP had chosen the southwest location of Bangladesh as the base. Like some other comrades, I was deputed in that location for much-preferred field activities, more as a strategic decision.

'This operational area also included Sundarban, the largest single halophytic mangrove forest. The Sundarban forest territory stretches across the deltaic coast of Bangladesh and India with a complex network of tidal waterways, flora, and fauna.

'PBBP, after making that political decision, had three major encounters with the authorities and suffered major setbacks. That was primarily because of an ostensible mismatch between opposing forces in terms of manpower, training, logistic, resources, quality and type of equipment, and reliability of needed replenishment. But more significantly, the leadership faced the vagaries surrounding the concept of popular support, the essence of classless struggle.

'I was the divisional leader of one of the many operational divisions into which Sundarban was strategically divided. Apart from anything else, each of the aforesaid divisions had an invariably good stock of small ammunitions and communication equipment. The specific priority during any deployment or retreat was to carry them along, even sacrificing other stores and food items. We were motivated and trained to consider food as secondary, live on indigenous vegetation, and, as necessary, starve without unnecessary exposure. Our numerical strength was nominal. The avowed strategy was speed, shock, and severity.

'I was taken aback when I first met my assigned security personnel. Clad sacrilegiously in a very ordinary *tateer* [handloom-made] sari without pleats was a rustic and determined young lady, Rushni. Her style of draping the sari, following prevalent rural practices, was unique. The *anchal* of her sari, which was pulled up from under the right arm and slung over the left shoulder, created a unique distinction. I was not familiar with that way of draping the sari. It was very rural but sufficient to bring out and highlight her suppressed frustration and anger that I came to know later on. Rushni's style of interaction had the smudge of brevity and was mostly confined to singular utterances. She was about my age, unusually reserved, and did never indulge in light conversations, even when provoked. I found out within the first few days that besides her duty as my security-in-charge, she was assigned with all other responsibilities about my life and living in that particular section of Sundarban forest. During lunch and dinnertime, she would, from a respectable distance, silently push the *shanki* [a round clay plate] containing my food. Similar actions were repeated when she would occasionally serve me tea. But there was one act about which she had always been very particular—the occasional exposure of a revolver she used to carry, ostensibly as a defensive weapon, and the open exhibition of a vintage hand sickle. She had a typical way of keeping the revolver in a semi-hidden position with the nozzle inside her sari and the shaft visible. The parking position of the revolver was at her waistline, where her petticoat and the sari were tied. The *anchal* of the sari used to always camouflage the shaft of the revolver.

'I had no inkling from whom Rushni received orders or to whom she reported—i.e., her chain of command—but she was always around me wherever I was within my command area. During such patrol, she would always carry openly her officially assigned arm, a "three-knot-three" [.303] vintage rifle. She carried and handled that rifle with ease and assurance that was exceptional but more significantly was of significant deterrent to others in the vicinity. I gradually started feeling safe and secure under her constant surveillance, even though our interactions never crossed the periphery of operational and functional needs.

'My positioning at field level was unexpected and sudden. I landed in Sundarban with a theoretical perception and rudimentary knowledge about people's war. I had to respond to the call of duty as the time was very challenging, threatening PBBP's very existence and known ideals with objectives focusing on a common good for common people. During pre-position briefing in a dilapidated building in the Shutrapur area of Dhaka under total secrecy, I was told about the reasons for my field-level sudden deployment. The more relevant and important members pronounced a long-term shift in operational policies and the need to groom young leaders for the eventual taking of responsibility in pursuing the ideals and objectives for which PBBP stood. What surprised me during the briefing was a total separation of policy and management matters, contrary to the general understanding of authority concerning command and control.

Whatever might be the provocation or the justification, no action was to be initiated or undertaken at the field level without explicit authorization and approval of the party's high command.

'The stage-one role of my future position, like similar positions in other operational areas, was to analyze facts and situations and forward information to the party high command. The stage-two rule was to execute the approved plan as envisaged with total operational responsibility and flexibility. However, all matters pertaining to logistics, supplies, and strategies for propagational work among civilians were to be ensured by the field-level management team—a completely separate command structure dealing with supplies and provisions. The operational structure of PBBP had a pyramid design of responsibilities. The field operational strategy highlighted total compliance with two requirements—infrequent and equally short duration communication and efficient and organized retreat. The first requirement was to minimize the chance of being identified by the evidently superior organized opposing force. The second was more importantly to confuse and mislead any advancing force. Special emphasis was on eliminating or at least minimizing apparent signs of direction of retreat. We were to cover or remove all footprints and signs of the destined direction while keeping visible foot signs with multiples of them in a wrong direction. A quick scouring of operational areas and retreat direction for loose weapons and the adequate cleanup of other evidence were emphasized, and we were to pretend to be civilians.

'It was difficult for me to understand the rationale of the operational design. But it soon dawned on me that under the circumstances where direct confrontation with organized, well-trained, and superior government forces was not a prudent and militarily viable conflict proposition, it was only prudent to have scattered operational groups keeping the army on their toes and to be continuously uncertain as to where and how the next encounter would take place. Also, since the supply of arms and ammunitions of PBBP were limited and it was absolutely binding to ensure secrecy in their supplies and use, the designed separation of logistics, supplies, and strategies were a response to the dictum of the situation. I had my initial constraints in appreciating the organizational pattern but soon understood the rationale and was able to reconcile.

'PBBP's operational strategy had three other unspoken but strictly enforced guidelines—lie low and remain invisible; deception, intelligence, and espionage are the trait of preparedness; and the undertaking of all assigned activities from the perspective of small-unit tactics. The support of the local population, which is the essence of guerrilla tactics, was not high in priority.

'I was befuddled observing Rushni at one of the many encounters that my command was involved in, getting entranced in exchanges of direct fires with the government forces to ensure adequate cover for my small unit undertaking safe withdrawal. Her bravery and firing of shots from varied nearby locations possibly sent a wrong signal as to the number of people we had in our position. After a while, shots from the other side stopped. Rushni negotiated her return, bypassing many bushes, plants, and trees besides innumerable waterways, being totally oblivious of the presence of tigers in that area. Finally, she had the barrier of a midsized river known to be infested by crocodiles. Rushni did not hesitate for a moment. She jumped into the river with her submachine gun [an air-cooled, magazine-fed automatic carbine designed to fire pistol cartridges, commonly known as an SMG] but dropped the SMG at the midpoint of the river to hasten her own retreat and reported to my command safely.

'I was at sea, looking at Rushni, clad in her drenched combat outfit of trousers and a shirt with long dripping, flowing hair. Very naively, I asked, "Are you alive?"

'Rushni kept quiet, but I wanted to provoke her. I shot out, "What was the need for you to face the enemy? You could get killed."

'In the presence of some of my comrades and with a rare exchange of looks with me, she responded, "There is no one in our group who knows the terrain better than me. So I thought it to be my responsibility to ensure needed counter-defense as soon as you ordered the retreat without proper command for providing cover. You referred to my death. Possibly, you had concluded so until I reappeared. Sir, for your information, I emotionally died many years back. My determination to take revenge kept me physically alive so far. What you see is an extension of my life, so I am not afraid of death."

'What Rushni said and what she alluded to during that encounter preoccupied my thoughts for many months. Any discussion on personal and family matters was forbidden per ground rules of PBBP. That was all the more relevant in this case as it involved the most notable lady comrade of the group. The feeling slowly neutralized. There were other pressing concerns that had sidetracked my thinking. Those concerns started putting greater pressure on the core of my feelings and commitment that had earlier aligned me with PBBP.

'PBBP suffered both unexpected and repeated setbacks in encounters in two strongholds. Success by government forces was magnified by print and electronic media. That partly was the outcome of pressure that the government could exercise while allocating significant public sector advertisement funds among the media entities. It was worsened by the unforeseen arrest and the government's prompt execution of PBBP's top leader. All this shook the core base of the organization. The central political leadership was in total disarray and mostly got disintegrated outwardly. The field-level operational and management structures were disheveled with evident signs of estrangement. I faced the challenge of keeping a small force in action-driven motivation despite a state of inactivity for an indefinite period.

'My learning of left-oriented movements was evidently short in details about survival strategy in the situation where PBBP was. It dawned on me that a policy has no relevance to desire. It has always been a product of necessity. I, thus, assumed the operational leadership of my unit and started acting independently but adhering to broad guidelines of PBBP. However, I had no inkling about the management structure of field-level activities and preparedness in support of the political objectives of the party.

'All decisions in life do not necessarily yield preferred results even though very much desired. That happened in our case too. Assuming leadership in a small sphere was easy, but to act effectively in attaining desired outcomes became a most thwarting experience. Lack of clarity about the persistence of the goal and direction of the movement; the miniaturization of the area of operation; the ambiguity about the flow of arms, ammunition, and other supplies; and the inability to have new recruits against the much-trumpeted success of the government forces were our immediate impediments.

'I opted for mini periodical meetings with our comrades in different locations and times to keep their commitment and enthusiasm intact. The plodding erosion of passion among some comrades for PBBP's political objectives and actions was nevertheless palpable. This period in national life started witnessing an emerging ethos of predominance of self over everything else. Money started overtaking ideas, individual interests steadily crept in over broad national objectives, and societal approval for personal attainments over social causes were perfunctorily being accorded.

'The ugly relevance of money in the related peripheries of individual and national lives started pervading with the slow and tolerant endorsement of the evolving social system. It had, across the board, a plausible effect on PBBP's political goals, plans, and actions. My small force was no exception. I started slowly losing comrades. With not many new recruits, my force gradually became a decrepit one. I could sense an erosion of commitment at the same time. Some of those who stayed back with me were mostly victims of circumstance—many having police cases against them. There was, however, one exception. That was Rushni. Among all my comrades, she continued to be the most loyal, trusted, and committed. I had a nice feeling having her around in that dismal setting of our organization.

'Rushni appeared one day with an unknown person and briefly introduced him as Ukil Mia. After the introduction, Rushni stepped back with her .303 rifle in position, and it was Ukil Mia who had to introduce himself and explain his presence. The substance of that preliminary discourse was that he was from the same group with field-activity responsibilities and had been deputed to be the temporary replacement of Rushni, who was in urgent need to go to Panchkhira General Hospital, where her mother was seriously sick. She would be away for three days. Ukil Mia would report back for field duty once Rushni returned. He did not fail to convey that his selection as temporary replacement was the result of Rushni's recommendation.

'Ukil Mia was just the opposite of Rushni in his social interactions. He was generally gullible and open to conversation, a trait very useful for a field worker. To become friendly, gain his trust, and establish the needed rapport, I jokingly asked him about the story of his being named Ukil Mia, sidetracking numerous popular Arabic-based names that were common in the Muslim society. In his response, Ukil Mia said, "The name of my father was Munshi Mia. As Father grew up, it dawned on him that the title *munshi* [like clerk or assistant] was not sufficiently high in esteem and named me Ukil Mia, the title of *ukil* [lawyer] being generally more respectable. He did not stop there. Before his death, Father made a *nosihat* [last expressed command] requiring me to name my son Joj [judge] Mia, a position of still higher regard, but since I have joined PBBP, there is probably no hope of having a family life and a son, so that command of my late father will always remain an unfulfilled one."

'Ukil Mia's other conspicuous reason of frustration was that he spent most of his growing-up years as a political activist supporting independent Bangladesh. Subsequent circumstances were such that he had to commit his youth to achieve a fair and sustainable political, economic, and social environment in sovereign Bangladesh. His last statement about himself was "I am a live witness of what we experienced in Rupaipur in particular and in Bangladesh in general. The new country started experiencing awry actions in the name of social justice. What was hortatory overtook the principles and objectives, which were the core of the fight for Bangladesh. With the passage of short time, a mind-set was predominant, stating and repeating that everything the establishment is doing is hunky-dory. Because of the patronized distribution of booty, a group of touts soon dominated the political landscape. Being dismayed, I have dedicated my youth and aspirations for the greater good with no expectation for reward. I am a content person as a field-level comrade of PBBP."

'As Ukil Mia was struggling to open up, I could not help but inquire specifically about the sudden absence of Rushni. With a lot of hesitation and after obtaining solemn assurance from me, he started narrating the backdrop, which, in essence, opened my mind and feelings for her. He hesitatingly started Rushni's story but continued without any wavering. As he started opening up candidly, detailing her life and activities as known to him, and as he heard from others, he possibly could not control himself. He went into details beyond my expectation, saying, "Rushni's mother is seriously ill and in Panchkhira General Hospital. Our field command normally looks after her mother. On being apprised about the critical health status, command decided to let Rushni be by the side of her ailing mother, taking all shielding arrangements for the safety and security of one of its most noted and committed comrades. Command, at the recommendation of Rushni, deputized me to look after you and also sent a burka [veil] for use by Rushni on her journey to and from Panchkhira, avoiding police vigilance. They made arrangements for undercover escort during the journey and for adequate security cover for her visit to the hospital."

'Ukil Mia unexpectedly—and contrary to party dictates— became very emotional and continued his prattle unknowingly. In his pidgin style of communication, he continued. "Leader, Rushni is not only a committed comrade but a determined and a ferocious one too. The vintage hand sickle that you see in her hand is neither a toy nor for show only. She beheaded two of our enemies single-handedly with that hand sickle. But she's not like that. Rushni is a victim of events beyond her control.

"Rushni and her mother were living in one of the partitioned properties of her grandfather as a consequence to the untimely accidental death of her father. She was about fourteen years old, with her widow mother being about thirty when the War of Liberation broke out in 1971. People, mostly the Hindu population around Panchkhira and other border areas, started leaving their homes around mid-1971 for safe haven across the border. That was because of a very natural fear syndrome as a consequence to the vicious decisions and actions of the Pakistan army of the time. That psyche of fear got aggravated by actual and fabricated stories of atrocities committed by the advancing army from military bases around the area and the positioning of untrained and uneducated militia from different rural settings of what was then West Pakistan.

"One of them, a middle-aged person from Nagar Thole of Gilgit-Baltistan, was Sher Didar Khan. He replaced the militia commander of the area where Rushni's family lived. Sher Didar Khan took over the command around mid-1971. Most of these militia personnel had little knowledge about the physical setting or any orientation about prevailing conditions in East Pakistan. They were motivated with the responsibility of saving the religion of Islam from the onslaughts of Hindus with covert support from India. So most of such militia landed in East Pakistan with the misplaced mind-set of jihad [holy war] embedded in their minds, thoughts, and actions. That resulted in widespread carnage all over Bangladesh and caused the large-scale migration of the Hindu population, followed by Muslim inhabitants in greater number of mostly border areas.

"Rushni's extended family had no penchant for leaving the home of their forefathers or their own country to be refugees in another country. That possibility never came in their dream. As insecurity engulfed the surroundings because of mayhem created by militia, Rushni's entire extended family decided to cross the border too. In a rare display of open dissent, Rushni's mother decided to stay back with her daughter. The innate confidence associated with the place where one's home is located, familiarity with the surroundings, and the horror stories emitting about life and living in refugee camps worked as deterrent. Her own youth was an important factor in the absence of a direct male member of the immediate family.

"Life was neither secure nor easy for the vast majority of the population of then East Pakistan as 1971 progressed. It was true that reckless and reprehensible acts and deeds of militia and their wide publicity by the Shahdeen Bangladesh Betar [Free Bangladesh Radio] aggravated the situation. But worse was the involvement of *razakars*. *Razakars* were those selected from local people to help the militia and mostly recruited from Urdu-speaking refugees who settled in East Pakistan after 1947 and a conservative segment of the local population. The *razakars*' involvement and role were conceived as a supporting arm for the efficient operational deliverables of the militia. Because of unanticipated urgency and resultant lack of planning, those militias were airlifted suddenly, without proper orientation about engagement paradigms and responsibility. In an unknown place, unfamiliar terrain, and unsympathetic population with a totally different topography, climate, and cultural behavior patterns, the militia was evidently dependent on *razakars* for nuanced intelligence, field-level reconnaissance, and sporadic interventions to ensconce authority and control—but the whole strategy boomeranged. The *razakars*' role and responsibility got flirtatious. The degree and nature of that was dependent on each local militia commander's caprices, desires, and feebleness. The *razakars* gradually started functioning more as spooks and soon mastered the art of fakery. Most of them took advantage of the situation and primarily focused on taking political revenge, occupying vacant properties and settling personal, family, and clan-related vendettas. This seriously impacted the morals of the vast majority of the predominantly Muslim population of then East Pakistan, and some of them left for India. These *razakars* have since then become obliquely and infamously known as *dalals* [collaborators] in Bangladesh.

"Sher Didar Khan, the local militia commander of the area where Rushni's grandfather had his abode, unlike most militia commanders, was a very different and consummate person. This area was known as Rupaipur Thana [akin to small county]. "Sher Didar Khan was, by nature, a reticent personality and not susceptible to the alluring propositions of the *razakars*. His approach, attitude, and preference had been in complete contrast to his predecessor from the Jhang district of Punjab. As communicated later by the *pesh* imam [according to Muslim tradition, an imam is appointed by Allah as leader for all nations, and a *pesh* imam is one who leads the prayer in congregation at the local mosque], Sher Didar Khan suffered a sense of oddity in reconciling his mission of fighting to save Islam, observing the ground reality around Rupaipur Thana. He had no doubt that what he observed in his command area is generally applicable for the most parts of then East Pakistan. Sher Didar Khan's resolve to fight slowly became tepid with each engaging and melodious diction of *azaan* [public Muslim call for prayer five times a day] from adjacent mosques. That feeling was all the more congealed in his thoughts during his maiden visit to the abode of Rushni's grandfather.

"The visit was orchestrated against the backdrop of some local *razakar*s' sustained and roguish insinuation of the established link between the owners of the house and anti-Pakistan elements based in India. Leaving the home of their ancestors without the widow daughter-in-law and young granddaughter was painted as sufficient corroborative evidence. That sort of open allegation had the inherent objective of convincing the militia commander to allocate the vacant portion of the property in favor of one extreme conservative but poor elite of the area, Haji Ramzan Ali by name.

"There were two broad understandings between Haji [he who has performed pilgrimage {hajj} to Mecca is known as haji] Ramzan Ali and the *razakar* leaders piloting the deal. Those were that once Haji Ramzan Ali gets the possession of the property and the militias are gone, the former will part off one third of that property in favor of two senior *razakar* leaders. In exchange, the *razakar* leaders committed to provide Haji Ramzan Ali protection if and when the owners ever return and want to reclaim the property.

"Sher Didar Khan's first act on arrival in Rupaipur was to perform *asaar* [late afternoon prayer] in the local mosque. He was very pleased with the upkeep of the mosque, the overall attendance, and the conduct of the prayer by the local *pesh* imam, but what impressed him most was the rendering of *monazat* [submissions before Allah after each Muslim prayer], parts of which were spoken even in Arabic and Urdu. That took Sher Didar Khan aback, and doubt started creeping in his mind about the purpose of his mission. Since that evening, Sher Didar Khan bonded very well with the *pesh* imam and took him into confidence in matters of concern. This particular relationship enabled Sher Didar Khan to understand the nuances of the local culture and the values and way of social paradigm. He was consequentially able in managing his group of militia well and earned due local respect in spite of subdued overwhelming dislike for anyone from then West Pakistan.

"Some of the local leaders, at the behest of Haji Ramzan Ali, were pressuring for quick action on the pending request of Rushni's grandfather's vacant property. Sher Didar Khan told the *razakar* leaders that he would have an inspection of the property before deciding either way. He also made it clear that the day, time, and presence during that visit would be determined by him only. He did, however, assure them that it would be done soon. He requested Pesh Imam Shaheeb during a social discourse to see him after the *asaar* of the upcoming Friday. Neither did he detail the reason, nor did Imam Shaheeb ask for one. That was standard practice during those tense and security-sensitive days of late 1971.

"With an SMG in his left hand, Sher Didar Khan politely put his right hand on the delicate shoulder of Imam Shaheeb's fragile physique on that Friday afternoon, and whispered to him to take him to the property. He suggested taking a diversionary direction to camouflage the real intent. Imam Shaheeb complied. During that brief walk, Sher Didar Khan inquired and obtained information about the family of Rushni's grandfather. Most of what Imam Shaheeb stated was in contradiction to what the *razakar* leaders and some of their civil elders had told him for so long. That agonized Sher Didar Khan, but he was equally happy for not taking action solely based on what he had heard earlier.

"While crossing the relatively large property, a definite symbol of social standing, from the northeast to southwest periphery, Sher Didar Khan was astounded, seeing Rushni reciting the Holy Quran with melodious elocution. She was sitting in the veranda by the side of her widow mother, who had just finished post-*namaz* [prayer] blessings [reciting various *suras* {verses of the Holy Quran} and a *sunnat* {a way, deed, custom, or epoch following Islamic injunctions}]. The mother was in a state of total submission while making her *monazat* [submissions before Allah after each Muslim prayer].

Seeing Sher Didar Khan with his dangling SMG, Rushni became scared, stopped Quran recitation, clung to her mother's sari, and moved closer to her. The devotion and submission of her mother while closing *monazat* was absolute and inconspicuous, devoid of problems and anxieties that normally shroud life and thinking in a setting of lonely living on a large homestead, also because of her age and having a growing daughter. That was heightened by a pronounced sense of insecurity surrounding the society in view of military operations and the presence of militia. Rushni's moving close to her and ceasing the Quran recitation annoyed her. She quickly finished her *monazat* and turned back to notice both Sher Didar Khan and Imam Shaheeb standing silently on the other end of her courtyard. Uneasiness engulfed her total persona as she saw the unknown and huge non-local guy—with clear feeling as to who he could be—along with a local guy. She heard many stories as what such a combination of people could do in harming helpless ladies of the land in the name of saving Islam. She promptly increased the covering of her head by placing an enlarged additional *anchal* on top as a symbol and gesture of modesty. In a sudden state of quivering, she immediately stood up and was about to hold the hand of Rushni to drag her in.

"Imam Shaheeb politely said, 'Salai malai kum' [the local version of the formal Muslim greeting of "Assalamualaikum"— peace be upon you] and then introduced himself as the *pesh* imam of the local mosque and the accompanying gentleman as the militia commander of the Rupaipur Thana area. He explained the background of their presence in her mostly empty homestead. As additional elaboration in support of their continued presence, he went on to say, 'The gentleman, Sher Didar Khan, is from West Pakistan. Seeing your daughter reciting the Holy Quran, he immediately remembered his own daughter, of about the same age and body structure except the complexion, in the far-flung rural location of Gilgit-Baltistan. Contrary to his physique, he immediately experienced an emotional breakdown. That is evident from the fact that during last few minutes we are standing here, he incessantly only talked about his daughter. In the process, he has also become very thirsty and would like to have glass of water to drink.'

"Rushni, in the absence of any male family member, brought the glass of water. Sher Didar Khan bowed significantly to accept with an all-embracing smile. He finished drinking and, while handing over the empty one, placed his right hand on the head of Rushni and blessed her. He also, as translated by the *pesh* imam, said, 'I do not know your name. To me, you are Raunak [an expression meaning light], the name of my daughter. From now on, both you and your mother's safety are my responsibility.'

"Saying those words, Sher Didar Khan left the premises along with Imam Shaheeb but did not say anything else. Sher Didar Khan's subsequent decision not to accede to the earlier proposition of allotting the empty property of Rushni's grandfather in favor of Ramzan Ali infuriated the local *razakar* leaders and thwarted the right-leaning civic leaders. Both indirect threat and pressure failed to change his position. Systematic efforts were launched by disenchanted stakeholders to spread small talk—hypothetical spicy stories concerning Sher Didar Khan's presumptive relationship with Rushni's mother. Some even crossed all the limits of civic propriety by getting Rushni involved in such stories. But all these were very hush-hush exchanges as the militia was dreaded by the local population. Anonymous communications started flooding the desks of higher authorities, arraigning Sher Didar Khan of being involved in all kinds of concocted stories with common culminating apprehension about the continued security of Pakistan. That was late November 1971.

"Sher Didar Khan unexpectedly received an urgent communication informing him that December 20 would be the last day of his assignment in East Pakistan. He would proceed to the rangers' [paramilitary armed troops] headquarters at Gilgit-Baltistan.

It surprised him but did not disappoint him. The element of surprise was predicated on promptness of action, and disappointment was premised on the absence of opportunity to defend him and to tell the truth, but it also made him happy. That was for two specific reasons. Going back earlier than scheduled had the pleasure of an early reunion with his family, most particularly his dear daughter, Raunak, his only offspring. The other reason was getting away from a totally wrong war in which one Muslim is being motivated to kill another Muslim in the name of saving Islam.

"Sher Didar Khan, accompanied by Imam Shaheeb, visited Rushni's house to share the news and took respective seats on a chair and a bench kept on the veranda. That was the practice of the last few times they were occasionally in that house. Sher Didar Khan was unsure about the modicum of classifying that particular news either as good or bad. But he was conscious of one thing that always made him happy. In a very unknown and hostile place, that house gave him peace of mind by accepting him as a harmless individual and the dignity he enjoyed in this house, as if he was an extended family member. The intermediation of Imam Shaheeb in this process was helpful but not the determining element.

"The sudden presence of Sher Didar Khan and Imam Shaheeb was of no surprise to Rushni and her mother, but the content of the message caused anguish in the mind of Rushni's mother. She suddenly became worried about retaining the ownership of the homestead and their security. Among the neighbors and village folk, Rushni's mother was generally acclaimed as a resolute and confident lady. Not many eyebrows lifted when she decided to stay back in the relatively large homestead, all alone with her growing daughter in the midst of raging civil war, but this specific news unexpectedly shook her beyond words. She was almost in a frozen state while standing behind the entry door, thereby observing modesty as per local custom.

"Total silence, indicative of both concern and uncertainty, engulfed their discourse. Sher Didar Khan could sense her shock easily and told Imam Shaheeb to convey to Rushni's mother his sentiments with the words 'I have had been to this house only to see

Rushni as in her presence, I see my only daughter, Raunak. That has always given me a lot of mental peace. She is a daughter to me, and her mother is my sister. So long as I am alive, no harm will befall them. Before I leave for West Pakistan as presently ordered, I will make arrangements so that my successor will protect them the same way I would have. Please assure my sister.'

"Rushni's mother was overwhelmed by the statement of assurance, even though, like all previous occasions, she was hiding herself behind one of the double doors. She could feel that Sher Didar Khan was not only tired and exhausted but also had a dry mouth, affecting his statements. Seeking excuse from Imam Shaheeb, she went inside and brought a glass of water [*pani*] and two *paan*s. She told Imam Shaheeb, 'Please tell Khan Shaheeb that I do not have a brother. He has made me enormously happy by taking me as a sister in the presence of a pious man like you. So as a sister, I would, if you so permit, like to serve the *pani* and *paan* myself.'

"That was done, and everyone present was very happy.

"Since launching the ruthless military operation, an emerging sense of Bengali nationalism had pervaded throughout East Pakistan, contrary to the determining factor of Muslim nationalism, which singularly resulted in an overwhelming mandate in Bengal of undivided India for the creation of Pakistan in 1947, which rapidly underwent startling changes, emotionally and physically. With the passage of time and because of the misgovernance of military rulers, the passion for liberation accentuated, and the civil war took the turn for liberation. That intensity was reflected in the esoteric changes of popular support and actions, giving the war a new dimension and focus. The physical changes on the ground motivated even otherwise neutral individuals to increasingly support the war of liberation. The widespread presence of illiterate militias from various parts of West Pakistan on the plea of war for saving Islam, the constitution of the ruffian support-group *razakar*s, and planned killings of local intelligentsia were the fatal certitudes that hastened the liberation of Bangladesh, with, of course, the unlimited diplomatic support and military help of India.

"The whole of East Pakistan became ungovernable by late 1971. The more force that was used to clamp down the alleged rebellion, the greater the erosion of control and authority. That was more visible in some border adjacent areas, and Panchkhira was one of them. Rupaipur Thana was no exception either.

"Sher Didar Khan and his associates were aware of the increasing vulnerability they were being exposed to. With the passage of time and increasing military setbacks, Sher Didar Khan's trust in the allegiance of *razakars*, as was throughout the province, became increasingly doubtful. He started doubting many of them as counterspies.

"In this setting, the Indian Air Force literally crippled Pakistan air capability, and the Indian army routed the Pakistan army to the western front while helping *mukhti bahini* (freedom fighters) liberate East Pakistan and establish Bangladesh as a sovereign country on the Eastern front. That happened on December 16 when the Eastern command of the Pakistan army formally surrendered to the joint commands of Bangladesh and Indian armies in Dhaka. Bordering areas of Bangladesh were liberated earlier, mostly starting in early December 1971, and that happened with Rupaipur Thana and other adjacent areas of Panchkhira.

"Most *razakars* sensed the impending military debacle and gradually disassociated with local militia command. The skeleton militia presence of Rupaipur was emotionally decrepitated with every passage of day. While some could escape with uncertainty looming large, others were killed by mobs celebrating liberation. Major elements of that mob had one common characteristic—many were desperate to portray themselves as freedom fighters. This was more applicable in the cases of those who were close to militia command, curried favor of the militia, and were benefitted by the militia's decisions and actions.

"Unlike many of his comrades in arms, Sher Didar Khan had a clear premonition about the imminent upshot of misplaced military intervention. Since his arrival and observing the commitment and conduct of Bengali Muslims with regard to their faith and adherence to faith-related rituals, he was certain of the misdirected conduct of operations in the wrong premise of fighting for salvaging Islam. Unlike many of his compatriots, Sher Didar Khan was more sympathetic and respectful to the local population. That prompted some extreme elements from among the civil elites and a group of *razakar*s to write anonymous letters against him to high commands. That was the background of the order stipulating his premature transfer back to Gilgit.

"Any war, notwithstanding exuberance predicating it, is always a traumatic experience for the country. That was significantly piercing for Pakistan with two wings [East and West Pakistan] separated by about one thousand miles of hostile enemy territory. With the initiation of formal war around December 4, 1971, the central government's authority and control on East Pakistan just withered away. The same was the case with military command and coordination with the significant dent in fighting spirit. All the fighting forces were from West Pakistan with no grassroots support or sympathy in East Pakistan.

"Like other decisions, Sher Didar Khan's transfer back to Gilgit was stalled, but more significantly, he was not afraid of what was going to befall on him and his colleagues. He had candid foresight about the futility of any war to keep a large population subjugated by sheer force and that too on a false pretext. Still, he was hoping against hope that their command would at least ensure the fighting force's safe retreat and security. But something dawned on him a day before Rupaipur and adjacent areas of Panchkhira were liberated. It came to his thought suddenly that he did not visit Rushni's home for quite some time because of the chaos and confusion prevailing everywhere. So as he did always, Sher Didar Khan sent a message to Imam Shaheeb to see him after *asaar* that day.

"In a brief exchange, Sher Didar Khan frankly told Imam Shaheeb about his earnest yearning to see Rushni once more before anything happens to him. Because of the rapidly evolving situation with unquestionable certainty of the emergence of Bangladesh as a sovereign country, Imam Shaheeb fell hesitant to accompany Sher Didar Khan but eventually could not say no. Because of unfavorable developments everywhere, Imam Shaheeb, on his own, minimized contacts with Sher Didar Khan in the immediate past, but on being specifically told the purpose, he thought. Imam Shaheeb quickly revisited all past discussions and visits but could not identify a single incident or utterance that could be the excuse for his refusal. He, thus, accompanied Sher Didar Khan without waste of time, and both of them agreed to return before sunset.

"Sher Didar Khan's subsequent statements during that ephemeral walk made Imam Shaheeb happy, which testified the nobility of his desire. He addressed Imam Shaheeb as Bhai-jan [brother at heart] for the first time and said, 'I am not sure what destiny has for me. Though consciously I have not done anything wrong or did not show any disrespect to any local, I hope Allah's blessings will take care of me. But my *iman* [faith] is not that strong as many of yours. I have dreamt of my daughter, Raunak, last night, and she was crying. So I decided to see Rushni once more, and that could possibly be the last time too. In Rushni, I will try to find my Raunak before anything befalls me.'

"Imam Shaheeb was dumbfounded by what was stated and was about to react with some soothing and reassuring words, even though he had absolute clarity as to what was going to happen soon. As Imam Shaheeb was struggling with words and expressions to console him, Sher Didar Khan looked at his companion with body language, which was antithetical to any form of verbal consolation. They silently continued their journey.

"On reaching Rushni's house, both of them took their usual seats in front of the main entrance door of the home. Rushni appeared with a broad smile, and her mother positioned herself inside the house. She was not hiding anymore behind the partition of the door.

"In initiating the discussion, Sher Didar Khan first said, 'Salaam malikum,' to Rushni's mother and then repeated the contents of his dream of the previous night. In finishing his introductory remarks and deviating from past practice, Sher Didar Khan continued to say, 'Both local and national situations are momentous and equally perilous ones. In spite of certain imminence of an uncharacterized hazard that is looming large, I ventured to be at your place with a few specific intents. In a very unknown place and unfamiliar setting, your home gave me peace of mind, and the presence of Rushni always drew me close to my dear daughter and only child, Raunak. I remain thankful and grateful to you for that and to Imam Shaheeb for making my past visits possible. As you are gracious enough to accept me as a brother, this house means something special to me. Wherever I may be in future, your home will be my identity in East Pakistan. I am unsure and equally nervous about our future. The local population will have information about us, so I am leaving behind the address of my family with you. If you are so willing and consider it appropriate, please let my family know of our fate. The communication should be in English, and Raunak will be able to decipher that and, if not, could get help from others. That will be a tremendous favor for which I will remain ever grateful to you all.'

"After saying those words and handing over the address to Rushni's mother, which passed through the hand of Imam Shaheeb and Rushni, Sher Didar Khan appeared to be at ease with himself and relaxed. Looking at the horizon, he said, 'We need to be back in our camp much before sunset for security reasons for me and for Imam Shaheeb to be at the mosque to conduct *magreeb* [sunset prayer]. When I visited this house the first time, I had a glass of water. Who knows? This may be the last visit of mine. So I would like to have a glass of water this time too.'

"As the voice, words, and body language of Khan Shaheeb, since his arrival, sounded very ominous to Rushni's mother, she was momentarily oblivious to the normal custom of treating a guest with *pani* and *paan*. She rushed inside and then came out with some. Imam Shaheeb, who was both tacit and solicitous all through during the gathering, quickly, more as reactive spontaneity, finished the drinking and put the *paan* in his mouth, while Sher Didar Khan slowly glugged down the *pani* as if he was taking something very sweet and tasty. He then took leave from the family after blessing Rushni by placing his hand on her head. Before leaving, to the astonishment of Imam Shaheeb, he decided to undertake a reconnaissance of the major vacant portion of the said property. Observing a rather odd-sized windowless small construction with thatched roofing in the midst of nice houses, Sher Didar Khan asked about it.

"Imam Shaheeb said, 'This is locally called *gola* [storage]. Most affluent families have such *gola*s to store paddy for round the year. Because of its specific nature, *gola*s have only one opening.'

"Sher Didar Khan looked at it intently and left the premises.

"As he was finishing his ablution ritual, prior to saying *magreeb*, Sher Didar Khan noticed two bushed *razakar*s speaking very intently with most of the remaining panicky militias of the camp. The location of where the conversation took place was something similar to a hideout, with unintended cover of a bunch of mango trees at the periphery of the camp. The ephemeral setting of December dusk and the leery and shrunken body language of the crowd was indicative of an upshot of yet unknown but definitely grotesque consequences.

Convulsion

"On that evening, after return from Rushni's house, Sher Didar Khan took an unusually long time attending to his very regular command-related tasks and personal errands. That included the ritual of ablution and saying his prayers.

"Adult Muslims are obligated to perform prayers [commonly known as *namaz* but perhaps more correctly called *salat*] five times a day. The ritual of *salat* constitutes the framework of a day for an adult Muslim, beginning with predawn prayer and ending with prayer preceding sleep at night. The root word of *salat* is *silat*, meaning 'connection.' *Salat* is the pathway to connect with the Creator, Allah. The ritual of ablution and other requirements purifies a worshipper to connect and converse with Allah [the Divine] and his messenger. Mandated daily *salat* can be performed individually or in congregation.

"There are two different forms of prayers in Islam. *Salat* is strictly governed by prescribed time, specified implementation mechanics, and the ordained command. The other form of prayer is called *dua*, supplicatory for open-ended communication with Allah, irrespective of time, place, requirements [purification, direction, the fundamentals, and humility], or restrictions [covering and attire].

"Of the five principal elements of the faith of Islam, prayer is ranked as the second one. Others are testimony of faith [*iman*], pilgrimage to Mecca [hajj], month-long fasting every year [Ramadan], and paying poor tax [*jakat*]. These fundamental elements of Islam are believed in and complied with by all Muslims of the world, irrespective of geographical locations, skin tone, physical features, language, and ethnicity.

"Prayer has always been the central constituent of Islamic faith and practice. It is referred to seven hundred times in verses of the Holy Quran. *Salat* is performed with specified physical and worship-related postures and submissions, involving both standing and sitting positions. These are quintessential components of Muslim prayers. Of the physical ones, *ruku* signifies bowing down without bending knees while placing hands on knees. The other one, a more significant submission, is called *sejdha* [prostration], having the forehead, nose, both hands, knees, and all toes touching the ground together. In essence, *sejdha* is a symbolic physical posture to praise and glorify Allah [the Divine] and humble oneself before him. It is perhaps one of the most complete forms of spiritual connectivity, with physical ability and response under one's command.

"In performing *magreeb* on the return from Rushni's house, Sher Didar Khan committed mistakes twice, both in *ruku*, in spite of solemn devotion. It had never happened in his adult life. That made him edgy and created an irksome pounding feeling about possible portentous happenings. His eyes were suddenly filled with sniffles, and, for reasons obvious, he started having blurred vision. At that moment of emotional anguish and mental breakdown, it was difficult for Sher Didar Khan to relate symptoms and reactions. He singularly blamed himself for those two slipups while performing *magreeb* and took it as something ominous because of the unexplainable recent erosion to his *iman* [faith]. Sher Didar Khan's inner reaction to such happening had all the elements of fretfulness, irritation, frustration, and foiling. This was plausibly augmented by the perceptible body language of his skeleton militia comrades and very brief occasional visits of some *razakar*s to the camp, avoiding him. Some of these *razakar*s were involved in the unsuccessful pursuit of Ramzan Ali's case for the allocation of Rushni's grandfather's homestead and, as such, were very unhappy with Sher Didar Khan. By being nice to other militias, they were laying a defensive strategy against the backdrop of a changeable situation, as well as cautiously inching forward with plans to take revenge if the parameter alters otherwise.

In December 1971, most of these *razakar*s were unsure about the course to be pursued. That was compounded by frequent broadcasts by Radio Pakistan about the movement of the U.S. Seventh Fleet in support of Pakistan and the ground-level reality of looming sounds of shelling from guns of advancing armies under the joint command of India and Bangladesh. By planning to help leftover militias escape to the district-level militia command post for enhanced security, the *razakar*s maintained their visible allegiance to Pakistan military authority. On the other hand, by leaving out Sher Didar Khan, they ensured a pawn in their hand to prove themselves as supporters of war of liberation. They were certain that if the India and Bangladesh forces were to succeed, they need some salable item at that moment of impetuous euphoria to cover up all their past heinous delinquencies.

"The local *razakar* group, thus, opted to exclude Sher Didar Khan from the escape plan and convinced fellow militias that he would be helped, but that needed separate arrangement in view of the high visibility of the commander. An agreement was worked out in that evening's meeting for the militias to quietly abandon their camp immediately after *magreeb*, with Sher Didar Khan's escape to follow soon. The latter was just a convenient subterfuge.

"Sher Didar Khan continued sitting on the *jai namaz* [prayer mat] since finishing his *magreeb*, totally oblivious to his immediate surroundings. Most of the time, he was praying by counting beads of his *tasbee* [prayer beads tied together, numbering ninety-nine and close to a rosary in meaning and form], keeping his eyes closed. All his thoughts encompassed what was going to happen to the country, his own safety and security concerns, and the prospect of how and the possibility as to when he was going to be united with his family in Gilgit-Baltistan. Because of his prayers and resultant total devotion to Allah, seeking mercy against persistent constraints and beleaguered expectations, Sher Didar Khan overlooked the protracted absence of movement of any of his fellow militia associates. He mused for a while and stepped out with hesitation and nervousness but did not find trace of any other individual in the compound of the militia camp.

"He hurriedly returned to the camp office, took possession of his SMG, along with additional magazines, and stepped out once again with all gusto. He surveyed the camp premises very penetratingly, notwithstanding the incipient darkness of the early December night with dominant presence of miasma. Cautiously, devoid of the command posture of earlier times, he called his fellow militias one by one, by name, with no response. He then surveyed the camp premises to note that while the gate was closed, neither of the gate lamps had been lit nor had the national flag been brought down and folded, usually coinciding with sunset. Both these noncompliances were against the strictly adhered-to standard operating procedures of the armed forces. Sher Didar Khan returned to his office room in the surroundings of dominant darkness, placed his SMG on the table with the trigger guard nearest to its usual sitting position, and took slow shattered steps toward his office chair, a symbol of power and authority. As he drew close the familiar chair, he lost control of his somatic self, his robust muscle started tattering, and he just collapsed on the chair like baggage. His bucolic physical build, a tall and muscular presence, the prowess of his race in bravery and military skill, the presence of his much-adored SMG, and the existence of other arms and weapons were of no relevance. All those were lost with the precipitous erosion of poise. Seated vulnerably with opened eyes in the midst of total darkness, he was lost within himself, engrossed with the thought of circumstances and conditions that prompted his otherwise loyal colleagues to abandon him in such a situation.

"In that debasing mental condition, Sher Didar Khan recuperated the residue of his physical strength and positioned himself on the *jai namaz* to say the night prayer [*asher*]. For abstruse reasons, he could not keep standing and went straight to *sejdha* without performing the ordained rites of that prayer. He was in *sejdha* for an indeterminate time, seeking pardon for past intended and unintended sins, as committed, and begging the *raham* [mercy] of Allahpak for future safety and security, with fondest thoughts of reunion with his family. In the process, the only conspicuous indication of human presence in that room was his asymmetrical raucous sound of crying and the uncontrolled continuous flow of tears. He was unsure about the time he spent in *sejdha*. Nor did he bother to look at the wall clock. Somehow that unqualified submission rejuvenated his thinking and physical intensity. He stepped out of the camp office, positioned himself in the open veranda, and looked outside in the midst darkness and haze.

"A thin line of light and the echo of an intermittent clamoring sound, something close to political slogans, from the far-flung western territory of East Pakistan drew his attention. Though not particularly sure about the reason and nature, Sher Didar Khan had an unreserved mental conclusion about the impending emergence of the sovereign new state of Bangladesh. The erosion of management and control and the chain of command that gave him authority and confidence in the past was very much palpable. That more pronouncedly impacted his personal life and security, more particularly with the most shocking disappearance of his comrades in arms. That made his own life vulnerable to all sorts of possibilities. Worse was the high negative orientation of most of these possibilities. The increasing brightness of the line of light and the slowly impending sound of slogans with the noticeable movement of people around the camp area made him more concerned about his own safety and security.

"With perceived negative attributes overwhelming his own life and security in the implausible and vulnerable situation that was fast emerging, Sher Didar Khan's thought process, bewilderingly, was very clear and candid. He immediately concluded that the emergent new country Bangladesh, with all honest objectives, would invariably encounter initial chaos and confusion created mostly by fifth-columnists. Identification with the euphoria of liberation and some related acts to demonstrate alignment with that would most likely be carried out by fifth-columnist in a most incongruous fashion and far in excess of the dictum of civility as much would be used to pronate and establish their new identity as *mukhti bahini* [freedom fighters]. He mapped out possible scenarios—an advancing mob rushing to occupy the militia camp, taking possession of arms and ammunition, and taking hostage of militia personnel for revenge. He also thought of the reaction of the mob not finding any militia except him and their possible immediate acts. Sher Didar Khan soon became scared for his own life.

"Propelled by such portentous eventuality, he promptly thought of the *gola* of Rushni's house for safe refuse during the initial few days at the least. He took some small dry items from his militia rations, a bottle of water, and his pride and traditional identity, the *pagree* [headwear], along with the much-cherished and revered *tasbee*. He then tossed his favorite SMG between two hands and decided to leave it behind. The most fearsome and effective weapon to attack an enemy and defend oneself had become most ineffectual and unworthy.

"That decision was inimitable for a person like Sher Didar Khan, who was born in surroundings dominated by gun culture. He grew up with guns, played with guns, conducted social dealings based on the quality and types of guns, protected the family and tribe honor with guns, and even developed the mental frame to trade land for guns. When he was ordered to be in East Pakistan, he opted to bring his own SMG to fight for the cause of Islam as he and others like him had been told. This SMG was a prized gift from his in-laws during his wedding, and he himself went to Bara, a famous habitation of the Northwest Frontier Province [now renamed Khyber Pakhtunkhwa] for the indigenous manufacturing and unfettered trading of guns of all types, names, and brands. His decision to abandon his SMG at the critical juncture of life was perhaps the most cataclysmic for him. The best option would have been, in the context of sprouting scenarios, to commit suicide, but because of teachings of his faith, he had to refrain from that.

"In the midst of distressing sheathed darkness, aggravated by loneliness and the evident signs and sounds of total collapse of the authority he was familiar with and accountable to, Sher Didar Khan just continued reacting based on his embryonic immediate impulse. It was neither the moment nor the setting for him to think about the inner truth. The moral strength and backing emanating from the cause of a fight is stronger than any arm, however sophisticated that might be. He wrapped himself with a local handloom *chador* [shawl] and prayed to Allahpak before stepping out of the militia camp office.

"He moved forward with slow but firm steps as if he was going to get lost in the darkness. As he was getting to the main road, he stopped suddenly, thought for a while, and decided to take a circuitous route through dry farmlands of the winter. In his calculation, that was a safe approach in concealing his journey and identity. He slowly approached and quietly entered the *gola*. By employing his rudimentary military expertise and recalling the features of structure he could briefly reconnaissance during that afternoon's visit, he was successful in managing rather the most delicate entry into the *gola* without any clatter. His nervousness and difficulty was the outcome of two most plausible factors—the smallness of the entry access and his significantly large body. As the *gola* was half empty, awaiting a new harvest, he had no problem in making himself comfortable in the given situation. The *chador* and *pagree* he carried with him became very handy as a base and headrest, but he had to struggle to maintain total silence to conceal his presence.

"By the wee hours of that night, as Sher Didar Khan assessed with trepidation, it was all over around Rupaipur and most of the Panchkhira areas. With the progressive advancing forces under the joint command of Bangladesh and India, assisted by *mukhti bahini*, the Pakistan army retreated without much resistance. People in general were relaxed and jubilant, came out in large numbers on the road, and were talking freely in their own environment.

"Sher Didar Khan had no doubt about the outcome with each louder utterance of 'Joy Bangla!' ["Victory for Bengal," the famous and most oft-repeated political slogan epitomizing Bengali aspirations in totality] by thousands of jubilant voices and shrank within himself, thinking about his destiny. He closed his eyes, pictured his dear daughter Raunak, and continued to pray for safety and security. In the process, he dozed off as a consequence to sleeplessness the night preceding.

"He woke up feeling a sense of commotion around the property. The restlessness and frustration of the people was most perceptible with frequent shouting, tensed movements, and relentless screaming. In monitoring, he could easily identify the voices of two *razakar* leaders involved in Ramzan Ali's case. His fretfulness multiplied hearing his name being uttered. He had no qualms that the groups of people under the leadership of the two *razakar*s were looking for him.

"Sher Didar Khan was in a state of severe internalized edginess, and his physical self-experienced involuntary muscle movements. He started quivering and shrank further. The prime reason of his refocused disarray at that stage was the most unexpected turn of events that allowed the *razakar*s to have visible presence and participation in the jubilant celebration of the liberation of Bangladesh that they had opposed in all emotive and material terms. The small-framed brown-skinned young *razakar*s were much more perceptive in their thinking, assessment, and actions compared with the big and robust—with an air of bravado—fair-skinned militias [commonly known as *khan shena*s]. As the civil war progressed with the triggering of visible increase in support within the country for liberation per se and overt support of India for the cause, the emergence of Bangladesh as a sovereign country was no more an 'if' but 'when' to anyone with common sense. The *razakar*s were no exception. Most of them sensed the inevitable emergence of Bangladesh around the tail end of 1971. That was more applicable for those who were from border areas like Panchkhira was.

"The bellows that characterized the initial robust search to find *khan shena*s, more particularly Sher Didar Khan, within the militia camp compound or the abode of Rushni's grandparents soon degenerated into a tepid and disheveled effort, manifesting frustration and subdued anger. The thwarting expressions embodied in the physical expressions of the two *razakar* leaders were more pronounced in their stomping off and equally conspicuous actions.

The failed effort in finding the favored catch was a disaster for the *razakar* leaders as their game plan was predicated on handing over either residue *khan shena*s or Sher Didar Khan alive to advancing joint command forces and, thus, have a permanent seal of being dedicated *mukhti bahini*. The immediate objective was getting instant reprieve from the atrocities and crimes committed in the past. They were frustrated and jumbled while unknowingly getting involved in the common act of biting respective fingernails, sitting in the *kachari* [meeting space] of Rushni's grandparents.

"Inside their part of the homestead, Rushni and her mother were both confused and nervous.

"In that particular edgy situation, a junior follower of the *razakar*s came running into the *kachari* and informed that he had noticed a small filament outside the entry space of the *gola*. Both *razakar* leaders rushed to the *gola* and were convinced that those filaments were the tail ends of Sher Didar Khan's *pagree*. Though they were certain that Sher Didar Khan took refuge in that *gola*, both of them had the instant feeling of being anesthetized and refrained from uttering a single word but had resorted to visual exchanges. Their predicament was how to face their boss of the last many months, arrest him, and hand him over to the advancing joint command. That was an embarrassing situation for them beyond comprehension, more so for Sher Didar Khan, both as a person and a commander. He was an admirable individual, except that he did not act as per the desire for allocating Rushni's grandparents home to Ramzan Ali.

"It was in their self-interest to shed immediately the ignominious burden of being *razakar*. The inner urge to optimize immediate access to benefits associated with being a *mukhti bahini* propelled their immediate thoughts and actions. They were certain that neither pallid denials nor unconvincing contrition would be of any practical value. There was the need for evidence-based actions, and there could be no substitute of an act like handing over Sher Didar Khan to the joint command in a public gathering. Based on such a public act, stories could be circulated as to their role and activities in support of the creation of Bangladesh, playacting outwardly as being *razakar*s. Both of them smiled at the junior follower and, by physical gesture, asked others present to be in the *kachari*. Those who were not in the immediate vicinity were also called in. The assembled people of that gathering consisted of genuine enthusiasts, totally oblivious of the past and overtaken by the joy of the emerging new country of Bangladesh. Some others were traditional followers of the locality without having definite perspectives about reigning political issues, and some others were those who were brought in by handing over a little money. A sense of euphoria was omnipresent. Joyousness everywhere was overpowering. No one had the mind-set of visiting the past and gravitating toward the activities of others.

"The *razakar* leaders involved took full advantage of this and tried to strengthen their position by openly demonstrating their love for the new country, the creation of which they had opposed only a few hours back. Their principle predicament was how to get Sher Didar Khan out of the *gola* unharmed and hand him over to the joint command. Between them, the two debated a lot as to whether Sher Didar Khan was likely to open fire when confronted and so on. Their conclusion was that the best option would be to get hold of him without any confrontation and then take him to the Rupaipur High School playground to publicly hand over a *khan shena* commander to the joint command. That would instantly make them local heroes. Based on that, stories could be circulated vouching for their loyalty and commitment to the cause of Bangladesh.

"As all the followers and jubilant enthusiasts assembled in and outside the *kachari*, the *razakar* leaders opened their mouths for the first time, breaking the silence observed during most of the past intense moments. One of the critical points they debated, prior to opening their mouths publicly, was whether Sher Didar Khan had his SMG with him. Keeping in view his temperament, behavior, and leadership traits, the consensus was that he would not resort to opening of fire, even if he had the SMG with him.

"The carefully articulated line of actions emphasized during the group deliberations were the vigilant but cautious approach to *gola* by a select group and to persuade him to come out and surrender, simultaneously assuring him safety and proper treatment as a prisoner of war. They were to avoid the exchange of fire power as the objective was to hand over Sher Didar Khan alive to the joint command and to observe due decency while taking him to the school grounds but with his two hands tied behind him. They would send an advance team of a few followers to make public announcements regarding the imminent handing over of a *khan shena* commander to the joint command on the playground by two courageous *mukhti bahini*—erstwhile *razakar*s.

"The two *razakar* leaders selected a few trustworthy, loyal supporters and local youths to be the members of the group in handling matters and actions pertaining to the incarceration of Sher Didar Khan. They also confided that during the entire process, from initial coaxing for surrender to the handing over at the playground, both of them would remain indiscernible to avoid any emotional breakdown on the part of Sher Didar Khan and consequential disablements. With that sort of logic and stratagem, they conveniently shrouded their innate sense of guilt and embarrassment in facing and handling Sher Didar Khan. Consciously, they opted for a quick transaction. That sort of approach was needed to protect and preserve their much-cherished new identity of being members of *mukhti bahini*.

"The select group took control of the situation. Before proceeding toward the *gola*, tensed assembled people were confined by them in and around the *kachari*. Following instructions, the select group, divided into batches of three, approached the *gola* by crawling on knees to avoid probable gunfire and persuaded Sher Didar Khan to come out successfully.

"His first symbolic gesticulation consequent to the polite persuasion was his showing empty hands to assure the assembled people that he was not carrying any arms. That was a significant act and had a startling reaction among the crowd. The uneasy calm of the last few minutes amazingly turned into a situation of ease and reassurance. Totally oblivious to the earlier instructions of the select group, people slowly walked toward the *gola* as Sher Didar Khan maneuvered himself out with an acute sense of nervousness. To conceal from people ogling him, he took out his *pagree* and *tasbee* and kissed the locally made *chador* before leaving it inside. The more Sher Didar Khan wanted to be upright and straight while standing outside the *gola*, the more shaky and pliable he was. That encouraged the assembled people to move forward, defying earlier instructions, and soon, they surrounded him. As a last act of being a militia commander, Sher Didar Khan placed his *pagree* on his head and had a passive look at the people around him.

"Many among those present were astounded, seeing for the first time the orange-colored hair of Sher Didar Khan. Those who had been closer to him were used to his orange-colored beard, but none could think of his having orange-colored hair. The regular application of henna made the gray and white hairs have an orange twist. But that did not have any impact on the select group. They concentrated on their undertaking.

"As the short brown-skinned leader of the select group faced the tall light-skinned and well-built domineer with the flowing beard, famous for warfare-related skill, strength, and bravery, one thing was obvious—the confidence and strength that emanated from the reality of the emerging situation predicated on victory was much beyond physically built mortal strength. The leader of the select group had total control of the setting, while the militia commander was evidently wobbly and jumbled. As the former started whispering some words, Sher Didar Khan arched his body and nodded. On being gestured, another follower moved forward with a rope generally used to secure cows. He took possession of both hands of Sher Didar Khan, placed them at his back, and tied his hands with that rope. That was quite demeaning, but he had no negative reaction at that time.

"The two *razakar* leaders witnessed the whole episode from a secured position of the *kachari* and, being satisfied with the outcome, quietly left by the back door. The expressed justification was the need to supervise arrangements for handing over the militia commander to the advancing forces of the joint command. But the inherent objective was to avoid Sher Didar Khan as much as possible and to orchestrate the short event in a way to ensure their public endorsement as significant members of the *mukhti bahini*.

"The event was slated for pre-twilight on the cool mid-December evening for security reasons, as well as coinciding with the estimated arrival of the joint command forces. Sher Didar Khan was kept standing near the *gola* with his hands tied at the back. To begin with, there was a sizeable crowd. Then the spicy news of finding the militia commander in the *gola* of Rushni's grandparents and being kept there, standing with his hands tied behind his back, spread like wildfire. People from everywhere started pouring in. Soon, hundreds of people were there from nearby locations, causing a total collapse of authority and control. As the crowd grew larger, bedlam started to set in. The ever-increasing crowd was uncontrollable. Unruly children and some adults started teasing and enticing Sher Didar Khan. Those who had never dared to be around the periphery of his militia camp started touching his hand and belly, making a mockery of the situation. Some played with the hanging end of his *pagree*. The uncontrollable crowd unleashed a torrent of gestures and parodies representing grotesque imitations and gaping travesty.

"The pervasive common euphoria of the victory of *mukhti bahini* over the superior Pakistan army unleashed both ecstatic joy and appalling comportment among the crowd assembled. Locally, that was heightened by the news of arrest of militia commander Sher Didar Khan and seeing him standing near the *gola* with both hands tied at the back. In that situation, general attributes of decency in social behavior evidently became the first casualty. People started going inside Rushni's home at will—as if not only Sher Didar Khan was apprehended alive—but they took possession of the house too. They drank water from *kolshi* [traditional earthen jar] and opened tin containers to have *muri* [puffed rice] and *cheera* [pressed rice] without seeking permission from the residents.

"Seated on a *pattie* and closeted together with nervousness permeating in all expressions, the bewildered mother and daughter observed the incoming and outgoing traffic indulging in all sorts of despicable acts. The only action they undertook from time to time was to enhance respective *anchal*s to cover their heads.

"The increasing number of unruly young people of varied backgrounds unnerved the select group. They decided to commence travel to the playground on foot, slightly ahead of the time earlier indicated by the *razakar* leaders. The select group surrounded Sher Didar Khan to ensure his safety and security before commencing the journey on foot. But that was of no consequence. As the walk barely started, vicarious words and contentious gestures from among the crowd, with desperate effort and focus to be near Sher Didar Khan and to touch and tickle him, took the shape of a fracas. That was evidently the upsurge of a hidden psyche turning fear of yesterday into arrogance of today. The hidden craving for taking vengeance was at its zenith. As the young people started pushing and jumping, the bellows grew louder, and the mob became more unruly. Some elements of the mob started lugging the hanging end part of the *pagree* that Sher Didar Khan so respectfully—and as symbol of power and prestige—always put on his head. It was the same during the walk, though neither power nor prestige carried any significance in the changed setting. As the *pagree* fell on the walkway, it was mercilessly trampled by hundreds of bare and dusty feet.

"Sher Didar Khan was surprisingly tepid to all those shouts and roars and remained nonreactive for the initial few moments, even when his *pagree* was tugged away. He probably could not make sense the nature and types of reactions the crowd was initially agitated with. In his earlier brief talk with the select group leader, Sher Didar Khan made an ephemeral confession about his agonies and fear of last night and how and why he took shelter in this *gola* without anybody's knowledge or consent. He had received assurances from the select group leader of his safety. Moreover, his greatest solace was that he did not participate or get involved in any wrongdoing—but the jubilant crowd was behaving contrarily.

"Sher Didar Khan suddenly stopped walking as he realized what was happening. In the momentary standstill position, the jubilation of the crowd grew brasher with what doubtlessly was an outburst of joyful anger. Unraveled by the ordeal, he looked around but did not look back for his *pagree*. He evidently controlled his vitriol and remained reticent, balancing a delicate compromise between reputation and reality. He concentrated on his only earthly possession, a *tasbee*, and possibly made a total submission to God, thinking, nevertheless, about his daughter Raunak.

"The walk hardly crossed the boundary of the pond located in front of the extended home of Rushni's grandparents when suddenly, rowdiness overtook the control of the situation. Overenthusiasts started throwing small stones, small chunks of dry mud, or whatever they could lay their hands on at Sher Didar Khan. Much of this was misdirected toward members of the select group and their followers in proximity. They became preoccupied with the twin tasks of protecting him as well as themselves. The sudden upcharge of chaos and pandemonium caused confusion, providing an ideal setting for the consequential ruckus. One of enthusiasts in the crowd unexpectedly encountered a half-broken brick and, possibly without any premonition and more as a part of uncontrolled exuberance, threw it at Sher Didar Khan. That half brick struck the vital section of his head. He loudly uttered, 'Allah!' and fell flat on the pathway. He died soon thereafter in the same place.

"One person witnessed the whole episode but from a hideout at a safe distance. He was the *pesh* imam of the mosque and regular companion of Sher Didar Khan. The abrasive words hurled at Sher Didar Khan and the abusive gestures to tease him pained the *pesh* imam immensely, but he could not come out to help for the sake of his own security. Fighting members of *mukhti bahini*, along with supporting Indian forces, were yet to arrive. Earlier, the prevalent command and control structure had rapidly collapsed with the unexpected outcome of the short-lived war. Local political touts of divergent shades jumped in to take full advantage of the vacuum. In those prevailing social conditions, elderly people, generally those having beards, were suspected as pro-Pakistani. Being a *pesh* imam of the local mosque and his periodical but open association with Sher Didar Khan was double jeopardy. The *pesh* imam did not waste time in realizing that. So he prudently exercised the option of remaining unobtrusive, even though that hurt him very much.

"That episode of Sher Didar Khan's sudden death had its precipitous reactions. Pin-drop silence descended in the immediate vicinity. Some were shocked, while others were dumbfounded. As the news of the imminent arrival of the forces of the joint command at the Rupaipur High School playground reached the scene, the crowd rushed to greet them—totally insensible to the dead body of Sher Didar Khan.

"The *pesh* imam of the local mosque observed every bit of the outrageous homicide. The rapid evaporation of the crowd with children and young corps running and the elderly people lumbering toward the playground without an iota of unplumbed degree of empathy after getting the news of arrival of the joint command forces pained him most. Sher Didar Khan was the center of all acts and attention when alive. His body in death was of no significance to anyone. The corpse was most negligently left behind unattended and uncared for. The *pesh* imam kept on waiting in his hiding spot to see whether people would come to undertake religiously ordained actions for his burial. He was thinking that Sher Didar Khan could be an enemy under a changed situation but deserved all religious rituals and decency in death, being a Muslim. The *pesh* imam waited for quite a while in his latest hideout. He slowly mustered enough courage to be near the lone body of Sher Didar Khan.

"Contrarily, people, both male and female, were continuing to pour in the sprawling playground of Rupaipur High School, irrespective of the cold climatic condition and rather late hour. Many of them were competing and struggling to greet the forces of the joint command. Most ladies and girls had garlands of red roses and marigolds, while others had bunches of other winter flowers like jasmine, *shiuli*, China roses, and tuberoses. Those who could not manage flowers had small stems of various native plants having green leaves. A temporary stage was built. Loudspeakers were tied with posts, erected to support the plank of the stage. Unknown random speakers were at the height of their zeal in welcoming the forces of the joint command without missing a single opportunity to make public their commitment to support the cause for Bangladesh. They were particularly mindful in quantifying their role and contributions in support of the liberation war.

"The two *razakar* leaders played the leading role in all matters pertaining to welcoming the joint command forces, even though they were, for a while, unnerved and muddled when told about the unexpected killing of Sher Didar Khan. They also did not fail to articulate every detail in portraying themselves as the local protagonists of the war of liberation. Taking space of that, they loudly said, 'We have monitored the local militia and implanted in them gradually a sense of disarray, impacting their fighting will. We arrested their local commander to hand over tonight to forces of the joint command. We decided to do that as we were certain that he had important intelligence about war-related assets and crimes and could be a credible source of information for the joint command. Unfortunately, fifth-columnists are active in this liberated soil much before the whole of Bangladesh is liberated. Conspiracies started creeping in this liberated soil of golden Bengal. Pretending to be active supporters of the war, the conspirators pushed our security guards and reached closer to the local militia commander and killed him by throwing a brick. We see this as conspiracy, as how does one find a brick in a farmland?'

"With that note of interrogation, they assured the command of joint forces that they are there and are always available to share whatever information they have about war-related assets and crimes. The whole crowd listened with raft attention and started shouting, 'Shobuz Bhai Zindabad [Long live Brother Shobuz]!', 'Khoka Bhai Zindabad [Long live Brother Khoka]!', and 'Joy Bangla [Victory for Bengal]!' The crowd was at its ecstasy in expressing joy. Happiness was pouring in the words and actions of Shobuz and Khoka, the erstwhile *razakar* leaders. Public proclamation and endorsement of their being members of *mukhti bahini* in the presence of the forces of the joint command put a permanent seal on their new identity. Their happiness emanated from being able to wash away the stigma under the changed situation from being *razakar*s, notwithstanding the failed effort of the much-treasured handing over of Sher Didar Khan in person.

"The joy was intense. The resultant stupor was beyond comprehension. The sporadic setting and unplanned presence of tea and snack stalls everywhere in the cool hours of the night, initially done to entertain joint command forces, added color and festivity. Nobody knows who was serving whom or who was paying for such services. The demented exuberance got a startling boost when the commander of *mukhti bahini* took position on the stage and announced that the Pakistan command in Dhaka decided to surrender to the joint command of Bangladesh and Indian armies, bringing an end to the war of liberation on the following day. All present around were happy and relaxed for varied reasons.

"The *pesh* imam continued to be in a bewildered locus, sitting on the side of the pathway close to the dead body of Sher Didar Khan. He was very alert and kept the required close watch on the dead body, fearing blitzes by animals. He had two plausible reasons to be in that state of thought. First, he had no idea of what was happening in the playground except about the advancing of victorious joint forces. Second, he had the burden of divergent priorities involving religious duty and obligation concerning the burial of a fellow Muslim, with possible vulnerability to his own security. His moments of internal strain soon were relieved as he saw two upcoming people with kerosene oil lamps in hand. They were two elderly gentries with a close relationship with the *pesh* imam as regular participants in the congregation for prayers, as well as being neighbors. That was a happy reunion in a very pitiful moment. Exchanges among the three elderly individuals were short and specific about ordained religious obligations concerning the dead body of a fellow Muslim and a possible burial place. Based on the background of outrageous happening, the consensus was for one of the visitors and the *pesh* imam to go to Rushni's house, seeking their help in burying Sher Didar Khan, and for the other person to be in position to guard the dead body.

"As Pesh Imam Shaheeb was trying to detail his proposition, Rushni's mother intervened. She quietly but firmly said, 'Sher Didar Bhai-jan took me as a sister. His last statement was that my house was to be his last address. I have been treated by both of you as a sister since the first day of our encounter, so I give you permission to bury him in our family *koborostan* [cemetery], but that should be done quickly and without publicity. Alternative to that had unthinkable risks and ramifications, including tearing off different parts of Bhai-jan's body by the frenzied public or wild animals. I, being his adopted sister, can't allow that to happen.'

"After saying those words, she went inside and brought out two *kodal*s [shovels] with Rushni's help and handed them over to the *pesh* imam. Everything was done as ordained by the religious edicts and in a time-efficient manner, with compromises needed. Sher Didar Khan's body could not be cleaned and washed because of time constraints. Similarly, the practice of putting the body in the grave in a white shroud had to be dispensed with, given the need for speed.

"As they were carrying the body to the *koborostan* area for burial, one of the visiting gentlemen had found a big piece of cloth. That was the material used to wind the *pagree* of Sher Didar Khan. It had been trampled earlier with all the zeal of victory just before the brick fatally hit him but was somehow spared from being torn. The piece of cloth was retrieved, whisked in the air, and used as a partial shroud for Sher Didar Khan's eternal journey. That tangled-up piece of fabric, the significant constituent component of any *pagree*, symbolizing power and prestige in the life of Sher Didar Khan and his tribes and communities, became the lone and much-revered mortal thing to partially cover his body for burial, complying with Islamic religious injunctions. The relative importance of anything in life is the upshot of the evolving situation. That was the lesson of life for all three gentlemen involved in the burial process with universal application. The needed activities pertaining to burial were quietly and hurriedly completed, and all the three individuals promptly left the place after handing over the *kodal*s to Rushni's home. That was past midnight.

"About a mile farther south, the jubilation and jollity were at its peak in the playground and adjacent areas. The forces of the joint command were evidently happy but exercised due restraint in expressing their elation. They camped in vacant farmland areas for the remaining night. People around, even those who witnessed the death of Sher Didar Khan, somehow were completely reticent about any concern pertaining to the care of his dead body. Hard that it might sound, there was no discussion, and not even a query was made by anyone. Both Shobuz and Khoka even overlooked that need during the emerging night.

"The forces of the joint command left the place early the following morning. Both Shobuz and Khoka, like a score of others, went to brief sleep in the school premises once the forces marched forward. Most others returned to their respective homes. The collapse of the previous administrative structure and the departure of the joint command forces created a plausible but precipitous vacuum in local authority. As the proclaimed *mukhti bahini* members, both Shobuz and Khoka assumed open-ended authority and started passing on verbal orders and instructions.

"In following discussions over a cup of tea after snapping their brief sleep, Shobuz expressed his satisfaction as to the way the events of last night were conducted. He particularly expressed special happiness for being able to get general acceptance as genuine members of *mukhti bahini* in the presence of the forces of the joint command.

"On listening to that, Khoka poured two teaspoons full sugar in his cup of tea and stirred vigorously, creating obvious noise and drawing the attention of all present. Shobuz silently expressed his discomfort but agreed with Khoka to have a private follow-up conversation in the office room of the school headmaster.

"In that private discourse, Khoka became very emotional, contrary to his character and personal traits. He started by saying, 'Shobuz, we grew up in this community and have been socially and politically active together for many years. We became very close because of our association with involvement as *razakar*s over the last nine months and up until this point in time. Although you are younger than me, I have always been respectful of your views and complied with decisions taken. But I am not in a position to share your unrestrained happiness related to our endorsement last night as members of *mukhti bahini* in front of the forces of the joint command. The reactions of some among the joint command were not very warm when people were chanting, "Joy Bangla!" as we were being introduced. We should reasonably be prepared to tackle any adverse fallout of that in the future. Also, it would be unwise for us to forget that to a group of people, we are known for having the cunning qualities of jackals. Anyone can betray us anytime. It is evidently perilous and so not advisable to take things for granted. We ought to think of actions continually to protect ourselves. Our inability to present Sher Didar Khan last night might haunt us in future and could conveniently be used by others to demean us.'

"As Shobuz was about to reposition himself to respond to what Khoka had just said, their attention was diverted because of an unexpected commotion outside. Both of them came out, and one of their trusted cohorts came with the ominous news that Sher Didar Khan's body was not in the place they left last night. The obscure impact of this in future and the subtleties inherent perturbed Shobuz and Khoka, particularly against the backdrop of the immediate past discourse. A prompt decision was made to commit resources to resolve the whodunit as soon as possible.

"Not much time was needed to trace the dead body. As the chosen followers started scouting the areas adjacent to the point where the body was left last night, they soon found a new grave in the family *koborostan* of Rushni's grandparents. Because of the freshness of the topsoil and length of the grave with no known immediate death in the community, they concluded with full conviction that it was the grave of Sher Didar Khan. That was promptly reported to Shobuz and Khoka.

"Elevated by the reassuring and positive fresh news, both of them decided to discuss future options privately. As the obliging followers were waiting outside eagerly for further instruction, the two went to the office of the school headmaster and spent a rather long spell of silent moments. They were debating the options between what was socially and religiously desirable and what was politically expedient.

"Finally, Shobuz opened up, saying, 'Khoka Bhai, I am thankful for your past understanding and support. The words of caution you articulated a while back concerning the need to remain alert always were most apposite. I gave serious consideration penetrating probable circumstances and events, which could cause peril to both of us in the future. As I was debating internally, Allahpak [the Lord] blessed us with the good news relating to the ossuary of Sher Didar Khan. Now the onus is on us to exploit this unexpected opening.'

"Khoka continued to be in disarray, more trying to assess what Shobuz meant by his last statement.

"Taking note of the baffled expression on Khoka's face, Shobuz continued, saying, 'We need to create mayhem in the community focusing on the secret burial of Sher Didar Khan. That would pave the way to reassert our *mukhti bahini* identity and to refocus on our contribution to the cause of the Bangladesh liberation war, even though we were known as *razakar*s. The presence of Sher Didar Khan's grave in the family *koborostan* of Rushni's grandparents is our potent opportunity. Through trusted associates, we would sow juicy stories of a relationship between Rushni's mother and Sher Didar Khan. That story's critical focus would be to malign Rushni's family based on the presence of that grave, projecting them as real *razakar*s. Repeated assertions by our associates pronouncing our principled commitment and secret role in support of the war of liberation would be an emphasis. First would be a spicy story, bound to create interest among the people. The grounding of effort and action in burying Sher Didar Khan secretly and with such promptness, when most of the people were participating in the merriment concerning Bangladesh's victory in the war, would act as supporting justification. Second, we would need to ensure that ordinary people get used to hearing about our *mukhti bahini* identity, which is needed to be ingrained in their thoughts and recollections. After this is achieved, we would tell our trusted supporters various made-up harrowing tales as to our secret involvement and activities in support of the war of liberation. We would also encourage them to repeat that during blather in local tea stalls and bazaars. The passing-on of advance critical information pertaining to the positioning of Pakistani troops and movements of other war assets and helping in planning strategic engagements to disrupt local infrastructures would be the highlight of such propagation. All this would be portrayed in the context of persistent risks to our lives. That would go a long way in creating our images as *mukhti bahini*, and over time, it would become irreversible.'

"Shobuz and Khoka did not waste a moment in pursuing their agreed agenda. They asked followers present to be at the same venue after *johor* [noontime prayer] along with other supporters as they had important information to share with all. That instruction was carried out in totality as was evident from the size of the crowd. Both Shobuz and Khoka showed up without any vacillation. As they stepped in, the crowd started chanting the slogan 'Joy Bangla!' every time the close associates uttered, 'Shobuz Bhai' and 'Khoka Bhai.'

"Shobuz and Khoka started addressing the crowd alternately, with each one taking over from the other. In addition to a glorious welcome, the highlight of their initial commentary focused on the contribution and sacrifice of all present in attaining freedom from Pakistan. As part of undercover *mukhti bahini*, they had meticulously observed the behavior and actions of all in the community and were very pleased to see most of them last night and in this assembly called at short notice. During the process, Shobuz made up stories highlighting Khoka's daring acts though outwardly was known as a *razakar*. Khoka glorified the decisions and actions of Shobuz because of which Rupaipur could avoid most of the vicious tumult of war. Their well-orchestrated gig predicated on the focused objective of being acknowledged as *mukhti bahini* was astounding and mesmerized the assembly. Mutual peddling reached its zenith, showering assumed credit to all present, and Shobuz took over the lead in making public what they knew for quite some time.

"He said, 'Brothers, we planned this urgent assembly not to relate our specific acts of valor as undercover *mukhti bahini*. We called you for two specific purposes. First, to thank you all and through you to those absent with our profound gratitude for last night's participation in welcoming the forces of the joint command. They were very happy about the spontaneous welcome and asked us to convey that to you all. Second, a very sad and appalling piece of information we kept closeted within ourselves. While all and sundry like you spared no hardship and sacrifice in getting rid of

Pakistanis, there were some among us who deliberately betrayed the cause of Mother Bangladesh and actively collaborated with the Pakistan army and militia. One of them is the mother of Rushni, who frequently entertained militia commander Sher Didar Khan and hosted him. We tried our best to confidentially restrain her, but she never listened. Perhaps that was a reason why, in spite of repeated indication, she continued to live in their big homestead with her daughter instead of crossing the border with the rest of the family. We also got indication from Sher Didar Khan about her oft-repeated request to get the whole property in her name through his good office. But that was not all. Even when the Pakistan army was defeated and Sher Didar Khan was killed, Rushni's mother could not forget her lovebird. When all of us were busy in welcoming victorious joint forces last night, she somehow got the dead body of Sher Didar Khan shifted to their family *koborostan* and buried the *jollad* [butcher] in the holy soil of *Shonar Bangla* [Golden Bengal].'

"The assembled crowd roared outpouring protests, expressing their anger and hate. Sensing the mood of the crowd, Shobuz threw the ball in their court. He said, 'We do not like to take any decision as to a future course of action as that could be misinterpreted. We leave that to you. You decide and guide us. But remember, there is no room for collaborators in this golden land of Bangladesh. We need to teach a good lesson so that the suspected people think twice before talking or taking any erroneous step.'

"A surge of fury among the mostly young assembled people was palpable. Rather than suggesting anything specific, they were mostly preoccupied with various versions of slander associated with the allegation and shouting for revenge. That precisely was what both Shobuz and Khoka were looking for. They intervened, suggesting that the crowd go to Rushni's home, get mother and daughter out of the house, and demand explanations. They would put them on a cow-driven cart and parade them through the community as being proclaimed collaborators. That would be a great lesson for all others like them. The enthusiasm for punishing them was much more heightened than the pronounced punishment. Some enthusiasts suggested that the mother's hair be shaved off with a simultaneous application paste of ashes on the face. That was agreed to without any reservation.

"Rushni and her mother were in their *ranna ghar* [kitchen in a separate shack], mutely spending their time. Though together in a lone setting, their minds were scanning two divergent aspects related to the killing of Sher Didar Khan. Rushni was thinking of Raunak losing her father, as she had a few years back, and her mother was engaged in self-inflicted guilt for not being able to do anything to save the innocent life of her embraced brother. That state of mind suddenly was shaken by the fast-moving boisterous sound of slogans. Rushni's mother initially thought that to be one of the many celebratory events related to victory in the war of liberation and moved to the main house with Rushni to have a better view. But that would prove to be wrong. Innocence of thinking just evaporated as they saw through the small window of their house a large twitchy gathering assembled near their family *koborostan,* with *razakar* leaders Shobuz and Khoka pointing to the grave of Sher Didar Khan. The more the two pseudo *mukhti bahini* members were detailing imaginary facts with impudent gesticulations, the more raucous and frantic the gathering became. Rushni's mother sensed susceptibility outright and, as a caution, took refuge in the side bedroom, bolting the entry door from inside.

"The agitated mob moved forward and besieged Rushni's home, impulsively hurling abusive words and tenuous allegations. They were screaming, asking the mother and daughter to come out. Those swipes and sacrilegious utterances, coupled with rampant rage, made mother and daughter flabbergasted, and they instinctively took refuge in a remote corner of the floor of the room. Except occasional exchanges of looks, they were speechless, uncertain about what was going to happen.

"On getting the signal from Shobuz, a few from among the crowd positioned the bull-driven open cart in front of Rushni's home, and three young guys went inside, breaking the entry door to the room where mother and daughter had sheltered themselves. They lunged at them, grabbed their long hair, and brought them out simultaneously, expectorating on them. On seeing them in that condition, the whole crowd burst into jubilation. They were forcibly put on the cart. From the slurs uttered by the crowd, both mother and daughter had the explicit hint of likely cogency of the mob for treating them like that. In their thoughts, they were clear about the clobbered reality they were in and concluded that showing any veneer of ironic tenacity in that situation would be of no relevance except enhancing the rage and worsening the antiphon. Both of them remained unmoving.

"On the cart, the local barber promptly started shaving the mother's head. Two of the three young men who brought them out got engaged in making paste by mixing ashes and water. Once the shaving process was over, the surrounding people started putting that paste on the head and face of the mother. That unbridled enthusiasm propelled some to put the paste on the hair and face of Rushni too. The frenzied mood of the gathering crossed all limits of decency and civility with oft-repeated flirtatious comments and remarks. A few among them even took the chance of momentarily touching private parts of the mother's body in the pretext of putting the paste.

"Rushni observed that but refrained from reacting because of eye indication received from the mother. She just kept a solemn posture.

"The procession of rowdy people kept the cart in the middle of the path, with mother and daughter in a standing position to ensure their identity, and optimize the intended humiliation. Intermittent ugly rattles with sadistic elations were the hallmark of that march.

"It was difficult for Rushni and her mother to be in stable positions because of the rudimentary nature of pathway the cart was trailing. As they were trying to keep them steady, adjoining people around extended their hands ostensibly to help them, nevertheless taking advantage of touching them physically. That was a great opportunity for many. There was therefore a rush of people to be close to the cart. In that ruckus setting, a few nearby people snatched off the sari of Rushni's mother. Humiliated by that unexpected act and standing with only petticoat and blouse to cover her, Rushni's mother had firmly looked at those people and, instead of saying anything, put her two hands in a cross manner on her chest to minimize the apparent shame.

"Shobuz and Khoka, notwithstanding being the scalawags, always maintained a safe distance from the infuriated crowd and enjoyed the evolving progression. They were happy for the turn of events. The more was the humiliation of Rushni and her mother, the greater was their happiness as that was going to put a seal of permanency to their new identity as *mukhti bahini*.

"Their much-valued mental peace suddenly experienced a jolt, seeing Kalon Master, a teacher, hurriedly approaching the riotous crowd by crisscrossing the barren paddy fields. That was an ominous sign. Insulting and humiliating Rushni and her mother was their latest strategy to establish themselves as real freedom fighters. It was their second effort to have an unblemished identity as *mukhti bahini* but that could as well be confronted with startling hindrance once again if Kalon Master got involved. They conveniently hid themselves behind the torso of a nearby big tree, observing the moves of the master.

"Kalon Master was a popular history teacher in Rupaipur High School. He was a vibrant young teacher with social interaction across the board. Politically, he was sensitive and a firm believer in the ideology favoring independent Bangladesh and openly discussed that. One of his favored places for sharing political thoughts was the homestead of Rushni's grandparents. Kalon Master was known to all who lived in the homestead by name, even though his association was mostly with Rushni's elder uncles. He casually encountered Rushni and knew about her as uncles had shared their thoughts and plans with matters related to taking care of orphan Rushni as she was growing up.

"When the war broke out, he initially took refuge in India, got enlisted and trained as a *mukhti bahini*, and was sent back to Panchkhira by the high command. He was embedded there with a broad spectrum of responsibilities but had focus in and around

Rupaipur. Kalon Master soon became known as a legendary *mukhti bahini* around the locality. Among many others, his daring acts in blowing up one of the Pakistan army's convoys carrying arms and ammunitions and his frontal fracas with Pakistani soldiers, suffering three casualties, soon became a mythical story continuously prattled. His ferocity was likewise a common story. He did not hesitate to kill a number of collaborators during the war of liberation. Besides being popular, people generally were scared of him.

"The band of people accompanying the bull-driven cart with Rushni and her mother in a traumatized standing position were engrossed in their joy and merriment, totally oblivious to developments around. They were tempestuous and licentious in their words.

"Kalon Master was in Panchkhira most part of that day. As he returned to his small abode near the Rupaipur High School, a trusted associate told him what was going on in Rushni's house. That prompted him to rush without wasting time. Before leaving, Kalon Master took his SMG and some magazines. He tied the magazines to his chest and waist and held the SMG under the *chador* draping his body. His searching mind and *mukhti bahini* instinct did not fail him. He easily identified the frenzied procession from a far distance as being the one linked to the episode he was told about earlier. Coming nearer to the moving procession and seeing Rushni and her mother in that browbeaten condition, Kalon Master just could not control himself. He growled at the rampageous and riotous crowd. He shuffled across the procession, boarded the bullock-driven cart, took out the SMG from under his *chador*, and opened immediate brushfires to unnerve the crowd.

"He shouted, 'What you all are doing to these two ladies? Don't you have mothers and sisters back home? Are you not ashamed for your reckless and deplorable behavior? I am not saying that they are innocent or guilty. If there are allegations against them, then we should have a *salish*. Who are we to degrade them like this without a trial? If a trial takes place, I will give witness regarding their contribution to the war of liberation. During the last six months and when I was hiding from public appearance being a *mukhti bahini*, I spent many days and nights without food. I went at late hours of many nights to Rushni's home and whispered being the Kalon Master and requested food. These two ladies never hesitated in feeding me. One night, Rushni and her mother even brought their moveable *chula* [a clay cube with a round hole for cooking] from the kitchen and cooked rice for me in their bedroom to avoid public attention. And now you are insulting these two as being collaborators.'

"He paused for a second and concluded his deafening statement by saying, 'You know that I have killed many collaborators and some Pakistani soldiers in frontal engagements. I did so, not caring for my life. The country is free today, but I am still ready to die for a right cause. So I warn you, if anyone among you raises a single voice against these two ladies, then have a look at these magazines. I will not hesitate to kill many more this evening and here. Also note that if anyone utters a single word against these ladies or I see anyone around their house in the future, this SMG would be activated without further warning.'

"With manifested anger oozing from physical reaction and frustration at its pinnacle, Kalon Master did not obfuscate in addressing the disheveled crowd. It worked in creating a sudden besieged shock and fear among the crowd. Being aware of the unpredictability and impulsive reaction traits of Kalon Master, the tousled crowd was in a total silence, as if they went into hibernation precipitously. Soon, the demented crowd meekly vacated the place. The panic was intense, and even the cart owner left his cart unattended.

"Kalon Master, keeping his eye focus down, gently took off his *chador* and wrapped it around the body of Rushni's mother. He descended from the cart, extended his hand, and helped exhausted Rushni and her mother in stepping down. A total silence prevailed as they returned to Rushni's home, just before *magreeb*. Rushni's mother sat on a *choki* [a simple wooden bed], and Kalon Master was given the lone chair. After wiping their respective faces with the tangled sari that had been dishonored by the crowd, Rushni went inside and brought a glass of water and handed it to Kalon Master.

In sipping that water, which tasted much better than well-prepared sherbet, Kalon Master initiated first direct exchanges.

"He recalled his few secret visits to this house at the odd hours of some nights and began the discourse by saying, 'When I used to come for food during dark hours of nights, I always whispered and addressed you as Ma [Mother]. I had no idea about your age and no inkling about your demeanor. As I see you today, you are too young to be addressed as Mother by someone of my age. But you eminently fit in as an elder sister. Since elder sisters in our culture are given the honor and dignity mothers deserve, I will continue, if you permit, to address you as Ma.'

"As Kalon Master was finishing his statement, the *chador* slipped from the shaven head of Rushni's mother. She was embarrassed in front of Kalon Master while she had audaciously remained nonchalant before the maddening crowd. As Rushni's mother was riveted in putting back that *chador* on her bare head, covering part of her forehead and anchoring the sides of the cover behind her ears, she just nodded without any word. The tensed and embarrassing experience gradually faded away, facilitating more congenial milieu for a normal discourse. Matters related to their future well-being was the focus of that conversation.

"Kalon Master repeatedly assured Rushni and her mother about their future safety, saying, 'So long as I am here, no one would dare to touch you. But one thing is bothering me. Why did neither of you protest or resist publicly?'

"Rushni's mother softly said, 'We were overtaken by the speed of unforeseen developments. We could never think that we were their targets until the last moment. Evidently, our option was limited. We had no time to think and discuss. We opted to keep quiet, surrendering ourselves before the will of Allah.'

"Rushni added, 'Any resistance by us would have infuriated the crowd, and one could have even set the house on fire. We totally lost our senses once they dragged and put us on that cart. The only thing I remember was the subsumed distress embodied on the face of Sher Didar Khan as he was taken out of our property and the internal anguish triggered within him. We undeservedly experienced something worse than that.'

"Kalon Master listened carefully and said, 'So long as I am here, you do not have to worry. But one should know and be prepared to fight for oneself, whatever may be the downside.'

"After saying this, Kalon Master, to the immense surprise of both mother and daughter, brought out a vintage hand sickle from his waistband. It had been hidden, being positioned between his body and the trouser belt, with his shirt providing immediate cover. He handed it over to Rushni with firm advice that she should carry it always and never hesitate to use it for the sake of her honor and life, especially when he is not around. As he was leaving Rushni's home, the mother requested Kalon Master to have dinner with them the following night. He agreed and left without his *chador*, still covering part of the mother's body and shaven head. Both mother and daughter felt embarrassed that they had forgotten to return it.

"After necessary cleansing, both mother and daughter sat down for their dinner, sharing the residue of rice left from lunch, but could not swallow. Their wretched mental and physical conditions were just not genial for eating. They silently withdrew from the process and opted for the immediate alternative of going to their respective *choki*s [beds] to sleep. But sleep, what they wanted desperately, was not forthcoming. Mother was engrossed with thinking as to what could have happened to them had Kalon Master not shown up at that critical juncture. More than life, she was preoccupied with thoughts of squalor in front of hundreds of people. In that situation, she would have been emotionally dead though perhaps physically alive. The related thoughts of how they would have treated young Rushni made her body shake. She turned herself on the bed to get out of that thought in trying to fall asleep.

"Rushni was also struggling to fall asleep. But her thoughts were centering on her first touch with the rugged hand of Kalon

Master when he helped her in getting down from the cart. That was her first touch with an adult male person. She recalled with full sensitivity her second touch, when she handed him the glass of water. Besides those, she was thinking about his manliness, courage, and determination in facing that maddening crowd and taming them like a herd of sheep. His handing over of personal hand sickles as something ultimate to protect made her happy as that was definitely reflective of his care and concern for her. Rushni fell asleep easily after a while.

"Kalon Master's visits to Rushni's home initially were occasional but became regular after a few times. Those were mostly for dinner, and the visit attained a pattern in terms regularity and time. He conveyed his discomfort in visiting them regularly once the extended family returned from a refugee camp in India.

"Rushni's mother brushed off that uneasiness and, contrary to her normal demeanor, firmly insisted that he should continue coming. She said, 'No one has any right to say anything about who is visiting us or not. When our life and dignity were at stakes, no one came forward except you. So you have every right to visit us.'

"As a supportive justification, she encouraged Imam Shaheeb also to visit them more often and, in that process, indirectly alluded to Imam Shaheeb about the possibility of a relationship with Kalon Master. Though Rushni was upfront and guileless in her interactions, Kalon Master was somewhat reserved, especially pertaining to emotional aspects of a possible relationship. In one of his discussions, he indicated to Rushni's mother about something he had in mind to tell her but needed some more time as things around him were yet to be settled. The constraints were related to emerging socio-political conditions and his role and responsibility. Rushni took the unstated matter as things related to their possible union. Kalon Master's polite decline to take back the *chador* with which he covered the body of Rushni's mother with reasoning that he has many back home was taken as a positive signal. All these made Rushni happy.

"While interactions and exchanges were warming up at the end of Rushni's home, both Shobuz and Khoka spent grisly time. Two successive attempts to publicly demonstrate and establish their *mukhti bahini* identity ironically failed at the very last moment. They took the first one as something providential. Both Shobuz and Khoka could not reconcile with the second one. The blame for it explicitly centered on Kalon Master. It was the consensus that any effort to reach an understanding with him would be futile as Kalon master has a one-track mind-set. Their sleazy feeling about Kalon Master was the centerpiece of discourse. The immutable conclusion was that Kalon Master is the principal impediment in the process of attaining *mukhti bahini* status, both present and in future. Shobuz and Khoka became very clear that for the sake of their own existence, they could not remain tepid and lumber away from their main objective. The domineering decision was to physically eliminate Kalon Master.

"Shobuz metaphysically observed, 'Kalon Master's dead body would give us the much-needed third chance to publicly cry and howl for a dead comrade, emphasizing the conspiracy by fifth-columnists around.'

"Notwithstanding being half literate, both Shobuz and Khoka exhibited their sly aptitude when they discussed the details of the killing operation. Both of them agreed that it would be unadvisable for them to be directly involved in the operation. They were to remain on the sideline, plan the details based on reconnaissance results, and get it done by their trusted but illiterate followers, alluring them with handsome rewards. They selected two after due thought, and those two, for all purposes, worked as their spooks. The following actions were taken meticulously. Kalon Master's time for visiting Rushni's home most of the evenings was monitored, and a trend was established. It was agreed that the operation would be undertaken during the dark moon cycle to conceal visibility. As evidence of their noninvolvement, they decided to be in Panchkhira on the night the action was planned. Most of their shrewd planning was the outcome of their training and operational experiences as *razakar*s.

"The two trusted recruits positioned themselves on the designated evening at a reasonable opposite distance from the sparsely trafficked rural pathway that Kalon Master normally followed. The strategic objectives of that positioning were to monitor the sudden presence of unknown individuals, ensuring, when needed, calling off the operation for the sake of secrecy, and to enable them to dislodge Kalon Master easily by attacking from both sides.

"Kalon Master was on his way to Rushni's home that evening as he had in the recent past. He was in a relaxed and happy mood, thinking about the time and venue for talking to Rushni's mother. He argued with himself to hasten the process as the pressure of the war and subsequent embryonic frustration pertaining to the evolving social conditions had convinced him to shape up his own life by getting married soon. Internally, he was exhausted and somewhat disillusioned. The impulsive flashing of Rushni's face made him happier.

"Observing him, the two recruits started walking from the opposite directions, measuring their steps to enable them to traverse him at the same time. They did so precisely. One of the two collided with Kalon Master, who thought that to be accidental because of darkness and shrugged it off. He was destabilized promptly by a simultaneous attack from both sides. Kalon Master was taken aback, and his immediate maneuverability was constrained by the *chador* with which he wrapped his body, as normally done during winter nights. He instinctively placed his hand at the back of his waistline to get a hand on the sickle, forgetting that he gave it to Rushni a few days back. Unarmed and struggling, Kalon Master continued to resist unforeseen aggression when one of the men brutally attacked him with the machete.

"Unnoticed and uncared for, the brave son of the country who dedicated himself to die for its freedom succumbed to a most heinous attack by fifth-columnists soon after its liberation. The dead body was pushed into the adjacent dry farmland of *shonar* [golden] *Bangla*, with the dust around his dead body absorbing the oozing blood.

"Rushni and her mother continued waiting for Kalon Master. As time passed, Rushni's mother suggested that they should better eat and go to bed as perhaps Kalon Master either was constrained by some developments or might have gone to Panchkhira for urgent work. Rushni refused to agree, with a feeling of uneasiness and fear within her. She could not sleep properly that night.

"Both of them woke up early in the morning to hear unfamiliar noises outside. Rushni's mother opened the door and was told by the group of people standing outside about the killing of Kalon Master. On hearing the news, Imam Shaheeb rushed to Rushni's home from the mosque. The assembled people were comprised of family folks, elderly early risers of the community, and some children. The notable exception was the presence of those two who had killed Kalon Master that night. Evidently, they wanted to have the seal of innocence by their presence.

"Rushni's mother was stunned and speechless. Losing her husband in an accident a few years back, the shocking death of a brother-like well-wisher, Sher Didar Khan, in a mob violence, and now an obvious planned murder of an angel-like soul, Kalon Master—this series of catastrophes was too much for her to endure and handle. She unreceptively looked at Rushni.

"Rushni remained steel-framed but not frozen. She was intractable but emotionless. Her vitriol was shadowed by irresistible moxie. Rushni's thought wave traversed in a variety of directions without any physical outburst. She was overwhelmed by the thought of not 'what' and 'why' but more by 'who.' As she was gazing at the crowd to find an answer within herself, she noted the presence of those two associates of Shobuz and Khoka. Rushni suddenly went inside and came out soon, holding the sickle that Kalon Master gave her a few nights ago. She held it with all rigidity and firmness.

"As the initial surprise and shock of the assembled people from the sudden killing of Kalon Master was slowly taking the tone of a whisper, Rushni passed on a signal to her mother to go inside. Before complying with the indication, Rushni's mother softly desired the presence of her elder brother-in-law and Imam Shaheeb in the house for discussions. Without sparing any more time, Rushni closed the entry door but did not forget to display her sickle prominently, even though she had no inkling about the perpetrator.

"The discussion inside the house was brief and direct. Rushni's mother firmly said, 'As details of Kalon Master's family are unknown and as he saved our lives and dignity a few days back during the unexplainable ordeal we suffered, it was our wish that Kalon Master be buried promptly in our family *koborostan* and by the side of brother Sher Didar Khan.'

"That was agreed to, notwithstanding the expressed hesitation by the brother-in-law, premised on likely social repercussions of having two sepulchres of contradicting relevance, one dedicated to oppose the creation of Bangladesh and the other being a freedom fighter in support of the cause. The affirmative decision was propelled because of insistence by Rushni's mother and bolstered by justifications put forward by Imam Shaheeb stating that the religious injunctions require a Muslim burial soon after death and that past enmity or identity should not be a determining factor in deciding the rituals of the ultimate disposal of a dead body.

"As arranged, the burial took place after *johor* [midday Muslim prayer]. Once the burial was over, the assembled few people, led by Imam Shaheeb, had their *munajat* [seeking divine peace and blessings for the departed soul].

"After the *munajat* was over and the assembled people were about to disperse, they noticed Shobuz and Khoka running toward the *koborostan*, howling and beating their chests in demonstration of their shock and grief. Both of them fell on the grave, cried incessantly, and, holding the clay in their hand, loudly proclaimed their determination to find the killers and take revenge. They publicly concluded that it was the work of fifth-columnists and that their revered *mukhti bahini* brother Kalon was the first *shaheed* [martyr]. People around consoled them. All present gradually dispersed, with gloom and sadness overwhelming Rushni and her mother in different ways.

"The episode was observed by Rushni and her mother from a distance, with other female family members, as detailed later by her cousins. Rushni listened with utmost attention, but she was in a confused mind-set. Kalon Master had never shared with them about having a very close and warm relationship with Shobuz and Khoka to impel them to have such a tumult. Rushni was evidently confused but kept it to herself. In spite of her outward stubborn physical posture, she eventually gave in to the involuntary flow of teardrops. Her mother was relieved.

Conversion

"Rushni was burdened by the thought that Kalon Master's brutal murder was the outcome of some local conspiracy, and moving her palm restlessly on the sickle, she made a promise to herself to unearth the truth. Observing the agony being suffered, her mother pressured Rushni to get married soon as a way out of her current angst. Rushni flatly rebuffed that and stated that getting married was not her immediate objective. Her prime focus was to unearth the secret of who killed him and to take revenge. One thing continued to persist in her thoughts—the identity of the presence of two unknown young men in the assembly of neighborhood people on the early morning of Kalon Master's death.

"Time passed. The economic conditions of the new country worsened. Social decency and propriety took a nosedive down deep. Law and order all over the country overtly became subservient to political maneuvering. Pseudo *mukhti bahini*s like Shobuz and Khoka came into prominence, increasingly monopolizing most of the economic and political opportunities. That gave rise to open conflict in the top hierarchy of the political establishment.

"The disillusioned, dissenting group broke away and formed the Purba Bangla Bonchito-der Party [PBBP]. PBBP was headquartered in Dhaka and mounted a number of political movements. Some such movements had overt militant character. In the face of serious impairments, ranging between summary imprisonment and killing, PBBP turned its course from typical political opposition to need-based military resistance. As a strategic move against the sustained tough policies of the government, PBBP branched out its operations in various parts of the country with a special concentration in townships around Panchkhira and Sundarban. The pronounced idea was to militarily confront the government to embrace scientific social systems to ensure equity among and well-being of all people.

"Simultaneously, PBBP undertook a concerted effort at the field level to establish contact and motivate disoriented youths to oppose the policies and actions of the government. Based on such groundwork, selected youths were recruited and trained by area commanders and were inducted as members of PBBP. New recruits were to undertake assigned responsibilities under total command and strict supervision of each area commander.

"One of Rushni's cousins, a college student during the war, returned from a refugee camp in India with a lot of negative impressions and irritation. That was multiplied by experiencing and observing evolving socio-political conditions. He soon joined PBBP. Rushni had a very supportive rapport with him. Whenever they had discussions—and that was not frequent—she would invariably raise the issue of who killed Kalon Master. Her cousin told her that she would never have the answer to that query by staying at home and lamenting about it.

"Her cousin told her in confidence about his joining PBBP and stressed that if she wanted an answer to her question, she should consider joining too and, through the contacts and links of the organization, try to find out the people behind Kalon Master's death. He also emphasized that carrying the sickle always would not have any relevance unless she has the determination to decipher the conspiracy, even staking her life in the process. Her cousin emphasized that going out of her home and finding those culprits would be the best she could do in repaying the debt owed to Kalon Master. It would be the most befitting reward of the care and love the sickle was given with. Considering the startling challenge her cousin had put forth and to seek a temporary redress, Rushni diverted the discussion by asking him for the reason that motivated him to join PBBP—without the family's consent and secretly.

"The cousin responded by saying that he would like to deal with the last question first. He said that had he discussed that with family, the response would have invariably been negative as no family would allow their grown son to join such a movement where death is always a probability, so he did not ask. His explanation on the first point was that in spite of good rationale for the war of liberation, he was totally frustrated observing the lifestyle and behavior of leaders who took refuge in Calcutta.

"He continued, saying, 'I went many times to listen to them and get direction as to a future course. Most of the time, it was an annoying experience. Life in the refugee camp was miserable, with the focus not on the care and welfare of the refugees but more on political exigencies and financial benefits. The insouciance demonstrated was very frustrating. I reconciled with it on our return from the war. The initial few months were unblemished. Because of political maneuvering, as time passed, the committed leaders and workers had to take back seats, creating space for new patriots. The worst was that it happened with the blessings of the establishment. At the local level, I find it awful to see people like Shobuz and Khoka dominating the political and social landscapes of Rupaipur and adjoining areas. When they are in public places, people bend to *salaam* them. Their ignorant followers are continuously prattling in tea shops and bazaar gatherings, telling and repeating the daring acts of both. If one sums up those stories, one might be inclined to think that the war was won only for their efforts. It pains me that no one talks about or refers to the real *mukhti bahini*s like our dear Kalon Master.'

"He was about to conclude his statement when he unwittingly said, 'Do you remember two young guys in the morning gathering of local people in front of your home giving the news of Kalon Master's death? I have been observing that those two people are always with Shobuz and Khoka since the sad demise of Kalon Master.'

"That insinuation shattered the thought process of Rushni. It appeared to her that she had a soupçon of tracks in pursuing her objective. Her mind was agitated by related thoughts—how and why those two people were in that early morning gathering as they were not from the community and, if showing sympathy was the reason, why they never came a second time. If the howling and crying of Shobuz and Khoka on the day of Kalon Master's burial were so genuine, why did they not visit the grave even a second time for *kobor ziarat* [a Muslim's practice to pray for a departed soul by standing in the vicinity of a grave]? What brought those two young guides so close to Shobuz and Khoka if they were not known to each other before? The questions were open ended. The answers remained unclear. They were relevant, though, in establishing a link yet without evidence.

"Rushni took the initiative to pursue these unanswered questions with her cousin. After some exchanges, she proposed to join PBBP with the twin objectives of unearthing the mystery surrounding the assassination of Kalon Master and eradicating self-seekers and self-proclaimed leaders from the social setting to ensure a more peaceful and livable environment in which innocent lives would remain safe. Seeking help in getting enlisted as a PBBP comrade, she assured her cousin that she would get the consent of her mother.

"She raised the issue with her mother. Being persuaded and based on a moral obligation to unearth the conspiracy shrouding Kalon Master's death, her mother reluctantly agreed but expressed her worries about Rushni's getting married. Her mother emphasized that in the absence of her father, the onus is on her to get Rushni married.

"She was quiet for some time and then responded, 'Mother, I agree with what you said, but think about me too. The growing-up phase of my life was very short, and within that short span of life, I lost my father in an accident, witnessed the brutal killing of one whom I respected as a father figure, and have had to handle the merciless killing of one for whom I developed love and care and was fondly hoping to have a family with in the near future. I am so unlucky and deprived. If it is so ordained, I will definitely get married but only when I have been able to take revenge for Kalon Master's death and if I meet someone who loves me and cares about my feelings.'

"No further discussions took place. With some cooked-up stories for her absence from home, Rushni went to Sundarban, got into PBBP, underwent training, and slowly started taking part in offensive missions. Initially, those were for threatening rogue elements and the liquidation of enemies, touts, and pseudo-leaders who were causing havoc to ordinary people. Notwithstanding her access and permission to use high-grade weapons as needed, Rushni consciously developed the habit of always parking the sickle at the back of her body, as used to be done by Kalon Master. She never defaulted, irrespective of whether she was wearing a sari or trousers and a shirt. During the process of her field assignments and through contacts of her cousin, who was also a field worker, she developed a close relationship with some field workers of PBBP whose job was intelligence gathering. In exchanges with the field workers, Rushni entreated for specific surveillance of the ruling party's local stalwarts to gather information pertaining to Shobuz, Khoka, and their activities.

"With astounding successes behind her, Rushni soon earned a name as a devout insurrectionary fighter. Her physical adroitness, mental resoluteness, and ability to handle various weapons soon became a common tale within the band, reaching the field high command. Increasingly, she was given more challenging missions, which she successfully carried out, demonstrating a very high norm of engagement skills and a profound sense of strategic maneuvering. Very unusually, she was assigned command responsibilities for skirmishes and encounters with the government forces.

"Around this time, sustained information was pouring in about the high-handed activities of Shobuz and Khoka, marauding the properties, assets, and businesses of ordinary folks and harassing and threatening people. They became the talk of the community as loud boors. Both created an environment of trepidation and bullying. No one dared to challenge or confront them. Local command took the decision to respond to that. It was decided to monitor them carefully, ambush effectively, and bring them before the people's court for trial. At her pleading, Rushni was given the task to accomplish the mission. She was a natural choice, being the leading militant with a series of success stories in a short time.

"Members of the mission, under Rushni's guidance, did intensive field reconnaissance, which established that Shobuz and Khoka returned to their homes rather late in the evening on most Fridays after spending time in their Gobindapur burrow, enjoying the free flow of local drinks. The other two who had killed Kalon Master were their regular companions on their return trips. Shobuz and Khoka used to be ecstatic and carefree during their return trip to home each Friday, often demonstrating a common characteristic of being demented. They often shuffled their feet, under the influence of native drinks, and never hesitated scoffing at local leaders of both establishment and oppositions, including PBBP.

"After vigilant scrutiny of their movements and activities, Rushni planned their ambush on a Friday evening, harboring the hope to get the accomplices as well. She concluded that to be the most opportune day and hour to undertake the operation as the time was late evening and there were marked portions of less traffic in their usual passageway.

"That was done as planned. The ambush was a total success without major resistance as the influence of liquor was both the prime destabilizing and supporting factor. Rushni and her comrades had a smooth operational success.

"Shobuz, Khoka, and their two associates were taken to Rushni's area command and were soon remanded for intensive individual interrogation prior to trial on the following day in the people's court. Succumbing to the brute tactics of interrogation, the two associates admitted to having killed Kalon Master and, to save their own lives, also confessed that it was undertaken at the specific direction of Shobuz and Khoka. As the remand process became more intensive, they even said that neither Shobuz nor Khoka were *mukhti bahini*. They had served the previous establishment loyally as *razakar*s but became desperate to be known as *mukhti bahini* after the liberation of Bangladesh. Realizing that Kalon Master, a genuine *mukhti bahini* member, was the main impediment in the process, they spread false stories about Kalon Master and then decided to eliminate him permanently. The considered and oft-repeated view of Shobuz and Khoka was that Kalon Master should be removed physically so that he could not derail them from being members of *mukhti bahini* now or in the future. Shobuz and Khoka had enlisted them to do the job, alluring them with recognition and rewards.

"Rushni came to know promptly about this interrogation outcome and made a firm determination within to take fitting revenge. As the people's court was in session in the presence of other comrades without bearing arms, as per the operational guidance of BPPB, Rushni, contrary to PBBP's standard practices, made a passionate statement about the brutality committed by Shobuz and Khoka in killing a genuine and committed *mukhti bahini*. She argued that in view of the unequivocal confessions of both associates, there was no need for further process-related deliberations to establish the guilt of Shobuz and Khoka. Narrating Kalon Master's singular effort in protecting her and her mother from unspeakable humiliation, Rushni candidly and with irrepressible tears flowing down her cheeks confessed, 'It was a nascent but unspoken desire and dream of both Kalon Master and I to have a permanent family bonding. And at that stage, Kalon Master was brutally killed.'

"That was the first time that her comrades and superiors ever saw Rushni succumb to emotion. The automatic outcome was unbounded sympathy.

"She continued, pleading, 'I have joined PBBP, aligning myself fully to the ideals of PBBP, and have remained faithful to that. But honestly speaking, I have also a palpable agenda—to find out the killers of Kalon Master and take equally brutal requite.'

"Having said that Rushni, clad in a *tater* [hand oven] sari as per the rural and traditional way of draping it around the body and visibly unarmed, made a passionate submission, stating, 'The command may decide the fate of the two associates, but I should be given the permission to deal with Shobuz and Khoka.'

"She emphasized as justification for her request, 'I am not seeking a favor for my full commitment to the ideals of PBBP. I am asking this for the simple reason that there is no thin line between certainty and doubt. It is more than certain that Shobuz and Khoka are the masterminds for the killing. Their statement that the two associates went beyond their mandate without sanction from them is not sustainable. These two associates continued to be Shobuz and Khoka's closet confiders since the killing of Kalon Master, and that is enough to ignore their latest entreaty.'

"After consultation, the command agreed with Rushni's pleading. As she desired, Shobuz and Khoka were tied to two big trees in the midst of incessant loud begging for pardon as they regretted the killing, and their two associates went beyond their expressed directive not to cause physical harm. Their other point was that their two associates implicated them to save their own lives.

"The trial venue puzzlingly was in a state of absolute silence. All present were racking their brains about what Rushni was going to do while Shobuz and Khoka were crying and begging for mercy. The only noisy sounds in that setting of hush were the shivering cries and loud pleading for mercy by those two, unequivocally manifesting the universal truth that the greatest fear of a mortal is death.

"Rushni took slow but firm steps to position herself close to Shobuz and Khoka, the guileful felons. Everyone present was familiar with the single-minded determination and capability of Rushni but were astounded to see her in an accreted physical posture in front of the strapped Shobuz and Khoka. Without any dithering, she took out the hidden sickle from behind her and tightened her grip. Unhesitant and with ironic grit, she beheaded them one by one with the sickle that had belonged to Kalon Master. After that, she desired that bodies be taken to the roadside where the ambush had taken place and left with a note to read 'These are the killers of Kalon Master.'

"The severity of the actions or the presence of a host of others failed to have any disheveling impact on Rushni. She did that without any reaction or remorse. She brushed the sickle on the grass, wiped it with a tattered piece of cloth nearby, and put it back behind her body. Placed in its previous position, the sickle went out of sight, but everyone noted its permanent presence. Rushni quietly walked away, her sari dotted with spilled-over blood from Shobuz and Khoka. She went to her homespun of living in the deep jungle and washed herself, spilling water from a rudimentary pail. She changed to her usual dress of a shirt and trousers and lay straight on a *pattie*, experiencing mental peace for the first time since the killing of Kalon Master."

'Ukil Mia continued his story, "In conveying the news of your posting as field commander, Dhaka emphasized that you are a highly educated comrade with no experience of field operations. Hence, a specific suggestion was mooted to ensure your continuous security. Based on that, the regional command deputized Rushni for your security. Rushni told me this before leaving for Panchkhira, emphasizing the magnitude of responsibility being reposed. That is why I have told you this long story."

'Ukil Mia had palpably become sapped after narrating the whole story. He, however, continued his submission before concluding, "All he said were the outcome of his field work, with specific interest in knowing the reasons for Rushni's unabashed determination prompting her joining PBBP and stentorian efforts to carry out related missions. His important sources were the cousin of Rushni and Pesh Imam Shaheeb. But being an experienced field worker, he made efforts to check and recheck all events told to him by various sources, including gossips of tea shops. So he is certain about what he detailed."'

"After narrating what Ukil Mia had said about Rushni, Logic Sir resumed his part of the story, saying, 'Rushni returned three days later than her original schedule with the sad news of her mother's death. Sadness was ubiquitous in her thoughts and actions. I tried naively to bring her out from that bemoaned mental condition. Slowly, I noticed some changes in her responses and acts. That was palpable when Rushni musingly said, "You will not be able to assess my feelings. I lost my loved and dear ones at a tender age. Having my mother, though away from me, I had the mental peace that there is someone who loves me and who prays for my safety and security. Now I do not have anyone."

'As the time passed, I started noting signs of perceptible waning in her intractable disposition traits. With a decline in operational engagements and the noticeable desertion of comrades, I had not much choice but to have recurring exchanges with Rushni on varied matters. She also showed a penchant to look at me, smile insouciantly, and talk a little occasionally. Her unflappable comment of being alone had an unusual impact on my subsequent thinking. My nascent sympathy for her created a window of feeling within me which innocuously had a deep mark. That was notwithstanding evident negative aspects—my age, frustration, way of life, and the related uncertainty, which are reality and omnipresent in my journey of life. This continued to baffle me. I was conscious of the cerebral gap between us but had solace in thinking about the existence of a sentient mind in that rural young lady, partly motivating her to join the movement and cause for which PBBP stands. On that score alone, I found a comfort zone.

'Rushni impressed me most when she suggested that I should now disassociate myself from PBBP and have a normal life, trying to influence social changes from another pedestal. The miasma being experienced by PBBP had a surprising common-sense reaction from her. During that discourse, to my utter surprise, I realized that Rushni was talking to me, premised on her shaped skepticism with an unfathomable degree of empathy. She also had said I should not think about her. In spite of all current negativity, she was determined not to be upended by current setbacks. Further, she was clear in her mind that there is no one in the party that is on her side, and she was taking responsibilities as life dictates. She concluded that discussion with the comment "Today or tomorrow, I might get killed."

'She excused herself to cook for us as it was already late by normal standard. It was relatively late for my dinner that evening. Rushni came with a *shanki* [round clay plate] containing rice, dal (lentils), some vegetables, and two burned red chili peppers. Since coming to Sundarban and experiencing the food with less spices and oil, I had resorted to having burned chilies, adding a specific flavor and taste in otherwise bland food. Even though I had a premonition about the taste of the food, I focused on eating immediately without hesitation. Rushni exchanged looks with me.

'With an insinuated smile adorning her lips, she said, "It is not like other normal days. I have cooked these with utmost care and decanted a good amount of spices and oil."

'I nodded as a sign of noticing what she said and continued eating. Rushni, to her horror, noticed a moving object passing close to my body. She had encountered numerous types of reptiles and animals since living in the deep forest areas of Sundarban. She had mastered the art of tackling them, and the sickle in her hand was always very helpful. She perhaps got panicked seeing the moving object very close to my body and held the tail end of it with the intent of throwing it away. After pulling the tail of the moving object, she realized it to be a snake. The snake reflexively responded and instantaneously struck her with a venomous bite. In that dreaded moment, she released the tail, and the snake vanished.

'I immediately took charge of her shivering body but was unsure of what actions I could take in that secluded hideout of my command. Few minutes passed in that condition, and I observed, even in that semidark setting, the swelling of her limbs, face, and lips, an increased level of wheezing and breathing discomfort, and then the eventual loss of consciousness. After a while, Rushni breathed her last in my embrace with oozing saliva between her lips.'

"As narrated by Logic Sir, he was in a bewildered and perceptual mind-set in thinking about life, living, and associated cruelty. He was sitting in the same spot under the big tree where Rushni had breathed her last. Speechless, he was searching for answers as to what fault this young girl committed to experience, mostly in equal proportion and periodicity, all the sorrow, dismay, and humiliation a life can offer and then death at this young age.

"With the help of some comrades, Rushni was buried in an unknown and less trafficked area of Sundarban, draped in the same sari she was wearing at the time of her death."

Cognizant of Aleena's emotional stress, Tanveer decided to take a break before detailing the remaining portions of what Logic Sir had told him that night. But the following day and during noon naptime, Aleena again raised the issue.

Tanveer resumed narrating the unfinished part of the story, telling her, "Logic Sir was evidently drained in recalling the sad demise of Rushni. He had narrated with a very calm disposition and, in the process, made a deliberate effort to subdue emotions, which nevertheless had overwhelmed him throughout the story. Logic Sir said, 'I was sitting quietly with a few of my close comrades nearby to the place where Rushni died. Suddenly, there was a commotion. My quick response had my SMG raised up to my chest to tackle the probable challenge. As I was looking for the target, I was taken aback, seeing Ukil Mia standing with an expressed feeling of profound sadness. The reason for Ukil Mia's presence was obvious, but what he had to say had taken all present by surprise—it appeared to be a premonition.

'Ukil Mia said, "As part of preparation for the travel back to my field assignment after Rushni returned, I went to her to say, 'Khuda Hafeez' [a Muslim's way to say goodbye]. At that time, she impulsively called me back and said, 'If anything happens to me, you should come and take over the charge of the commander immediately until a permanent one is assigned by the regional command.' Soon after hearing about Rushni's sad demise, I rushed to comply with her last wish to me. That is why I am here.'"

"Logic Sir intensely thought about Rushni's last advice to him to leave this armed struggle and to lead an alternative life, still working for ideals and objectives upheld by PBBP. Instead of holding any assembly, he opted to talk to each of his remaining comrades, passing on guidance and advice about their future role and responsibility. He meticulously urged them to go back to the society in view of the current priority of the party. In this connection, he shared his thoughts with each one of them about the mode of doing that and what each one could achieve to further the cause and ideals of PBBP as a robust movement. For his part, he confided to Ukil Mia about his plan to leave the Sundarban area. Simple-minded Ukil Mia took that as an order coming from the regional command and confidently assured him about his readiness to accompany him until reaching the first habitation point of Murad Nagar. It was done in secrecy with his help.

"During this later part of the discourse, Logic Sir appeared to lose his cool, and he started exhibiting an occasional mix of being disheveled and intractable simultaneously, bemoaned and ornery, concurrently with a frequent expression of vitriol and chill. That confused me totally. I just could not make out such incoherent expressions from a teacher for whom I have only the utmost respect. Since he had opened up about his nascent but smoldering feeling for Rushni and detailed her sad death in his lap after saving his life, I could not find any justification for that sort of continuous imbalance in Logic Sir's subsequent expressions. I started showing signs of uneasiness.

"Logic Sir took note of that and, as a diversion, observed, 'The time is now late evening. You may not get much to eat in your hostel dining place at this hour. Let us share whatever Bua, the household help, has cooked.'

"That was a surprise proposition. It had made me happy for unknown reasons, and I readily agreed.

"As we were eating, Logic Sir said frankly, 'My normal food is very simple, but I had a feeling that you may stay longer tonight, and so I told Bua that I might have a guest for dinner. She is used to this as I sometimes had late night visits from some of my close comrades.'

"I was not interested to know details of how the dinner was arranged but readily started eating. In conveying to Logic Sir my happy feeling, I said, 'Sir, I have neither seen your Bua nor know much about her, but whatever it is, she has a natural gift to cook. After many days, I have the feeling that I am eating food prepared by my very dear Pori Khala.'

"With dinner finished, Logic Sir lit his kerosene stove, put a kettle with water on, and prepared two cups of tea with utmost ease. I was astonished as I had never done that or even thought about it. Sir noticed and said, 'I was also like you. Living in the jungle, I developed a passion for tea. Rushni also liked tea. It was a commonality that bonded us.'

"As we were sitting quietly, there were three mild knocks on one of his bedside windows. Logic Sir appeared to be familiar with that. He immediately put a large book as a barrier to the light traveling through the entry door. Taking the cover of shadow, he very slowly and carefully opened a part of the door. The messenger outside passed on a small piece of paper, and there was no exchange of words between the two. Sir kept waiting for some time in the shadow and slouched in his chair with an uneasy posture after returning. He slowly positioned himself on the chair and glanced at the few words written on that piece of paper while continuously rubbing it with his thumb and middle fingers.

"While sipping tea, I kept quiet as Logic Sir appeared to be struggling with unknown predicaments. Noticing his ever-varying facial expressions, I had no doubt he was struggling to be both open and secretive at the same time, becoming leery within and rankle outside, a clear indication of being both unhappy and less complacent in the process. I decided not to interject. The book continued to be serving as a barrier to the light traveling to the front end of the accommodation.

"Sir quietly signaled me to be close to him. As I moved closer, Logic Sir had a long look at me and then started talking in an unusual low voice. He said, 'I have had many things to tell you, but lamentably and unexpectedly, time is the main constraining factor. So I am going to be very brief with one request. Consider each of my words, think about them, and try to apply in life as you consider appropriate, with no obligation to take them as they are. That will be your discretion and decision. As a younger brother and with no probability of seeing you in the near future or ever, I would like to emphasize that emotion is an essential element in pursuing life, but that should not overtake the realities around you. Emotion's real value is when it helps one augment abilities and move forward. Second, every individual has some capacities in life. Do not ever forget to celebrate your own capacities, however mundane they appear to be. Third, materialism is necessary for progression but shun away from too much focus on material things. Everything has a price to pay.'

"As Logic Sir nervously paused, looking around his small rented accommodation, he drew himself close to me further and said, 'My real name is Shabuddin Azraf and not Dewan Tasleem Ahmed, as you all know. As part of taking responsibility in my new position in the Sundarban area, I was sent to the Sherpur administrative area [district] to take part in a live operation. That was my orientation to the armed struggle.

'Besides being a very likeable place, the Sherpur township stands on the bank of the river Mrigi. The district's uniqueness and diversity were significantly enhanced by the presence of indigenous Garo and Hajang tribes. During that operation, I got a hold of a university certificate for a master of arts postgraduate degree. That certificate was issued to one Dewan Tasleem Ahmed, and the subject was philosophy. I just kept it in my custody and do not recall the reasons for doing that. As I was thinking of leaving the command assignment of PBBP and knew very well that the police were looking for me, I had the immediate idea of using this certificate by faking my name. That was easy. However, the subject became a significant impediment as I did my master's in economics. So I went to most northern part of Bangladesh and pretended to be a schoolteacher looking for a job, including that of lodging master [a house tutor who teaches the family's children residing in the same homestead]. I got a position in the Pramanik Poriber, a local respectable family of the Sonakandi area in the administrative region of Tanchagarh. At the very outset, I told the head of the Pramanik family that I would attempt to appear in the ensuing degree examination as a private candidate and hence would remain preoccupied with study during my off time. He readily consented, expressing happiness simultaneously. I slowly started procuring and borrowing books on philosophy, with a focus on textbooks covering the syllabi of intermediate and degree classes. I not only read them but also made all efforts to absorb them, to intellectually replicate Dewan Tasleem Ahmed. I continued to make progress and soon mastered various nuances of philosophy as a subject of study within the frame of a syllabus outlined by the university for learning at the college level. I soon noticed an advertisement of your college asking for applications from interested qualified individuals for the position of professor of philosophy. That appeared in the premier English newspaper of the time. Your school was still a community college just before its present transformation to a government college. I applied and was interviewed and selected as Dewan Tasleem Ahmed. At this point in time of my life, I realized that lying once, for whatever good reason, is perhaps a trap and is a precursor to more lies later for the sake of consistency if not for anything else. I traveled to Tanchagarh under a false name. I became a resident house tutor with a false pretext. I got my job with the false educational background, but there was no duplicity in my going back to a place called Panchkhira. I felt a strong urge, despite inherent risks of it being in a place very close to Sundarban. I decided to join and took cover of another lie in leaving Sonakandi, saying this time that my mother is very sick and I need to be by her side.'

"Logic Sir kept quiet for some more time with intense focus on the floor as could be assessed by the shade of the book still in its place as a cover. He then signaled me, stood up, embraced me, and asked me to leave.

"I naively walked out and took the usual way back to the student's hostel of the college and soon retired, telling my roommates that I was not feeling well. But falling asleep was the most difficult job for me that night. The more I wanted it, the more it became difficult for me to sleep. The changing mode of Logic Sir's physical gestures, tone of conversation, and words of wisdom recurred in my thoughts like the playback of scenes in a movie. I had the feeling of restlessness. With the passage of time, unknowingly though, I fell asleep, only to wake up very early in the morning from an unusual commotion around.

"In no time, most hostel residents came to know about the unexpected police presence around the accommodation of Logic Sir. We rushed to the place. I did not even change my night outfit, and that was common for most other resident students. We were all surprised and shocked. We assembled outside the police-cordoned area and wanted to know what happened during the night and why the police were after Logic Sir. Information flowed in more as impressions with significant individual additions and deletions in each stage of sharing. It was all so confusing.

"Our whispers and low conversations were suddenly overtaken by loud words from the police inspector shouting, 'Mr. Professor, please come out of the house with your two hands raised! I will count up to five. If you do not, my force will break open the door and arrest you.'

"He then started slowly counting, taking pause between each number. Bystanders were curious local onlookers. The congregated student folks were tensed and bewildered. As he finished counting to five, the inspector instructed his forces to close in and authorized them break the entrance door. That order was carried out with all care and promptness. However, the outcome baffled everyone. There was no one in the house. The police inspector was totally thwarted and agitated. He loudly started telling the untold story everyone was keen to know.

"He said, 'Our intelligence people were working for many months to build a foolproof case against this professor on two counts. First, he is not Dewan Tasleem Ahmed, as you know him. His real name is Shabuddin Azraf. He had no postgraduate education in philosophy, and his field of study was economics. Second, he is an active senior leader of PBBP and was stationed in Sundarban. But he just vanished at the peak time.'

"The gathering was surprised by those exposés. They wondered how he could do all those things and silently praised Sir's vigilance, farsightedness, and promptness in decision taking. It appeared to me that like many actions of the public authorities, this one of the intelligence department had also its inherent deficiencies. It just moved at its own pace, irrespective of the importance. Hence, the intelligence outfit of PBBP got the upper hand. There was no doubt in my mind that the small slip of paper Sir had received the previous night carried the message and instructions. That was probably the reason for his edginess after the silent exchange of the slip took place. Sir patently vacated the house much before the police force arrived to haul him."

Tanveer continued, saying, "That is the story related to my association with Logic Sir, from whom, directly and indirectly, I have learned a lot about life beyond textbooks. I respect him very much, notwithstanding his palpable misrepresentation of certain facts. To enable me to lead a decent life, I, in addition to erudition and a wife, need a friend to keep an eye on me and to guide me from time to time. That is why I told you that I want to see you as a friend in addition to being my wife."

While detailing the last moments of Rushni's life, Tanveer could sense an enhanced level of emotional burden engulfing Aleena's facial reactions. The sudden death of young Rushni flummoxed her. He could understand and appreciate that sort of reaction when he himself had encountered that when detailing the moments of last meeting with Logic Sir and his escape.

She moved closer and rested her head on Tanveer's chest with his left palm held firmly in between her two hands. Emotionally charged body reactions found their escape in the form of tears flowing from Aleena's eyes. The teardrops traveled down Aleena's cheeks and landed on his palm.

Conjunction

Life has its own unique sense of humor. Any given experience immediately amps up one, while another tamps down with not much long-term bearings on personal emotions and societal outcomes. That happened with Aleena Qulsum and Tanveer. Her flustered emotions concerning Rushni's fate bleached within a short span of time. She was besotte by the daily chores of family life, frequent thoughts and unfettered aspirations about her own world with Tanveer, and periodical engagements with reading, besides spending time with younger brother Tauseef. Likewise, Tanveer's warm attachment to Logic Sir as being a teacher of distinction and a person of great attainments lost intensity because of the pressure of an upcoming intermediate examination.

This backdrop and the fairly long winter recess, the first long vacation after their wedding, provided a unique opportunity for knowing each other more intimately and laying the foundation for a very content and happy conjugal life. That intimacy caused an unpredicted and passionate departure experience as Tanveer was returning to college after the winter break. He told everyone that this time he would not be home soon as he was to prepare for the school board–conducted final examination scheduled in three months. All informed took the news easily except Aleena Qulsum.

This caused visible unhappiness and warranted a mischievous side comment from Tauseef. "Why are you so depressed? I am here as Bhaiya's [Brother's] substitute."

Qulsum laughed and said, "You do not have any idea about a wife's feeling. To be a brother-in-law is one thing. To be a husband is completely different. It is advisable to keep your mouth shut." She said that in a friendly manner and then walked away.

The geniality around Biesh Moisher Bari remained pulsating under the pragmatic interference and astute guidance of Kazi Azmat Ali Shoudagar. He was respected very much by the local inhabitants of Apurba Neer. Biesh Moisher Bari literally reigned supreme in that local setting.

Kazi Azmat Ali Shoudagar was happy with the positive turn of events in life. Though married at a relatively early age, Tanveer had proven to be responsible and steadfast in all respects—family, education, and overall social matters. Kazi decided that Tanveer should pursue his degree-level study before taking over the responsibility of running the family business. That was not the outcome of solely his thinking and position, however. On this subject, he had an initial disagreement with Hashi Banu. It was she who wanted Tanveer to continue a higher level of education. Kazi Azmat Ali Shoudagar eventually agreed. He originally had wanted Tanveer to discontinue his college education after the intermediate level and slowly get involved in business so he could have time and exposure to matters related to running a successful business, with the unavoidable emerging need of having congenial social and political contacts, and that too, without identifying with any group. That, to him, was a good reason. Another reason for his earlier position was more personal to Kazi Azmat Ali Shoudagar. He frankly shared his past wariness with Hashi Banu about Tanveer's conjugal life.

He said, "It is more than a year since they got married, but still, there is no news about our having a grandchild. If they stay together permanently, that is bound to yield some result. My soul will be an unhappy one if I am to leave this world without seeing a grandchild."

Hashi Banu brushed off that reason. She confided knowing the reason why they were still not blessed with grandchildren. She assured him that she would take care of this concern as she too would like to play with grandkids, but she maintained her position with respect to higher studies for Tanveer. In a rare moment of having protracted incongruity, Hashi Banu demonstrated her wit in reasserting the aptness of her proposition by touching the soft corner of her husband's priority of life. That was family tradition, family value, and the influence of the family on the local setting of Apurba Neer. She was certain about the cogency of the point she was making with respect to his first concern and was very calm in articulating her reasons. She used common and meek words in framing her justification and unleashed them in a soft, low voice with pause and space.

She said, "Biesh Mosher Bari, our home, has influenced the social setting of Apurba Neer and adjoining areas for a long time. It started about four generations back, principally premised on relative financial affluence. That role and resultant social recognition have been enjoyed by each generation with an enhanced level of standing, premised on the relative increase in wealth. As I know and witnessed, you introduced a unique feature in that role. You cultivated a new sense of aristocracy in public dealings, emboldened by the title of *shoudagar*. You, thus, spontaneously received enhanced respect and consideration from ordinary folks, but the time is fast-changing. Societal values that we are familiar with are upending. Now people generally are engrossed in multiplying wealth. It is very likely that some people whom we may now consider ordinary could outshine our family in financial performance. So for Tanveer, being the son of Biesh Moisher Bari alone might not be adequate to remain relevant in the changing social setup. To ordinary people and for when we will not be here, Kazi Tanveer Ali, with a BA degree suffixed to his name, will likely be more knowledgeable, intelligent, trustworthy, and capable. If you want to ensure that the good name of Biesh Moisher Bari, our home, not only continues but remains relevant in the changed social conditions, then you should agree with me."

After saying those words, she pushed the *paandan* (special plate for serving *paan*) toward him, stood up, enlarged her *ghomta* (head cover), and walked away. It so appeared that Kazi Azmat Ali Shoudagar enjoyed this unusual physical insouciance on the part of Hashi Banu. He was also certain that she would immediately park herself by the side of Pori and detail everything confidentially with a mischievous smile adorning her lips.

Kazi Azmat Ali Shoudagar had no qualms with what Hashi Banu articulated. He was thankful that while his focus was on the immediacy of the need, Hashi Banu had a visionary assessment, and her proposed actions, in many respects, would ensure continuity of the prominence of Biesh Moisher Bari, notwithstanding the lack of impressive and easily recognizable titles adored by the society. He was very happy, put a *paan* in his mouth, and started puffing the extended pipe of his favorite hookah.

Tanveer was enrolled as a freshman in the pursuit of his much-desired degree level of education after attaining distinction in his intermediate examination. Since the college was the same and the social setting was a familiar one, Tanveer had no problem in the admission and settlement processes.

Time passed with happiness and fulfillment proliferating all around Biesh Moisher Bari, particularly because of the successive good news of Tanveer's higher education and confirmation of Aleena Qulsum's pregnancy. The pronounced exhibition of that happiness on the part of the grandfather-to-be was visibly marked in the noticeable increase in his chewing of *paan* and indulgence in puffing his favorite hookah.

That sense of happiness was bolstered high in Tanveer's mind, when he received a letter from Qulsum conveying the much-desired news of her pregnancy. But the essence of that happiness was very personal as the college atmosphere was not conducive for such news, nor had it any relevance in the immediate surroundings. Young fellows were mostly floating in respective lives of dreams and hopes concerning and pursuing the unknown and unfamiliar. Tanveer quickly summed up that he had no commonality with the mainstream students. He enjoyed the happiness of being a father-to-be within himself. Recounting the words and statements of Logic Sir and his guidance, Tanveer was exultant in the increasingly enhanced level of maturity and confidence in Qulsum's thoughts, words, and actions. The specific news of pregnancy made his feeling for Qulsum even still more absolute. With perfect felicity, he was discovering the friend and partner in life that he had so desperately wanted.

With experience and maturity of his own, Tanveer had clarity about his future educational pursuits. He was certain that having a bachelor-of-arts degree was all that the family was expecting from him, and he was sure he could do that easily. High-level attainment in the BA examination had no relevance for him as he would be joining his father in running their business. So he visited Apurba Neer more frequently than earlier years and, in the process, sustainably built up a very warm, understanding, and mutually respected supportive relationship with his dear Aleena Qulsum. Even though immediate feelings pertaining to interactions with Logic Sir had faded away, his firm diction in vocalizing life's events, decisions, and actions were always fresh in Tanveer's memory. He was very impressed in recalling Logic Sir's choice of words and expressions detailing his feelings about Rushni with total openness and no stigma assigned to her. He was in awe in reentering Logic Sir's sincerity and openness in trusting a young fellow like him with his real identity.

The manifestation of joy as a result of Qulsum's pregnancy was completely different in Biesh Moisher Bari. On being advised, Kazi Azmat Ali Shoudagar's first act was to say a few *rakat*s (repetition of a unit of *namaz* prayer, also called *salat*, consisting of prescribed actions and words) of *nafal* (additional prayer) *namaz*, conveying his thanks and gratitude to Allahpak (the Lord) for blessing Biesh Moisher Bari with a new generation. Hashi Banu and Pori got involved in making arrangements to send Badsha (Pori's husband) to Nobi Nagar with the good news. As per tradition, he was needed to carry love and good wishes from the in-laws' house of Aleena as she is known there. So Badsha was sent along with sweets, *paan*, and *shupari*. Tauseef was nonchalant, however, being nonresponsive to such undulated happiness and unrestricted excitements. Aleena Qulsum started enjoying the spontaneous outpouring of love and care with the internal feeling of a new recognition as mother-to-be of the new generation. Syrupy happenings had been all pervasive in the surroundings of Biesh Moisher Bari since the time of the great-grandfather of Kazi Azmat Ali Shoudagar. That accentuated during the time of the present owner. The good performance by Tanveer in his intermediate examination, the delivery of a baby boy by Aleena without much complication, and continued success in business and social attainments made Biesh Moisher Bari a matter of admiration of many and of envy of some among the community.

The only exception was Tauseef. His reactions to most good events for the family were somewhat starchy. Ever since he came to know about the decision of his great-great-grandfather to not divide Biesh Moisher Bari—and consequently, he would have to move out of this homestead sometime in the future—he could not take all events as good. He always harbored an attitude of aloofness and moved in his own world of hopes and aspirations besides being preoccupied with studies. Tauseef's focused desire was to excel in a secondary school certificate examination as a precursor to convincing his father to send him to Dhaka for higher studies.

Though Tauseef harbored a sort of a sheltered attitude in the genial family setting, he maintained a warm and supportive relationship with Qulsum besides being very considerate to his dear Pori Khala. That caused his very unexpected presence and tangential participation in a discussion that he had with Qulsum after the baby boy was born. The subject of discussion was naming their newborn son. It was the decision of the family, contrary to local practice of naming newborns by family elders (mostly grandparents), that Qulsum and Tanveer should name their own son. That decision was made public before the baby boy was born, and that made Qulsum very exuberant. She spared no time in informing Tanveer about the decision and desired that he should think through it before his homecoming for the ensuing vacation. She did not fail to indicate that whatever name Tanveer chose would be okay with her but that she would very much like to have Azmat as part of the new name besides family title Ali.

Muslims follow the Islamic tradition of sacrificing an animal (one sheep for a baby girl and two sheep for a baby boy) on the occasion of a child's birth. This is called *akika*, a process of pledging a baby by means of which she or he is closely linked to Allah (the Creator). In essence, it is an act to remove harmful things from the baby. By Islamic injunctions, it is a *sunnah* (acts, deeds, and practices of Prophet Muhammad [peace be upon him]) to be performed on the seventh day after birth, with the rituals involving the naming of the baby and shaving his or her head. It can be delayed because of capabilities but should be done before puberty.

The discussions between Qulsum and Tanveer were centered on that topic as the date of *akika* was near. They had reached understanding in naming their son after working on a name that met relevant needs and expectations. The indicative chosen name of the boy was Tauheed, followed by two names of paternal and maternal grandparents and suffixed by family title. Both of them complimented each other, while Aleena Qulsum went out of her way to express gratitude for taking note of her family in naming their son.

In that moment of exalted contentment, Tauseef entered the room with some periodicals in hand for Aleena's reading and sat by their side. The happy new parents exchanged looks with each other, and Qulsum promptly said, "Tauseef Bhai [Brother], we have labored hard in working on the name of your nephew and have agreed on one that is very nice. That is Tauheed Azmat Mansoor Ali."

Tauseef, in his usual way, was nonchalant about the outcome and kept quiet. Tanveer had a very annoying feeling for not having a much-expected prompt and positive endorsement from Tauseef. He winked at Qulsum, signaling a query.

Qulsum coughed to draw attention and enquired, "Tauseef Bhai, why do you not have any comment? You do not like the name?"

Tauseef smiled and said, "No, that is not the case. I am trying to understand and digest the full implication of that complete name. The middle two names and title are revered ones in the context of both our families and the surroundings we live in. It will be inappropriate for me to comment on those. So far as my nephew's name is concerned, Tauheed is a very sweet and meaningful one. I like it."

Both Qulsum and Tanveer were happy with Tauseef's endorsement. They internally concluded that it would make things easier for them in steering the name with Tauseef's endorsement paving the way.

Tauseef observed the unadulterated happiness in the expressions of both and promptly decided to play a droll game. While stepping out of the room, he turned back and, in a rare address of Bhabi (sister-in-law), said, "You have chosen the formal name after due consideration of all plausible variables. As his only uncle, may I have the privilege to suggest a nickname?"

Qulsum consented readily without even looking at Tanveer. Tauseef, standing outside the entrance door, said, "I do not have the ability to go deep in searching an appropriate nickname for my nephew. I am conscious of my limitations in this regard. Nonetheless, I can't miss this opportunity. I would like to suggest the nickname of Tama [copper], taking the first alphabet letter from each component of the proposed name."

He gleefully left the room. Qulsum's half smile responding to this derision of Tauseef abruptly froze, observing the unexpected and sharply levitated racking manifested in Tanveer's facial reactions. Instead of saying anything, Tanveer started gnashing his jaws, a precursor of something ominous to happen soon. Qulsum was stunned but decided to provoke Tanveer to release his anger at that moment in their private setting without allowing it to smolder and then to have an outburst later on to the dishonor of the family. She slowly and cautiously took possession of one hand of Tanveer, put that on her lap, and held it within her palms as if to assess the internalized level of his anger.

Tanveer looked at her and wanted to say something, but she stopped him, saying, "Tauseef is your younger brother, and he needs your understanding and love in his journey through life—"

Tanveer did not allow Qulsum to finish what she wanted to say. Cutting her short, he said, "Yes, I agree. I love him more than possibly anyone else in this family. I accorded all indulgence to his growing-up aspirations and showed full consideration, even if sometimes I had hesitation. Now you see what he has done to insult all of us, including the newborn baby boy. Do you know the applicable inferences that are related to the term *tama*? *Tama* (copper) is a ductile metallic element with a malleable feature that occurs abundantly in large masses. In relative assessment of importance and value, it is significantly inferior to other metallic elements. So by proposing that name, he has insulted the innocent newborn, shown disrespect to us as his elder brother and *bhabi*, and dishonored our parents besides harming the good name of this family. I can't allow a free passage to his roguish behavior. His awry suggestion obliquely slighted the very base of my unmitigated love for him. I will definitely talk to our parents. He needs to face consequences for his insularity."

Unleashing his anger in those words, Tanveer appeared to have calmed down. Qulsum had maintained endearing eye contact when Tanveer was expressing his disdains with respect to the name Tauseef just suggested. But in her inner self, Qulsum was trying to comprehend the reasons for such shrill reactions from Tanveer as that sort of behavior was contrary to the normal traits of his persona. She soon came to the conclusion that being a person of modest bearing and a down-to-earth mind-set, Tanveer lacked the ability to see things differently and to enjoy the sublime allusions of certain annotations mentioned casually. She became certain that structured growing-up parameters focusing on "good" in all actions and deeds, with holistic emphasis on obedience to family elders, may have molded him differently. She recalled reading earlier that a limited behavior pattern during the growing years, with a focus on compliance, could influence personality development and, in some cases, could as well be a person's greatest weakness. It is not unlikely that this may cause unwarranted complications in real life. She decided to touch base with that in making her points.

She once again tried to finish what she wanted earlier to say by breaking the anguishing moments of silence but could not as Tanveer was in the mood to vent out his frustration. In articulating reactions to what he had just forcefully said, she unwittingly premised her observation to the most vulnerable stance of his current expectation. Softly and lovingly, she said, "Normally, I would not have made any observation, but you have always emphasized your fondest desire of having in me a friend and partner besides a wife. That prompts me to say frankly what I think to be appropriate. My observations, against the backdrop of your expressed frustration, shouldn't be taken lightly or adversely. I request that you listen to what I have to say and then decide. I will not expect you to make a decision just to make me happy. You should make one that you consider appropriate. In assessing any comment or suggestion, one needs to consider two things—premise and motive. To understand these two, one must step into the shoes of the person making the comment or suggestion. Any quick reaction to the exclusion of these is bound to be slanted, causing misjudgment and resulting in erroneous decisions."

Aleena Qulsum abided briefly but was happy, observing that Tanveer was listening intensely to what she was stating. She resumed, stating, "Everyone is aware of your love for Tauseef, and more importantly, he himself has confided that a number of times to me, but in the context of our present discussion, one needs to take into account my relationship with him. I am his loving *bhabi* [sister-in-law], and he is my only very adorable *debar* [a word obscurely derived from two Bangla words: *deitio* {second} and *bor* {husband}]. I have a special relationship, as is the case with most *debar-bhabi*s, with him. Most part of that is grounded on the lighter aspects of a relationship—fun, laughter, teasing, galling, and so on. We never have had any straight and socially acceptable communication between us. We twist our comments to amuse each other and enjoy that. More interestingly and once in the midst of such exchanges, Tauseef surprised me by suddenly opening up. I discovered the real Tauseef on that occasion and have premised my feelings for him and our relationship as unconditional since then. I could not take one of his subtle comments concerning our marital relationship. My facial reactions were sufficient enough to unnerve him.

"He came near to me, sat by my side, and said, 'Bhabi, did you ever think as to why I sought your consent to address you as Aleena in private settings instead of Bhabi? I am tired of the surroundings of this house. Ever since I started assimilating in the setting of this house, I have had to listen, at every step of my progression, about the good name of Biesh Moisher Bari, the obligation to uphold that, and the onerous responsibility to carry that forward by our acts and deeds. The more all these were emphasized and repeated, the more my feelings adversely levitated. Since I am the youngest of the family, my most adored response has always been yes. That invariably made my family members and well-wishers happy. I am tired of this value and culture of Biesh Moisher Bari. I want to revolt. I want to break away from that but could not do so far as I am too young. But trust me, I will do that when I get the opportunity. I have been brought up in a culture where everyone—from schoolteachers to friends of Father and all the sundries of this house, including Badsha Chacha—are my revered seniors and are to be treated accordingly. I had no way to disagree on any matter. I desperately looked for one who is junior to me or at least equal to me so that I can have free exchanges in social dealings according to my choice or preference. Your arrival in this house was a matter of unfettered joy for everyone, but for me, there was an addition. That was in seeing someone who would be of my age or could even be junior to me. I had instant felicity. But that feeling was short-lived as it dawned on me that as per prevalent cultural norms, a *bhabi* is esteemed and treated with due carefulness, irrespective of age. The address of *bhabi* is a permanent emotional barrier in having the equal and friendly relationship with you that I had in mind. It was because of this reason that I requested your consent to address you as Aleena, at least when we are alone. That enabled me to have a remarkable and pleasurable relationship with you. It helped discovering a new identity for me in this tradition-laden home."'

Delineating the premise of a specific relationship with Tauseef, Aleena said, "I do not have exposure to a sustained higher level of education like you. I never had the opportunity of being blessed by the good wishes and love of someone like your Logic Sir. But certainly, I have been blessed by genetically inheriting the urge to read. I not only read everything that comes by my way but also subject every aspect of that writing to an internal but very neutral assessment before I take a position on any matter that I come across. Thus, I learned to distinguish between emotion and prudence. From various situations encountered in that reading process, it candidly became clear to me that as human beings, we ought to have emotions, but prudence in managing that emotion is very important in pursuing a meaningful life. Life just laden with emotion is a recipe for instant despair in its every bend and shade. Before feeling short-changed, we need to assess any pertinent comment from the position of the other person—the time, the setting, the relationship, and the overall parameters of life and living. Often, it is helpful to give some space before reacting. I have also learnt the wise lesson forbidding pointing a gun to anyone unless one is sure and willing to pull the trigger. I am saying all these to put on canvas the innocence inherent in Tauseef's proposition. Our relationship of *bhabi–debar* has socially sanctioned limited latitude in communication. He just availed of that. It was not you, but I had asked him about the name. He responded to me and not to you with the suggested nickname of Tama. The nickname suggested might have tormented you but does not bother me. It is coincidentally a product of the first alphabet letter of each of the four names we have chosen, as indicated by him . . . but look at it from another angle. Will Tauseef be at ease with himself being identified in the future as the uncle of Tama? I do not think so. He just told that to annoy me for the moment. Moreover, what is the relevance of a nickname in your family setting? Both of you have names of Manik [gem] and Hira [diamond], but nobody, out of probable reverence, ever calls you by that name. So in the confluence of traditions in this house, nobody would address your son as Tama. If we raise this issue at the level of parents, it will almost amount to pulling the trigger on our relationship now and in future. Soon, it would become an open secret. Everybody will speak about it, and probably, it will involuntarily travel outside with divergent manifestations. That would certainly cause dishonor to the family's good name, could have a long-term impact on your relationship with Tauseef, and might be used by fellow friends to taunt our son while he is growing up. My suggestion is to forget the Tama episode as if it never occurred. I am more than certain that Tauseef himself will forget it too. We should propose the name as we thought of. If still it bothers you, we may change my father's name, Mansoor, by his other name, Shafiul, to read as Tauheed Azmat Shafiul Ali."

Emotionally exhausted, Aleena reclined her head on the shoulder of Tanveer as sort of an assured parking lot, more to escape from self-doubt about the consequential reactions of Tanveer. Her internalized agony was centered on possible rejoinders of Tanveer to her millennial propositions. She had confidence in their cheery relationship, but that was mostly premised on the softer aspects of life's bonding. The present discourse was significantly divergent, having bold positions that were contrary to the emotional antiphons of Tanveer. Those bold propositions could be blistering or beautiful, depending on who is judging and from what angle.

Life is a strange mix of happiness and concern. The former often ascends with unbridled joy premised on oneself's ability, while the latter is caused by occasional torments because of shrouded fear. That precisely was the position of Aleena Qulsum after unleashing those convincing words in support of her position. She was unsure and somewhat diffident of Tanveer's reactions but unhesitatingly sought refuge on his chest.

Tanveer, while casually looking at bunches of green coconuts through the window of their bedroom, affectionately put his hand on her head, casually playing with loose ends of her plaited long hair. As he noted her long breaths, Tanveer quietly bent his face down and looked at her acquiesced face, which, for that moment, looked exquisitely bravura with both eyes closed.

It is very common that adorable moments, good happenings, and happy feelings do not last long in life. That happened in the case of Tanveer as he was about to be lost in uncontrolled romantic feelings after a focused assessment of his wife's face. Then the baby boy woke up and let everybody know by crying loud. Tanveer, for a while, became engrossed in understanding why a baby cries immediately after waking up. The baby stopped crying as soon as Qulsum picked him up and held him warmly close to her chest. Though there are a number of reasons for a baby to cry—hunger, a dirty diaper (in the setting of rural Bangladesh, it could as well be an underlayment sheet or pad), tummy trouble, the need to burp, not feeling well, and so on—Tanveer soon realized the sensibility, even of a baby, when he is positioned in a warm close embrace. He had the feeling that crying from a baby is possibly a nature-ordained means of countenance.

Though Tanveer's immediate response to what Aleena Qulsum had alluded persuasively to was short-circuited by the sudden cry of the baby, he did not miss a moment in conveying a response to her. Their post-dinner private discourse was all about signifying total consensus between the two and making Tanveer happy and content in having in his life a real and genuine friend. Qulsum expressed her content by being increasingly close to Tanveer, making their private discussions the foundation of their lasting relationship based on trust and mutual respect.

A common characteristic of the setting of life is to take happiness as something due and deserved and to handle distress with discomfiture but mostly as a precursor of something good to happen soon. That is how life moves on. That is how societal beings conduct themselves, and residents of Biesh Moisher Bari were no exception. The unabated success and glory that typified the house since its earlier times were taken for granted as each successive generation did outshine his forerunners in most economic and social aspects. The all-round and unbridled success of Kazi Azmat Ali Shoudagar, the current generation, augmented that. In the latter case, there were more, which accentuated that with zest. Continued success in various business ventures, successive family weddings stringing at higher social strata, the congenial grooming of two sons with academic excellence, and the birth of the first grandson were some of these. In that moment of realization and happiness, Aleena recounted the dismay her mother had undergone for not having her dear husband by her side, the related agony of not being formally acknowledged as the daughter-in-law of Khanbahadur Monzeel, her own birth in the far-flung abode of Imam Mama (uncle), and growing up in various locations. Against such an infelicitous backdrop, she was enormously thankful to Allah (the Divine) to have blessed her with a home like Biesh Moisher Bari and a husband like Tanveer. Happy teardrops slowly rolled down her cheeks as she took refuge on his chest.

Catastrophe

Against that backdrop, time passed in the midst of uninhibited contentment. Tanveer was finishing the first year of his bachelor's course. Tauseef, after attaining distinction in his SSC examination, went to a district college with the understanding that if he excelled in the exam, he would be sent to Dhaka University for higher education. Tauheed started taking small but unstable steps to the amusement of grandparents and all others at Biesh Moisher Bari. Kazi Azmat Ali Shoudagar started enjoying his hookah with more regularity and relaxation.

That was the phase of the family's life and the time and the moment that the most bewildering traumas in quick successions befell them. Biesh Moisher Bari, since its identification five generations back, had never been smarted by any negativity. The impact of sudden bewildering traumas was overwhelming and nerve-breaking and shattered everyone, irrespective of age or status.

The first trauma related to the family's very successful business—making bricks. Kazi Azmat Ali Shoudagar, after a pragmatic assessment of local economic opportunities, concluded an upcoming construction boom for all around Apurba Neer. As the backbone of major nonfarm activity in a rural setting is construction, he had no doubt about the emerging demand for bricks locally. The hectic preparation of plans for offices, schools, and health clinics everywhere had convinced him of it.

Brick is a significant building material in Bangladesh and is commonly used. There are different types of bricks, such as common burnt clay, sand lime, engineering, and concrete ones, but the one most common and popular in Bangladesh at the time was the burnt clay bricks. From a cursory assessment, the making of common burnt clay bricks may appear to be simple and straightforward. But they are exceptionally technique-oriented, vulnerable to unspecified risks, and susceptible to weather-related uncertainties until the bricks are ready. All these works are very labor intensive but equally rely on human ingenuity. The first major challenge in making bricks in

Bangladesh at that point in time was to find suitable open and unused land with appropriate topsoil. The production process begins with workers hacking mud from the base with shovels and depositing it near the production site by balancing heavy loads atop their heads.

It was a difficult and risky business venture involving a risk-prone decision. But Kazi Azmat Ali Shoudagar had unique positive thoughts about the outcome of this new venture. He was certain that if successful, it would be game changing for his business. The inherent risks, the susceptibility to weather, and the uncertainty that hinges on the pace of an anticipated construction boom could not deter him. He had singular focus and determination to launch that business with enormous potential. His main premise was the availability of both suitable clay and cheap local labor.

Though he was an ardent Muslim by faith, Kazi Azmat Ali Shoudagar continued his ancestors' practice in following *ponjika*, a much-trusted and much-respected annual Indian astronomical almanac. *Ponjika* is ritually used by Hindus and some other faiths of the Indian subcontinent in determining the dates and times of important pursuits of life, such as travel (an infrequent and exceptional experience in the past) and marriage, in addition to important dealings and acts. Kazi Azmat Ali always quietly consulted *ponjika* in determining the dates and times of important events of his family as it usually contained much practical information and always had positive results. Against repeated concerns expressed by many close to him about the vulnerability of the proposed business to nature's vagaries, Kazi Azmat Ali Shoudagar remained steadfast in his goal of launching the brick-manufacturing business. His sole safety bulb was his unflinching trust in *ponjika* and its forecast. He annually assessed *ponjika* forecasts with due diligence concerning matters specially related to seasonal storms to delineate dates for brick making. Locally, such storms are known as *kal boi sha ki* (tornado accompanied by heavy wind and rain, so named after the Bangla calendar month of Boishak) and generally follow the Bangla calendar month of Choitra, the hottest summer month, annually. He had been fortunately right on all past occasions. Slowly and steadily, Kazi Azmat Ali Shoudagar invested more capital and reaped high returns.

It soon became his most important business venture, followed by construction contracting and trading.

Tanveer got into his second year of bachelor's education, and Tauseef had just enrolled in the district college, and it was the closing days of brick making. Three different clamps were prepared and insulated for firing the following morning, which was a Friday, considered auspicious by most Muslims. In the midst of a sense of accomplishment and merriment even in that sultry afternoon, workers noted the sudden emergence of dark cloud formations in the northwest horizon. Heat started building up quickly, indicating something ominous. Indigenous efforts were made promptly to cover clamps and kilns with whatever materials they could lay hands on, but that was not of much help. Suddenly, and contrary to *ponjika* stipulations and the solemn faith of Kazi Azmat Ali Shoudagar, *kal boi sha ki* hit the area with all force, accompanied by heavy rain. All the clamps and kilns were damaged, and apprehension was overriding as to the loss of most investments.

Kazi Azmat Ali Shoudagar was dumbfounded and sat in his favorite cane easy chair with a blank and nonresponsive look. He even did not respond to the many indications of Hashi Banu. Pori showed up quietly with her *bhai shaheeb*'s (respected brother) much-preferred hookah, with the top vessel blazed by aroma of tobacco cake, and placed it by the side of his chair. He did not look at it and, contrary to elegant interactions with Pori since his wedding, remained nonchalant. Bleak uneasiness set in Biesh Moisher Bari, which, for generations, had only blessed with happy events and blissful experiences.

The sun shone brightly the following early morning against a light blue clear eastern sky as sort of a riposte to what happened the last afternoon. Kazi Azmat Ali Shoudagar glanced at it with an insipid half smile and closed his eyes while waiting, as was the practice of many years, to convey decisions and guidance to Badsha. But his mind was preoccupied, thinking about the extent of the loss and immediate and long-term impact on the business and the unremitting social standing of Biesh Moisher Bari. As the night before was distraughtly haunted by all negative possibilities, Kazi Azmat Ali Shoudagar had a sleepless one. He was physically and emotionally drained, causing him to fall asleep in the easy chair while resting with his eyes closed.

Badsha Chacha came rather late for his usual early morning consultation and guidance from Kazi Azmat Ali Shoudagar before going to the business place. He was fully aware of the extent of financial catastrophe caused last evening by Mother Nature and was initially hesitant to face the boss. Persuaded by Pori, Badsha was taking reluctant steps to meet his boss of many years when he noticed two bewildered senior staff of the construction branch of the business standing just outside the *kachari* of Biesh Moisher Bari. Their facial expressions and body language were unnerving. What they told Badsha was too traumatic for anyone to digest, more particularly after the most unexpected catastrophe of yesterday. The onus of conveying this to Kazi Azmat Ali Shoudagar suddenly appeared too heavy for the feeble shoulder of Badsha, a very trusted staff and close family well-wisher who spent most of his life conveying good news and complying with directives of all Biesh Moisher Bari, particularly that of Kazi Azmat Ali Shoudagar.

An unexpected challenge, in some cases, brings out the best in a person. Likewise, unparalleled responsibility and obligation very often even provoke deep thinking in some other cases. Badsha engrossed himself in deep thoughts, trying to delineate a possible reasoning for consecutive bad news shattering the core of the respected house. He positioned himself silently on the outer side of the entrance door. That was his usual place to meet with Kazi Azmat Ali Shoudagar every morning for many years. With eclipsed deep emotion and anxiety having immediate similitude on Kazi Azmat Ali Shoudagar's face with eyes closed, Badsha neither moved nor caused any sound. The internal agony of how to break the unexpected and most distraught news just conveyed to him was his most immediate challenge.

After a while and to the great relief of Badsha, Kazi Azmat Ali opened his eyes and kept ogling Badsha as if looking for a berth to unburden his bane. Even in that dismal setting, Kazi Azmat Ali Shoudagar was conscious of the need to uphold the inherited prestige of Biesh Moisher Bari. He concluded promptly that sharing present worries with a member of the staff, even with someone like Badsha, with a position akin to a family member, was below the dignity and values that Kazi Azmat Ali had inherited.

To thwart any immediate emotional vulnerability, he softly asked Badsha for a service of his hookah. Badsha rushed out, prepared one with the help of Pori, and tried to return hurriedly. The more he wanted to hurry, the more lethargic he felt in taking steps. Hashi Banu, sitting on the *choki* in the *ranna ghar* (kitchen located in a separate structure), noted Badsha's very weird gestures but refrained from making any query.

Hashi Banu became enthralled in her effort to scan the rationale for Badsha's very uncommon behavior. Contrary to his usual practice of smiling at Hashi Banu while saying "Salaam mali kum" every morning, he had avoided any interaction or exchange of looks with her. Even last night, with the backdrop of disaster that prodigiously shattered everyone related to Biesh Moisher Bari, Badsha had plenty of soothing and reassuring words to console Hashi Banu, more to ensure her role as a solid support to her husband at this hour of crisis. She wondered about what could have happened during the night to cause such a change, but instead of asking, she continued sitting on the *choki*, praying to Allah for mercy. Hurriedly counting the beads of her *tasbee*, she fervently prayed to the Divine to spare the family from further calamity.

Sitting at the far end of the room, Kazi Azmat Ali Shoudagar continued observing Badsha. When Badsha placed the hookah by his side and was in the process of handing over the mouthpiece, Kazi Azmat Ali unwittingly made a casual observation, inquiring as to whether there was any additional news.

At this, Badsha could not control his aplomb anymore. The mouthpiece tube fell from his grip, and in a frenzy, he started crying. That took Kazi Azmat Ali Shoudagar by total surprise. He wondered what Badsha could be thinking to trigger such an outburst after his simple and unspecified query. Hashi Banu and Pori rushed in, expecting something more ominous.

Badsha yielded after persistent queries by all present as to the reason of his crying. Gusting initial shuddering and sadness, Badsha slowly informed them that the latest two-span beam bridge constructed on the *baduri khal* (canal) by the Shoudagar Construction Company had collapsed yesterday. The connecting pier had buckled, to the surprise of all.

Since the beginning of the nineteenth century, the design of bridges underwent significant innovations and improvements based on transportation needs, structural elements, load factor, material availability and cost, and design requirements. The bridges are now generally identified as beam, truss, cantilever, arch, tied arch, suspension, and cable-stayed and are generally made of steel, concrete, fiber-reinforced polymers, stainless steel, or a combination. Such bridges are common now, being omnipresent in most places. That was not the case with areas around Apurba Neer. The two traditional bridges, until this time, were single-span horizontal with beams supported at each end by substructure units. The bridge on the *baduri khal* was the first double-span bridge in the surrounding area, unique from that perspective, and constructed by SCC within time and costs. That was marketed effectively as something exceptional, done by a local company. The good name of SCC spread quickly, and additional contracts were bagged by the company, cashing in on that good performance.

Premised on such successes, Kazi Azmat Ali Shoudagar had been beaming with happiness, foreseeing a bright future for all his business enterprises and a secure and safe life for his offspring. That happiness, however, experienced its first significantly major setback last afternoon. Kazi Azmat Ali Shoudagar, relying on his rudimentary knowledge of arithmetic, made a mental estimation of capital, assets, and loss of last evening and was relieved to feel that though the *kal boi sha ki* affected immediate liquidity, he would be able to recoup that—if current problems could be tackled promptly.

Badsha was naively oblivious of the possible repercussions of what he had said to all present as most of the time, he was looking down. He had an urge to tell everything and disclose all facts as told to him by construction people a few minutes earlier. He had the impulse to live up to his reputation of being an honest and sincere person.

Kazi Azmat Ali Shoudagar had straightened himself on hearing the news, clasping his two hands on the two arms of the easy chair he was sitting on, but he wore an apparent posture of reassurance in his physical demeanor, obfuscating the raging internal agony. He had no idea of its evident severity and possible catastrophic impact. He asked Pori to pick up the flexible tube of the hookah and give it to him after cleaning. While saying this, he looked at Hashi Banu with a half-expressive smile, more to reassure her about himself.

Badsha, beholden to the irresistible urge within to narrate facts and the source of information at the earliest possible to his *hujur*, continued, saying, "This incident not only tainted the good name of SCC but is sure to have a denting impact on the future of our construction outfit. Reliable oral reports indicate that most government departments have already decided to suspend their contracts with SCC, and others are likely to follow. Decisions are likely to be communicated soon."

That was too much for Kazi Azmat Ali Shoudagar, who, all through his life, had enjoyed inherited prominence and had acted and reacted only to positive outcomes to enhance that image both economically and socially. He was not attuned to handle adversity, let alone two consecutive cataclysms. He possibly saw the collapse of the edifice of social and economic prominence that Biesh Moisher Bari was, nurtured by generations.

Badsha was just finishing his last statement when he noticed the flopping physical mien of his revered *hujur*. He shrieked impulsively and rushed forward to hold the falling body of his *hujur* before his head could hit the emblazed vessel of the hookah.

The precipitous uncontrolled outcry of all three present traversed throughout the property, impelling other household staff to rush to the site. The cry multiplied with the partaking of others seeing their *hujur* in that pitiable condition. Overcoming initial surprise and shock, Badsha commissioned his cool and took actions that were needed. With the help of others, he carried the insentient body of Kazi Azmat Ali Shoudagar to his bed, asked Pori to put a soaked folded piece of cloth on his forehead, and rushed to get the local physician. Hashi Banu, riveted in a confused state of mental agony, sat by his motionless body and systematically massaged his palms and chest while droplets of tears rolled down her cheeks in spite of words of reassuring consolations from many present.

Qulsum, so known to everyone in the house as such, except in private moments with Tanveer and personal discourse with Tauseef when she was addressed as Aleena, could not sleep much during the previous night. The thrust of *kal boi sha ki* of the previous afternoon, the resulting consequences, particularly ones related to the making of bricks, and the restlessness of her father-in-law and other family members were pedantically ascribed in a long letter she wrote to Tanveer, to be posted first thing the following morning. The surroundings of Biesh Moisher Bari during that night appeared to be too heavy and burdensome for the first time. Not only that, but it also continued to cause a sense of disenchantment and angst within her. She got up from the bed at the usual time, quietly finished her ablution as a prerequisite of saying daily Muslim prayers, finished her *fazar* (early morning) prayer, breastfed her son, and unwittingly went to sleep again, with her right hand on the body of the infant.

The cracking sound of sudden shouts from the formal sedentary room of the house jostled her, and she woke up with a befuddled state of mind and rushed out. She was appalled to see the stalwart persona of Biesh Moisher Bari, the pallbearer of the traditions of the house, without whose consent or command nothing happened in those surroundings, lying motionless, with well-wishers surrounding his bed. She quickly went inside, brought out the *tasbee*, and handed it over to Hashi Banu, softly putting two hands on the traumatized shoulders of her mother-in-law. Qulsum was unsure about her responsibilities and obligations in such a situation. Local traditions and practices of Biesh Moisher Bari had laid out a framework of a very formal relationship between father-in-law and daughter-in-law, encouraging neither to be informal in routine dealings. The relationship between Qulsum and Kazi Azmat Ali Shoudagar was very much fashioned by that framework, even though informality in contacts was encouraged with respect to others of the immediate family. She very much wanted to put the wet folded cloth on the forehead of Kazi Azmat Ali Shoudagar as Pori was doing but was hesitant to propose so, being unsure of the propriety of such an action. She silently left the room and called in one of the staff, asking her to take care of her baby. She performed mandated ablution and sat on the *jai namaz* with the Holy Quran on the balustrade. She totally got lost, involuntarily isolating herself from the immediate surroundings, and started reciting the Holy Quran with all consecration, intensely praying for the prompt and full recovery of her father-in-law.

By the time Badsha came back with the local physician, the large *uttan* (courtyard) of the house was full of people: employees, business associates, community elites, and ordinary folk who had always either admired or meekly criticized Biesh Moisher Bari and Kazi Azmat Ali Shoudagar. Many ladies came through the back entrance and were in jumbled groups in the sprawling space of Biesh Moisher Bari.

The reactions of those present were as dappled as their compositions. The marvel of such spontaneous reaction and opinion was that no one from the house had asked for them, nor had they any relevance in that context. Each set of assembled people had a veiled reason for Kazi Azmat Ali Shoudagar's sudden illness. Others had specific opinions about taking prompt religiously mandated actions, having *Quran khattam* (immediate reading of the whole Quran with total submission, seeking the mercy of Allah [the Divine]) and giving *sadka* (sacrifice of an animal in exchange for the life of the ill). The most intriguing was related to immediate treatment with implicit conclusions about his recovery or possible demise.

With the endorsement of the gentry present, Badsha went inside and requested the ladies present to vacate the room to enable the physician some space. The physician, the center of attention in that setting, had an unusually grim facial bearing, with spectacles hanging on the tip of his nose and a stethoscope dangling at full length. Badsha was delicately holding the black box containing immediate medicines and items needed for administering injections. His posture was notable, the way he was holding the black box with the care and passion reflective of curing Kazi Azmat Ali Shoudagar.

The physician conducted his medical examination and vacated the main bedroom, enduring the somber expressions, with no exchange of looks or words with anyone. In the courtyard, he took his seat on a chair in the midst of local gentries and still kept quiet, to the agony of everyone present. Direct and indirect annotations were made to provoke a response from the physician. Finally, he said, "I have examined him thoroughly. The findings concerning all relevant indicators are unfortunately negative. He has suffered a severe shock, which has affected and possibly damaged his vital body organs. Life and death depend on the will of Allahpak [the Divine], so I can't say anything about his physical condition. But besides being a doctor but also a friend and well-wisher of Kazi Azmat Ali Shoudagar, I have two suggestions. Recite the Holy Quran and seek the mercy of Allahpak and send someone to get both his sons back home immediately."

Tanveer sensed something portentous when he saw Badsha Chacha waiting for him in his hostel room. Before he could ask any questions, Badsha Chacha started crying like a child with accompanying hiccups. Tanveer concluded within himself that whatever might be the news, it was of immediate concern, with possibly ominous implications. He positioned a chair in front of Badsha Chacha, sat, and kept quiet to give time for emotion management. Seeing Badsha Chacha wiping his eyes, Tanveer straightened himself, looked directly at Badsha, and asked point blank, "Is Abba [Father] alive?"

Badsha responded affirmatively by nodding and said, "He is physically in a critical condition," and detailed briefly what happened in Apurba Neer and continued, saying, "I have been sent by Hashi-bu to fetch you both immediately. Here is a letter for you written last night by Bou Ma [daughter-in-law]. It might have some more details about what happened in the late afternoon of yesterday."

The three boarded the same auto rickshaw that had brought Badsha to Tanveer's hostel and started their excruciating travel to Apurba Neer. Although the three were heading to the same destination, their minds had significantly divergent thoughts. Seated in between Tanveer and Tauseef, Badsha somehow had a tranquil feeling, despite the jerks and shakes of the auto rickshaw with its mundane suspension and ubiquitous potholes in the road. He narrated the incidents and continued to pray for the immediate and full recovery of his *hujur* and was planning for a grand *milad mehfil* (*milad* is the most common way to express collective gratitude to Allahpak [the Divine] where believers voluntarily sit and recite praise. It can be for seeking mercy or thanking Him for graciousness) to celebrate his recuperation.

Tauseef had a sort of detached thinking, though his feelings were profound. His premonition about his father's health had no qualms about the severity of illness narrated, but he had no doubt about a possible overblowing to convey disquiet, as local traditions dictate. His veneration for Badsha Chacha unresistingly bourgeoned, even though his oft-repeated soliloquy could have some elements of meandering.

Tanveer had no exchange of looks or words with his companions on the journey. Tanveer was mostly gazing at the fast-ebbing landscape, holding firmly the enameled frame back of the driver's seat of the auto rickshaw. He occasionally nodded as Badsha Chacha continued intermittent narration. Tanveer had no incredulity about the acuteness but was edgy in thinking of variable possibilities. Different forestalled problems and challenges jumbled up in the rapidly mutable milieu, unknowingly causing a physiological convulsion within.

The upshot of that was palpable to all present when they disembarked from the auto rickshaw. As Tanveer straightened himself and took firm steps toward the home, Tauseef gently followed him. Walking through the sardined assembly of people, both of them exchanged *salaam*s with community seniors, family friends, and well-wishers. Tanveer's startling personality took most of the assembled gentries by surprise, while some others were dismayed. The ostensible reason for some to be dejected was not getting the chance to shower words of wisdom and consequential advice during a distressed time, as per local culture, bestowing special privilege that elders are privy to, by sheer age and position. They expected that both Tanveer and Tauseef, on hearing the news of their father's sudden illness, would be bizarrely hectored and opened up the much-desired opportunity to hold them in arms publicly and to portray each of themselves as the true well-wisher of the family. Each one of such gentries was certain about their own ability to win over the brothers easily because of their youth and inexperience. The long-term objective, obviously, was to make an in-road to the family's flourishing business and assume societal prominence that Biesh Moisher Bari had enjoyed for generations.

Tanveer's unwavering gestures were just the opposite in all plausible manifestations. Tauseef, always being less enthusiastic about material things and societal preferences, the two pivotal priorities of their home, was nonchalant and did not offer any window of expectation. The two quietly approached the bedside of their wilted father without any exchange of words with those present. They stood there in total silence for quite a while, perhaps prophesying and absorbing all possible consequences. The only limited exchanges the two boys had during this phase of total silence was with their mother, Hashi Banu, and with the local physician, who were sitting in two chairs near the headboard of their father's bed. On the receipt of the signal from his mother, who was murmuring Arabic words of *doa* (blessings) with rapid rotation of beads of her *tasbee*, Tanveer exchanged looks with the physician, seeking his approval to talk to their father. The physician nodded silently. Tanveer bent down slightly, lifted the two inert hands of his father, and kissed them with full intensity. He moved those torpid palms to the surface of his closed eyes and placed them back tenderly on his father's chest.

During that emotionally charged moment, Tauseef quietly kept his two hands on his brother's shoulders, as if ensuring his own participation, and providing additional support in that poignant journey of which he was also a silent part.

Qulsum had been engrossed in reading the Holy Quran since that morning, besides visiting her ailing father-in-law for brief periods in between. She came out of the room on hearing the arrival of Tanveer and Tauseef and positioned herself at the far end of the bed, next to her mother-in-law. She was pleased with Tanveer's initial response but had a feeling of uneasiness, observing a lack of follow-up action. She moved forward and exchanged looks with Tanveer, beseeching him to talk.

He placed both hands on his father's body and lowered himself to be close to his father's chest. That position was maneuvered to place his face near his father's ear, feeling and sharing respective breathing.

Once the setting was right, Tanveer impetuously released words from his heart, "Abba, please open your eyes to see all of us around you. Get well and come back to us. Enjoy your life. I promise to you that I will take full responsibility of Biesh Moisher Bari in all respects, in preserving and protecting the traditions and values that our progenitors nurtured and you cherish so much, in enhancing the social prominence of this illustrious *bari* [house], and in expanding your business, in addition to taking care of our mother, sisters, and Tauseef by delivering not only what is socially desired but everything else to make them happy."

As Tanveer lifted himself away, something very inexplicable and sudden happened for a brief moment. The closed eyes of Kazi Azmat Ali Shoudagar opened partly, and two tears flaunted the corners and fell, and the lids reverted to the previous closed position. That was immediately taken as a sign of the beginning of his recovery. All present were elated. Movement of beads in Hashi Banu's *tasbee* gained sudden momentum. Pori had some mixed feelings and took loath, slow steps toward the kitchen to prepare food. Qulsum exchanged looks with Tanveer, and they returned to their room. Tanveer hugged his mother and went inside, while Tauseef quietly settled himself in his own room. The only apparent exception was the local physician. In the atmosphere of feigned positivity, he had a sort of negative proclivity but refrained from speaking out. He hurriedly undertook a follow-up checkup, sat quietly for some more time, and then took edgy steps outside without saying goodbye to anyone. His quiet departure did not allure any particular attention as most took that as a possible reaction to being there for a long time.

Tanveer entered his bedroom, lifted his son, softly pressed the tiny physical frame against his own chest, and placed the toddler back in his bed. He then went to Qulsum, had a direct but passionate look at his dexterous life partner, and said, "I now need you by my side more as a friend than a wife. You are not only to take charge of all household responsibilities of my family but also equally be a trusted friend of mine in my new journey of life, which would not have any link with my past. For all practical purposes, my formal education has come to an end. In my journey back to Apurba Neer, all shared advice from Logic Sir, those related to emotion, individual capacity, and relevance of material progression, as emphasized by him during our last meeting, flashed in my thought process. I remembered each of his words and revisited them in the context of realities that I will probably face and have decided accordingly, much before reaching home. Now and at this challenging bend of my life, I would like to have you always by my side as a friend. Please do not deprive me of that."

Qulsum moved close to Tanveer in the private setting of their room, remained hushed, and very impulsively placed both her hands on the two sides of his head. Because of the closeness and her very sincere touch, he experienced a sudden feeling of equanimity and closed his eyes. He was evidently experiencing an escape from the protracted sustenance of anxiety and uncertainty that the future held for him and the resultant responsibilities.

She slowly drew his head to her chest, pressing it against her bulging breasts, and said slowly and firmly, "Please be assured of that. I am not just saying something affirmative to console you at the moment. This is not your family. This is our family. All through this journey, you will always find me as a support, as a friend, and as an honest critic for the betterment of the family to uphold your dignity and honor. You should have trust in me, and the repetition of this request in the future will be treated by me like inveighers with faceless acquisitions."

Responding to a buzz from Pori Khala, Tanveer went to have his food and was pleased to see Tauseef sitting. Both Pori Khala and Tauseef were having slow voice exchanges concerning Badsha Chacha. Tanveer's alert ears picked up the thread of that discourse, and he requested an additional plate, clearly saying that all three would eat together. That took Pori Khala by surprise as what Tanveer stipulated was a major shift in the age-old practice of Biesh Moisher Bari. In that house, the most likeable relationship was practiced within prescribed bounds and the limits of specific dos and don'ts. That boundary was never crossed.

Tauseef went out without giving Pori Khala any chance to react or comment. He soon returned with Badsha, who was both embarrassed and reluctant to have food with members of the master's family. Tanveer, with the assumed demeanor of being the future master, signaled to Badsha to take his seat. That was done without any eye exchange so that the gesture was valued not as a right but as a favor. The latter complied gladly but with gargantuan hesitation. The intrinsic message was loud and clear: the values and practices of Biesh Moisher Bari are all set to undergo some changes. Badsha, being humbled, took the gesture as a lifetime favor, setting a greater standard for loyalty and commitment. He was enormously happy with prospectively better status and a more proactive role, both in relationships and matters related to the house.

Responding to the suggestion of Qulsum, a decision was made promptly to send special emissaries to his sisters conveying the news and bring them back at the soonest possible moment.

In line with an understanding reached during the partaking of food, Tanveer went to his father's bedside and whispered to his mother and then stepped out abruptly to go to the brickfield. During the travel, Tanveer behaved like the de facto head of the family. He said to Badsha, "Chacha, you must be wondering what I am doing. Instead of being by the side of my ailing father, I am going to the brickfield site. I am very clear about my priorities. It is in no way preference for something at the cost of others. Abba is the prime focus for all of us, but it appears we can't do anything medically at this moment. Life is to move on. Our business should not be affected by the lack of decisions. So I decided to have a brief visit to send a very positive message. And that is important for the family and its well-being."

Upon arrival, Tanveer was surrounded by loyal and dedicated workers who were sad and dismayed because of the unexpected *kal boi sha ki* storm of yesterday and the inexplicable ailment of the *malik* (master). The assembly soon became a sizeable one, with workers scurrying to the spot upon hearing the news of Tanveer's arrival. That was easy as most workers were seasonal and, thus, resided in transient accommodations around the brickfield.

The labor *sardar* (leader) explained the impromptu preemptive measures taken to minimize the damage by *kal boi sha ki* and reported proudly that subsequent inspection revealed that the damage was much less than expected because of those efforts. He finished his submission, lamenting, "Time was just not enough. By the time we finished checking and assessing and were preparing to share the good news with him, the *malik* fell sick."

Tanveer briefly touched upon the reason for his sudden visit with rationale indicated earlier to Badsha. He thanked all present for their spontaneous efforts in substantially protecting the assets of the brickfields from the direct onslaught of *kal boi sha ki* and promised that Biesh Moisher Bari would never forget this. Just before leaving the brickfields, Tanveer sought everybody's *doa* (blessings) for the early recovery of his father. The labor *sardar* did not want to miss the opportunity for a general demonstration of their love and respect for Kazi Azmat Ali Shoudagar and his family. He immediately raised his two hands, followed by all present, recited a few verses from the Holy Quran, and made a devoted *monazat* (submission) to Allah (the Divine), seeking the immediate and full recovery of the *malik*.

In life, reality often is in variance negatively with expectation. The upshot is mostly disheartening and devastating to unsettle people involved. Precisely that happened in this impromptu gathering around Tanveer. Hardly had they finished their *monazat* when a special messenger came running and whispered to Badsha. Tanveer was briefed accordingly, and most of those present, except ladies, rushed to the house.

Tanveer crossed a number of people on his way home, and most of them passed him, keeping their heads down. He was still hoping for the best, beseeching the long life of the father. The ultimate reality was crystal clear to him as he stepped into the courtyard. The vociferous family outbursts became louder as they saw Tanveer stepping in. The message was loud and clear when the local physician also passed him without any word. He stepped into the room in the midst of sustained bawling and looked at his stone-faced mother, having no outward expression of grief. She continued to sit on the same chair, with the marked exception of having her *tasbee* on the chest of her deceased husband.

Tauseef, standing opposite his mother, held the sluggish right hand of the father with tears uncontrollably flowing. That was a rare sight for someone noted generally to be unemotional. Upon seeing Tanveer approach, Tauseef moved to create necessary space for his elder brother. Tanveer, notwithstanding his resolve otherwise, could not upholster the composure, and his internalized torment of the whole day succumbed to irrepressible emotion. Lowering his body close, Tanveer embraced the immobile cadaver of his father and burst out in expressing his grief. He kissed his face innumerable times and raucously said, "Abba [Father], you can't leave me at this stage. Wherever you may be, do not deprive me from your blessings. I promise once more that I will do everything to fulfill your dream and uphold the prestige of Biesh Moisher Bari."

Tanveer, like all others present, had extreme anxiety in observing the impassive, static stance of Mother in reacting to the sudden demise of her loving life partner. Marshalling composure, he moved to her side, abetted her affectionately rise up, and embraced her caringly. Stony-faced Hashi Banu placed her head and upper body on the chest of Tanveer and openly broke down for the first time since the demise of her loving husband. What a twist of life. For so long, Tanveer sought shelter in the warm embrace of his mother. Now the mother was seeking solace in the embrace of her son. As Tanveer was reiterating his earlier promises, Hashi Banu started shivering with the uncontrolled flow of tears flowing through her cheeks and passing down to his chest.

After some time, he unfastened the embrace, looked at his mother, and comfortingly said, "What happened, however sad it may be, was as ordained. It is the will of Allahpak [the Divine]. We are to accept his decision, and that will bless the noble soul of Abba. Continuous lamenting would only signify our dissatisfaction with the act of God. We should rather accept the act of God and move forward to fulfill his dreams and desires. That is the best we can do."

Hashi Banu involuntarily stopped both crying and shivering. She was astounded in seeing a new person positioned just in front of her with a new sense of identity, confidence, and command. That was just opposite of the docile, soft-spoken, and obedient son she knew Tanveer to be. He was fixing the *anchal* of his mother's sari as a departing act. A big teardrop, an apparent sign of happiness even against the backdrop of the surrounding sadness, graced the opposite side of his right palm. With lights everywhere, that tear looked like a sparkling *manik* (gem), the nickname of Tanveer fondly chosen by Pori at his birth but seldom used.

Challenge

All processes and rites concerning the burial of Kazi Azmat Ali Shoudagar were carried out with due assiduousness and solemnity. That included *kul khani* (Muslim religious ritual of communal prayer on the fourth day of death). The daughters, who had rushed to Biesh Moisher Bari with their respective husbands and children on hearing the sad news, gradually left for their respective homes. The Biesh Moisher Bari slowly returned to the usual chores, notwithstanding the persistent pain and agony. The most shaken was Hashi Banu, who, in spite of angst, tried to get relief, observing Tanveer handling and tackling all family and business matters.

Without wasting time, he called a family assembly with the participation of all, including Pori and Badsha, bestowing on them a new identity of being members of extended family, as well as a key indication of change in the stance and focus of Biesh Moisher Bari. Addressing Tauseef directly, Tanveer made the most profound statement. He candidly outlined the state of the family and future course by saying, "We have lost the torchbearer and symbol of everything the family and our home is known for. While we will have feelings of grief all through, we should try to move forward so that by our deeds and achievements, we can not only maintain but also enhance the image of this house. That will be the greatest tribute we can pay to the noble soul of Abba. Thus, I have decided to take over the family and business responsibilities, ending my pursuit of further education. There is nothing to lament as by itself, that objective has limited goals. Irrespective of the family finance situation, I undertake the need to fulfill Tauseef's dream of studying in Dhaka University. So instead of losing more time, Tauseef should go back to college with singular determination to excel in his intermediate examination. Badsha Chacha will accompany him to bring back my belongings."

Things were not as straightforward as Tanveer initially thought. His initiation to business was a convoluted experience, made worse by the varied nature of advice from ostensible well-wishers with a discerning overt objective of harming the Biesh Moisher Bari. He opted for an approach of propriety in dealing with such well-wishers as many were friends and associates of his father and considered his relative youth and inexperience in business. The initial few months were both confusing and dispiriting for him. In his enthusiasm to set things right, he made many decisions, some of which backfired. For example, the decision to market smudged bricks of that season at a lower price neither had market response nor could uphold the good name of Kazi bricks. Another quick decision to not go for brick-making the following season sent the wrong signal to the market, in addition to helping his competitors. His most challenging predicament was concerning the tackling of the quagmire created by the bridge collapse and the follow-up actions taken by the government agencies. Family, friends and well-wishers visited him many times, even at home, urging him not to pick up a fight with the government, the sole source of all construction in the vicinity. The common nature of advice emphasized the early reaching of a contrived understanding with them. That indirectly envisaged accepting blame for the bridge collapse, paying some damage to the department, and making others neutral by pleasing them unofficially. Friends and well-wishers volunteered to lobby with various government departments to take a lenient approach and to give the young successor a chance in consideration of the family's name and standing.

Distraught and unsure, Tanveer returned home rather early on a particular day. Qulsum was happy but somewhat apprehensive as it was the middle of the week, and normally, he returned on a very late afternoon or early evening. Creating necessary space, she asked him whether his early return was just for relaxing or because of some stress. Tanveer gave a passionate look and detailed the tenor and nature of advice he was receiving from many. On specific query, he confessed his inclination to follow the advice for working out a compromise with government departments to get out of the current quagmire. Hearing that, Qulsum repositioned herself, kept looking at Tanveer without any twinkling, and kept unusually quiet for a while. Surprised as he was, Tanveer had a natural query for the reason of her rigid and silent posture.

Qulsum could not maintain her composure or conceal her frustration and said, "I promised to be your friend, and that promise has had both the elements of love and commitment. As I know you and recall each word of your vow to Abba at the time of his demise, this is the least I ever expected from you. By accepting the undetermined blame, you are undermining the good name and social standing of Biesh Moisher Bari, which you pledged yourself to uphold at his deathbed. Why compromise? If so necessary, we can get out of the construction business. We have other businesses and enough property. We can and will survive. There is no need to accept any blame without investigation."

Saying those words with all firmness, Qulsum left the room. Sitting alone, Tanveer was in a stance of befuddled trauma, trying to navigate between what Qulsum said and what others had advised.

Badsha Chacha showed up unexpectedly, saying, "There are two young men who had a very scary bearing and want to talk to you directly."

After a thought, Tanveer nodded. The two, exhibiting unusual body deportment, said rather coarsely, "Our leader will be visiting you tonight at around ten o'clock, have food at your place, and stay about an hour. This is to be carried out in total privacy. Your *chacha* should wait near the bamboo bush on the other side of your big *pukur* [pond] and escort Leader to your home. We will be giving him cover from a little distance."

Saying those few words, they left hurriedly, giving no chance to interact. It was evident that they were in a rush to leave. Perhaps that was the reason for their being restless and apparently rude.

The distraught mind of Tanveer was encumbered by the newfangled development. He proceeded to Hashi Banu's room along with Qulsum and briefed mother and wife as to what transpired. The consensus was that since the person had indicated his desire to have food in Biesh Moisher Bari, his planned sojourn would not have any sinister motive. Mother called Pori and instructed her to make a proper dinner and arrange service in a low-key manner as desired. She also advised that Tanveer should eat, even though very late, with the guest, whoever he might be, as manifestation of the good gesture for which the house is known and famous for.

Tanveer and Qulsum returned to their room. He reclined on his easy chair, while Qulsum positioned herself on the end of the bed, ensuring direct eye contact. Observing undue strain in his body language, she said, "Could that person be your Logic Sir?"

Tanveer thought for a while and said, "I do not think so. Sir does not know about my family or my roots at Apurba Neer. He never asked anything about my family, except having casual interest to know about you. I do not have any contact with him since he escaped the arrest on that night. Logic Sir, if alive at all, is a fugitive and would not risk such a venture."

Time passed in that emotionally charged setting. Tanveer was both weary and hungry. Badsha showed up and drew his attention by a typical low vocal clatter and stepped aside. Following him was the most unexpected visitor—dear Logic Sir.

Badsha closed the door and stood outside, guarding the entrance as earlier instructed by those two young men. Tanveer was dumbfounded and speechless. Logic Sir was calm, quiet, and steadfast. He took confident steps and brought out his two hands from inside his *chador* (shawl) to have a very heartfelt embrace with his most adored pupil. They were quiet for a while, with Logic Sir sitting on the easy chair and Tanveer in another formal chair with delicately carved woodwork. While Tanveer was absorbing the suddenness of the most unexpected encounter, Logic Sir was wearing a mischievous smile, being happy in seeing his pupil and giving him the surprise. Through the movement of his hand, he conveyed to Tanveer to lower the light of the room. A moment of total silence masked the scenery.

Logic Sir opened up in a very low voice, saying, "My time here is very limited. You are always in my mind and thoughts, and I always felt appalled for not being able to have a formal uncoupling with you, but one never knows what providence has in store. I had no idea about your address or other usual family details. So whenever you came to my mind, I only yearned for your good and happiness. That is more so as I have no family and not a son. I was undertaking a surreptitious travel from the Hatbazari area to the Anantapur village to attend to some organizational concerns of immediate importance. The two comrades who came to inform you about my visit to your place are my local guides, facilitating my journey. Our strategic approach in such travel is to uphold secrecy, and for that, we travel either at night or when traffic is heavy, such as an event like a local *haat* [open-air informal market on specific days of a week].

"There is such a *haat* about two miles from your home. When we reached there, it was just past sunset. My two local comrades suggested having a break. We went to one of the makeshift tea stalls. Because of the need to avoid unnecessary queries from the local residents, in which they mostly excel, I deliberately took my seat on a rudimentary bench located slightly away from the main section of the tea stall, while one of my comrades went for tea and the other one stayed with me to provide necessary cover. The local customers were sitting together and enjoying their time and gossip in loud voices, outshining each other, each proving oneself more knowledgeable and authentic. I just could not help but listen to those mundane utterances.

"Suddenly, your name was said, detailing your current predicaments after the death of your father. Hearing your name, I paid rapt attention to what they had to say. It soon became apparent that those people know everything about you and your family. That, of course, included the catastrophic bridge collapse. What amused me were their utilitarian opinions and options to redress your glitches. I asked for a second cup of tea to buy some more time in listening. I felt an urge to see you. Surveying the surroundings in the darkness, I asked my comrades whether we could break the journey here for a day. The option was to take a night's rest in a mosque. One of my comrades became very excited. He has a dear cousin in this locality and is a very influential person. He opined that possibly, we could take rest in his home safely. That comrade, asking us to stay put, went to meet his cousin and returned with affirmative news.

"I gave them the task of finding you. They undertook required scouting, identified your person standing outside here, and met you. That is how I am in your place. I am not saying anything about myself as that will be a waste of time. There is only a bullet between my life and the end of my journey. I dreadfully made the decision to meet you to see whether I could be of any help to you in view of the diverse nature of the problems you are faced with."

Tanveer was unsure as to how to respond. His predicament was in knowing Logic Sir as an idealistic individual, with limited relevance to practicality or business matters. While having dinner served by Qulsum, Tanveer came out of that quandary and raised the issue of the bridge collapse, it being a matter more of policy than business. He briefly articulated the advice he heard from local elders and friends of his father versus quite the opposite view of Qulsum.

Logic Sir looked at Qulsum directly and smiled. He quietly said, "I am proud of Ma [Mother] Qulsum for her perspective about the more appropriate step forward concerning your bridge episode. That is why I had encouraged you to groom your wife as a life partner. Only in that scenario, a wife can disassociate herself from the immediate interests to larger perspectives. You have a gem of a life partner, and so give due consideration always to her opinions and suggestions."

There was a moment of silence before Logic Sir resumed his monologue, "In life, do not take the words of others as they sound. Always make a determined effort to put yourself in the shoes of those people to understand what prompted them to say so, and only then should you articulate your own views or response. As I see— and this is a hunch only—your well-wishers may have a malevolent motive in suggesting you to accept the blame and reach a compromise with the department. If you do so, you will get immediate relief, but that may continue to haunt you for a long time. The negative assessment as documented now will not be erased, and more so, it could be brought to the surface by others whenever needed. In the process, your putative well-wishers will have the opportunity to establish themselves in the lucrative construction field, and your company will just wane out. Because of this, I find plenty of merit in what Qulsum suggested. There is no apparent reason, without proper investigation, to blame your firm for the collapse of the bridge. Like most construction and engineering works, any bridge project may have vulnerability for one or multiple reasons. Some of these are design deficiency, inappropriateness of the site because of the lack of required soil testing, inadequacy of supervision, deficiency in undertaking construction work, and axle load of traffic using the bridge. Of these five factors, your firm is related to the fourth one only. I am not saying that your firm is not at fault, but it could reasonably be any other four factors too or a combination. So I suggest that you send a strong representation to all the departments, urging them to withdraw suspension orders, request the bridge construction department to institute an investigation, followed by a lawyer's notice, and, if required, file a case.

"Mr. Fazlul Bari Chowdhury of the district is a renowned lawyer, besides being my good friend. I will write to him immediately that you are likely to see him, and he should do everything to help you out in your quest for legal redress."

After saying those words, he suddenly stood up, saying, "I am running out of time and should go." While thanking Qulsum for a very tasty meal and nice evening, he unexpectedly expressed his desire to see their son. Qulsum brought him, and Logic Sir tenderly held him to his chest and said, "Qulsum, I have nothing to give to your son. I am giving him a most heartwarming kiss as manifestation of all my love and best wishes for him."

Saying those words, Logic Sir covered himself fully before stepping out of the house with Badsha as an escort up to the point of the bamboo bush.

As the night descended, a relaxed and reinvigorated Tanveer approached his bed for a jocund night but found Qulsum sleeping. On a closer look, he was certain that she was not asleep but was pretending to be so. He lay down slowly by her side, turned himself toward her, and attempted to hug her and put his hands on her body.

She was yearning for such action since the demise of her father-in-law. She enjoyed the slant but, to convey the point of disdain, disengaged at the earliest moment. Her prompt action convinced Tanveer that she was not sleeping at all. He forcefully turned her toward him, hugged her intensely, and kissed her profusely, saying repeatedly, "I am so lucky to have someone like you as my wife. I will continue to value you more as a friend and will always take note of your considered advice in future. This is my promise."

It was Qulsum's turn to overtake Tanveer. She positioned herself on top of him, started scratching his neck and chest, and put one of her paunchy breasts in his mouth. They finally had the real, mutually desired, and fulfilling physical engagement they had been waiting for.

An estimably changed Tanveer, with confidence overflowing in his facial expressions, stepped out of the room the following morning. His physical bearing had all the pluck to confront the challenge and convert it to opportunity, determinedly envisioning sweetly savored rewards. He met his mother, recounted his discussions with Logic Sir last night, enunciated his positions, and left after seeking her blessings.

Stepping into his business establishment, he called core associates to share his vision about the future of the business and spelled out the strategies he would be adopting. Emphasizing that the past was past, he articulated his determination to reinvigorate the business. Reversing his earlier decision, he opted to continue the brick-making business with needed input of fresh capital to ensure better technology and lesser risk. He confidently emphasized, "Kazi Brick must be in the market again, exceeding its past glory."

With respect to the problem of the bridge collapse, he summarized a position consistent with what was stipulated last night by Qulsum and Logic Sir. Though he followed their reasoning and technical confines, due caution and care were exercised in those discussions, and he only shared the relevant details. The news of Tanveer's pronouncements concerning his approach and determination to carry on the business with enhanced determination spread quickly. His business associates and workers took that positively, but some purported well-wishers and friends of his late father had negative reactions. Some said Tanveer made immature decisions; others predicted further doom for the family as the son was going to squander the assets so arduously acquired and left behind by the late Kazi Azmat Ali Shoudagar. The obvious premise of those negative comments had inherent reality with related frustration. Tanveer's decisions had thwarted their objectives of phasing out Biesh Moisher Bari from the panorama of dominant business activities in Apurba Neer. His earlier decision of getting out of the brick-making business already encouraged some to commit resources for that business. They had the definite credence that once SCC accepts blame and enters into compromise, the escalating prominence and monopoly being enjoyed would certainly be impaired, opening up opportunities for some of them. The frustration of friends and well-wishers of his late father was evident as their frequent visits to the business establishment with loads of good wishes and earthly wisdom markedly declined within a short span of time. With that, Tanveer had an even more definite indication that he was in the right course. That confidence energized him, and he devoted full attention and even more time to business matters.

He labored hard to draft a convincing representation against suspension of all construction contracts, took that to the lawyer friend of Logic Sir in the district town for vetting, and sent it to all concerned. In that representation, he requested for the constitution of an interdisciplinary inquiry team to look at all aspects of the bridge work, including design, soil testing, supervision, construction, and load pressure on the bridge in terms of capacity and strength. He also emphasized that it would be helpful to determine deficiencies that caused the collapse and assured that SCC would fully abide by the decision of the proposed committee. He was extra careful with his approach in drafting that representation as he was conscious of the long-term consequences of standing up to government departments. He was always polite in affirming that inaction on this proposition within the next one month would compel SCC to send a legal notice, to be followed by formal filing in the district court. As a supporting effort, he started enhancing his contacts and interactions with all the departments concerned.

Surprisingly, the outcome of that submission astounded all who knew the case, particularly Tanveer himself. Other departments concerned withdrew their suspension orders, convinced by his reasoning. The department directly involved with the bridge construction sought an extension of time, being in the process of submitting an affirmative note for approval by the divisional engineer, including the proposition for an inquiry committee. The latter proposal was framed to respond to the need of identifying real issues for better outcomes in the future. That immediately engraved a status of prominence for Tanveer in the society and among the local community. He was no more just the son of the late Kazi Azmat Ali Shoudagar but a well-respected businessman of the surroundings, bolstered by better exposure, higher education, and broadened intelligence. People also commanded his confidence and intelligence.

During his visit to the district headquarters to consult with the lawyer concerning the representation, he met some prominent businessmen and discussed prevalent brick-manufacturing problems and issues. He came to know about the use of a new machine for brick making and was told that it had become very popular in cities and urban growth centers. Before his return, he also met some of his old teachers, discussed the same issues and, at the suggestion of the hostel superintendent, who was also a chemistry professor, visited a bookstore to see whether there were any reference materials and publications on the subject. With the help of the genial manager of the store, he found a business journal containing a detailed article on the problems and prospects of brick making in Bangladesh. He took that with him for his office.

Based on discussions he had in the district headquarters, as well as reading the comprehensive article in the magazine, Tanveer was convinced of the bright future of brick making. He decided to invest substantial new capital by liquidating some fixed assets, such as farmland. Though his understanding and focus were absolutely clear and firm, he considered it necessary and prudent to keep Mother and Qulsum informed beforehand and decided to have an in-depth discussion with both before making the decision public. It was also considered important because his proposed line of action would mean liquidating farmland to capitalize his new initiative. He needed their consent and advice and the blessings of Mother. Tanveer took his time and, in the process, always looked very stressed out. His main concern was fear of the unknown: whether or not he was going to commit a portion of the family fortune to chase a business venture. That triggered a marked and impulsive presence of crudity in his behavior, though he did not mean any umbrage to anyone. He was importuning himself and, for the first time, felt the absence of Father.

The wince on his face drew the attention of Pori Khala. She just could not help but bring it to the attention of Qulsum directly. Qulsum concurred with what Pori Khala had observed and also stated how worried she was about his recent peripatetic behavior pattern. She maintained that knowing and understanding him as she did, he would open up in due time and that pestering at this stage would not be of any benefit.

Hashi Banu was in the secluded locale she had chosen for herself since the death of her husband, mostly concentrating on prayers, delegating full responsibility to Qulsum to the care of Pori. She had no inclination to be involved in such mundane matters.

Qulsum remained nonchalant against the backdrop of the sudden change in Tanveer's gestures and was beleaguered by the thought of losing her loving husband to the challenges and commitments of upholding the name of Biesh Moisher Bari. She had no one to share with, except raising the issue with Tauseef during his recent short visit. She was suffering within herself, patiently waiting for Tanveer to open up. Months had passed since the demise of their father, time was running out, and the need for a definite decision about an additional investment into the brick business became imperative.

Finally, Tanveer told Qulsum that he had pressing matters concerning business to discuss and desired having a meeting with her and Mother. All three sat together, and Tanveer formally advised them, though the contents were mostly known from other sources about positive things that had happened, and gave them a preview of his thinking and slant about future growth to keep the image and relevance of Biesh Moisher Bari in the traditional context. In particular, he reiterated his earlier decision to continue with the brick-making business and put forward the justification for additional capital to ensure a continuous presence in their business.

In support of the last point, he recounted his discussions and research on the issue and said, "Brick making in Bangladesh, though hundreds of years old, still follows a primitive way. The prevalent kiln technology that is commonly in use is a century old, inadequate in terms of quality, inefficient in terms of cost, vulnerable to natural hazards, and, most significantly, low in productivity. Though there are varied types of kilns in use in countries like China and others, Bangladesh brick manufacturers still prefer the primitive method primarily because of the lack of initiative and capital needed.

Bangladeshi brick manufacturers generally rely on this old clamp type of kiln as the concept of a permanent kiln structure is neither known nor practiced. This type of practice is common in faraway semi-urban areas like Apurba Neer, even though a steady move is being made to modernize brick making in areas surrounding big cities and urban growth centers. The result is gradual progression in developing a user-friendly brick-making machine. The product of this new machine is called Bangla brick. This machine, operated by diesel engine, among many advantages, has definite lower operating costs. Other proven advantages are a significant increase in brick making, better quality of products, reduced susceptibility to hazards and risks, and saving on fuel wood. The impact is bound to be far reaching as with the rising population and better communication, there is an evident desire for better homes across the board. Also, there is bound to be an increased demand for bricks because of the significant surge in infrastructure-related development projects in most of the adjacent areas. The market is there, and it is the need of the business to respond. As the major brick maker of the area, we need to take the leadership."

Mother and Qulsum listened to Tanveer with rapt attention. With her mother-in-law present, Qulsum refrained from making any upfront comment. Hashi Banu closed her eyes and continued to move the beads of her *tasbee* as if she were seeking guidance from Kazi Azmat Ali Shoudagar. She opened her eyes and softly said, "You are in charge of the business. Whatever you think best, you should do that. Moreover, what you said makes sense. I can only say that brick making was very dear to your father in making progress in the business. In fact, this business ushered the most successive progression. His soul will definitely be happy to see you are following his footsteps. I do not have much to say except you have my blessings. The rest depends on Qulsum."

Saying those few words, she looked at Qulsum as if to give a window to state her own views. Qulsum politely nodded and said, "I fully agree with what Amma [Mother] just said. It is your judgment and decision, and we will always be supportive. You please be rest assured of that."

Tanveer's reaction was unobtrusive, and he kept mum for a while and then said, "For the planned invigoration of the business and procurement of the new brick-making machine, we need a good amount of liquid funds. Though our present business is slowly turning around after unforeseen incidents, it is not advisable to divert funds from existing business. The only option I have in mind is to sell the parcel of farmland in Uttar Khand [another habitation outside Apurba Neer]. But our property is jointly owned. I will not like to be seen as squandering assets acquired and left behind by Abba [Father] for all of us. As you know, business is always an indeterminate venture where things may go upside down against all calculations. It is vulnerable to unspecified uncertainties and is always shrouded by unpredictable miasma. It is no doubt a diaphanous proposition. I want to keep you informed and need your endorsement before taking any action."

All the surrounding sounds of the room suddenly ceased. An implicit hush hovered around them. Qulsum suffered an internalized shiver and, to conceal that, kept her eyes focused on the floor. Hashi

Banu closed her eyes with the enhanced rolling of *tasbee* beads. Tanveer maintained a calm posture. He was certain that irrespective of the decision concerning his proposition, he was determined to pursue the brick-making business and bring it back to its previous position. What he had proposed was a security to ensure that the objective was achieved quickly and sustainably.

Hashi Banu opened her eyes and coughed a little, more symbolic of drawing attention. She said, "Brick making was a very dear business venture of your late father. Against all advice, he sold some land at the time and started his new business. That paid us enormous return. Most of his later success was triggered by this new business venture. As Muslims, we believe that longevity is determined by Allahpak [the Divine]. But the damage done by the *kal boi sha ki* of last year shattered him, and that perhaps was the immediate cause of his death. Unexpectedly, the whole burden of taking care of the family and business landed on your lap. There were many issues that needed fixing, many deficiencies that needed tweaking, and many ideas that needed testing. You may be young but well-placed because of better educational attainments in assessing business opportunities in the changing business setting. You have done wonderfully well, as I know from Pori. I am sure you will continue to do so in the future too. You sought my endorsement of your proposition. I give you my unequivocal permission to sell that land and invest the proceeds in the business. I will bear all responsibility in case of a negative outcome. You have my blessings."

Saying those few words, she lay down on the bed, ostensively to take rest. Tanveer and Qulsum went back to their room. Qulsum was tranquil and happy in observing a sense of relief in her husband's body language. She was relaxed not just because of the positive outcome but more because of the trust that Mother had in Tanveer and the implications of the decision. Any negative or reserved position would have impacted on his morale and commitment to the business, to which he devoted all his time and energy lately.

While having a follow-up discussion, Qulsum emphasized the need to ensure the proper training of key staff to run the new expensive machine and suggested the need to ensure such training. Tanveer was very happy. Taking note of her suggestion, he indicated that he would ensure the provision of such training in the purchase deal by having direct negotiation with the manufacturers.

The subsequent story was short and positive. A better quality of Kazi brick with lower costs flooded the market. All would-be potential local brick makers faded away. Kazi brick not only gained back the previous market but also accessed markets beyond.

Tanveer sensed that the time of doing business while just sitting in the office was over. He focused on developing social relationships with pertinent government functionaries. Simultaneously, he quietly started developing connections with political entities, often quietly sharing boons. But as a strategy, he kept himself aloof from identifying with any political setup, whether in power or in opposition. Consequently, he also increasingly engaged in various social works with community institutions. Pending the findings of the inquiry committee constituted to look into the bridge collapse, SCC continued competing and getting new contracts. His pluck and luck, coupled with vigorous hard work, started yielding sweet rewards beyond expectations. Biesh Moisher Bari started to regain its previous social prominence and prestige. All these necessitated his spending more time outside, and very often, he would be tired when returning home.

There was an evident slide in interactions with Qulsum too. Some of his responses had the shade of squabbles and, on other occasions, sounded condescending and peevish. She lost her jubilant and easygoing husband to his newly acquired success and prominence. Nevertheless, she opted to endure that as a true friend, not just as wife. Her understanding, accommodation, and sacrifice helped Tanveer achieve what he wanted. In the process, she lamentably lost her ever-gregarious husband and life partner. She could not restrain the teardrops springing from her emotion-laden eyes from spilling over.

Complications

It was time for planning Tauseef's pursuit of higher education in Dhaka. That aspirational focus of life encountered a most unexpected obstruction by a precipitous change of position from a most unexpected quarter, highlighting the glorious uncertainties of life. The process of decision making had to suffer undue uncertainties, causing qualms to many.

Tauseef excelled in his intermediate examination much beyond expectation. He hurried back home from his short visit to district headquarters to share the good news with all. His first stop was the family's business premise to keep Tanveer informed, who obviously was very happy and proud, hugged him very warmly, and ordered the distribution of sweets among staff (following local custom). Both brothers kept quiet for a while, reminiscing the reactions of Father—had he been alive.

Tauseef rushed home to share the news with Mother and, on his way to her room, told Qulsum and Pori Khala. All three of them cheerily entered Hashi Banu's room and gregariously imparted the news. Qulsum, as an expression of happiness, alluded to Tauseef's long-harbored and cherished inclination to go to Dhaka to pursue higher studies. Hashi Banu's response, paraphrased in somber peroration, stunned all three present.

Unexpectedly deviating from a foreseeable reaction of joy and happiness and demonstrating specific insensitivity, she said, "Why should he go to Dhaka? He can finish his higher education in the same college that Tanveer tried in. His father left behind the flourishing business for them. Through ferocious hard labor and total commitment, Tanveer has successfully arrested the invariable slide the business faced at the time of your father's demise. Now the onus is on both to take care of it. Why should Tanveer shoulder the entire burden? It pains me to look at him. All the pressures and challenges being faced have already made a diaphanous mark on his physique and facial expressions. Tauseef is not going to Dhaka for studies. He should finish his studies locally and join Tanveer in the business after graduation."

Saying those few words with all the unsullied reasoning and moral strength she could master, Hashi Banu lay on her bed and turned away to avoid further eye contact. Qulsum and Pori Khala left the room. Tauseef stood for a while with the hope of pleading but refrained after Mother had deliberatively shut down further communication. He came out of the room as a blunted fellow. All dreams of higher education in a challenging academic environment withered away in a moment. That frustration was too much for him to absorb. By nature, he had a detached mind-set from his early growing-up stages, exacerbated by the expressed lack of interest in family business, acquisition of properties, and overt preference for social prominence. He always had qualms with the priority accorded to uphold family traditions and values. In his thinking, all these priorities for hereditary tenets were predominant barriers to much-needed changes in his life and practices. To his judgment, all round, social settings were constantly evolving, but Biesh Moisher Bari remained afoot in the values and practices enshrined five generations back. He wanted to break from that and taste the mutable world outside the parameters of his ancestral home.

Hashi Banu was the most depressed. It caused agony within her to give that negative decision, knowing Qulsum had, on many occasions, indicated Tauseef's intense desire for higher studies in Dhaka. She was thinking about this against the backdrop of her husband's sudden death and her bestowed new responsibility. She decided internally that when the time comes, she would oppose that, and she did exactly that. Her prompt gesture of avoiding further eye contact with her dear ones was not an act to insinuate anything. It had relevance to her health conditions, which was not known to anyone in the family. That was another ascendant factor influencing her negative decision about Tauseef. She was persistently encouraged by words of wisdom and material support from Qulsum in daily living and had fought with herself to get out of the weakness syndrome caused earlier by frequent pregnancies and her *shutika* illness. Her ardent willpower was premised on the need to be in good health to support Tanveer in his journey of life and to ensure the early settlement of Tauseef with a supporting hand. Most interestingly, Hashi Banu slowly started treating this as her own reasoning to try to live longer. More importantly, she was making steady progress, except that she started feeling weak and disconcerted if anything stressed her. The decision of Tauseef's going to Dhaka was one such matter. Thus, soon after detailing her position on that heavy subject, Hashi Banu lolled in her bed to manage her stress and to overcome evanescent exasperation.

Some parents have inclinations to overtly demonstrate a special bond with the eldest and youngest children of the family. Though their love for other children is not to be doubted, that bonding with the eldest and youngest has visible expression and significant latitude. That was not the case of Hashi Banu so far as Tauseef was concerned. That rather deviating type of her feeling and love for him was not the subject that predicated her negative decision. She never thought about Tauseef's growing up and his perceptible indifferent behavior pattern. She always thought that Kazi Azmat Ali Shoudagar would be the right person to handle and mitigate that when the time is right. His demise made her responsible to think more astutely about that in the context of traditions, values, and the good name of Biesh Moisher Bari. That feeling accreted with a leery reaction when she recalled Tauseef's blunt discussion with *ghattak* Bakshi Mia (BM), who was a shrewd operator. He did not fail to show up for a timely expression of sympathy and participate in religious rituals on hearing of the demise of Kazi Azmat Ali Shoudagar. He did that to further bond his relationship with Biesh Moisher Bari and earn the trust of Hashi Banu under the changed circumstances.

On hearing of Tauseef's good performance in his HSC examination, *ghattak* BM visited the house and had a discussion with Hashi Banu within the framework of *parda* (modesty) and in the presence of Badsha. The subject of that discussion was a marriage proposal for Tauseef. As they were talking, Tauseef ignorantly came in with a smiling face. As he came to know the reason of all pervasive happiness, he pointedly told BM, "Bakshi Chacha [Uncle], you are a trusted man of our late father and arranged the marriages of our three sisters and my brother. They have had been very remarkable, especially the last one. We have one of the nicest daughters-in-law. But that is it. Please do not waste your time and raise the expectations of others by trying to do something similar for me. I am not interested in marriage, at least for now. Notwithstanding that, you are and will continue to be a well-wisher of this family. We are thankful to you."

He left the room after uttering those very specific words, to the utter surprise and dismay of those present. That especially unnerved Hashi Banu. The experience and resultant reaction made a huge dent on her thinking process concerning Tauseef and his future. She concluded to herself that it was time to reign him in for the sake of the good name and standing of Biesh Moisher Bari. She, thus, unhesitatingly concluded not to allow Tauseef to go beyond her periphery of influence. That was the backdrop of her negative decision, without discussion, when Qulsum mentioned Tauseef going to Dhaka in pursuit of better learning.

A dispirited Tauseef retreated to his room, shattered by the vocal decision from Mother. He was anguishing himself with thoughts about his future and what he could possibly do. Right at that moment, Qulsum entered the room without any premonition and quietly sat on the only chair in the room. Both of them were quiet.

Finally, Qulsum opened up by stating, "I really do not understand Amma's [Mother's] quick and firm position about your going to Dhaka. That proposition was not a surprise to her. I have steered the issue in the immediate past while talking with her about your future to prepare for your going to Dhaka for higher studies. I had, all along, the feeling that she was agreeable. It took me by total surprise when she diverged so promptly—and the way she did it too."

Tauseef was looking at her without much reaction, with the feeling that she showed up to console him. Qulsum's follow-up discourse took him by surprise when she continued, saying, "I did not respond to Mother's negativity immediately simply because that would harden her position. Generally, people in such a situation neither expect nor encourage dissenting stipulation. The most prudent approach is to align with the negative position of the other party, to give one the comfort of having some support, and then to win the trust of the other party. Slowly pursue the matter, step by step, facilitating a possible change in the stipulated position. This is definitely a path of least resistance and most likely to yield positive outcomes. I, along with Pori Khala, intend to do that. Give us some time and let us work through it, including the unconditional and convincing alignment of your brother. I am more than certain that I will be successful. In the meantime, you start taking slow but subtle preparatory steps for going to Dhaka."

Tauseef thanked Qulsum profusely. He was given an inkling of the light at the end of the tunnel, though it was somewhat blurred. He said, "Perhaps Mother did not take graciously my direct communication with *ghattak* Chacha conveying an expressed negative position on marriage. My problem is that I have grown up with a definite censorious perception about much-revered values and common practices, as outlined by our progenitors. They were perhaps right at the inception, but times have changed. Present-day snags and related challenges are now totally disparate and require an evolving approach. Thus, I want to challenge them. It is important to know what we are, but it is equally relevant to be aware of and strive for what we could be. The ultimate for Biesh Moisher Bari is just not to remain germane within Apurba Neer but to position itself in the greater settings that time opens up for. I want to be a part of that process without having an onionskin-insinuating position, without ratcheting others or showing umbrage, avoiding any squabble. I will do so in my own way, confining the fallouts within the edge of my life."

After saying those words, Tauseef was unsure about Qulsum's intellectual ability to digest what he had just articulated. So he made a plain statement, saying, "While I would like to conduct myself according to my proclivity, I will entrust Bhaiya [Brother] to handle all other family matters, whether pertinent to business or properties and social engagements, without preconditions or other stipulations. With you as being a wise counsel by his side, I am more than certain that he would do what he would consider best to keep up the name and flourish the image of our home. I will never question any of his decisions, even in the unlikely worst scenario. This is my solemn promise."

As a diversion and to tease his *bhabi* (sister-in-law), Tauseef alluded to his inevitable physical parting from the traditional family home. He said, "As you know by this time, I am only a guest in this abode. Hereditary rights and policy were laid out when this house was built by my forefathers. Five generations back, it was stipulated that this *bari* [house] would never be divided. The eldest male offspring will be the owner of this house, and other offspring are to be located at separate new homes. So I do not have any right to this house. In that sense, I do not belong to this house. Saying goodbye is inevitable for me, today or tomorrow. From that reality, it does not matter whether I live next door, in the next village, in the next town, or, for that matter, even in Dhaka."

His last statement was laden with suppressed emotions and stifled Qulsum. She kept quiet, avoided eye contact, and left the room inaudibly. She was bemused not because what Tauseef had just said was new but more because of the resoluteness inherent in its future application. She gradually appreciated the rationale of value changes Tauseef had always emphasized. She had no qualms that though both brothers were born and grew up in the same setting with the same set of parents, they were downright two very unalike individuals. Tanveer was, in every sense, a traditional son that a customary family like Biesh Moisher Bari aspired to have, being committed to the values, traditions, and cultures as passed on from generation to generation. Contrarily, Tauseef, though respectful of family mores, grew up with an open mind and had a penchant to assess things from a broader perspective. He savored change in all manifestations. Mostly because of such personality traits, the passed-on family creed regarding inheritance had troubled Tauseef from early childhood. The following thoughts and assessment made Qulsum reach two definite conclusions: first, Tauseef has a reason to be different, and his strong preference for higher education in a more challenging setting needed to be strongly supported; second, the family decision pertaining to residency in Biesh Moisher Bari was so strong, valued, and respected that it would be futile to raise this issue with anyone. She decided to pursue the first one without atrophying anytime.

To be sure about her conclusions, Qulsum decided to consult Pori Khala, who agreed with Qulsum's position after being apprised of Tauseef's inner feelings and approach to life. Both agreed to have a sustained but very delicate initiation of the process without, in any way, hardening the known stance of Hashi Banu. It was also agreed that Qulsum would try to gradually align Tanveer's thinking into supporting Tauseef's higher education in Dhaka, more so as he had done extremely well in his HSC examination. That was pursued as planned.

Hashi Banu, though mellowed down from her previous firm position, was still dithering in indicating an affirmative decision. As time was running out, Qulsum became very twitchy. For the first time in her four years of married life, Qulsum broke away from traditional behavior pattern and took the atypical step of not only making her points but more significantly asserting their relevance. It was not that she planned it that way; it was Hashi Banu who raised the issue of Tauseef's studies when Qulsum went to serve her mother-in-law her ritual late morning tea. Expressing her persistent concern on the issue of his departure, she wanted to have Qulsum's shoulder.

Without looking at Qulsum, she moaned, "Tauseef has no interest in the values and acts that made this house what it is today. Once gone to Dhaka, I might lose my son."

Contrary to the prevalent practice of keeping one's head down in listening to what a mother-in-law has to say, Qulsum had a direct look at Hashi Banu and said, "Amma, in the absence of Abba, you are the guardian of the family. I understand your concern and fully align with what you have in mind. We, however, need to see things from a larger stance. Because of family decisions made five generations back, Tauseef is to leave this house today or tomorrow. I know from discussions with Tauseef that the eventuality disturbs him persistently. It is one reason that he is so aloof from everything pertinent to Biesh Moisher Bari. If he leaves this house with that mind-set, social crosiers will easily take full advantage of the situation and help create unnecessary misunderstandings between the two brothers, and that may as well result in the division of business and properties, to the great dismay of all of us, and unwanted detriment in the good standing for which Biesh Moisher Bari is so famous for generations."

Hashi Banu had developed the habit of having a *paan* after her late morning tea. Since Qulsum did not return after serving tea and was still in her room, Pori entered with *paan* for her Hashi-bu (sister). With a wink by Hashi Banu, Pori quietly took a seat near her bed and listened to what Qulsum was detailing. What she said caused Hashi Banu's open-mouthed apprehension.

Qulsum reasoned, "The social setting has undergone immitigable changes in the recent past, shredding all past values with which you are familiar. Just think of the recent happenings related to our business. So-called well-wishers of family and friends of Abba [Father] gave all sorts of wrong advice to Tanveer, veering our business soon after he took over. It was good that Logic Sir came and Tanveer listened to what he and I had to say. In essence, one can't trust any other person anymore. Though I am new in this house, I have had more interactions with Tauseef than any other. I have discovered in him a gem, contrary to perception otherwise. His eventual leaving of this house does bother him, but it does not shadow his feelings and love for you and Tanveer. He even told me that he would, without any qualification, repose his trust in his brother and would never question his decisions, even in the case of adverse consequences."

Pori interjected by saying, "Hashi-bu, what I am going to say may sound condescending to you, but I must be honest with you. I am an illiterate person whose life and living have been orchestrated by your love and generosity and the care of Kazi Bhai. I can't wish anything but for the good of the family. It is a question of time for when Tauseef will leave this house. In that situation, it is inconsequential whether he is located in the next settlement or any other place, near or far from Biesh Moisher Bari. The fact is that he will be away from here, so let it be now as he prefers. That will ensure amity in sibling relations. In my humble opinion, what Bo-ma [daughter-in-law] Qulsum is saying makes a lot of sense but, of course, is up to you to decide."

Hashi Banu slowly retreated from her earlier firm position. With precautious and persuasive follow-ups by Qulsum and Pori, she thoughtfully avoided any churlish response and did not demur their points. In her consideration, she consciously did not resort to any thwart and just remained unobtrusive with an apparent focus on the logic made by the two. The obsequious muteness was both onerous and strenuous for Qulsum. Her thoughtful mind concluded it would be inept trying to pepper any more on the subject. She exchanged looks with Pori Khala, and they both stood up to leave the room.

As they were about to step out, Hashi Banu called them back and said, "I have given due thought to the points that both of you alluded to earlier. I am willing to let Tauseef pursue his life as he wants to, but one concern continues to engulf me. Am I going to lose my son by allowing him to go to Dhaka for higher studies? Keeping in view his disposition and demeanor, am I going to commit a gaffe? I have my qualms about whether he will keep a link at all with Biesh Moisher Bari in the future."

Qulsum and Pori were delighted to take note of her changed mind-set. Qulsum promptly said, "Your affirmative decision is the best one under the given circumstances, but your concern about his keeping a link with Biesh Moisher Bari is valid. I suggest that while conveying your decision, you should predicate that, imploring a firm promise from Tauseef to keep link with his roots, irrespective of his future position and residency."

That made Hashi Banu happy. She felt relieved of a huge emotional burden and blessed Qulsum profusely for facilitating it. Pori expressed her happiness by nodding. Qulsum and Pori left the room merrily, feeling gratified.

Pori had no premonition of what was awaiting her. Though she wondered about the reason for Qulsum's sizzling smile and bubbling physical gesticulation since leaving Hashi Banu's room, Pori kept the usual distance both in physical proximity and in conversation, being conscious of her standing in the family and assigned role. Nevertheless, she could not hide her obfuscating feeling in finding rationale for Qulsum's impulsive comportment. Pori was taken aback when Qulsum, contrary to past norms of interactions, came close to her and stood face-to-face and suddenly hugged her with ubiquitous happiness. Pori was evidently happy with such a flaunt of happiness but remained leery about the spasms. She was certain that Hashi-bu's affirmative decision concerning Tauseef could not be the only cause but opted to keep quiet while cuddling.

Slowly unraveling, Qulsum said, "Pori Khala, I am happy for finally getting Amma in line with us on the issue of Tauseef, but I have other news to share. It was my thought that I would do so while serving late morning tea to Amma, but as she raised the issue of Tauseef, I could not tell her. I just can't hold it within myself anymore and would like to tell you."

Having no clue whatsoever, Pori was in a state of bafflement. She held the hand of Qulsum and lovingly conducted her to the kitchen—her world and domain. Giving Qulsum a *mora*, she looked at her with all adulation and requested her to sit. Still wearing a penumbra of doubt, Pori focused herself toward Qulsum without any words.

Qulsum steadily opened up. "Pori Khala, for the last few days, I have had a scratchy feeling within me, something similar to the early days of my pregnancy with Tauheed. With my normal appetite for food slowly withering away, I have a craving for sour foods. Now I have missed two monthly period cycles. This morning, I had a bout of trivial vomiting too. I think I am pregnant again."

Pori could not control herself and was about to react, but Qulsum stopped her by saying, "No one except you knows about it. I would much prefer to tell Amma and Tanveer more or less at the same time. Or Amma may take it otherwise as normally, widows are extra-sensitive to protocol, order, and respect in dealing with or handling family matters. My unbounded happiness could easily be blemished. Not only that, but my telling you first before Amma may be wrongly construed, impacting on your long-standing relationship with her."

Both of them decided that the best course would be to take advantage of the usual post-dinner chat time of the family. During that chat, Qulsum would raise the issue of Tauseef's going to Dhaka for higher studies. As Amma would convey her consent, everyone would be happy. That happy setting would be the most apposite moment to divulge the news of the pregnancy and make all present euphoric.

Qulsum did the spadework. She met Tauseef and indicated to him about the likely positive outcome for his studies in Dhaka. When Tanveer came back home from his daylong commitments, she likewise shared Amma's agreement allowing Tauseef to go for higher studies. About the pregnancy, she was not specific but left sufficient indications, like not having appetite and the feeling of needing to snooze at odd times.

Qulsum said, "Since Mother has consented to allow Tauseef to go to Dhaka and let everyone know about it, Pori Khala made some special food for tonight's dinner. I would like you to ask Badsha Chacha to join the family dinner."

Tanveer easily agreed. Pori entered with *paan* for Hashi Banu and hot tea for Tanveer, a post-dinner ritual she meticulously performed. Tanveer asked her to have a seat too. On specific inquisition by Qulsum about Tauseef's future plans, considering the time constraint, Hashi Banu gladly indicated her consent, allowing him to go to Dhaka in pursuit of his life's ambition, but expressed specific yearning to have a firm commitment from him to maintain links with his roots under all circumstances. Everyone was happy but remained equally uncertain about the response.

Tauseef was both relieved and exultant. He did not take the time to respond to Mother's specific precondition. In his unusual detailed response, he not only explicitly dealt with that stipulation but also touched base with other probable and related matters— to the surprise of all except Qulsum. He unhesitatingly indicated his position, saying, "I give you my most solemn commitment that wherever I may be and whatever my profession, I will always maintain links with my roots. Neither you nor, for that matter, anyone of Biesh Moisher Bari should have any doubt about that. But please bear in mind that the nature of that might have variances. I have full trust in Bhaiya [Brother] in managing the affairs of our family, business, and related social standing. My association with Biesh Moisher Bari may not always follow the traditional route, but my commitment will remain unabated. I will always be proud of being a son of this house and will do whatever needed to enhance the name and prestige of our home. Please have your blessings with me."

Saying those few words, Tauseef stood up, went near Mother, and touched her feet (the Bangladeshi Muslim way of performing *salaam*, expressing gratitude and/or seeking blessings from a senior and dear one). All were astounded except Qulsum, who had better communication with and appreciation of Tauseef.

In that setting, even Qulsum was taken aback when Tauseef, returning to his original position, resumed his unfinished statement by saying, "I take this opportunity to make another point clear to all and for all time. I know that I do not have any right on this homestead but have proportionate share, along with Bhaiya and our sisters, in the properties and other assets left by our father as per Muslim law of inheritance. So far as my share is concerned, I give Bhaiya irrevocable right and authority to manage and use them as per the family's need and his acumen. I will never question his decisions or actions, even if, God forbid, things do not work out as perceived. There will never be any need to keep me informed or get my consent. The presence of Qulsum Bhabi [sister-in-law] in our house, which is her own house now, makes me doubly sure that Bhaiya will always act judiciously. As you all know, I am not an acquisitive type, both by nature and choice. Thus, what I stipulated earlier is the final position, and there is no room for any discussion on this."

Saying those words, Tauseef was about to leave the assemblage when Tanveer drew his attention, saying, "I have something to say. I am thankful for what Tauseef has indicated. My love for him needs no reiteration. I would like to reassure him that I will do everything and support him in every way to fulfill his journey through life. I have promised it at Father's deathbed. I will do that, irrespective of any constraint."

Hashi Banu was pleased to note that both her sons were on the same page in relation to mutual feeling, care, and trust. She happily exchanged looks with Pori, never thinking of what she was going to be apprised of.

Pori looked at Qulsum with a suggestive smile, and the latter immediately and involuntarily extended her *ghomta* (traditional covering of head by positioning the *anchal* [end-portion of the sari]) on her head. That did not escape the attention of Hashi Banu. Being somewhat amused, she inquired about the reason—if there was one.

Pori took her time and manipulated an insinuating story, not to create any unforeseen misunderstanding, by saying, "During the dinner service tonight, I observed some inconsistency in Qulsum Betty's body language, including a visible mysterious facial expression. What she told me on being questioned is suggestive of good news, and Biesh Moisher Bari should get prepared to welcome a new arrival. There was no time to tell anyone earlier, so I thought this happy setting tonight is the best time to inform everyone about it."

Hashi Banu called Qulsum to her side, hugged her daughter-in-law intensely, and blessed her profusely. Tanveer had his sober reaction in knowing that he was going to be father a second time but refrained from reacting because of the presence of Mother. Tauseef wore an impish smile, waiting for space to tease Qulsum.

Badsha immediately left for the bazaar to get some sweets. Exhilaration was all pervasive. That assemblage ended with all joy and happiness, collectively and individually shared by all in totality. The sweets brought by Badsha added extra flavor to that unqualified happiness.

The following morning, Tanveer, keeping in view Qulsum's suggestion from the night before, discussed their desire to invite all three sisters to be part of the unrestrained joy and happiness that was overpowering the surroundings of the house. Hashi Banu cheerily consented. Letters were promptly dispatched from Tanveer, imploring all three sisters to come visit Apurba Neer with their husbands. A time frame was indicated, keeping in view Tauseef's impending departure for higher studies in Dhaka. The letter was guardedly drafted in not divulging the news of Qulsum's second pregnancy to serve as surprise news and an additional item of happiness, augmenting all pervasive exhilaration.

Events were planned, and actions were being taken to make a wonderful family gathering against the backdrop of the sad demise of Kazi Azmat Ali Shoudagar and the dismay and uncertainty that followed soon thereafter. All the extended family were exuberant. The only exception was Tanveer himself. Some nameless anxiety appeared to cause a sort of pensive reaction in him. This did not escape the attention of Qulsum.

At time opportune, Qulsum raised the issue with Tanveer, whose immediate reaction was a feeble smile without words. She persisted, "I made the query just not being your wife but equally a friend in your life's journey. I do not find any reason for you to be relatively detached from things we are so ardently doing to make the family gathering a joyful one. Why can't you tell me what is bothering you?'"

Tanveer replied, "You did not have opportunity to know much about or interact with my three brothers-in-law. You met them during our wedding but, that was an occasion of joy outshining formalities. The second time that you met them was during the sad demise of Abba [Father], and that was brief as well, in a setting of sadness and grief. All my brothers-in-law are individually very nice people, and they love Tauseef and me very dearly, perhaps because of the age gap. But the relationships among those three are somehow always strained. Each of them is very sensitive to issues like seniority, prestige, and intelligence. That, perhaps, has been aggravated by their pronounced political preferences and affiliations. The eldest brother-in-law aligns himself with the political position that no one is a true Bangladeshi except his party and its members. He is strictly principled and would like to be respected as such. The second brother-in-law believes in Bangladeshi nationalism and in making the nation united and moving that forward. By nature, he is more affable and accommodating in discussions. The youngest brother-in-law is aligned to political philosophy in which state and religion should have a common identity and goal. He is pronouncedly aligned to stipulations and edicts based on *sharia*. They tend to be cordial to one another in brief discussions, but the presence of all three in any gathering invariably sparks heated arguments as Bangladeshis love to divert all social discussions to politics. Because of this, Abba had judiciously worked out an informal protocol for their traditional visits to Apurba Neer and once shared this with me. The eldest sister and her family generally would have their annual visit coinciding with the *nabanna parban* [harvest ritual], commonly taking place on the first day of the Bangla month of Agrahayan [very close to the advent of winter]. My second sister and her family were supposed to visit us coinciding with the beginning of the Bangla New Year [the first month of the Bangla calendar, Boishak, falling between mid-April to mid-May]. My youngest sister and her family's usual visits were always during *Eid-ul-Fitre* [the Muslim religious festival at the end of a month-long fasting]. This is the first time in many years, and that too in the absence of Abba, that all three brothers-in-law will be in Biesh Moisher Bari, not being involved or preoccupied with any event or other commitment. My worry centers on how to keep them apart and avoid any sparking of controversy that can mar the endearing jiffies of this gathering."

Tanveer and Qulsum had in-depth discussions and agreed that Tauseef should be apprised of this predicament, evoking his understanding and support to avoid possible mix-ups. The details of the proposed arrangement were also agreed to. Tanveer was to look after the eldest brother-in-law and take him to the office every day and would gradually share with him his future business plans. This would give the eldest brother-in-law a feeling of comfort as his personal ego would be elevated, sensing Tanveer was looking for his advice. Both of them would spend the rest of the days with selective local gentries and government officials. Tauseef would be looking after the second brother-in-law, taking him to his previous school, showing him various interesting places around Apurba Neer, and spending time in tea shops in the company of friends, ostensibly to introduce his more social brother-in-law. Imam Shaheeb from the mosque would be advised to look after the youngest brother-in-law, keeping him engaged on how the religious base and education could best be made more prevalent and effective against the current slide. With that sort of planning and preparation, the visit of all three sisters was happily undertaken. The news of the second pregnancy of Qulsum added expected hilarity, invoking snapshot side comments from all the brothers-in-law, varying in focus and content. Most of the jokes were from the second brother-in-law, to the amusement of Tauseef.

All preparations were afoot for Tauseef's departure for much-cherished higher studies in the challenging setting of Dhaka. Societal ethos was complied with under the astute planning and guidance of Tanveer. Both he and Badsha Chacha were to accompany Tauseef up to the district headquarters to see him board the train for his maiden journey to Dhaka. Pori Khala was intensely sad, seeing her dearest Hira—Tauseef's nickname, by which she always called him—leaving his hearth for an unknown place and setting. Qulsum, with a baby boy on her lap, was very happy seeing her only *debar* embarking on a journey of life, both unknown and challenging. Her happiness emanated from observing a sense of determination and confidence with which Tauseef was shaping his youth and was certain about its positive outcome with possible variances in shapes and shades.

Tauseef moved forward, took his Tama (the hilarious nickname he jokingly suggested earlier) from Qulsum's lap, lifted and hugged him, and returned him to his mother after bestowing him with loving kisses. After taking leave from all, Tauseef stood face to face with Mother, reassured her about his commitment to maintain links with his roots, and bowed obediently and thankfully to *salaam* Mother. Hashi Banu put her hand on the head of her son, raised him up by tugging his shoulders, and hugged him with unrestrained tears flowing down her cheeks. Tauseef passionately and respectfully wiped those tears with his palms as if he was taking those with him as Mother's blessings.

Circumspection

Concerns premised on the uncertain track of travel he was embarking on motivated Tauseef to prepare himself amply by having peripheral information about the challenges of life and living in Dhaka. But of all that effort and information proved to be derisory. He was not surprised by the gargantuan size of the station per se and the multiplicity of railway tracks and platforms as he stepped on the platform of Kamalapur Railway Station in Dhaka. Tauseef had prior ideas about that from congregated information, but what took him by surprise were the practices and interactive parameters of people around him.

As the train slowly came to a halt on the designated platform, Tauseef quickly stepped out of the compartment with his luggage. In that quick action, he was totally oblivious of scores of red shirt–attired *kuli*s (porters) facing stationary compartments while standing in a horizontal line. Noticing the distance he would have to cover, he made an effort to hire one, but there was no response. All *kuli*s were looking at the stationary compartments, waiting for the call to pick up luggage. After repeated failed attempts, he was told by a sympathetic bystander that *kuli*s were not to pick up luggage from the platform without first serving passengers in side compartments. Tauseef sensed that what he was told by the bystander was something totally different than what he observed in their district town railway station. After waiting for a while, he dragged his luggage, took them outside the platform, and negotiated with a rickshaw puller to take him to Mia's Hotel (something like an inn with minimum facilities) near the old campus of the Dhaka University.

While slouching on a single *choki* (wooden bed) with a hardened thin mattress and equally hard single pillow, after having food consisting of abundant rice and lentil but limited fried vegetables and one piece of fish, Tauseef, for the first time in life, realized and appreciated all that had been bestowed on him without asking and all that he enjoyed in Biesh Moisher Bari. As he had ideas about life in a hostel from reading and other sources, he did not suffer any qualms.

The nonchalant shy young man from Apurba Neer started his following day in an unknown setting but with brimming determination. He walked to the arts campus of Dhaka University, taking the main road and bypassing a number of buildings and other structures. Everything looked to him as being huge, and he started having a feeling of not being ever able to belong to the place.

Things dramatically changed in a short while. Outstanding attainments in his HSC examination made Tauseef a very welcome student in most of the departments he visited. His preferred subject for higher studies was history because of his Biesh Moisher Bari background and exposure. But the chairman of the economics department talked him through, convincing Tauseef to opt for economics as his chosen subject for higher studies. The chairman emphasized that the study of economics by a good student like Tauseef would make him more meaningful in the emerging surroundings, particularly because of emerging globalization. Tauseef's conviction was without any disinclination, but he felt that having an opportunity to share that with someone knowledgeable, prior to taking the decision, would have given him needed comfort.

That realization implausibly made him confront another veracity of life that he had charted to pursue. Being the subject of a setting devoid of family elders and known social elites, Tauseef unequivocally realized that it was he who would possibly have the distinction of deciding many aspects of his life and pursuits all by himself and consequently would have only himself to blame for any unforeseen shortcomings. That cognizance itself reticulated his thinking, making him aware of the responsibility and consequences of present and all future decisions pertaining to his life. Tauseef geared himself accordingly but did not fail to inform Tanveer about the change in the focus of his future study. That made everyone of Biesh Moisher Bari happy.

Tauseef had other reasons to be happy. His hassle-free admission to the economics department, getting a seat in his choice of residential halls, and prompt familiarization with the surroundings made him exultant. He was not only delighted to realize that the path from his temporary place at Mia's Hotel to the university arts campus and vice versa became very familiar, but he also came to know swiftly and intimately the surrounding buildings and structures.

The time came for Tauseef, like many others, to move to the residential hall of admission. Residency in a student's dorm has all along been a requirement as Dhaka University was established as a residential one. Though some relaxation was made in the years to follow, a student has all along been primarily identified with reference to a hall, either as a resident or attached. Moving into the hall of residency had all the match and mix of happiness. But for some strange reasons beyond comprehension, Tauseef, for the first time, felt a sense of anguish in leaving the very mundane Mia's Hotel and its tiny *choki*, hard thin mattress, and equally hard pillow besides the rationed service of fried vegetables and principal curry items of the day. Tauseef did not fail to question himself about such an odd but strange reaction within. He recalled that he did not have that sort of feeling even when he left Biesh Moisher Bari for Dhaka—a separation from his roots, which had all the possibilities of being a protracted one. Subsequent thinking resuscitated a distinct element of acquiescence in his thoughts. A sense of genuine harmony totally divorced from a condescending attitude and an approach of slavish mind-set made Mia's Hotel a home away from home for ordinary guests. Congenital politesse demonstrated by all concerned involved in managing and running the small hotel naturally stoked the feeling of comfort and strengthened the bond between the hotel and its ordinary guests, notwithstanding apparent shortcomings. That was something that had a deep mark in Tauseef's mind during his short stay and accentuated as the time for parting drew close. He realized that genuineness, even in a setting of simplicity, could propel love and sympathy, earning the trust and confidence of people. Even in the situation with a lack of many amenities, Mia's Hotel amply demonstrated that a spectacle of simplicity could as well be spectacular, provided one has relevant attributes. That feeling and realization gained during his brief stay in Mia's Hotel guided Tauseef through the subsequent journey of life.

As the medium-built simple young man from Apurba Neer, clad in ordinary pajamas and a full-sleeved top shirt, stepped into his room of future residence along with an accompanying suitcase and other luggage, he was warmly welcomed by a two-year senior fellow roommate. Tauseef was not surprised as he had prior indication that as a freshman and most of the time thereafter, he would have to share his room with three others. The senior student first inquired about Tauseef's roots and his chosen field of study and then, exceeding all congeniality, swamped him with all sorts of information and advice directly and remotely related to living in the hall.

He started by saying, "My name is Afzal, and I am a third-year honors student of general history. The other roommate is Zahoor, also a third-year honors student of political science. You are our new first-year honors in economics roommate. Even if we do not know as yet about the fourth one, there is no doubt that having students of history, political science, and economics in one room by itself is a very exciting setting."

After exchanging looks with Tauseef, the senior roommate Afzal resumed his monologue, stating, "Since we are your seniors—and following common practice—you can address us as brothers, and we too will treat you like a younger brother. This bond among us as roommates is very important since each of us is here all alone and far away from family support. We are to look after one another in both good and challenging times."

Afzal then shared some information about the hall, its facilities, and related practices. He said, "Each hall of the university is administered by a provost. For ease of management, each hall is generally divided into two houses, supervised by separate house tutors. The dining hall has an informal layout, separating food service arrangements for the two houses. The hall contracts our breakfast and afternoon tea services but in the space provided. Similar is the arrangement for laundry services. The common room facility provides newspapers and radio and television facilities, a number of tables for playing ping-pong and carom boards [a "strike and pocket" table game originated in the East], besides having lawn tennis courts."

The other roommate, Zahoor, stepped in as Afzal was finishing his statement. With the introductions over, at the behest of Zahoor, all the roommates went to the hall canteen to have tea. To his glee, Tauseef observed a startling semblance in the food service patterns and practices as he had experienced in Mia's Hotel.

Tauseef's induction to hall life and, for that matter, his university education pursuit got a smooth start with the intermittent guidance from the chairman of his department and the precipitate and unreserved succor and care of both Afzal and Zahoor. Tauseef evidently was happy, but that happiness was all-pervading around Biesh Moisher Bari after the contents of his latest letter were known to all. Hashi Banu was happy, even though the letter was written to Qulsum. Pori, upon returning home, performed four *rakat*s (*cycles*) of *nafal namaj* (additional prayers), thanking Allahpak (the Divine) for taking care of her dear Hira.

The happiness, however, was not an all-permeating one. It had its accompanying curmudgeon, with posits of more consternation than grievance. A specific incident that took place in the first tutorial class of an honors study paper on economics theory had a deep mark on the ingenuous mind of Tauseef. That incident was premised, pure and simple, on an oblique association with unalloyed fun. All present enjoyed the moment and moved on, but that was difficult for Tauseef. He had no time to understand and absorb the urban panoply of comedy. The embarrassment that tingled him in the first tutorial class, due sheerly to his rural simplicity, had an indelible mark on Tauseef's behavior pattern and interactions with fellow students, particularly the girl student who was the focus of that hilarious incident.

The honors classes of most liberal disciplines are divided into smaller groups of students to constitute tutorial classes with provision for more intense study, undertaking periodical tests and assigning marks in addition to the normal class for each of the eight papers of study during academic evaluation. As the professor was having introductory exchanges—and perhaps more to create an ambiance of informality—he suddenly wanted to know whether most or any of the students had nicknames. The genuineness embedded in the rural upbringing impelled Tauseef to stand up and let everyone know that his nickname was Hira (diamond). Tauseef's unpretentious background was evident from his outfit of a simple top shirt and pajamas, contrary to the more smart and modern dress-up of other students. Of the three girl students of that tutorial class, one was fairly tall with long straight hair and a very desirable light complexion. Other attributes of her persona were very attractive physical features, perceptible expressive eyes, an ability to hold an alluring smile, and candor with social skills. That made her a point of attention and attraction to many. Most students, except Tauseef, made attempts to be friendly with her. He had noted her presence in the class. Something attracted him to her, but his own personality trait of being standoffish and congenitally reclusive precluded any attempt to say a simple hello to the most attractive, smart, and confident fellow classmate, even though she was very open-minded and approachable. He could not even have eye contact with her on the previous few occasions when they crossed each other's pathways. Every time such an incident happened, Tauseef promised to himself not to repeat it, but it was invariably replicated.

The rest of the class was in a quiet mode. The professor once again followed his question by stating, "We have a Hira [diamond] in this class. Are there no other gems in the class?"

Tauseef committed the unintended gaffe by confirming that his elder brother's nickname was Manik (gem). The whole class had a gaudy laugh, to his embarrassment. The gregarious fellow girl classmate turned toward Tauseef, gaped at him, confidently stood up, and informed the class that her nickname was Mukhta (pearl).

The professor chuckled and said, "So what a nice class we have! Both Hira [diamond] and Mukhta [pearl] are physically present in this class, while having a close connect with Manik [gem]. What else we can hope for? Let us now start our class with the aim of attaining outcomes matching those."

That was the first time Tauseef had his first direct eye contact with the girl, who, for indeterminate reasons, engulfed most of his current thoughts, causing an unintended predicament within. He harbored all keenness to be close to this specific girl classmate, but his confidence was always battered by a fear of uncertainty. Such emotive backlash minimalized over time because of frequent study related exchanges, particularly in the tutorial class. Tauseef was very happy with each such exchange but could never convey his sense of glee. He gradually came to know that her name was Chandni (moonlight). Some of his other classmates later told Tauseef that her saying that she too had a nickname was a response to the predominant and rueful, gaudy laugh of the class. Tauseef neither tried to reconfirm the fact nor could express his gratitude to Chandni. He was contended within himself.

That was somewhat different in the case of Chandni. Her standing up with the concocted nickname of Mukhta was a response to the frolicsome reaction of the class, to what was irrefutably an unpretentious statement of fact. Growing-up predicaments, challenges, and gravities embedded within shaped up her persona with an urge to stand up for any just case or cause she had an affinity with or believed in. It was one such reaction at that moment, without expecting any kudos or thanks.

Initially, Tauseef was a loner both in his general and tutorial classes. Being unfamiliar to almost all the class and unaccustomed to relative social etiquettes, he was not easy, even with himself. His dressing up in ordinary shirts and pajamas was an obvious handicap and an inadvertent limitation in cultivating needed contacts.

As time passed, the ordinarily dressed simple class fellow from an unpretentious rural setting started making his marks, especially in tutorial classes. Tauseef's comprehension of fundamentals of economic theory, his discerning ability to generate queries relevant to on-the-ground predicaments, and his thought-provoking articulations impressed his professor and fellow students. The tutorial professor even reported to the chairman of the department about Tauseef's academic attributes. That resulted in more frequent meetings with the chairman, boosting his morale and confidence level.

There was a congenial change in attitude and approach of fellow students, and Chandni was no exception. Tauseef took that easily. He liked the occasional interactions with her, for whom he naively developed a fondness. Those exchanges were always brief and specific-issue related as Tauseef always suffered from some unsigned hesitations. Another specificity of her persona was beyond his comprehension, triggering shielded misgivings. Her guilelessness and congeniality in interactions with a varied spectrum of students, irrespective of subjects and years of study, were both conspicuous and universal. That caused an element of disquiet in Tauseef's thinking but did not unnerve him. What dampened him was her visible propensity to pass on the signal of allurement to all she came across. Her physical attractiveness, pleasant personality, and smart assertion in varied types of social interactions cut a deep mark on the minds of many. Tauseef concluded that she was someone quite different from most he knew and that she had no special feelings imbued to her words and actions. While Tauseef charted his way forward without being bothered by thoughts concerning Chandni, he just could not wipe her off from his occasional contemplations.

His initial settlement process progressed satisfactorily with periodic glitches, some being addressed by the passage of time and others unraveled by his own decisions and actions. One of the latter groups related to his switchover to trousers and dress shirts as daily wears. That soundly facilitated his total amalgam with the larger student community as being one of them. With happiness imbibed in his words and expressions, Tauseef had a pleasant visit to Biesh Moisher Bari during the first winter break.

The surrounding academic equations, however, started getting deranged soon thereafter. Social discontents emanated from concerns focusing on the autocratic rule of many years started stoking student body politics. The decisions of and actions by student entities gradually realigned to a greater demand for the resignation of the autocratic ruler. The management and control of student politics moved out of campus, and future protests and agitations were tailored to the primary objective of ensuring early abdication by the autocratic ruler instead of academic issues, which caused the movement to start with.

Tauseef initially enjoyed the palate of protests and sporadic strikes. Consistent with his own personality traits, he started to have a vibrant feeling about social and political awareness in a setting of pure academic pursuits. Tauseef quickly established an analogous association of his mute protests with the many values and practices of Biesh Moisher Bari and the framework of ongoing student protests. He was happy to be in an environment where there was scope for expressing a dissenting voice.

The happiness soon became an issue of concern and anxiety for many. The ongoing protests and strikes took an obdurate stance with each unbending decision of the government. Spasmodic strikes took the turn of unremitting adverse impact on planned academic pursuits. To begin with, it affected a few classes, and then it was days and months with no resolution on sight.

Spending a few days with a mixed feeling of uncertainty, excitement, and challenge, Tauseef's quixotic mind refocused on the winnowing of options and concluded there was no easy and singular way to leapfrog over it. His frustration and anxiety took him back to Biesh Moisher Bari instead of idling time in Dhaka with no immediate purpose. He went home after borrowing a number of books on economics and social sciences from the library.

In the midst of reading those books, Tauseef took out time to have friendly colloquies with his dear Bhabi (Qulsum). While most such discussions focused on family- and neighborhood-related matters of common interests, Tauseef, being impelled by his robust affinity for Chandni, could not help but open up to Qulsum. He enjoyed every bit of Qulsum's banter, in spite of his forceful denial of having any inkling of a veiled feeling for Chandni. The discussions would mostly rest at that stage, with one common feature: a request to

Qulsum to keep the matter private. Qulsum would wear a mischievous smile and nod gently.

During one such discourse, Qulsum left her room to fetch a cup of tea for Tauseef, a taste he developed since his stay in Mia's Hotel. Seated on one of the two chairs kept by the side of the reading table, Tauseef started leisurely glancing through some publications on the table. As he was casually shuffling those, a full-page advertisement of a private university drew his attention. Among many highlights contained in that advertisement, two drew his attention: forbidding student politics and strikes and the additional assurance of completing the course within the time and cost estimate. That ordinary advertisement caused an unexpected one-hundred-eighty-degree twist in Tauseef's thinking. He was wondering why the option of studying in a private university did not embrace his thinking, more so when certainty in public university education was increasingly becoming a hostage of larger political decisions and actions. Engrossed in resultant thoughts and conscious of possibilities to get out of the current quagmire impairing his academic pursuit, Tauseef got lost within himself and did not even recognize the stepping in by Qulsum.

Placing the teacup on the table, Qulsum did not miss the chance to tease Tauseef, saying, "My *debar* [brother-in-law] is so mesmerized by his faraway lady classmate that my presence is of no relevance to him anymore."

Tauseef looked at Qulsum, held her wrist, and requested her to sit on the other chair. Their relationship had been congenial, premised on unqualified politesse. The sudden holding of her hand by him had no repercussions within, even though she liked the unexpected touch.

Taking the seat on the other chair, Qulsum stated, "Now tell me what you want. Should I talk to your *bhaiya* [elder brother] about that girl?"

Tauseef was quiet and then slowly responded, "Bhabi, perhaps you do not have, as yet, a comprehensive understanding of who I am or the characteristics that make what I am. Yes, I like the girl, but that is just so. If that liking stands in my way of achieving the larger objectives of life that I have in mind, then I will not hesitate to bypass that emotional feeling. Maybe I will repent in subsequent life, but for the present, my reactions and options will always be clear and focused. It is not that girl issue I want to talk to you about. I need your candid views on something that dawned on me during your brief absence just now."

Saying those words, Tauseef placed the magazine in front of Qulsum, drawing her attention to the advertisement. She had an in-depth look at the advertisement and did not notice anything bizarre. It was just like many other advertisements she had encountered whenever she opened up any periodical. Being unsure about what Tauseef was aiming at, Qulsum shot a look at him, conveying an abstruse reaction without any words.

Tauseef got the message and said, "Bhabi, what is an ordinary piece of dreary advertisement to you is in fact of special significance to me, particularly in the situation I am in. I only wonder why the message contained in the advertisement did not come to my mind earlier."

It was still difficult for Qulsum to comprehend what Tauseef had in mind. She continued to wear a queasy posture. Tauseef resumed, saying, "You see, I am in a most unpredictable situation at this moment concerning my study focus and future plans. The academic environment of my university is overtly susceptible to broader and equally capricious political scheming. Things are absolutely uncertain. Session gridlock is a major problem presently. Current indefinite strike would worsen the situation. While uncertainty hinges on the completion of my study, it is most certain that both time and eventual costs would escalate disproportionately. Contrarily, possible study in a private university would ensure the timely completion of study, though immediate costs would be high. That is my predicament since reading that advertisement. I am hesitant to raise this issue with my brother at this stage. I just do not know what to do. That is the reason I tried to draw your attention to the advertisement."

Qulsum stepped out ostensibly to reheat the tea she brought earlier but more truly to have some space of time to think through her possible response to Tauseef's dilemma. On her return, she placed the hot cup of tea on the table, imploring him to finish it before it got cold again and then said, "As the taste of the tea is palpable when it is hot, so the solution of any problem is more apposite when the same is identified instead of when it has intensified. There is no gainsaying in alluding to my experience and exposure. But as I could read your mind and your concern, I get that your preferred option is to switch from Dhaka University to a private university, but the immediate pressure pertaining to financing drove the choice outright. It is also right that neither the problem you have will be resolved in a short time nor will there be any preternatural intervention. Instead of being ambivalent, causing irresolution, let us have unequivocal clarity in fathoming the options and move forward based on best judgment. It would be unwise to treat the extant position as something calamitous. In the long journey of life, our ability to handle it prudently will shape our path. Considering that, it is my suggestion that before you articulate your position and discuss it with your *bhaiya*, you should go to Dhaka and visit some private universities and assess their respective standings and costs. You may like to have additional discussions with your teachers and well-wishers. That will give you some clarity and certainty concerning the option you have in mind. In the meantime, I will do everything I can to ensure all initiatives to steadily bring your apprehension to your *bhaiya*'s attention so that he is not taken by surprise when you raise the issue with him, as well as the relative analysis of cost and time in line with what we discussed, and prepare him mentally to be responsive favorably."

That made Tauseef very happy. As he was unleashing his impulsive words of thanks, Qulsum stopped him by saying, "Do not blame me later on for encouraging you to opt for private university education. That evidently signifies your physical separation with Chandni, possibly your first love. That may haunt you for a long time."

Tauseef sported a thin smile and replied, "I am more focused on my long-term objectives of life. The separation you alluded to is perhaps the price I will pay, but that may not have any effect on her. By nature, she is friendly with all, a feature of her trait that often sends wrong signals. She may not even notice my eventual absence, but I will always ruminate her."

Actions and decisions were taken, primarily consistent with broader understandings between *debar* (brother-in-law) and *bhabi* (sister-in-law). Once the decision was taken, Tauseef moved to the most reputable private university of the time and finished his local academic pursuits with distinction and as scheduled. The cost was much higher, but Tauseef had the satisfaction of being on his own.

Soon after the result of his master's degree was out, Tauseef got an offer to work as a research fellow in one of the top research organizations in the country, funded and run privately. The specialization was in areas of poverty, income inequality, and gender disparity, the same areas of Tauseef's academic focus and future interests. He kept the family informed after joining the research organization.

Tanveer expressed his discontent to Qulsum as he wanted Tauseef to compete in a civil services examination for a well-recognized job in the government. It was his view that had he consulted him, he would have suggested so. That would have considerably enhanced the image and influence of Biesh Moisher Bari, a very treasured focus for generations.

Qulsum had no qualms with what her husband said but had to keep a window open to leave way for Tauseef's desires. Agreeing with Tanveer, Qulsum quietly said, "Tauseef has grown up with a different mind-set. He is a mature person now and is competent enough to make decisions about his own life. Possibly by doing things differently, he will enhance the name and fame of Biesh Moisher Bari in a way quite unlike what we have in mind."

That dialogue between Tanveer and Qulsum did not proceed further. Their occasional discourse with matters related to Tauseef was curbed to one agenda item: his getting married soon. In one of such discussions, Tanveer said, "My reason for his joining the government service was predicated with paramount emphasis on the discipline that routinely is related to that sort of engagement. I very much wanted him to be like many others in that profession. Now you see, he is getting involved in all mundane matters like poverty, gender disparity, and economic inequality. These have no focus in terms of life's direction, and thus, I am worried."

After a few months, Tanveer returned home one day in a very happy mood, holding an English publication in his hand. He called Qulsum immediately and proudly displayed Tauseef's first published article with his photograph and brief introduction, which mentioned both Apurba Neer and Biesh Moisher Bari.

Qulsum gleefully took that to Hashi Banu and repeated all that Tanveer said to her earlier. Hashi Banu expressed happiness by raising her two hands in a way Muslims generally perform *munajat* (denotes a particular informal way of asking something from Allahpak [the Divine] or thanking Him profoundly for anything bestowed).

Qulsum then rushed to the kitchen to show the publication to Pori Khala. Her spontaneous response bemused Qulsum intensely. When Qulsum finished her excited statement, repeating what Tanveer said, Pori Khala tenderly touched the magazine and asked Qulsum if she could have it for a while.

Qulsum gladly consented but equally wondered what Pori Khala would do with it as she did not know how to read. As the magazine changed hands, Pori started flipping through the pages with utmost passion. When she reached the page that contained the photograph of Tauseef, Pori lifted the opened magazine with all her passion, held it close to her chest for a while, and kissed the photograph of her dear Hira episodically. No one was particularly present to assess the inert feelings of illiterate Pori, but her exuberance took aback Badsha when they had the discussion with respect to the magazine.

Pori repeated her old statement, saying, "You will see one day my dear Hira will be known across the board, enhancing the name and fame of Biesh Moisher Bari."

Pori's aforesaid avowal was not something just wishful. It soon became a periodical practice for Tanveer to bring home English magazines containing articles written by Tauseef. The general interest was limited to opening and seeing Tauseef's photograph and simultaneously feeling proud of his accomplishments.

The only exception was Qulsum, with disappointing glances because of language limitations and her unfamiliarity with the subject matters. The magazines that Qulsum had access to hardly dealt with topics like gender discrimination, income inequality, or poverty. She lacked the necessary orientation and understanding, and it became a cause of overwhelming consternation. That was aggravated with marked changes in Tanveer's personality over the years. Qulsum acquiescently and gleefully reconciled with Tanveer's taking full responsibility of the traditional family and its engrossed business challenges coinciding with the demise of father, but she never thought it would the harbinger of the process of a change in which she would lose her young and vibrant husband.

Tanveer's initial handling of business challenges and the onerous decisions related to them elevated his status much above his age and standing. That brought him into routine contact with a somewhat elderly segment of the society's gentry. His easy access to and frequent interactions with government functionaries made him more preeminent. That increasingly made Tanveer more involved in social organizations and work. In doing all these, he scrupulously avoided involvement in any political party or group. That enhanced his image and status.

Everyone at Biesh Moisher Bari and others connected with it were very happy with Tanveer's success. Badsha, who never did miss opportunities to convey infinitesimal elements of success stories to Hashi Banu through Pori, was ecstatic. Hashi Banu always expressed her happiness and merrily started enjoying the success of her son with usual lamenting for Kazi Azmat Ali, a standard process for her sharing happiness.

A tired and exhausted Tanveer would return home most evenings wearing a staid bearing. Life for Qulsum slowly was taking a different direction. She started observing behavioral changes in Tanveer. An earlier time, simple talk on ordinary issues, frequent discussions on magazines she read, and matters highlighting waggishness and glee were no more the norm. He was not even regular in inquiring about their son Tauheed and daughter Malvina unless the issues were raised by Qulsum.

There was an exception in the midst of such milieu. Tanveer, to the surprise of all, ecstatically returned home one early afternoon and stridently called for Qulsum. As she approached, Tanveer joyously grabbed her hand and went to his mother's room.

His mother and wife were dazed by his demeanor. As an immediate and undefined reaction, Hashi Banu unbent herself from an afternoon nap posture, put a pillow on her lap, and straightened her *anchal* as a prelude to cover her head, according to the Muslim practice of observing modesty.

Tanveer saw Qulsum at the lower end of Mother's bed and positioned his chair in between mother and wife. He then weirdly picked up Hashi Banu's glass of water and gulped the whole thing down. After performing all these histrionics, Tanveer eventually opened up, saying, "We have very good news. I just received a letter from Tauseef informing that he got a scholarship to undertake his PhD [an academic endeavor focusing on further higher-level study] in one of the reputable universities of the USA. The funding is a mix of financial assistance and job opportunities to sustain his education for about four years."

Noting that both Mother and Qulsum were unable to digest the entirety of the good news, Tanveer went on clarifying that a PhD program stood for a doctorate program, which bestowed a particular discipline-oriented academic authority on an individual. It testified an individual's competence and authority to take lead in those areas of learning, research, and development. Being sure of conveying the essence of the good news to both Mother and Qulsum, Tanveer continued, saying, "Tauseef also wrote that he will have to leave for the USA in about two months and, thus, is presently busy in complying with requirements. Within that busy schedule, he will be coming next month to meet all of us for a few days and will communicate about the visit as soon the schedule is finalized."

Both Hashi Banu and Qulsum were exuberant on hearing the good news. Their full understanding of the opportunity triggered a sense of happiness far outweighing their respective sense of relief from the earlier concerns about Tanveer's actions. Many anomalous thoughts and spiteful apprehensions fraught both all through until Tanveer narrated the details. Those details had an immediate upbeat impact on both, but the essence of that remained somewhat vague in terms of implications. Tanveer could note that from their physical expressions. He tried to clarify, "PhD is the highest level of educational attainments, and only very few talented people get that chance. Tauseef has been chosen to be one of them, with financing and related opportunities. Once completed, he will be the first PhD holder in this region, and the name and fame of Biesh Moisher Bari will dazzle everyone downright. Simultaneously, we should be thankful to Qulsum. It was her persuasion and rationale that enabled Tauseef to undertake studies of his choice and pursue his life as he had in mind."

Hashi Banu readily agreed. Just before ending that meeting, Tanveer sought her blessings for a proposition he had in mind. He said that he would like to organize a big *jayafat* on the occasion of Tauseef's departure for the USA and would like to invite the elites of the locality besides community members. Hashi Banu agreed, and Qulsum was giggling, trying to maintain due propriety. She was so very proud of her dear husband.

Things were planned, and actions were taken for Tauseef's visit to Apurba Neer and his travel to the USA for higher studies. Everyone who was someone in the locality was invited to the party.

Even Bakshi Mia, the traditional matchmaker, was present. He was feeling very uneasy as he had an increased feeling of losing a prospective prized groom.

The family's happiness was overpowering. Hashi Banu, to the surprise of all, was more preoccupied in learning from Tauseef the duration of travel, where and how he would have food during the travel, and the arrangements for boarding in the place he was going to. Pori kept herself absorbed in making food items liked by her dear Hira. Qulsum was busy taking care of her two visiting sisters-in-law and some of their children. None of the brothers-in-law could make it because of short notice, and the other sister was unable because of a sad death in her extended family. Tanveer was proudly engrossed in making the arrangements for Tauseef's comfort and enjoyment at the *jayafat*. Unfailing Badsha Chacha was, as usual, the front person for executing all his decisions.

While playing with the new toddler niece Malvina and favorite nephew Tauheed, Tauseef drew the attention of Qulsum and flippantly but profoundly advised her not to follow the footsteps of her mother-in-law in getting pregnant too often.

Tauseef's suggestion was consistent with what Qulsum had in mind, with the informal indulgence from Tanveer, but she prosaically reacted casually, saying "Why you are advising me? Go and tell your *bhaiya*. In any case, we are not going to bother you about naming them if and when we have them."

Tauseef was taken aback by such a terse response. She took note of his immediate reactions, and to make things easy, Qulsum clarified, "Thanks for your suggestion. We have that in mind. Your brother also wants that. I was just joking with you."

As the setting of the discourse reverted to their traditional friendly tone, Qulsum inquired, "You will be away for many years. What will happen to our loving Chandni?"

That was a matter of inner anguish to Tauseef. Being focused on his own priorities, he unwillingly had abated contact with friends from his previous academic institution and, in the process, lost updated information about Chandni. Tauseef thought about her many times. Her very outgoing personal traits and sort of inkling, creating hopes and frustrations among many, did not encourage him to pursue the matter, even if his liking had always been as strong as on the first encounter.

In a voice reflecting a state of being stretched to stiffness, Tauseef, unruffled, was very straight and candid in responding to Qulsum's frivolous query. He said, "I presently do not know much about her, nor have I seen her since changing schools. I came to know from a common friend that besides her ostensible beauty, smartness, and open attitude, she is blessed by inherited financial affluence. That made her a subject of greater interest to many, including some eligible faculty members. Being conscious of that, I think she played with the emotions and feelings of many. I tried to forget her, knowing full well that by temperament and social outlook, she is different from me. I could not. She has always been present in my thoughts, even though I have not seen her since leaving Dhaka University. In fact, I was thinking about her when you asked that question. It is perhaps a desolate reflection of my first liking anyone from the other gender. Time has passed. It is late for me to try to know about her. So that's it."

Each word uttered by Tauseef and each of his expressions made a deep emotional mark on Qulsum. She knew Tauseef very well since her arrival at Biesh Moisher Bari, and it was he who first gave her the much-needed space of comfort in the new setting. A feeling of unpredicted grief overwhelmed her, and she sensed wetness in her eyes. Qulsum hurriedly picked up the *anchal* of her sari and wiped the drops of tears that were about to roll down her cheeks. She was evidently happy in being able to do so while avoiding Tauseef's attention. Her thought was that if he didn't see her tears, she could minimize the anguish that was hurting him.

Conciliation

Tauseef's departure from Dhaka to New York was preceded by meticulous planning and detailed preparations. Both Qulsum and Tanveer showed up surprisingly to wish a "bon voyage" to Tauseef. That made him both exultant and exhilarated.

In working out an itinerary through the assigned travel consultant of the funding agency, Tauseef planned a two-day break in London to have a feel of that city. People of Bangladesh, in general, have an affinity with London, starting with the trading operations of the East India Company and the development of Calcutta as the first urban township for resident British personnel. As the time passed, England, in general, and London, in particular, attained a congenital identity for all-round excellence with politesse, as far as Tauseef knew. In academic pursuits and social interactions, England and London had still an eponymous status, though exposure to and orientations in the United States were gaining ground.

Tauseef had clear ideas of his priorities during his stay in London even before embarking on his epic journey. Keeping that in view, as well as probable costs based on the information available in the British Council of Dhaka, he made two advance decisions: his preference for staying in any of the YMCAs in central London and to see as much as possible on a "hop-on, hop-off" bus tour, purchasing a forty-eight-hour ticket. He was certain that it was well-nigh impossible to see all that was to be seen in London in two days, especially for a person who had never been to that city. It was complicated by the varied nature and type of priority choices, ranging from the House of Parliament to Big Ben, Westminster Abbey, the British Museum, the National Gallery, Buckingham Palace, and Madame Tussauds, to mention a few. He was guided by his acquired wisdom of being easy when choices became busy. He zeroed in on two choices for in-depth viewing: the British Museum and Madame Tussauds. With respect to others, he kept them as probable choices. If any of them were in the vicinity of the tour plan of the bus routes, then he may consider the options possible.

Tauseef landed at Heathrow Airport and took a cab to Central London. The first thing he noticed was the proliferation of a matchbox type of black British taxi. However, what amused him most was the four-door design of these vehicles, with front and rear doors opening out from the center. These black British taxis have the reputation of being the most common sight in London for more than fifty years.

He enjoyed his two days, with things working out as scheduled and without fault-finding or blame games, a common experience of his immediate living. To top up his happy experience, Tauseef decided to have dinner on the last evening in one of the numerous Indian curry restaurants. Though commonly known as Indian restaurants, these were mostly owned by Bangladeshis, with English people being the most regular patrons. That made him even happier.

Tauseef's happiness burgeoned upon his arrival at JFK Airport in New York. Immigration and customs clearance went smoothly, but he was surprised by the experience with the staff at the airport shuttle services booth. As he approached the booth, one of the staff on duty greeted Tauseef with a full smile and inquired, "What can I do for you?"

That was surprising for him. In the environment Tauseef grew up, any contact with a person of some relevance or authority would be sure to allude to a question like "What do you want?" Thus, "What can I do for you?" was a very unexpected and equally pleasant statement, erasing all apprehensions he had in articulating seeking help. It was even more glaring as a few hours back, he was in London, notoriously famous for being very reserved, where most of the equations were premised on a strict sense of etiquette.

Tauseef politely told him about his maiden visit, his need for a place to stay overnight, and the need to avail a bus the following morning to go to New Haven. The employee not only gave the strange person a patient hearing but went out of the way to identify the bus number and the time to go to Central New York City and to suggest an inn-type accommodation in the vicinity, with directions to the bus stop for the following morning.

Approaching the visible and notable Triborough Bridge, Tauseef was in awe at the skyline of Manhattan. The bus passed by the side of high rises all around him, and he literally pressed his head against the glass window to see more of the heights the skyscrapers reached. The reality was much more gauging than photographs and movies. It was an astounding experience for him, and London, by contrast and for a moment, appeared to be minuscule.

The positive experiences of his initial days were just not an exceptional few. With every step of his settlement and academic progression, he thought that this was one exceptional nation. State ideals and people's practices were not on a collision course. In systematically navigating the water while looking deep into the focus of his life's pursuit, the evolving social setting, the deliverability of a political system in place, the neutrality and timelessness of the judicial system, and the opportunity to excel in life based on merit, Tauseef unqualifiedly realized the uniqueness of the USA. There may not be another country where words written in the constitution were so much in conformity with the individual citizen's aspirations and actions. In spite of periodical hype to the contrary, the singular focus of this nation remained firmly anchored to freedoms in all their manifestations, rights in all their applications, justices in all their delivery mechanisms, and assimilations in all their forms. This society had, by choice or chance, evolved a pattern of political and social discourse, which shook core values after periodical gaps. Once so done and fresh from that sort of shake, the country moved on with new energy and vigor, following the track the founding fathers thoughtfully charted.

Tauseef had no doubt about his astute assessment, even though some aspects of American life always bemused him. Every conceivable facet of life and living had been privatized in this country, with the market being the determining factor for access, cost, and quality. Even the universal social services for public good, like basic health care and education, had been privatized. In most cases, access had been constrained because of affordability. Efforts to address such impairments had mostly been lost in the evolving mirage of private intervention–based policy initiatives, which mostly failed to ensure harmonious relevance. Notwithstanding the perceptible negative attributes of uninhibited privatization in all spheres of life, Tauseef was smart enough to weigh in some of the inherent positive aspects. He acknowledged the excellence and achievements of private sector initiatives that made the USA the leader of nations in innovations and progress in all conceivable areas, including medicine, technology, and applied and social sciences. What impressed Tauseef most related to his micro-level experience based on the unofficial but generally applicable business practice that the customer was always right. Most business establishments allowed liberal times for customers to return or exchange purchased commodities without any question and mostly even without purchase receipts.

He was amused by specific variances between the UK and the USA with respect to some matters of mundane nature. It took him time to be cognizant of those and to understand from an American perspective. Some changes were predictable, while others were mind-boggling. For his easy understanding and assimilation, Tauseef identified them as "English English" and "American English." Before leaving home, he was familiar with the nature and type of some differences and more common ones like expressions, matters, and measurements. For example, he was aware of America's left-hand driving policy, expressing distance in miles instead of kilometers, and the flexibility in the use of a fork and knife as opposed to the strict protocol outlining the propriety of use under the British system. Also, reference in the USA to a higher university level learning unit of any specific discipline as *school* compared with *department* in the UK, and putting the month first followed by the day and then the year in recording dates did not cause any inelegance in his initial phase of assimilation.

Many non-Americans merrily embraced some spelling preferences of American English, and Tauseef was one of them. Some examples were *airplane* in place of *aeroplane*, *defense* in place of *defence*, *pajama* in place of *pyjama*, *tire* in place of *tyre*, and other words like *autumn* for *fall*, *subway* for *underground*, *candy* for *sweets*, *elevator* for *lift*, *baggage* for *luggage*, *movie* for *film*, *restroom* for *toilet*, and so on. There were numerous American English words and various number usages that Tauseef found to be in substantive variance with English English. Unless one had upfront clarity, committing an unexpected gaffe would not be unusual. He found that out while using the American English word *pants*, which, to his knowledge, meant *trousers*. He soon realized that *pants* in English English stood for what one wears under trousers. Tauseef knew that possibly all languages had one vague commonality: they underwent silent and soft changes in pronunciation, lexis, and idioms after about every forty miles. That sort of assessment was strengthened by noting differences in pronunciation, usages, and vocabulary among English spoken in various states, not to mention the discernible variances between New England and southern parts of the USA. He was not that surprised by the apparent differences in English English and American English.

Tauseef's liking of the USA was total, though he always missed the food prepared by Pori Khala. He spoke to his close friends about the excellence of Bangladeshi cuisine and the intricate spice combinations mastered over time. He did not forget to mention the mundane Mia's Hotel occasionally. In emphasizing that, Tauseef was always polite and predicated his observations with positive remarks about the local food of different tastes, initially patronized by immigrants of varied origins. He used to say, "I like pizza, burgers, and Chinese food. But the issue is that the spectacle of spectacular food loses its culinary specialty when the same is prepared day in and day out following the same recipe, both in terms of ingredients and measurements."

The USA had one popular local food item of New Mexico origin, known as guacamole—mashed avocado. Because the fruit had a mild taste, it easily compliments a lot of food. Notwithstanding Tauseef's favorable orientation for local food and the overall popularity of guacamole, he always felt uncomfortable with it because of an initial experience. He liked guacamole instantaneously when he tasted it the first time. His liking multiplied as guacamole, with a mix of jalapeño paste, became tastier. It made guacamole very spicy and, for the first time since his arrival in the USA, tasted something close to the spicy foodstuffs of Bangladesh, and he unknowingly overindulged. Consequently, he suffered from stomach disorder and became nauseous. The discomfort unfortunately lasted longer than usual and created a most disorienting problem for Tauseef, and he could not get out of it. His adventure with American foods soon got better with meticulous care and caution to quantum and frequency. He liked the burrito very much, a Southwestern cuisine made by rolling tortilla with foodstuffs like meat, scrambled eggs, potatoes, and onions. Tauseef used to bring it to his residence and heat it up to make the tortilla crunchy. He liked it very much but always exercised care in not having too much. The tortilla was a flour- or corn-based soft flatbread very similar to Bangladeshi *roti* (also known as *chapati*). In Apurba Neer, Tauseef had frequent breakfasts made of *roti* with fried potatoes and eggs, so burritos inspired a nostalgic feeling.

Though Tauseef made every effort to adjust with the USA way of life and living, one particular issue bothered him for a long time. The left-hand driving policy of the USA, which essentially meant that the vehicle was on the right section of the road, did not bother him as he was aware of that for quite some time. But what amused him was the term *tall* for something short or small. Tauseef was smart enough to realize that either one changed against the reality of emerging compulsions or got changed subsequently. The option was open but had no exception. He chose the first one.

His admission was in a full-time course of study with a higher degree of curriculum flexibility. That encompassed about four years' research and faculty work, with time flexibility for a defending dissertation. Engagement in faculty research was a vital task during the initial process, in addition to selective involvement in faculty-related work. The timely completion of initial requirements was achieved smoothly as Tauseef prepared well prior to embarking on the journey for his much-cherished doctoral study with a focus on being challenged and being ready to challenge others. The spontaneous help of the adviser and the guidance of the doctoral advisory committee facilitated the smooth determination of research objectives and requirements for Tauseef's area of interest and needed academic focus. This normally was the foundation of the post-doctoral amalgam process.

In this process and because of the excellence shown, he was increasingly exposed to the school's intellectual environment through participation in workshops and seminars where high-level outputs of fellow researchers were vigorously deliberated and debated. That was of enormous help. In Tauseef's adjusting with the American way of life and living, in his discovering the Unites States in terms of its values and traits, in his exploring opportunities and challenges that dominated the U.S. setting, and in his managing and handling academic trials and other tribulations involving dread and delight in completing his doctoral thesis, time just flew away. Nothing distracted Tauseef from accomplishing his avowed objective on time and with distinction.

With the successful completion of his PhD, Tauseef unwittingly landed into a situation of unanticipated challenge and involuntary jeopardy: unbounded opportunities for attaining academic excellence in the USA and the commitment given to maintain links with Biesh Moisher Bari in Bangladesh. The first one was premised on an offer to join his current university as a faculty member, made more attractive with the direct offer from his supervisor to be an academic member of his research team. This had the additional attraction of being a legal resident of the USA as a green card holder to lead to citizenship. These were peripheral to Tauseef. His uninhibited liking of the USA singularly hinged on the society's openness: the tolerance of divergent and conflicting color, creed, and views; the knack in encouraging and nourishing dissent; and the unreserved aptitude to respect ideas and innovation, even though at variance with established equations.

These were in direct conflict with the societal ethos with which Tauseef grew up in Bangladesh. The societal norms influenced his growing up as being somewhat introverted and shy, but his inner dissent and tenacious rebellion helped him be what he was today. So the USA was the place where Tauseef found his ease in breathing life. But the commitment, echoed as a solemn undertaking, to maintain a link with Biesh Moisher Bari was something much elevated and without inhibition, accepted as such by all present, including Mother. In an informal milieu with limited communication, that was the first commitment she had wanted from her son, and Tauseef had unhesitatingly complied.

The academic success and associated recognitions padded with attractive propositions made Tauseef happy but did not derail him from his love and link with family, particularly Mother. He recalled regularly his few conversations with Mother, the love and care from Pori Khala, and his latest dear association with Qulsum Bhabi. The inability to see one another had accentuated that. Tauseef was haunted by the solemn assurance he had given to Mother against the backdrop of lucrative propositions for post-doctoral life and living. He eventually opened up to his doctoral supervisor and sought his guidance. The consensus was that Tauseef should be back to Bangladesh and keep himself engaged in research-related work with a focus on publication and remain in touch with the supervisor regularly. Upon reaching Dhaka, Tauseef looked for job in academic institutions and research bodies. In that process, he went to Apurba Neer and spent a few days merrily with the family.

During one extended family dinner, Qulsum directly but unpretentiously inquired about Tauseef's plan to get married. In the inherited setting of Biesh Moisher Bari, matters like this were not for public discussion. It, thus, took all present by surprise but with no adversarial comment.

Reflecting maturity in thoughts and action, Tauseef took a sauntered approach to responding. He thanked Qulsum for raising the issue and said, "I know that I will have to face this question and have thought through this of late. I will let all of you know about my readiness as soon as I get a job of my liking."

Everyone was happy with that response. All present were gratified that their Tauseef had remained the same person as he was before and that four years of U.S. living did not adversely affect his thinking and values. Tanveer and Mother exchanged positive looks reflecting their happiness and relief. That was the case with Pori Khala and Badsha Chacha, though from a different pedestal. Qulsum was, however, the exception. During a later solitary conversation with Tauseef, she raised the issue of the girl he liked most during his first-year university education.

Tauseef posited, "Who knows where she is? Many years have elapsed. She must be a mother of many children by this time, simultaneously enjoying economic affluence and some social prominence through marriage."

That was the most direct and expedient response, but Qulsum did not fail to notice the rueful nature of his vocal sounds. She was smart enough to conclude that the response was premised on a xenophobic hypothesis giving him an expedient exit from the sudden reference to an emotionally laden past. Exercising her prudence, she did not prolong that discussion. On his part, Tauseef was both happy and relieved.

Tauseef soon found an opening in a prestigious national research institution with focus on areas of his specialty and interest. During the initial days of familiarization, he suddenly was assigned a task that had nothing to do with his position and seniority. The chairperson of that research institution was to be the chief guest in a book-launching ceremony. That specific book was reflective of poverty and income inequity syndrome–related research materials and, more importantly, was authored by a budding professional from the same institution. The chairperson and some seniors of the institution were required to meet the minister-in-charge of planning. The time collided with the book-launching event. It was, thus, decided that Tauseef would represent the institution as well as act as the chief guest in place of the chairperson.

The institution had the fame of being very selective in hosting events. Thus, whenever one was scheduled, the attendance was overwhelming in terms of the quantity and quality of participants. Tauseef kept his demeanor befitting the task assigned and launched the event successfully.

He was about to leave the venue when a whisper from behind took him by surprise. "Are you not Hira?"

Tauseef turned back and was stunned, facing Chandni from his first year at university. She indubitably created a mark in his thinking from the very first encounter and have had that sensation with unfailing consistency, despite the passage of time and living in different places. His response was expectedly guileless. Ignoring the high echelon of academic standing engulfing the institution's environment and the setting of the book launching, Tauseef's instantaneous affirmation was rapidly followed by "You had doubt about my identity, but I could recognize you even when you were sitting in the first row of audience. I was thinking about your presence at the launching event of a research work and was wondering about ways to know more about you. I maintained restraint because of the unaccustomed burden associated with representing the institution and being acting as the chief guest."

Chandni replied, "A nephew of mine works as a research fellow in this institution. It was from him that I came to know that someone by the name Tauseef Ali with a PhD from an American university had just joined his institution. To be frank, I vaguely remembered your formal name. The description of the person as being smart, handsome, and well-dressed created confusion in my mind. I, thus, decided to avail this opportunity to check on you but never expected to see you in the chair of chief guest. That confused me a bit, besides marked changes in your demeanor and dress, compared with the shirt and pajamas from before. To be absolutely certain it was you, I whispered from the back using your nickname."

Listening intently to what she was saying, Tauseef could not be oblivious to the many sets of eyes fixated on them. Perhaps that was his being the chief guest as well as in the presence of a very smart, outgoing, and exquisitely attractive young lady. The captivating nature of that private talk could as well be another reason. Tauseef promptly realized the delicate nature of the situation, exchanged telephone numbers with her, and left the venue with candid understanding to be in touch soon.

Elements of romantic uncertainties emanating from the unplanned exchanges were humdingers for both. Tauseef was pleased to note that his silent lovebird was still as beautiful and shining as her name Chandni (moonlight) was. Chandni was likewise exultant in noting positive changes in the ensemble and demeanor of the person she had been thinking about.

Tauseef took that sudden meeting as something preternatural. His curbed exuberance was because of the unexpected—and that too in a most startling way—reunion with the person he so silently adored and remembered all through. While pertinent and equally most crucial details of her life and living remained muffled in emotional predicament, he thanked his stars for being so kind and so soon since his return.

Chandni likewise had her feelings, but her related thinking had focus on Tauseef's personality changes. His outward and visible changes from dress to demeanor made her happy, but she was wondering whether he was still the same and simple Hira from the first-year honors course. In that short duration of their first-year tutorial class, Chandni noticed very clearly Hira's unexpressed eagerness to talk to her but could never muster the courage to do so. She used to giggle to herself whenever she thought of that simple pajama-shirt-clad class fellow, even though his academic excellence made him one of attention.

That happenstance encounter was something special. The inert contact subsumed in many years suddenly started to have a sublime boost in her thoughts and feelings. She was impressed by the way he conducted the event but also by the depth and the diaphanous diversity of his peroration as the chief guest. But one queer feeling made her bizarrely tense—was he married?

In the midst of such mixed antiphon, Chandni inadvertently dozed off in her couch, only to be awoken by household help as the usual dinnertime had passed quite a while back. She decided to skip the standard dinner and opted to have some fruits and milk. Then the telephone rang. She was overwhelmed to hear the voice at the other end. It was Tauseef, with all sorts of excuses for calling rather late at night.

He was frank enough to say, "I was not certain about the appropriateness of calling you, and the correlated agonizing thoughts only delayed my calling! Finally, resting all hesitation and complex to rest, I decided to call you. I hope it is okay with you."

Chandni laughed stridently and said, "While you spent your time agonizing with what to do or not do, I had a very pleasant state of mind after meeting you again. It was so nice and so fulfilling that I even dozed off untimely. My getting up rather late found me still preoccupied with earlier thoughts of you. Your call is, thus, timely and most welcome."

Tauseef and Chandni talked for a long time, reminiscing earlier tutorial class times and sporadic exchanges, mocked about the nervousness Tauseef always exhibited, teased Chandni for her flirtatious way of conduct in communicating with all and sundry, and relevant general observations about life since leaving Dhaka University. Time had taught both Tauseef and Chandni, though from different perspectives, to handle expectations with maturity. From their respective belvederes, both the personalities were coincidentally attuned to avoid the head-on dash of any inner liking and preference. Thus, both were vigilant and articulate in pursuing the mutually favored first-time discourse. Both carefully avoided reference to any substance, even though each was desperate to know the other's marital status.

As Tauseef continued to make wishy-washy references pertaining to the marriages of friends and relations, Chandni took the initiative to say, "Look, whatever you have in mind, please note that I was married and am now single without any children. I hope this puts to rest your predicament in asking me directly about my status."

Tauseef took that information with an altruistic attitude with an all-munificent feeling he could master without the inclination to know the details. He was quiet for a while and amused himself momentarily with options in mind. He came out of that only when alerted by Chandni inquiring as to whether he was still on the line. In response, Tauseef thanked her for the fact as it was and requested her presence in a brunch meeting the following morning at the elite local hotel. Chandni agreed readily, and that made him very happy.

He spent most of that night with a feeling of happiness that he seldom experienced, notwithstanding her divorced status. Chandni, on the other hand, was in deep self-evaluation of her past life and decided to open up fully to Tauseef to avoid unsought stalling in the future.

They met the following day at the appointed time and venue but had difficulty in continuing the discussions by last night's standard. The ambiance of the brunch setting was just not apposite for initiating and enduring a discussion of that nature, loaded with emotions and life-related implications. The obvious choice for them was to concentrate on food like many others present, and they did so. Even in that situation and as noted by Tauseef, Chandni was very tense. The internal pressure within her to open up to him was pulsating as she did not want to experience any frosty development.

Tauseef had learned in life that frequent and often direct follow-on queries tend to dilute thoughts and responses, and one seldom gets the correct one, so he refrained from making any redolent query and allowed time to take care. That worked.

Chandni, with a desolate scowl gracing her face, suddenly said, "Since meeting you, I have had deep thoughts within me. Are you the same simple Hira from first-year studies, or are you a changed person? I have something to share with you before our startling present contact is fostered further."

Saying those few words, Chandni invited Tauseef to dinner at her place. That was agreed to with the understanding that her personal transport would be on time and in place to fetch him.

Chandni planned all relevant locales according to her penchant without meddling with her principal goal. The dinner was planned as the first activity of the evening, to be followed by tea and dessert in the study. That was to be the setting for sharing with Tauseef what she had in mind. The study was a neatly designed, nicely kept, cozy trilateral room with a glass-top table housing a desktop, an office chair, and shelves full of books and journals. The other side had a love seat, a sofa, and a recliner overlooking a big picture window.

Even though this planned meeting was preset to know the unknowns of their respective lives spreading over many years, both were struggling to initiate the discourse. For Tauseef, it had always been difficult to initiate a conversation, but once done, he could easily carry on without hindrance. Chandni was always at ease in raising issues and unloading her viewpoint. Predictably, the onus was on Chandni this time.

While seeping tea, Chandni pointedly asked, "I thought that once you are aware of my divorce, you would cogently like to know the backdrop of that. But you did not. Is it any indication that my divorce status is a disablement that would have impact on our future contact?"

Tauseef gave a passionate look and responded spontaneously, "Your divorce does not matter to me. It has no bearing on my present contact with you or our future relationship. If divorce continues to be an emotional burden for you, I am ready to extend my support shoulder to lessen that. In a sense, the divorce has eased the process of knowing a person whom I liked at the first look and adored all through without knowing anything."

Chandni manifestly felt content. She took time to assess and absorb the real inferences of what he had alluded to. It was the first time that she could not have direct eye contact with him. It was not that she was hesitant; it was just that she could not do it in spite of efforts otherwise.

Those ephemeral moments of muteness were heart-throbbing for them both. It was the desire of Tauseef to make the silver-toned affirmative assertion about a possible future relationship, and that made him nervous. The pressing internal turmoil about sharing facts pertaining to her divorce made Chandni temporarily tangled. Keeping her eyes fixated on the floor, she firmly and without any inhibition resumed the discourse. "Before our potential interactions elevate our present contact to something more personal and emotional, I think, from my perspective, you should know my life's depressing experiences and sore facts."

Tauseef was taken aback. All along, he thought that she was just an outgoing, smart, and effervescent young girl from a well-to-do family without any desperation. That was how he knew her initially. That was how the related reminiscences involving images of her had been entwined in his thoughts. Those few unexpected words she uttered softly but with copious apprehension were most unnerving for Tauseef. The related melancholic tonal and facial expressions of Chandni made him both fretful and inquisitive. He exercised restraint by not making any spewing query. His strategy was more to give her space for unburdening per her convenience and predilection. It so appeared that Chandni had mastered assuredness and serenity with respect to the angst and stresses that had wedged the unbounded dreams of her youth.

She resumed her statement, saying, "To be honest, I am responsible for my divorce. I grew up with a feeling of hatred for men. There was a veiled but raging longing within me to nurture physical and emotional milieus to draw men closer and then to throw them off as dirt. I circuitously and naively internalized it from sayings of Nani [maternal grandmother], who often emphasized during my growing-up phase that women are not weak. The Creator has blessed the fragile body of women with unspoken attractions and unspecified strengths. If one could maneuver that feminine blessing wisely, then she can be more powerful than a man."

Chandni took an intended break this time, possibly to recall facts and arrange her thoughts pertaining to her life and its vagaries.

She resumed, "Destiny took me to the place of my maternal grandparents, under whose care and indulgence I finished my late teens–related two years of high school education and the two years of intermediate study before, like you, I too was admitted into

Dhaka University. Apart from the untrammeled life pattern that I enjoyed under the uninhibited love and care of my grandparents, I also observed one thing particularly as I was growing up—whoever passed me or came into contact with me always had an unusual look at me. My grandmother helped me understand what that meant. I got into the habit of positioning frequently in front of a full-sized mirror in my grandma's room. I used to observe myself taking various postures and enjoyed that very much. This, I used to do mostly when Grandma was not in the room. I was born in a socially recognizable family, with my father being a mid-level civil servant. When I was in grade seven, my father had to go to Northern Bangladesh for some official duty. At his insistence, my mother joined him. After finishing the assigned job, they wanted to hurry back both for me being alone and the day being an official weekend. The consideration was spending the whole day with me.

"They left the place of the visit very early morning by official car to return to Dhaka. It was the month of December. An unusual thick fog engulfed most of the northern parts of Bangladesh. Numerous dangling lamps of cow-driven carts and substandard headlights of occasional mechanized vehicles worsened the misty condition. That caused a situation of low visibility and conflicting signal. The driver of the official vehicle was cautious and driving carefully though at a higher speed to make his boss happy by reaching Dhaka well ahead of time. He misread an oncoming truck, which had only one functioning headlight. By the time the driver realized that it was an approaching truck, there was no time to undertake any defensive maneuver. Both my parents died instantaneously in the resultant head-on collision.

"My maternal grandparents reached Dhaka from Comilla on hearing the sad news. Among others, the family decision pertaining to my future was that I would stay in Dhaka with my maternal uncle to finish my school year and then would move to Chittagong to finish my education under the care of my paternal uncle. That happened as postulated, with the one major exception that I unexpectedly had to move to Comilla in the middle of grade eight. That was an unanticipated relocation premised on unusual circumstances.

"This aspect of my challenging teenage life was deeply swayed by shock, sorrow, and sadness. However, there was another aspect of my growing-up life that was affected by abuse, allegation, and angst. It is that part of my life that I want to unload today. You need to know that too, not for empathizing but more to know who I am and why so."

Chandni poised for a moment and checked the immediate surroundings again from a privacy point of view. She continued, saying, "My uncle's family in Dhaka consisted of an aunt and their three children—the eldest, the only son, reading in college; and two daughters, one of my age and grade in school. I was a temporary addition. My losing parents unexpectedly and transient status, which used to be repeated often by Aunt, made me someone special to my cousins. Still, my life in that setting was a routine and structured one with no one except the household help lady to share occasionally my sadness and frustration. My temporary physical indisposition compelled skipping a regular school day. I was alone in my uncle's place under the care of female household help, enjoying the local television program, lying on a couch.

"Unexpectedly, the young and abrasive brother of my aunt with the nickname Tulu showed up. After an exchange of customary salutations and even though he was advised of Aunt's absence, Tulu Mama [uncle], as I was to address him, occupied a sofa without hesitation, positioning himself diagonally. His extraneous queries were answered by me, remaining within the dictum of social propriety.

"Tulu Mama impulsively got up and went toward the kitchen. He asked the household help lady to fetch him a packet of cigarettes from the grocery shop and came back and sat by my side. Soon, he took hold of my right hand ostensibly to assess whether I had any body temperature. Tulu Mama's grip soon became a firm one, and he applied some force in placing my palm on the lower part of his lap. As he was pressing my palm against his lower lap and even in that tender age, I started having clear idea of what he was up to. I felt the inevitable touch of his twitchy dick. A sense of feebleness and fretfulness engrossed my thinking and carnal riposte. Before I could react otherwise, he grabbed me, pressed me against his chest, and tried repeatedly to kiss me. Being enraged by my persistent resistance, he threw me on the couch, enforced the separate positioning of my legs, jumped on my body, neutralizing my feeble resistance and taking control of my two hands, and molested my private part savagely and was unzipping his trousers.

"At that particular moment and as a divine intervention, the household help lady returned unexpectedly, recalling leaving the kitchen with the cooking range enflamed. While approaching the kitchen, she winked at the living area and got involved in self-talking, stating loudly in a vacuum the reason of her return. The roaring lion abruptly became a lamb, and his firm penis just withered away. Consequentially, I was released involuntarily.

"He drew the attention of the maid to tell her that he remembered an earlier commitment and would have to leave at that moment and buy the cigarettes on his way out. The related money changed hands without any other comment. He left the apartment immediately.

"As I was going to my room, the household help lady quietly advised me not to tell anything to my aunt. She told me, 'Your aunt has a biased feeling for her younger brother. Whatever you say would never be taken into account. She will always believe what her brother says. Ultimately, you will be a loser.'

"With those words and while conveying other things by varied physical expressions, she quietly left me. I had no doubt that she could very well sense what I was experiencing and going through. The experience of mine at that tender phase of life impacted my thinking and physical responses, but I was unable to assess the real impact. The only outward feeling that I recall was persistent fear in facing any male individual, irrespective of age or relationship.

"I sustained that ghastly feeling, thinking that it would go away. That was reinforced when I moved to Chittagong to be with the family of my paternal uncle for a sort of permanent residence. My paternal uncle and aunt had an unusually small family by Bangladesh standards. Their only son was an intermediate student in the reputable local college. My *chachi* [paternal aunt] had always lamented not having a daughter. She was, thus, very happy in having me, even though my presence was predicated on a colossal family tragedy. My slated move to Chittagong after my seventh-grade final examination was on time, to the immense relief of my maternal aunt. I myself was happy for unknown reasons, even though separating from friends had caused insuperable anguish. One specific reason for such baffling happiness was the bond of trust and confidence developed with my only cousin, Mahi, and that too in no time. I was happy to have a brother but even more so to be a sister. My suppressed feeling of anxiety in meeting and interacting with male acquaintances started to fade."

Saying those words with absolute calmness and assuredness, Chandni sipped some tea before resuming her unfinished statement, "I do not have any inkling about the philosophy of life. But I do understand that consistent with its journey pattern, each life has its due share of good and bad times. A good time often flashes away, while a bad time is prolonged because of its adverse impact. In my case, the latter is more applicable. My happy acclimatization with my paternal uncle's family was jolted brusquely beyond any thinking or probable apprehension. The resultant shock and anger are haunting me still today, severely shaking my living at its every bend.

"It was late summer of the year of my moving to Chittagong. My uncle abruptly postulated a visit to Bandarban, reputedly one of the more scenic places in the Chittagong Hill Tracts area of Bangladesh. Whatever he had in mind, the ostensible justification was to expose me to the beauty of hilly areas. He made an extra effort one dinner night by explaining his plan for our proposed trip. He said that about forty-five miles away from main Bandarban, there was a place called Nil Giri. In a flat terrain, it was situated at a height of about 3,500 feet on the Bandarban-Chimbuk-Thanchi road. It is surrounded by beautiful nature with overhead clouds most of the time and affectionately called "the Real Paradise" or "the Mountain of Blue." Chacha also explained that though our trip was to Bandarban, we would stay in the rest house located in Nil Giri and spend our time there.

On arrival and at first sight, both Brother Mahi and myself were overwhelmed by the scenic beauty of Nil Giri. We concluded that Chacha did not exaggerate in describing the beauty of Nil Giri and that the visit was worth it. For someone like me, born and brought up in Dhaka, this was a unique experience. Besides the elevation and the lush green setting all around us, I also enjoyed the cool breeze, the ever-embracing noticeable clouds, and a serene way of life of the local tribal habitants known as Mro or Murung. I had read in Bangla novels about comparable settings like this but enjoyed the reality for the first time in my life. My exposition was complete when the family took a stroll on the very afternoon of arrival. What impressed me the most was the way the ladies dressed up, the quiet manner of their movement and interactions, and the specialty that characterized their cooking. Principal items of daily food such as rice, beef, and mutton were cooked in hollow bamboo strands without water. I had no idea about such cooking and enjoyed witnessing the process.

"The family started the following morning very late and in a relaxed mode. Perhaps walking the previous afternoon on hilly terrain had caused grogginess to my *chacha* and *chachi*, and they were inclined to take rest. Standing on the veranda, I was having a long look at nature. The external locale in the late morning sunrays was enchanting for me. I had an urge to go out and explore more about the life and living of the Mro people.

"While my thoughts were floating between such engagement with nature and urges to reconnoiter more of the idyllic setting, Brother Mahi suggested a walk along the trails of hills around. My agreement was spontaneous. I accompanied him gleefully.

"In the convoluted walk, climbing and bypassing hills as encountered, we unwittingly moved far away from our rest house. The lushness of greens everywhere, a panoply of waterfalls, the frequency of water reservoirs, and the presence of a small lake kept us going. We realized we were close to the tribal habitation and their walk trail.

"The distance covered and uneven terrain was tiring, but the heat of the noon sun and the high level of humidity were even more daunting. The lack of support inputs made it more tiring. We felt like taking a break and so decided to sit under a big tree, resting our backs on its robust trunk.

"I had no impression of that tree in my memory except that for its size, the canopies had lighter foliage, providing dappled shades. That caused both of us to sit very close to optimize the benefit emanating from the shade. In spite of earlier discomfort and exhaustion, we were enjoying the serene setting of nature with a mild breeze embracing us. Then Brother Mahi took one of my hands and put that in between his two hands. He slowly started pressing my hand with specific annotation about my physique, beauty, and attractiveness.

"He said, 'You do not know how beautiful you are. I always wanted to be close to you but had neither the chance nor the courage. In this setting, there is no one around. It probably is a god-gifted opportunity.'

"Saying those words, he pulled me toward him and started kissing me, simultaneously pressing my breasts. I was totally unprepared for such action by someone whom I treated as a brother. Ruffled by the most indecorous acts, I was in a baffled situation. That obviously paralyzed my response. Contrarily, Mahi was breathing heavily as an outlet for exhilarated excitement. In his exciting follow-on acts predicating my relative vulnerability in a secluded setting, he was engrossed, unfettered. Mahi lost his body balance unexpectedly, and both of us rolled down from the base of the tree to a relative flat terrain. Whether it was the rolling experience in close embrace or an act of premeditated xenophobic design, Mahi's subsequent advances were most distressing and deplorable. Soon after settling on the flat terrain, he hastily unknotted the tape of my *shelwar* [traditional baggy outfit of girls/ladies], threw it down, and penetrated his male body organ into my ensnarled reproductive tract.

"I overcame that momentary shock quickly and forcefully threw him off my body, only to witness the most embarrassing act of ejaculation. I was relieved in realizing that my belated response was timely enough to avoid a calamitous incident in my life. Forgetting things for a moment, I found solace in being able to avoid an apocalyptic situation. Perhaps because of such thoughts or the appalling deceit, I, for a moment, became impassive. It became apparent to me that any charge of abuse would only cause countercharges and result in sniveling acts with no immediate redress. Based on my earlier reading of stories and incidents, I also had the immediate conclusion concerning possible ridicule premised on the negative attribute of a lonely setting.

"Instead of indulging in any diatribe, I managed not to rile. After readjusting my shattered outfit, I gave a serious but cool look at Mahi and started following the rudimentary track toward the rest house. It was difficult, but the sudden help of two tribal girls with whom I had exchanges and the commonly understood English words *rest house* made my return trip safe.

"In my muddled and stressed journey back, I just could not help the occasional flow of uncontrolled tears. I remembered my dear mother at every step of that journey and asked the Lord about my sins for taking away my parents so soon in life. That was the phase of my life I needed them most. That was the time I needed most their care, love, and protection. I was not only deprived of those but also undeservedly exposed to the most abysmal experiences of life in rather quick succession.

"The incidents of that day and the earlier one engulfed my thinking during the entire time of my return journey. A fixed and irreversible opinion about men by and large and their vulnerable proclivity of having no space for respect, sensitivity, feeling, and relationship was firmly entrenched in my thoughts and mind.

Unknowingly, I started to harbor a strong sense of hatred for men everywhere.

"Disconcertingly, the first person I encountered upon return to the rest house was my *chacha*, another man, anxiously standing on the doorway, awaiting our return. Seeing me coming back alone and observing my stiff facial expressions, he inquired about the reasons, specifically asking about Mahi. My oxymoronic response confused him totally, and he went inside his room without any follow-on queries.

"I went to the veranda, took a seat, and stared outside, focusing on the lush green natural setting, asking myself why it was to be so and why me. In that self-questioning situation, I soon grasped that with parents deceased, I was vulnerable to the support and sympathy of others to whom my life, my happiness, my security, and my success matter but not unerringly. I realized that notwithstanding compelling provocations, the pragmatic approach for me was to maintain solipsism in my future journey of life. I kept the whole incident to myself.

"Little I knew of what transpired between Mahi and his parents, but the otherwise genial family discourse was notably missing to the discomfort of all. To be fair, neither my aunt or uncle asked me anything, nor was I was exposed to any further vulnerable interactions with Mahi. The only notable development was our return to Chittagong earlier than planned.

"I tried to settle down in my Chittagong setting, notwithstanding what I went through and opted to breathe as normally as I could, sustaining a discomforting disposition. That was more visible in the case of my aunt, who did not miss any chance to glorify her son. Initially, I accepted that as normal motherly weakness, but the gradual enhancement of that and Mahi poking his nose in irritated me. It was difficult for me to live like that. I wrote a letter to my grandparents requesting an immediate visit by them. My objective was to unload pressing emotional burden, conveying more about sufferings rather than complaining about grievances.

"I was surprised by the promptness of my grandparents' response. They soon came to Chittagong to see me. In a private meeting, I told my *nani* everything that I had experienced since the death of my parents, with no insinuation of expectations from her or grandpa. Nani was an intelligent and confident lady. She absorbed the most acerbic information with grace, maintaining all calmness. What she told me took me by surprise.

"She firmly said, 'Remember for all time that we did not discuss anything. We will tell your *chacha* and *chachi* that the tragic death of your parents is scorching our day-to-day life. We are not at all at peace with ourselves. Hence, if agreeable, we would like to take you to live with us permanently, and we will take your full responsibility with their involvement and participation. We will justify that premised on our mental peace that your presence would cause.'

"What we discussed was acted upon. In follow-on discussions, both sides maintained social niceties and adhered to family decorum, and a desired affirmative decision was reached soon. The only lamenting element was repeated assertions from my *chachi* about missing the daughter of the house, an outward emotional expression with all camouflaged negative traits. Nani and I exchanged looks.

"Grandpa assured, 'Notwithstanding living with us, Chandni will maintain regular contact with you both.'

"The simplicity of that articulation by my *nana* took care of most likely and vulnerable accusations and arguments between two sets of close relations, jeopardizing my entire future happiness. I realized that simplicity was just spectacular, teaching me a lesson in life. Relieved from all emotional stress, I settled down effortlessly in the new social and academic settings of Comilla, the place of my grandparents. The social and cultural excellence of the city made that transition easy for me, and I did not miss my earlier associations with Dhaka and Chittagong. Missing my parents was largely compensated for by the unbounded love, care, and affection of my grandparents.

"I had a very open and cordial relationship with Nani. Perhaps my opening up to her with all bluntness and without any inhibition of everything that I had experienced in Dhaka and Nil Giri paved the way, in addition to the framework of a grandma–of granddaughter relationship. We developed a friendly and mutually supportive equation to the inner comfort and happiness of my *nana*.

"Nani occasionally joshed me, referring to my beauty and attractiveness. Once, she said, 'Allah cannot be that cruel. He has taken away your parents prematurely but blessed you with impeccable gorgeousness, attracting the attention of all, irrespective of gender, age, and relationship. As the days are passing, the splendor of your beauty is increasingly becoming more overwhelming. I am so worried about you and your future.'

"A few days after making that comment, she called me for a most unusual discussion. My jovial *nani* unpredictably became serious and said, "As I said the other day, I am really concerned about your future and possible vulnerability. It is more so as you will soon go to college for your intermediate study. In that coeducation setting, you will be in regular contact with young men and young male teachers, many of whom will go out of way to win you over. Remember not to trust men. Condition yourself not to be swayed. You must work hard to establish yourself first. You will get plenty of good people in every bend of life. There is no need to hurry. I am not telling you to take shelter under a hijab [veil that covers the head]. Since Allah has bestowed you with exceptional beauty, you may, as revenge to what happened to you, use that for making fun and abandoning the suitors appropriately, more as dirt. Do not succumb to temporary emotion. That will equally hurt us too as we would never be able to say no to your choice and preference. I insist that you should remember these always as a sort of recompense for all our love and affection, and I ask a promise from you.'

"I had no diffidence in acquiescing with Nani's proposition. That pledge was made spontaneously and with full earnestness. The love and care from Nana and Nani for me was overly passionate and euphoric, even when my parents were alive. Perhaps my being the only daughter of their only daughter made that more conspicuous, but I had no inkling about the extent and depth of their concern and support for me in the absence of my parents.

"The related realization dawned on me in a situation when all our concerns and anxieties centered on the physical well-being of my dear *nana*. I was finishing the study of my first-year intermediate course. Nana suddenly fell ill, and the diagnosis was an ailment related to his heart. My *mama*, his only son, rushed in from Dhaka. Blessings of All Merciful Allahpak prompted medical attention, and the utmost care and love of all family and community triggered an immediate stabilization of Nana's physical status. Medical advisers emphasized continued rest and less talking. But my dear *nana* was not to be daunted.

"While Nani was preoccupied with taking care of Nana, I was giving company to Mama in his rather late breakfast. Nani showed up and told us about the urgent desire of Nana for a meeting in his bedroom. That took us by surprise, and all of us exchanged looks with one another. A silent fretfulness preoccupied our thinking.

"We were assured, seeing a relaxed Nana sipping green coconut water and sitting in his favorite chair. All three of us sat around him in chairs obviously prearranged by Nani. To the surprise of Mama and me, Nana dithered to open up, contrary to his common style of direct communication, as if he wanted to have an apposite premise for what he was going to say. Nani maintained a composed posture, evidently giving indication as to her familiarity with what Nana had to say.

"Softly and slowly, Nana started his avowal, mostly repeating some facts about his family and own life, touching his current age factor and health status and the need to make clear the issue of the inheritance of his properties and assets in case of an unforeseen eventuality.

"He said, 'I was neither born to a great fortune nor married into one, but my life is a testament demonstrating that a combination of pluck and luck can deliver sweetly savored returns. I, thus, have managed to have two apartments and a vacant plot of land in Gulshan City in Dhaka besides this abode at Comilla. The farmlands that I have are ancestral.'

"He then focused his attention to Mama and reverted to his style of direct talking. He said, "All our grandchildren are very dear to us. However, Chandni has a special place in our mind and thoughts. She is not only the only child of our only deceased daughter but is also a constant reminder to us, though for no fault of her, of what life's vagaries and vulnerability in all aspects could be. Nothing can compensate for the loss she suffered at her tender age. It is the common position of both of us that Chandni would continue to need guidance, education, and economic security in pursuing life. While we are sure that neither you nor her *chacha* would be found wanting in guiding her through life's path, both of us feel that we have responsibilities in ensuring the unimpeded pursuit of her education and the future provision for her economic security. We have, thus, decided that since you have two children, you should inherit the two apartments located in Gulshan City. We will unconditionally bequeath the vacant small plot of Gulshan and this Comilla abode to our dear Chandni. The income from inherited farmlands will continue to be used for the upkeep of our ancestral home in the village. After this meeting, I will take necessary steps to document this decision, meeting the legal requirements of the land, both civil and religious.'

"With those few words, leaving no room for discourse, Nana looked at Nani, who nodded. One by one, we left the room.

"Mama appeared to be happy as neither the Comilla abode nor the vacant plot at Gulshan was of interest to him. I had no idea of what I was going to inherit nor had specific interest in it. Shattered by the bewildering demise of my parents very early in life and the subsequent physical assaults by close relations at a phase of living when a girl's life is swamped by unfettered dreams, I could only hope to lead a normal life.

"But my *nani* would not allow that. All through our even usual sophistry, she would unfailingly persist on two points—playing mischief with male admirers and then abandoning them precipitously and also the upcoming financial relevance of the vacant land of Gulshan, sheerly because of demographic reasons. She said, 'Your ownership of the Comilla house has been thought of as a safety net—lest you commit any major gaffe in managing the vacant land—besides being a testament of our love and affection for you.'

"In spite of my palpable triviality concerning material things, more specifically properties gifted, Nani used to insist that I attain knacks in understanding life and abilities to handle its vagaries. She would often remind me about the two incidents that had already blemished my normal upbringing, emphasizing always that our social system was such that for all happenings in life, more particularly physiological ones, girls ware always easy prey for parking even assumed blames.

"As the time passed, I unknowingly started espousing what Nani used to repeat and understood the need and relevance of economic security she used to emphasize. I appreciated better the gestures of Nana and Nani in bequeathing a portion of their properties to me and became more serious in my thinking and academic pursuits. Simultaneously, I nurtured a specific personality trait that commenced distinguishing me with the added attraction of my inherent beauty and glamor. I started enjoying this very much in my college life. It always enticed me to observe the sensuality and susceptibility of men of all ages and standing and quickly mastered the art of flirting while keeping myself safe and secure.

"That transition process of mine got a sudden shock with the demise of dear Nana after a brief ailment. It was very much a reality, but we never expected it to happen so soon. I realized that the persona whom I always thought as a feeble one, in fact, was the umbrella that was protecting me from all the trials and tribulations of life. My depressed feeling was transitory as Nani soon put the *anchal* [tail end] of her sari over my head, a symbolic gesture reiterating her pledge to guide and protect me in the future.

"With such care and love, I merrily pursued my life in Comilla, finished my intermediate study, and then moved to Dhaka University for honors study in economics. This was the outcome of the expressed preference of my late *nana*, carefully nurtured by Nani after his death. I also wanted to fulfill his earnest desire in envisaging a life of self-sustenance for me.

"We shared the initial few months in the Dhaka University, and the highlight of that association was the incident related to your nickname. In your face and personality, I discerned a simple soul oblivious of inner-city public communication skills, social etiquette, and fashion preferences. That was the reason I stood up, pronouncing Mukhta as my nickname, evidently a false one. It was a spontaneous reaction to silence of the class and to minimize your embarrassment. Though I did not mean anything at that time, it definitely paved way for occasional interactions with you concerning study matters. Our study schedule was affected by protracted strikes and follow-on political turmoil. When things settled down and classes resumed, all of us were back except you. I missed you initially, more because of the previous habit of getting some study matters clarified, but got over that soon. I was more preoccupied dallying in varied settings and with swelling numbers of admirers. Among many of divergent backgrounds, the most unlikely one was our professor, who jovially inducted us in tutorial class by asking for nicknames.

"My panoply of discursiveness and unhampered social discourse caused visible irritation among some, but the 'tutorial sir' never exhibited any demur. He was very open, friendly, and supportive and always encouraged me to focus on study. There were other reasons too, which encouraged me to meet him rather frequently. One was the very casual approach to the profession he had chosen, contrary to others. Because of prevailing culture, most young teachers wear a miasma of sobriety, creating an artificial distance between them and their pupils. Tutorial Sir was not like that. So I started interacting with him even on nonacademic matters. Gradually, I came to know that he came from a flourishing business family and had opted to join the university just for fun. His family business, with a focus on real estate and transportation, would be happy to have him back at any time. I also came to know about his bachelorhood.

"It was the tail end of the third year of our honors course, a belated one. That, as you know, was because of resultant session jams and the successive disruption of class schedules triggered by frequent and prolonged strikes in academic institutions. Nani arrived in Dhaka without any prior indication and came to meet me with two well-dressed young men. She introduced them as officials of a renowned real estate developer saying that they had a good proposal for my vacant plot of land in Gulshan.

"I was amused but nevertheless listened to what they had to say. The proposition pertaining to the construction of a multi-storied apartment building in the vacant land immediately caught my imagination. But I proposed to have some time to consider before we got into the details of the deal. That was agreed to. Nani appeared to be happy, observing my initial response. On subsequent query, she confessed that my willingness to consider that proposal assured her of my understanding, self-confidence, and ability to take upright decisions in the future in varied situations. But she had no clue of the premise for that decision by me, and it was a different one. As I knew from earlier interactions that Tutorial Sir's family was engaged in a flourishing real estate business, I decided to discuss the proposal with him to get his guidance.

"The follow-on discussions with him were beneficial from varied perspectives, but what I did not initially notice was that the process enhanced my contact with him and made it informal and personal, and resultant interactions multiplied. That occasionally required visits to his home and their business office and having intermittent familiar exchanges with his parents. My casual decision to consult with Tutorial Sir on the proposed real estate deal was much more relevant than I had ever thought of. It was finally agreed that out of the proposed twenty apartments, I would get eight of them and some advance cash. Also, the construction outfit of Tutorial Sir's family company took full responsibility for finalizing the deal and overseeing construction from design to quality and safety standards.

I was lucky to own eight apartments and some cash before I even completed my master's degree. I thanked my deceased *nana* for planning and facilitating this. I was, however, totally oblivious of how Lady Luck was swaying and charting my destiny without conscious involvement. My frequent visits to Tutorial Sir's home, casual and open conversation with him, and friendly and respectful discourse with his parents and others in the abode had convinced his parents about our unrevealed romantic relationship. To give me a surprise, they drove down to Comilla privately, met Nani, and made a formal proposal.

"Nani had a reasonable idea about Tutorial Sir and his family as I frequently mentioned their help and guidance in working out a more favorable deal for the plot of land in Gulshan. She readily agreed with the proposal but with one condition. No one would tell me until she had the chance to divulge.

"Nani, of late, had developed a habit of visiting me without advance indication, but there had been a deviation. I had received a letter advising me of her proposed visit and asking me specifically to keep the afternoon of her arrival date free from all commitments. She said that she had something very special to share with me, besides treating me to my favorite *rosho malie* [milk-based special sweet] from Comilla.

"As I stepped into my uncle's place to meet her, Nani greeted me with exuberant gestures, contrary to her normal bearing. She hugged me most intensely, held my right hand, and literally dragged me to her bedroom as if time were running out. After closing the door, she sat facing me with a mischievous smile and her adoring facial expression and inquired, 'Why did you keep that secret from me so long? I have always prayed for your well-being. I am so happy now, knowing about your close feeling and emotional relationship with Tutorial Sir. Knowing that, I have blessed you both in absentia and consented to your marriage with him.'

"That was analogous to a thunderbolt for me, a startling pronouncement that froze my immediate response faculty. I sat for some time without any riposte but soon reassured myself, thinking of a likely misunderstanding. Avoiding contretemps and abusiveness, I softly inquired, whining nevertheless, about the premise of her statement. Nani, taken aback by my depressed reaction and response, detailed all that had happened in the immediate past.

"I was relieved. Neither Tutorial Sir's parents nor Nani were to be blamed. The cheery feature of my growing-up persona and the notoriety I had gained for having free and frank exchanges, more to entice some of my choosing, unknowingly misled many. My frequent visits to Tutorial Sir's home, spending time with him, and free mixing with all the household and the office had convinced the household of a romantic relationship. Tutorial Sir's parents were goaded by well-wishers to take action. They knew their son and concluded that there was no need to consult with him. So they went to Comilla to formalize what they had in mind.

"Their proposition responded to Nani's persistent frustration about her inability to get me married on time by local standard. According to her, I missed the eligible age of marriage by remaining unmarried for so long. Because of such feelings and based on earlier feedback from me about Tutorial Sir and his family, Nani did not feel the need to consult with me before consenting. Realizing all those, I immediately gained back my feeling of comfort and easiness. I could blame the whole episode on my utter lack of prudence in interacting with Tutorial Sir and his family, especially in their home and offices. In our social setting, that sort of behavior was taken as an unfettered expression of a future relationship.

"I took the initiative and explained to Nani the whole spectrum of our relationship. I also clearly told her that while I liked Tutorial Sir, I did not harbor any romantic feelings for him. I was, thus, not in a position to accept the proposition.

"Nani's follow-on reaction took me aback. That was not the Nani I knew so intimately since my location to Comilla. She continued looking at me with ever-changing but abrasive facial expressions as

I was unfolding the gamut of our relationship with the final notation of my inability to agree with the proposal.

"Maintaining visible rigid posture, Nani commented, 'It is no more a question of your agreeing or not agreeing. Your Tutorial Sir's parents made the proposal based on your affable interactions at their place. I accepted that premised on your sustained positive feedback over time. According to our family values and traditions, we can't walk out of that solemn agreement just because you have not been able to fix your mind yet. They are a good and respected family and economically well-off. The boy is well-mannered, has a respectable job, and likes you. His parents also love you, so there is no room for deviation. Since the sudden demise of your parents and sad death of your *nana*, responsibility landed on me to get you settled in life before I breathe my last. My soul would not be at peace if I cannot do it. So I beg of you and seek your consideration and concurrence. If I have done anything in life for you, I am now asking a repayment for that.'

"I did not return to the university residential hall that night. I opted to sleep in the study room, making a temporary arrangement, notwithstanding Nani's uneasiness. I consoled her, saying that I had a tutorial assignment and needed to finish it. Hence, sleeping in the study would be ideal. That idea was endorsed by my uncle, and all others took it with ease. Nani remained somewhat reticent with me but was quite gregarious in her interactions with my aunt and cousins.

"I did not sleep that night, except a trivial dozing-off in the wee hours of the following morning. Every word of reason and wisdom unleashed by Nani, my own behavior, Tutorial Sir's apparent empathy for me, and love and care of his parents dominated my thoughts and reasoning. The financial affluence of the family did not sway me as being the owner of eight apartments in Gulshan had made me economically secure. The absence of my parents and the same possibility with respect to Nani and her age haunted me. I recalled the brutal face of human feeling, response, and behavior in a growing-up phase, more particularly as an orphan. Nana and Nani not only rescued me from calamitous childhood but also provided me with all sorts of benefaction and guidance. Their love, care, and farsightedness in that emotionally turmoil-laden state of mind and growing up were incomparable. They enormously helped me. I not only got out of concomitant guilt and shame feelings but also was able to shape myself as a careful, confident, and motivated individual with a lot of self-assurance. They encouraged building within myself a sense of solipsism, which helped avoiding possible rueful vulnerability as there was no dearth of aficionados around me because of my beauty and attractiveness. At the end of a nightlong self-argumentation and assessment, I had no doubt that agreeing with what Nani had already concurred was the best option for me.

"I had a very early morning mesmeric shower in the most idyllic setting of the following tranquil morning with most family members still in sleep. In the absence of replacement outfits, I put on last night's but took time and made efforts to prepare myself, bringing out the best within me in terms of zeitgeist and politesse. With self-assuring perceptual preparation, I noiselessly entered Nani's room. I had the plan to wake her up but was astounded to find her sitting on a *jai namaz* [Muslim's prayer mat], in deep submission before Allahpak [the Divine]. She lifted both her palms in front of her chest with a *tasbee* [prayer beads] dangling between her fingers and, with eyes closed, was making her submissions most intensely and silently. What astounded me was her nonadherence with the usual and somewhat mandatory practice of closing the Holy Quran after reciting it and before making *munajat*. I silently sat by her side and tried to follow her in having a supplemental *munajat* of my own. It was evident that Nani sensed my stepping in and sitting by her side, even in the midst of her intense prayer. Being uncertain of what I was going to say, she kept her eyes closed for a while after finishing her submissions. Possibly, that was to prepare herself emotionally and physically to handle the repetition of my earlier negative position concerning the marriage proposal. After a while, Nani slowly and impassively opened her eyes and looked at me curiously without any verbal exchange.

"I was at a state of assuage because of the thinking and conclusions of last night. I inaudibly took possession of her two palms, lifted and kissed them as absorbedly as I could, and told her about my decision. I also emphasized that my decision to agree to my marriage was in no way just to gratify her or just because of a sense of gratefulness. I explained that this was a conscious decision of mine with full responsibility.

"Nani was speechless, being immersed in taciturn emotion. She softly freed her palms, closed the Holy Quran, put that on the wooden railing, and, to my utter surprise, went to *sejdha* [prostration]. Understandably, I was at ease with myself, even though Nani's nonchalant reaction puzzled me somewhat. She took me by bewildering surprise while standing up from *sejdha*. Nani held my hand, pulled me up, positioned me before herself, exchanged a look with me with absorbed ease and grace, and hugged me most intently for a very long time. While disengaging from the embrace, Nani told me that she was hopeful that finally, I would agree with her but could never think that it would be so soon and so easily.

"That morning setting of my uncle's home was full of jazz, heightened by the overflowing munificence of Aunt and Uncle, and the spontaneous giggling of Nani. All others in Mama's home did not fail in reacting to the good news either by words or acts. Follow-up events concerning my marriage with Aftab [Tutorial Sir] took place as per the choice and decisions of Nani and Mama, with minimal involvement from me. I moved into Mama's house a few days before my marriage to be close to family, especially my dearest Nani, and for the sake of wedding-related events.

"I will always cherish those few days that I spent with the family, an experience I never had in the absence of parents. The special significance of treasure was because of open discussions I had with Nani and the love and care of Mama and his family. In one of my intimate discussions during the stay, I raised with Nani my stringing discomfort for not letting Aftab know of the sexual incidents that I had encountered in my youth. I was very candid with her, saying that I had the feeling of cheating him. I raised the issue not as a grievance but more to get out of suffering within. It so appeared that Nani took that insinuation quite seriously as it was reflective of my internalized suffering. In responding to my anguish,

Nani, following her way of communication, shared with me two of life's experiences, more to guide me in my future journey rather than responding to my suffering directly. After a pause, Nani alluded to one dissimilarity and one similarity between our lives—one at its mature phase and the other one at the budding phase. She said, 'Your Nana neither was born to a great fortune nor did he marry into one. Whatever you see is the outcome of our joint efforts, joint understanding, and joint decision. We not only were able to lead a decent life but also acquired properties beyond our wild expectation. You are going to be married in an affluent family. The challenge for you is to nurture that in a sustainable manner. This is the difference between our lives.'

"My reaction to what she said was not stirring as the facts were evident. Nani noted the same but had no comment. She appeared to become absorbed in some other diaphanous thoughts. My apprehension was proven correct when she started saying, 'My point of similarity with you relates to early-life sexual experiences. It may sound dodgy to you, but I had also experienced a sexual incursion of a different type during my growing-up phase. But I did not tell your *nana*, as I believe that too much transparency may not always be helpful in life. If circumstances so warranted, I would have told him the facts, but no such situation arose. And we had a very secure and content conjugal life with the deleterious experience behind me. You may take any decision that your conscious dictates, but remember that voluntary disclosure of sensitive information sometimes might have involuntary consequences. Beware of that.'

"Against such a backdrop, I married Aftab with the presence and participation of all close relatives, including my *chacha* and *chachi* from Chittagong. As preparations were afoot for my leaving the house of Mama for that of Aftab, Mama stepped in and sat by my side in the chair courteously vacated by Aftab. I was somewhat taken aback. Mama kept his right hand on my head, saying, 'Ma [mother, as often daughters and the like are affectionately addressed], you were a guest in our family and home so long. Now you are going to your family and your home. Embrace all of new homes as your own, love each one as you loved us, and be permeating in your new setting. That is the only thing that I have to say. You are a smart and confident young lady. Aftab is a very compassionate person. So we do not have much to advise you.'

As I stood up to *salaam*, the ever-adorable Nani came forward, holding one hand of Aftab. She took my right hand and put that on his right hand, a traditional way of handing over the bride to a groom. Tears started rolling down my cheeks. The facial expressions of Aftab bore the signs of anxiety. Nani likewise was concerned as she never expected a girl of my proclivity to cry on the happy occasion of life, more so when I knew the groom. She inquired the reason. I told her, 'Since the death of my parents, you unswervingly loved and protected me. I never had the occasion to miss them. Today as you hand me over to Aftab, I suddenly felt their absence and could not help but cry. Never mind. You see, I am wiping my teardrops by these two palms and promise to you to look forward to life with positivity. I only need your blessings.'

"It was Nani's turn to cry. I quickly took possession of her teardrops and put those on my forehead with care and caution not to muddle my makeup. I stepped out Mama's home for that of mine to be in the company of Aftab and my new family. That is the complete story of my wedding."

Compendium

After unburdening her life's initial hopes, challenges and frustration, Chandni suddenly positioned herself in a state of muteness. Total silence overwhelmed the surroundings. Tauseef was dazed, seeing her switching off the room lights and switch on two small table lamps. The study room wore a unique shady vibe of its own. Tauseef liked it very much and commented positively as a way of encouraging further conversation.

That had no immediate bearing. Chandni quietly went to the kitchen, prepared new cups of tea, served them without words, and took a seat in her previous place, placing an ornate pillow on her lap. That was symbolic of her seeking needed respite from the agony she was suffering.

Tauseef observed all these minutely and decided that it was his turn to initiate the discourse. So he looked at her straight, saying, "I am thankful to you for sharing your life events with me so freely and frankly. I commend you for the way you grew up and have conducted yourself. But I have been wondering as to why you went through the process of divorce with Aftab. I am asking this as I do not know him well and have no idea about the depth and balminess of his love and care for you."

Chandni did not hesitate in responding as if she was waiting for initiation from Tauseef's side. She started saying, "No one in my life or surroundings was responsible for my divorce. It was me and my inability in spite of repetitive exertions. Divorce was painful for both of us but was the only option to ensure happiness and completeness for Aftab and his family. The reason is a very personal one. I do not know how to relate it to you or how you would take it."

Tauseef continued looking at Chandni unabatedly but had an obstinate feeling of dysfunction in thinking. He, however, overcame that soon, propelled by determination to know facts without losing time. He also decided to open up as subtly as he could without causing any discomfiture. He initiated his rendering by stating,

"One thing I am certain about is that I am the same inconspicuous person you first noticeably saw in the tutorial class many years back, notwithstanding what I am today. In that initial phase of my life in Dhaka, I suffered from a tweaking-related deleterious complex in the context of my peripheral surroundings, even though I had no qualms about my academic competence. Your coming to me occasionally for study help always made me happy, but I could never say how I felt. To be candid, my enrollment in the private university delinked me physically from the Dhaka University, but you were often in my contemplations. Thoughts about you gradually faded away as the time passed, coupled with determination to finish my study and give relief to my family from the financial burden that my decision for study in the private university entailed. Your coming from a supposedly higher echelon of society convinced me that a person of my standing had no relevance in your life. You reemerged in my consciousness once I spent some time in my U.S. academic school for the coveted PhD. It was in that setting that I discerned few remarkable social outlooks, many of which were in direct conflict with those I had experienced while growing up. Not that I esteemed everything that I experienced or encountered, but most of them, I definitely admired. I appreciated the challenge and opportunity for progression based on effort and performance and the constraints of income inequality being addressed by the voluntary discharge of social obligations. I admired life philosophy of relationships being premised on feeling, liking, respect, and compassion rather than wealth, outward beauty, and social standing. There was a typical genuineness and preparedness to help. I was initially astonished to know that my one-year senior Nick, hailing from a well-off family, is courting physically handicapped Maria who, in her early childhood, had a nasty encounter with polio. When I first went to the international student's office of my U.S. school, the lady at the reception desk promptly greeted me and said, 'Can I do anything for you?' That experience immediately took me back to my first visit to the office of the provost of my residential hall to be at my admittance in Dhaka University. The office clerk was busy doing his work and remained nonchalant to my repeated mild exertion to draw his attention. He only looked at me, at his pleasure, with the question, 'What do you want?'

"Notwithstanding other perceptible deficiencies, I started treasuring some of the positive aspects of the American social system. It was during such transition that you resurfaced in my thoughts, educing social and cultural attributes that precluded even normal communications with you in my early university life. During that period and from a distance, I admired your confidence, self-assurance, and openness but never understood your proclivity to momentarily enchant everyone who came across your path. Most of the time, I got out of these thoughts after scorning myself, being certain that by that time, you were not only married into an affluent family but also the mother of two or three children. I never had any inclination that I would meet you in such an environment, you still being single and I being unmarried as yet."

Chandni's reaction was a mix of happiness and reassurance. The last four words of Tauseef's latest statement were not only long awaited but also relieving to her at that moment. But that substantiation necessarily was not an undiluted opening. It affirmed something much awaited but gave rise to indefinite trepidations, accentuated because of the delicate personal limitations on her part.

He was determined to get to the bottom of Chandni's internecine anxiety. He was certain that this evening was the setting for that and that it should not be missed by lack of persuasion and support. He decided to be specific as the time at his end was also running fast, considering the family's pressure and the factor of his own age. He was convinced that by opening up his feelings without qualms, he could possibly unearth the veiled restraint. Tauseef repositioned himself on the settee and, like Chandni, placed a decorative pillow on his lap. He deliberately sipped the tea with conspicuous sound. That did the trick. He established eye contact with her after quite a while, with facial expressions bearing some signs of normalcy. That gave him the needed comfort. Armed with that sort of presentiment, he started saying, "I do not know why precipitously, you opted for sudden refraction or what is keeping you surprisingly unvoiced. If your equanimity is premised on predicament with your comfort level, then I will not insist you telling me what you have in mind."

Keeping quiet briefly against the backdrop of her persistent silence, Tauseef continued, saying, "I have no qualm about your awareness of my liking you from day one. I also had no problem with you not taking note of that as it was like hundred others you jovially played with, consistent with your grooming while growing up as reconfirmed a little while back. That negative realization reckoned within me sooner than most others. I have been blessed with a practical mind-set right from my childhood. I have had always clarity in my mind about what I should or should not expect or do. My unenthusiastic conclusion about the negation of a possible relationship with you premised on initial innocent liking was discernible because of a variety of plausible reasons. Some of them were my singular focus on completing academic pursuits early and with excellence and my social roots valuing family aristocracy and traditions compared with the urban setting esteeming connection, power, and money and, more precisely, your smart and open behavior pattern so unfamiliar to me at that stage."

Discerning Chandni carefully, Tauseef concluded that it was time for him to be direct without beating about the bush anymore, so he continued, saying, "You are the only girl in my life for whom I have had instant positive feeling. Over the time and under divergent surroundings, I made efforts to weasel out of that positive feeling for you. I even ridiculed myself, considering that as a disheveled feeling, and tried many a times to squirm out of it. But surprisingly, you resurfaced in my contemplations from time to time. Possibly because of that sort of very personal experience, I never felt the desire to look at others.

"I am under pressure currently from family to get married. While time is running short for me, destiny brought us together implausibly once more. So we need to be clear and candid to each other without wasting time. Earlier, you conjectured whether I am the same old simple man bearing the name Hira or have transformed into an unalike guise along with outfits. Though a specific answer was not postulated, I would like to give one. I come from a respectable traditional family with standards and mores passed on through generations, governing every decision-making process. Biesh Moisher

Bari adhered to that mind-set for generations, and my elder brother Tanveer, the current head of the family, is no exception. However, the silver lining is that my brother Tanveer has a more flexible mind-set, being swayed by my cerebrally alert sister-in-law Qulsum. The other important person in the family is my mother. Her very resiliently poignant position as being the custodian of passed-on traditions has, of late, shown some vicissitudes, influenced by her lifelong trusted household help, whom we address as Pori Khala.

In that backdrop, my growing up had indescribable variants. I continued to respect and value passed-over dictates of my traditional family and other social units of the type from early childhood but also have had a chant within against their replication, irrespective of variations in times, settings, and requirements. It has always been my conviction that there are different ways to adhere to and practice inherited values, but they become more relevant and sustainable only when required changes are respected and reflected. I also continue to believe that there are divergent ways to carry forward good names and values instead of repeating antediluvians. The penchant to repeat old traditions and values, ignoring current parameters, is self-defeating. This is true of both personal and social lives. Related milieus undergo inevitable changes even though one or a group pursues life while ignoring current realities and requirements. This invariably is a time-bound limitation. People generally get used to those resisted changes over time. In that sort of setting, options are limited, resulting in acceptance after a lapse of time. The major casualty in that process is the loss of valuable times and years.

I experienced other notable irritants while growing up, such as my mother's frequent pregnancies and the unwritten and implicit burden of the handed-down practices and traditions while seeing everything in the local context, confining one's thoughts and actions to what the seniors dictate and what the immediate social setting approves of. Open bedlams against those and recalcitrant comportment were not the attributes of persona I was bestowed with, but I always conditioned myself to be consistent with my inner thoughts. I have never dithered. Inclusive reading habits, the untimely death of Father, and love and affection of my immediate and only elder brother Tanveer helped the process. Sister-in-law Qulsum has always been quite an intelligent and indulgent supporter of mine. Mother has been somewhat reserved in her expressions but has never dissuaded me. My encouragement and support also came from a very incongruous source—my mother's illiterate household help from her parental house, who possesses a level of acumen that seldom one can find even among erudite people. Empathetic surroundings, thus, made a taciturn person like me a much more liberated individual. Within me, I remain the same person as you encountered the first time in our tutorial class. There is no doubt that with the passage of time and enhanced intellectual attainments, I have become more open, friendly, and poised, with changes in my personal bearings and ensembles.

"You have always been within my inner self, though intermittently. Thoughts about you and recalling our brief association from time to time always gave me gargantuan exhilaration, though I was always clear in my mind that your memory is just a mirage, having no relevance with reality. It was a most startling reunion in that seminar hall. Now the current private setting of this discourse, with your divorced status and my remaining single so long, are all perhaps outcomes ordained by divine design and tied to a single string for common good and bliss. It is now up to us to respond to that."

Having said as much, Tauseef went into deep contemplation and then resumed, saying, "From my side, I have no hesitation in marrying you. That will be the zenith of a long-held inner desire. As I said earlier, your divorce, per se, does not trouble me, even though I will need time to get the family along. That does not mean that I am suffering any self-doubt. I neither look forward to a condescending endorsement from the family nor foresee any denigration to my proposition. Rather, I am hopeful—though it may take a little time— that the family would objectify my inner feelings. On that score, I would heavily bend on the empathy and solid support of Qulsum Bhabi, my sister-in-law, and Pori Khala, a trusted person of my mother. Both these individuals have great influence on my brother and mother, respectively. I affirm without any inhibition that my life has never been infected by any creepy-crawlies, but I am of the view that perhaps you have had bugs in life that continuously impact your thoughts, words, and actions. Possibly, that is the reason you precipitously divulged your very candid narration of life events. You may have your skepticism in revealing facts, but I do not have any. I have never considered marriage just as a convenience to produce children as my father did. I recognize the relevance of sex in conjugal life, but to me, that is not the end by itself. I consider marriage, among others, more as a happy union of two souls with a common sharing of feelings and friendship."

As Tauseef was engrossed in articulating his thoughts while saying what he wanted to, there was a visible sign of cheerfulness in the facial responses of Chandni, neutralizing the plaintive feature that had been dominant so far in her expressions and reactions.

The sequel was extemporaneous, guileless, and without reticence. Chandni, most directly, avowed facts about her sensual limitations, leaving nothing to the imagination of Tauseef. Slowly and softly, she opened up, saying, "Though I got married beyond the prevailing marriageable age of Bangladeshi girls and knew Aftab and his family unlike most others, I had an agonizing feeling all through and suffered from a profound sense of edginess. It did not take much time for me to realize that the outward show of exuberance manifested in my noticeable openness, self-confidence, and carefree attitude were a camouflage for inner shyness, a sense of paranoia and an attitude of internecine in matters of behavior, trust, and social communications. With that backdrop, I positioned myself on our decorated wedding bed like most Bangladeshi brides. It initially took Aftab by surprise. He promptly marshaled his thoughts and tossed off a pesky comment. 'However hard you try and double down related efforts, you can never be a traditional Bangladeshi bride. Neither would I want to have you like that. You should be the same Chandni in my life as I knew so long ago—vibrant, confident, open minded, and, more importantly, loving.'

"Subsequent discourse and the gradual initiation process to our cherished conjugal exploits made sustained progression. Both

Aftab and myself were at the zenith of exhilaration and creeping forward to ultimate indulgence and contentment. They were so exciting and fulfilling that seldom I thought about or noted a lack of related response in other critical body organs. I experienced a major impediment when Aftab positioned himself for very natural vaginal penetration. Out of the blue, I reckoned the reality of having a very dry vagina, making the otherwise joyful experience of intercourse very uncomfortable. I sustained the discomfort without directly expressing any riposte. We passed the rest of the night assuming it to be a normal occurrence in the initial process of conjugal living. Similar experiences recurred with declining engagements. The more I was fretful about my sexual dysfunction, the greater was my inability to get aroused sexually or to have an orgasm. Our conjugal experiences were sporadic and equally painful. I could not bear that, seeing Aftab unceasingly unfulfilled and gradually observing a swelling gap in our relationship.

"Time passed. Family members started to whisper their concern, many times ensuring that it would reach me. But Aftab never uttered anything to disparage me. He continued to be quiet and reserved without any sign or symptom of denigration. The situation was a discomforting one. Based on discussions with Nani, I repeatedly suggested a medical consultation for apposite diagnosis, but Aftab would never agree. To my assessment, he was mortified to openly discuss this with anyone else. Gradually, he stopped even discussing this with me too, keeping himself ostensibly busy with reading and writing research papers.

"I had no other hitch with him and his family. I loved him and adored his family, but the consternation associated with our married life's problem gradually started to engulf other facets of our family relationship. It, thus, became incumbent on me to take a decision about our married life. Nani acquiesced with my decision to separate. However, what intrigued me was the laid-back way the family received the suggestion and consented as if they were all perceptive but just could not say. That was the end of my married life and all that I have to say—without blaming anyone or hiding anything."

It was apparent that Chandni felt relieved by divulging the most diaphanous aspect of her life to the only one whom she could trust other than Nani. Likewise, Tauseef was bemused while listening but was not piqued at all. He decided to buy a little time before articulating any insinuation, so discarding all paranoia, he suggested to suspend that evening's discussions, chivalrously proposing the next meeting for the following evening at the same place with similar arrangements. Both agreed, and he left with a feeling of nirvana, while she retired to her bed with a sense of respite.

The following meeting took place as postulated. Chandni was unusually dressed in a white sari. Another remarkable feature was her long dangling hair braid instead of a routine updo, commonly known as *khopa*. That was given a traditional Bangladeshi flare with two tubes of *rojoni-ghandha* (tuberose) placed delicately on the right side of the head, positioned by the ear. Most noteworthy was that her unusually subtle and sober bearings, physical postures, and emotional deportments were in sharp contrast with how she was normally known to be. Tauseef noted this promptly and decided that any hotfooted inquisition would be counterproductive. He was certain that her palpable demeanor was the derivative of a simmering enigma suffering within for hastily opening up her very private personal glitches. He also concluded that remaining unenthused in that setting could as well be misconstrued. His qualm since last night was not about what Chandni frankly stated relating to her sensual problem; he precipitously parked that in some unidentified inimitability on the part of Aftab and quickly concluded that by demonstrating unbounded love, understanding, and care, he would be able to make her comfortable in their future married life. His main concern was how to communicate with the family to be absolutely certain about reactions from Mother and Tanveer. Any proposition by him to marry a divorcee would cause a problem, even though he was certain that with the passage of time, Qulsum Bhabi and Pori Khala would be acquiescent, but that was not sufficient to ensure the esteem and dignity that Chandni deserved as a daughter-in-law of Biesh Moisher Bari. Though a person of liberal disposition, Tauseef even thought of justifying his resolution by educing Islam's unqualified sanction to marry divorcees. Notwithstanding the aforesaid validation, he could not assuage his apprehensions. Time and again, thoughts came to his mind about escalatory demurrals based on infelicitous annotations portraying him as perfidious to the good name of the family and the traditions upheld for so many generations. At the end of that disquieting night, he came to his final decision to marry Chandni and that he was not committing anything wrong fundamentally. If the family couldn't accept that, then it was the family's problem. Albeit possible reaction, he would keep his end of the turf clean and clear so far as maintaining contact and doing good things for Biesh Moisher Bari, even if indirectly. He resolved that the family's potential negativity would be countered by positive ripostes from his end as the situation so permitted.

Grounded in that premise, Tauseef did not want to harbor any more hesitation and so decided to convey to Chandni what he wanted. Entreating her to be seated next to him, he impetuously took possession of her hands and unexpectedly had a feeling of nervousness. For that moment, which appeared to be too long, Tauseef lost his confidence, and his coherence evaporated. His articulation, the singular most prominent feature of his persona, likewise drifted away.

Forsaking emotional elegance and romantic modishness, he uttered simple words, unwaveringly conveying in essence his final decision. "I have listened and assessed all that you have said since our discourse started. Weighing all that and other related challenges to the proposition that we may encounter, I am reaffirming my earlier decision to marry you. This decision is reflective of inner feelings and the recognition of my long-held admiration for you and what you are. I understand that carnal rapport is important in life, but to me, it's not the 'be all and end all' of a relationship. Moreover, observing my mother getting pregnant frequently, I grew up with an aversion to conventional sex, but that in no way wedged my liking of girls. That was perhaps moored in a corner of my stance and suddenly surfaced when you first interceded freely in class to salvage me from an unintended solecism I had committed. For reasons unknown, I nurtured that feeling all through, being absolutely certain that it had no relevance with reality. But destiny has its own way of shaping things. Here we are, after a long gap in contact, in a situation that enables us to act on such sensitivity and to bring it to a positive conclusion. I promise to respond to the arduous inner issues of our future married life with empathy, love, care, and understanding."

Tauseef could feel the softening of her hand clasped between the two palms of his hand. He could as well feel a sense of slackening and submission as she did not withdraw her hands, even though he relaxed his grip. Those were sufficient indications of a positive response from Chandni. He then continued, saying, "If you agree, we can marry any moment—this hour, today, tomorrow, next week—but I would much prefer to defer that for a while. I would like to inform the family about my decision first, seeking their participation and blessings. That is the respectful way to proceed, as I have learned, and the more acceptable way to ensure that you step into the house with due honor and dignity. If they say yes, there will be nothing like it. If they say no, I will marry you, keeping the door of understanding and reconciliation with the family open from our end."

Chandni was overwhelmed and, in the process, forgot the imperative need to touch base with her respected guardian angel, Nani, before even indirectly consenting to Tauseef's proposition. She suddenly was in a state of mind where the past had no germaneness and where only the future dominated.

Tauseef's letter, which conveyed his decision to marry, had triggered discernible tumult and despair in Tanveer. He was both appalled and exasperated, thinking about the loss of face in their surroundings and the disgrace it would cause to the generationally nurtured good name of Biesh Moisher Bari when people came know that the offspring of this noble house had married a divorcee. They would not hesitate to deride the house and inhabitants. Pressed by such thoughts, Tanveer involuntarily put the letter carefully in the inner pocket of his vest, closed his office drawer, and left the office for home quietly. While stepping out, he only nodded to respond to *salaam* but did not talk to anyone.

As a very exceptional gesture and with prior consent of her mother-in-law, Qulsum was on a casual short visit to Pori Khala's place. A household help came running to inform Qulsum about the unexpected presence of Tanveer at home. Both returned to the house, and Qulsum straightaway went to her bedroom, with prodigious anxieties disconcerting her. Pori Khala, as expected, went Hashi Banu's without showing any discernable disquiet.

Tanveer repositioned himself on the chair upon seeing Qulsum enter the room. Before she could make any query, Tanveer abruptly asked her with an obstinate tenor to accompany him to Mother's room.

Hashi Banu had prior information from household help about Tanveer's early return. Neither the untimely quiet entry of Pori nor the subsequent presence of Tanveer and Qulsum had any effect on her outward comportment. She greeted both son and daughter-in-law with a smile. Pori did not fail to notice the inner anxiety that was camouflaged by Hashi Banu's thin smile and was most concerned. Ice-cold silence dominated the setting of the room. Tanveer, following usual practice, sat near the foot of the wooden bed, a tradition and gesture reflective of esteem for his mother. Qulsum positioned herself near the headboard. Pori, more as a diversion, became engaged in preparing *paan*.

Tanveer broke the taciturnity ostensibly, taking blames for the tribulation he was about to reveal, saying, "My indulgence has spoiled Tauseef. I feel miserable that I could not live up to the expectation of our late father or fulfill the promise I made to him while bidding farewell. I would never think that Tauseef could propose something that totally conflicts with the pronounced traditions and good values that Biesh Moisher Bari has nurtured for generations."

He paused for moments, with the silence both arduous and intimidating for the three ladies present. With facts remaining obscure, their options were limited. The only thing that they could do was exchange looks with one another. That did not escape Tanveer. He quietly took out the letter from Tauseef and informed all present about its contents. He then lamented, "I would never imagine that Tauseef would propose marrying a divorcee. It is so dishonorable for all of us and especially ignominious for Biesh Moisher Bari."

Hashi Banu breathed deeply and said, "I had a hunch from his early childhood that he would likely do something that will cause a bad name to this noble house. He has always been different in his relationships with all of us. His focus and attitude toward our values and traditions have always been unresponsive, and his care and respect for the house were nonexistent. That was the reason that I had initially opposed his going to Dhaka for higher studies. What was the need for higher studies? His father left enough for him to have a nice life here. We have tolerated his capricious desires with the hope that things would settle down as he grows up, but now it appears he has crossed all limits. Without blaming, I must frankly say that the indulgence of Pori and the love and care of Qulsum are partially responsible. It is good that your father died without facing such a grievous situation."

Silence again befell in the room. Qulsum was still hesitant to react and remained pensive in labeling a pointer to say what she wanted without being seen insolent, but unlettered and loyal Pori did not waste the opening provided. To the amazement of all and as a very atypical intervention, Pori, who had established herself in this noble house as a family well-wisher through dedicated service and incontrovertible fidelity, civilly responded, saying, "Hashi-bu, I concur with your reflection about the cerebral reaction of Tauseef as being a family member—but only partly. He does not to have the same zeitgeist or views that Tanveer was blessed with, but we should not pass judgment on his attitude or priorities. We should try to understand him in the environment that he grew up in. He is the last of your five living children. The deaths of other children and your chronic illness had never allowed him to be close to you. Azmat Bhai Shaheeb was always preoccupied with business and social commitments. Our three daughters visited the house occasionally for too-brief periods. There was seldom any elongated family event in this house of noble traditions and good name. In that vacuum, Tauseef frequently sought refuge in my person. I have always encouraged him to concentrate on studies to enhance the name of this house. After Tanveer brought home Qulsum, Tauseef confided in me that for the first time, he had found a friend in this overladen traditional house. She gave him comfort and supported him all the way. Knowing him as I do, I can safely say that Tauseef has never been and is not at all disrespectful to this house and the many traditions."

There was a stiff taciturnity permeating the surroundings of Hashi Banu's room. Absorbing what Pori highlighted and taking advantage of the opening implied in the later part of her just-concluded statement, Qulsum delicately began to share her thoughts. She said, "In many of our discourses, we conversed on social, family, and personal issues but seldom talked about girls. The only exception was his first winter vacation visit after getting admitted into Dhaka University. There was a girl in his class by the name Chandni. For reasons unclear, he developed a liking for her from his first encounter, even though many of their known preferences and values were contradictory and interactions between them were few and far between. Our discussions significantly declined with his enrollment in the private university. In some follow-on discussions, he occasionally talked about Chandni, even though he had no update about her life. To my knowledge, Chandni was the only girl he was interested in."

The reference of Chandni with specific insinuation about Tauseef's liking triggered within Tanveer the needed avowal for what he wanted to say. He exchanged looks with Mother Hashi, and possibly being assured of implicit approval, Tanveer resolutely made his position known: a simple no. Tanveer made it abundantly clear that as a brother, he was sympathetic to Tauseef's desire, but he could not agree with it as the custodian to safeguard and preserve the traditions and reputations of this house, nurtured for so many generations. That irrefutably denoted the decision embodying the values, name, and reputation that Biesh Moisher Bari embodied and represented. There was no and could not be any follow-on discussions.

Qulsum was both distraught and thwarted. She had never anticipated such a quick and conclusive decision, even more so after what Pori Khala so courteously articulated. She was expecting a little more time for all to assess the proposition, ensuring the consideration of rational options, even having a hint of emotion. Such a premonition from Qulsum was premised on the understanding, compassion, and solicitous approach Tanveer had always demonstrated in handling subtle community- and business-related issues. But Tanveer's demeanor and tone during that late afternoon gathering were in sharp contrast to the affable and caring persona that distinguished him socially as she knew him since marriage. Qulsum concluded that certainly, the prevailing Bangla saying "Koila dhuley o moila jai na [The dirt remains even if coal is washed]" is appropriate in understanding Tanveer's instant behavior. The plushness in behavior that Tanveer personified through education and discourses with his logic professor could not shelve what he had in blood. Unknowingly, it was his genetic transmission of tradition and values of Biesh Moisher Bari. Having that sort of conclusion, Qulsum, after exchanging a passionate look with Tanveer, slowly moved out of Hashi Banu's room, repositioning the *anchal* on her head as a sign of modesty. But leaving the room, before the gathering was dismissed by either Mother or Tanveer, was evidently disrespectful under family traditions. Nobody was bothered as that was her first time gaffe and also because a more critical issue was being discussed.

While sitting alone near the kitchen, Qulsum lamented not for Tanveer alone but for the entire family of Biesh Moisher Bari. What happened in that *bari* typified the burden most families heightening in aristocracy suffered. That was the reason why her mother, for no fault of her own, could never set foot in Khanbahadur Monzeel, her rightful home. But Khanbahadur Monzeel unsuspectingly had to give in before time and the tide of events, and she, as the daughter of that mother, had her position of respect and standing in that house.

Growing up in Khan Monzeel and ruminating what happened to her mother, Qulsum comprehended something very valuable. Social and family values are bound to change whether one likes that or not. Attempt to resist is futile. Most changes face resistance but prevail in the long run. People and families become used to changes resisted earlier. The net impact is the loss of precious time and the warmth of relationships and experiences. Qulsum was certain that a similar experience would be repeated in Biesh Moisher Bari. Tauseef was the son of Kazi Azmat Ali Shoudagar and the very dear sibling of Tanveer. He was a part and parcel of this *bari*, and that would always prevail. Nothing could dislodge him from that position. Tauseef was and would always remain a progeny of this *bari* and would be so accepted in time to come. Moreover, present resentment and discontent most likely would be of less relevance with the passage of time. In the process, treasured time and the congenial bonding between two brothers would be impaired, serving no one.

Qulsum's affianced meditating mood was pried by the soft and polite query of Pori Khala for reasons to be near the kitchen instead of her room. Qulsum gave a taciturn look and refrained from responding orally. Pori Khala sat by her side and said, "I fully understand your position and agony. I also understand the reasons that stirred you to leave Hashi-bu's room early, but I do not know what to do."

Qulsum kept quiet, had a deep mien, and took Pori Khala inside the kitchen. In the familiar privacy, she unburdened herself of the thought that was permeating her mind since leaving the gathering. She said, "I have a plan for our joint efforts to save this noble house from impending catastrophe by minimizing the impact of today's decision. We will have to play respective roles in carrying out the plan. There are three elements to our approach. First, we need to be careful in undertaking any such effort. The strategy would be to give Mother-in-law and Tanveer an impression that we are on board with their decision. Second, we will slowly make points concerning family lineage, changes in focus and attitude, and the possible negative impact once the strain in the relationship between the two brothers becomes public. And third, we need to divide our effort by your focusing on Mother-in-law and me trying to cajole Tanveer."

Pori not only concurred but was in tears, saying, "Betty Qulsum, Biesh Moisher Bari is singularly fortunate to have someone of your astute competence to be our daughter-in-law. I will share this assessment of mine with Hashi-bu to assure her about the sustenance of values of Biesh Moisher Bari, even in our absence. But one point bothers me. How one would explain your conduct this afternoon, leaving the gathering first without any word?"

Qulsum smiled and said, "My position, as I would place, is that it was not meant to show any disrespect to anyone. I just felt bad thinking about the future bearing of the decision on sibling relationship. Hence, instead of creating any scene, I preferred to leave the room."

Pori Khala was impressed by the response thought through by Qulsum quickly and found that to be a reasonable one. While they decided to take a little time to initiate their efforts, Tanveer was very prompt in sending his reply to Tauseef, unmistakably conveying the family decision.

The contents of Tanveer's reply did not surprise Tauseef at all but caused grim dismay. Tauseef had his misgivings before initiating the action. Still, he was harboring hope against hope. That was premised on the family's eagerness to see him married. Without wasting time, Tauseef went to Chandni's place, apprised her of the negative outcome of effort to make the proposed marriage a consensual family event, and, more as a frustration, proposed to get married the following day.

Chandni's antiphon to Tauseef's irascibility had all the elements of being empathetic with equanimity and practicality as the hallmark of future passage. Her understanding, approach, and reasoning were able to calm down Tauseef. He even found a comfort zone in Chandni's words and reasoning, highlighting the predicament of Tanveer being the custodian of Biesh Moisher Bari. That bane day for Tauseef eventually ended with a clear happy note, notwithstanding initial disgruntlement.

The essence of their understanding that evening was a reconfirmation by both to get married and for Tauseef to write a second letter to the family communicating his decision to get married without, in any way, contesting the earlier negative decision of the family. They also agreed to have the wedding in about a month, giving the family opening and time to reconsider. In having such an understanding, Chandni unpredictably made an observation, which took Tauseef by surprise.

She said, "You should not write the letter to Brother Tanveer. Especially when you will be indicating a decision to get married against the family's approval. He may be only three years older than you, but in the local setting, he is now the head of the house. That has a special significance and relevance, so I suggest that you write the letter to your *bhabi* [sister-in-law] to convey your decision and requesting their consent and participation. We know the end result, but it will be a better approach. As you are not directly contesting the decision of Brother Tanveer, possibly in the future, we will be able to handle the waves that are likely to be generated."

That stance was acted upon promptly. In his emotion-laden yet polite letter to Qulsum, Tauseef renewed his commitment to Mother to be in touch and to uphold the good name of Biesh Moisher Bari. He beseeched, "My decision to marry Chandni in no way violates that undertaking. I am not acting against the faith and traditions of our noble house. The family may not be in unison with my decision, but that should not sully our bond and relationship. It should not spin us against one another or influence our fancying one another. So with indisputability, we urge and hope for agreement and blessings from all Biesh Moisher Bari and, as feasible, participation in our wedding on the twenty-seventh of next month."

Tauseef then discreetly conveyed the ultimate position concerning his marriage. He continued writing, "As you know, Chandni is the only girl I was attracted to from the moment I met her, in spite of some variances in our approach and attitude. During the intervening seven to eight years since I left for private university education and subsequent higher studies in the USA, we had no contact and communication. But unintentionally, she was always ubiquitous in the corner of my mind. Providence has brought us together after those many years, and we have evaluated our initial exchanges, likings, and differences before reaching the decision to get married. I cannot and will not think of marrying anyone else."

The letter was received by the inhabitants at Biesh Moisher Bari with varied reactions. Tauseef's decision to marry Chandni, albeit the family's disapproval, upset the house, especially Mother and Tanveer. Pori silently acceded but desisted from being vocal, anticipating possible backlash. Qulsum openly implored for introspection instead of making it a weighty family issue to be burlesqued by outsiders. Initial resistance to her suggestion soon withered away, even more when she emphasized Tauseef's final position that if not Chandni, he would prefer to remain unmarried.

The consequential tears rolling down Hashi Banu's cheeks had a softening effect on Tanveer too. The consensus was that the family would not object to the proposition anymore but would not be present at the wedding. In support of this absence, Tanveer advised for the first time about a plan he had to go to Mecca with the family so Mother could perform *umrah* (little hajj). This was carefully crafted to coincide with the date of the proposed wedding to avoid foreseeable misapprehension.

Addressing that letter to Qulsum had a positive imprint. It was taken as a symbolic gesture, confirming Tauseef's adherence to the values and traditions of the noble house. He demonstrated respect for his elder brother as the head of the house by not directly defying his earlier decision. All concerned were appreciative of that.

Qulsum wrote a letter in reply with adroitly framed lingos, which were neutral with respect to the agreement, and ensured space to escape participation without acrimonious feelings. In her prompt response, she recalled past association and understandings since stepping into the Biesh Moisher Bari years back but remained silent on the core proposition for participation. She did indicate clearly about the family's inability to be present at the wedding because of a finalized plan to perform *umrah*. She was particular in mentioning that they were scheduled to be in Mecca about the same time. In conclusion, Qulsum requested Tauseef to convey her love and best wishes to dear Chandni.

Tauseef was not alone in having a delicate exchange of communication regarding their marriage. Chandni had her share too. Her Nani was not opposed but had her reservations. She repeatedly insinuated about the principal physical cause of her divorce and forewarned her about the eventual reality. She counseled her about the veracity of sensual urge and the resultant experiences. Her conjoint homily was that both men and women were equally susceptible to erroneousness behavior in spite of sober and sensitive discourse or views expressed during a normal time. Sharing life when sensually aroused was a different domain and different experience. Chandni judiciously pursued her proposition and eventually succeeded in getting the concurrence of Nani. That made both of them happy, even though Tauseef had internal agony because of the certain absence of his own family.

Chandni consciously made efforts to console him, saying, "Our marriage does not mean the end of your relationship with Apurba Neer or Biesh Moisher Bari. We are getting married while informing them and seeking their blessings. Maybe this wedding will pave the way for a possible new and meaningful bond between your family and us. We will work on that with all sincerity. So please do not get upset."

Pursuantly, both of them became involved in working out the plan for a decent marriage, making the solemn occasion a memorable one. Since planning entails events and actions in the future, the place, time, and arrangements remain vulnerable to uncertainties. In some cases, such uncertainties have a positive outcome, enjoyed by those involved as glorious uncertainties, but in other cases, there can be a desolate occurrence or outcome, shaking the confidence and quintessence of those involved. The second one happened in their case as unexpectedly, Nani succumbed to a mild attack of pneumonia, to the shock and dismay of all concerned. The visible impact of her grievous loss manifested on Chandni's face and worried Tauseef very much.

Chandni, contrary to her personality traits and oblivious of social politesse, started reacting loudly, blaming herself for all that had happened in her life—the premature death of her parents, her separation after a most desired marriage, and the most unexpected demise of Nani just before her ensuing wedding. She all of a sudden became very lonely. Her *mama* (maternal uncle) had always maintained lukewarm contact with her mother and resultantly with Chandni. Her arcane emotive frenzy did not roil Tauseef's trust in her well-known cerebral qualities and pragmatic attributes. He resolved that it was the absence of any family shoulder in that critically emotional hour of her grief. Instead of being raked by Chandni's negative reactions, Tauseef demonstrated a sober and sustained positive approach and attitude in managing the situation. Perhaps it was an inherited skill. He recalled every detail of his and Tanveer's navigation out of a major family crisis after Father's death. The resultant experience of that approach echoed with sustained focus on an unwavering understanding of the position Chandni was in with meaningful support, including taking care of any of her immediate needs or errands. He soon concluded that the most effective way out of the current tangle may be to hasten the wedding.

That was meticulously pursued and patiently deliberated upon to reach a common understanding for an early wedding. Chandni's only caveat was the scale as she was in no mental state for a traditional Bangladeshi wedding. Especially in the case of families like Biesh Moisher Bari, tradition entails the involvement of the larger family and community participation. The proposition for a small-sized wedding was readily agreed upon as it also served the purpose of Tauseef. The absence of his immediate family in a traditional wedding would have been an embarrassment for him. The ostensible reason of *umrah* would have been taken by most as more of an excuse rather than a reason.

As acquiesced, the wedding took place in a very limited scale involving the close relations of Chandni and dear friends of Tauseef. He kept his family informed about the unexpected acceleration of his limited wedding because of the unexpected demise of Chandni's *nani*. He had no feeling of sheepishness or guilt. The wedding was small but complied with rituals, and the memorable event was beautiful for Tauseef and Chandni.

They commenced their conjugal living with a happy base that soon encountered the challenge of containment. Being conscious of Chandni's emotional inability for fully participating in sensual engagements, Tauseef's approach and attitude had all the elements of care, love, understanding, and compassion. He initiated conjugal living with low expectations and had been patient. More effort and attention were clutched to induce the emotional impulse of Chandni. Whatever a few engagements he had, the signal was transparent that Chandni did not enjoy any of it; rather, she silently sustained pain and discomposure. Tauseef took that as initial disablement against the backdrop of experience and related psychological impulse. Consciously, they spent many nights talking about the future, family, and married life. He availed every window of opportunity to discuss the germaneness of sex in emotionally bonding and fostering a happy and contented family.

Tauseef, taking refuge in made-up excuses, deferred his post-marriage visit to Biesh Moisher Bari to seek blessings from Mother. He was hoping for an unexpected turn of experience. As the time passed, that appeared not to be so soon except waiting for divine intervention. His initial anxiety steadily turned into frustration as the aberration between the soothing counsel of friendship and the reality of life after marriage started to creep into his feelings. His exasperation started scorching within as friends and close associates had begun teasing him for having such a beautiful, gorgeous, and, according to some, indulgent wife and for enjoying life blithely. Besides being annoyed, Tauseef started self-evaluation and examination. He questioned himself as to his current yearning for sex, which he spurned in most of his growing life. Tauseef garishly recalled that his negative feeling for sex induced a bad imprint of his father. He was a victim of that, now being frustrated for not having sex. He soon concluded that his early-age repugnance of sex was a weaseling feeling swayed by having observed Mother pregnant and ill regularly, depriving him of the golden experience of a mother's love. He also comprehended that sometimes life's different phases have unique finales. Notwithstanding that, life needs to be seen positively and pursued patiently. In that journey, there will obviously be the need for fixing, tweaking, and building new features. With that sort of thinking, Tauseef achieved impermanent tranquility with the current experience of life during the initial days after the wedding. But as he went to bed, night after night, every preceding logic and conclusion upturned repeatedly. Reflexes triggered by physical impulses consequent to sharing the same bed with the most gorgeous young lady and in the privacy and darkness of night bemused positions considered both ideal and logical during daytime. Tauseef continued to suffer from hushed pressure and frustration in spite of his public face of contentment. Initially, he had gullible conclusions for his continued infelicitous experience in married life. Why did he push the marriage proposition despite the opposition of family or marry a divorcee that ostensibly demeaned the name of Biesh Moisher Bari? Suddenly, his mother's unceasing frustration with him beginning in his youth began to perturb him. Propitiously, he overcame such mundane inhibitions while pursuing a course of forbearance and empathy in his dealings with Chandni.

Tauseef quietly focused on related research. His first broad understanding was that vaginal dryness caused by the inability to stimulate during intercourse further aggravated pain during penetration. It had a variety of symptoms such as the general lack of sexual desire or fantasies and the absence of signs of sexual arousal commonly noticed in vaginal lubrication. He learned about the factors that caused it either singularly or in combination. In Chandni's case, he could associate an autoimmune disorder that affected cells producing moisture and douching. He ruled out other possibilities, like allergies, reactions to medication, or the lack of enough foreplay. The research reassured him when he learned that the inability to be sexually aroused or to have an orgasm could either be a new development or a lifelong problem. Tauseef quickly concluded that Chandni's early twisted psychological experiences had a deep bearing on her emotions and physical responses. That conclusion made him happy; however, the inability to identify any medical process to overcome it made him depressed. He felt the need to share his views with a professional person and get some professional counsel.

Tauseef was coming out of the Institute of Postgraduate Medicine's hospital in Dhaka after visiting an ailing colleague. He suddenly encountered his once-close friend with whom, for unknown reasons, he lost all contacts. That friend was Associate Professor Alamgir, whose prominence and position were evident by the number of fellows and students following him.

Dr. Alamgir recognized him first and warmly embraced him, instantaneously recalling the good old days of intermediate college life without a single word about the lack of contact in the interim. During that brief discourse, Tauseef came to know that he was a renowned gynecologist in the city. Besides being part of the faculty of the institute, he also practiced. That opportune sudden reunion with Dr. Alamgir was just what Tauseef was looking for. He decided to share his fretfulness and agony with Alamgir and met with him privately.

The considered opinion of Dr. Alamgir premised on his professional expertise was not good enough for Tauseef in terms of his immediate objective of getting Chandni involved in a normal sensual life as soon as possible. Dr. Alamgir told his friend two things. First, the nature, symptoms, and other related issues pertaining to the current problem should not be discussed with Chandni at all. This would overload her mental anxiety, which would only worsen the situation. And second, most probably, this was caused because of psychological trauma experienced during her growing-up phase; perhaps another emotional or physical trauma in future would trigger her interest and participation back in sexual encounters.

Time lapsed. Anxieties burgeoned in the thoughts and actions of Chandni, recalling the reaction of Nani when the proposition for her second marriage was mooted with her first. Unwittingly, Chandni could never escape her anxiety concerning conjugal life and could not help revisiting the related gripping frustration that swamped Tauseef's social demeanors.

As an escape, Tauseef became more involved in research and writing, earning celebrity quickly. Coincidentally, he received an offer for consultancy from a Rome-based international development agency. It was a prestigious opening for him, but what interested him most were the terms of reference dealing with income inequality and applicable social safety nets, a subject matter of immense interest and very close to his heart.

Chandni was very happy. Tauseef informed Tanveer about his appointment, using it as an excuse for continuing to defer the already delayed post-marriage visit to Apurba Neer. Another taciturn reason for his nascent contentment was the space he would be getting from the thwarting in the bedroom he was suffering from frequently.

The three-month-long assignment passed too quickly. Apart from doing what professionally he was to do, Tauseef utilized the time and opportunity to get to know Italy, roam around the streets of Rome, and visit as many historical places, edifices, basilicas, and cathedrals as he could. The most striking discomfort for Tauseef was the culture of midday *siesta*, a Spanish word meaning "short nap." In Italian, this was called *riposo*, meaning "rest." There was a broad uniformity in the practice and timing of *riposo*. Most museums, shops, churches, and businesses, everything except restaurants, pulled down the shutters during *riposo* to go home or to a local trattoria (informal restaurant), café, or osteria (a wine bar also serving simple meals). The *riposo* usually lasted ninety minutes to two hours, varying between noon and two-thirty to four o'clock. The common practice had a sign posted—Chiuso (closed).

The culture of *riposo* did not trouble Tauseef during normal workdays as he was engaged in an international organization. It did hurt him most on weekends when his focus was to optimize the use of time seeing the thousand-year-old relics of civilization of which there was no dearth. Most appositely, wherever they were found, whether underground or on the surface, meticulous efforts were made and resources allocated to preserve them for posterity. He visited the most known vestiges: the Roman Colosseum, the Pantheon, St. Peter's Basilica, the Vatican Museum, and the Piazza Navona.

A piazza (meaning public or open space, mostly circular in shape) is the Italian version of what is meant by a town square in earlier urban planning. Mostly located centrally of any major habitation, piazzas are used for community gatherings and open markets. So far as Tauseef was concerned, piazzas were an instant hit.

He enormously enjoyed visiting various piazzas between his weekend promenades along various architectural edifices and cenotaphs. Though his main intent was to take a break in the long walks, he started to enjoy the setting and movements of the people everywhere, the occasional display of magic and burlesque, and the picture taking by locals and tourists alike. Unwittingly, he developed another new liking in the process. While sitting to relax, he started having great Italian coffee with biscuits. Tauseef's initiation to Italian coffee was an accidental one.

In one of his early days in Rome, he casually occupied a vacant table in an outdoor patio area of a coffee place. Sitting there for some time and monitoring the movements and expressions of the attending hostess, he felt embarrassed for not ordering anything but to occupy a chair. He was not sure as to what to order at the odd hours of the day. So when one of the attending servers asked him for his order, he was unsure about his reply. The server went inside and brought the *barista* (one who makes coffee) of the café as he had ability to communicate a little with non-Italian customers.

The barista had a compassionate look at Tauseef and directly asked, "Would you like to have espresso and biscotti?"

Tauseef, maintaining a pause, nodded. Soon, a server brought a warm wet hand towel and a glass of iced water, followed by the espresso and biscuit. He recalled his dislike for American coffee and so hesitatingly had his first sip. He instantly liked it and never tested any other type of coffee while in Italy.

His related exposure to and experience with biscotti was unique too. It took some time for him to get used to handle biscotti. The word *biscotti*, though it could have some link to the English word *biscuit*, means "twice baked" and can thus be stored and used over a long time. Because of baking twice, the cookies have a very hard texture. The most convenient way to enjoy a biscotti is to dip it in tea or coffee. Many indulge in this, even though some Italians despise dunking biscotti in any liquid other than *vin santo* (sweet late-harvest wine). Tauseef soon got used to soaking his favorite biscotti, made of hazelnuts, almonds, and pistachios, in his espresso without any feeling of guilt.

Tauseef came to know of Venice during his casual reading about the coffee derivation of the espresso. An unexpected inquisitiveness propelled an interest in him to know more about Venice. And he started his exploration, circumnavigating quantifiables of interest to him. In his quest to know Italy more intimately and based on his rudimentary knowledge, he decided to visit Venice, bypassing many other places of interest before leaving for Bangladesh on the completion of his assignment.

Modern Venice is the capital Veneto region of Northern Italy. This city was built over hundreds of years on a group of 118 islands located in a marshy lagoon of the Adriatic Sea. The habitation on this marshy land has been in and around water. There are no roads, and the numerous islands are connected by intricate canals and bridges. The distinctive geographical configuration of the city fostered its exceptional development and preserved structures and gave birth to unique artistic works. The most significant testament to that is the presence of lined-up Renaissance and Gothic palaces along the Grand Canal thoroughfare. The famous St. Mark's Basilica is located in Piazza San Marco, the largest square of the city. In the chronology of human ingenuity making progress through innovations based on need and experience, Venetians made their mark in erecting enormous edifices on marshy lands. Considering the saturated nature of soil and taking note of regular flooding the habitation has been exposed to, Venetians developed the use of wood as the foundation material. They first piled wooden stakes in the sub-soil and then built wooden platform on the stakes, and as a third step, structures were built on those platforms.

The abundance of water and its periodicity were surreptitious elements that influenced the said decision. As woods used for staking were mostly submerged underwater, they were never exposed to oxygen. Thus, those wood materials were immune from microorganisms as fungi and bacteria causing wood to decay could not survive without oxygen. Moreover, the flow of abundant saltwater with consistency as to level and duration petrified the wood over time, turning it into a hardened material.

Historically and strategically, the lagoon protected the city. Currently, the lagoon itself is a major cause of concern for its continued existence. Venetians are used to the periodic flooding of the city, which used to be about twelve times in a year. But current frequent occurrences of severe and lasting flooding because of the rising sea level, the recurrence of strong winds and storm surges, and the frequency and enormity of rain made that flooding a cause of serious concern. The water of the lagoon, which fostered the growth of this peerless habitation, is now threatening its very existence. This flooding is locally known as *aqua alta* (high water). The entire city and lagoon have been declared by the UN as a World Heritage Site, and international experts are working on options to save it from natural degradation.

Tauseef was exposed to the uniqueness of Venice soon after disembarking from his train. Stepping out of the train, he encountered the waters and canals of Venice. His ferry trip, which ran like a city-surface bus service, stopped at various points before berthing at Piazza San Marco, the disembarking point of Tauseef. During that journey of about thirty minutes, Tauseef just looked around, being awed by the nature and features of an urban development he had never thought of. He imagined that the whole setting of Venice from the sky would just look like a lotus plantation on a huge body of water.

He was thrilled by that exposure of two days and just could not resist the impulse to relate his experiences at the earliest to his counterpart of the agency, who had engaged him for the agency's job to begin with. On hearing his stories, the friend, who was from the south, smiled a little and suggested that if he were given the chance in the future, Tauseef should visit Southern Italy, particularly the Amalfi Coast—a forty-kilometer coastline on the southern shore, beginning at the town of Vietri sul Mare.

The friend said, "That travel takes one away from the churches, museums, and ruins of Italy to its natural bequests in undiluted form with captivating beauty. You have seen the beauty of Venice and enjoyed it, but the natural beauty of the South is so inimitable that one does not only enjoy it but also gets to feel it, absorb it, wander, and admire it. Go to the South if you have a chance."

Tauseef finished his assignment as scheduled. That was about ten days after his visit to Venice and was as per schedule with the funding agency. He returned to Dhaka with the only regret of having not visited the South, as highlighted by his friend.

Chandni was excited to have him back. Both soon realized and appreciated the positive outcome of intermittent space in connubial living. But that positive feeling withered away because of Tauseef's relentless repetition of his experiences in Italy, emphasizing how unique the country was, with its history, heritage, culture, architecture, innovations, society, fashion, and work ethos. He repeated his likings of piazzas and espresso. Chandni soon realized that for Tauseef, who had a marked character of being reticent, Rome had been an extraordinary experience and possibly his first love with any place beyond Bangladesh. She recounted that even though he spent about four years in the USA, he seldom referred to that country except its openness and opportunities and some girly talks, more to play with her reactions and peeve her. She, thus, stopped any vocal whining about it with just a decline in attention to what he had to say about Rome and Venice.

Tauseef took out the time and became engaged in planning his post-marriage visit to Biesh Moisher Bari, an obligation delayed for mottled reasons. He was determined to fulfill that obligation as soon as possible. Within his own thoughts, he reaffirmed his commitment to maintain roots with Apurba Neer, notwithstanding the irritating carry on burden of family traditions and related social pressures and the family's response to his wedding with Chandni. Everything was progressing as planned for the sojourn to Apurba Neer except the lingering frustration of wanting a conjugal relationship. Though conditioned to sustain the evident inadequacy with efforts to address it emotionally and somatically, he was definite that Pori Khala would be the one to identify his inner frustration, and it would be difficult for him to disavow that if confronted by her.

In that milieu, Tauseef was taken aback by the contents of an unexpected communication from the Rome-based agency. The content was simple and straight, appreciating the work he had done and offering a short one-and-a-half-month consultancy assignment in Rome again. The objective was to consider comments received on his previous paper, reflect on them as appropriate, and refine the draft policy paper—"Income Inequality and Applicable Social Safety Nets"—for circulation to the board for approval. He reacted promptly and advised the management of his institution, realigned some of his work schedules, accepted the offer, and genially informed Tanveer about a further unexpected delay in visiting because of the professional need to leave for Rome.

As he was ruminating about his previous visit during the flight to Rome, Tauseef precipitously recalled the suggestion to visit Southern Italy. He was amused, thinking that a chance would happen so soon. He had decided resolutely to visit Southern Italy this time and planned to accelerate his work at the initial phase to buy a little time for the weekend coinciding with the end of his assignment. He was confident that he could because after getting the offer, he devoted most of his Dhaka time to review and refine the earlier policy paper submitted to the agency, focusing on editorial facets like sequencing and the appropriate use of words and expressions besides deepening the policy aspects. Hence, he was ahead of schedule even before reaching Rome.

Once in Rome, progress was consistent with plan he had in mind. Tauseef found his initial Dhaka-based work very beneficial. He finished revising and updating the work ahead of schedule and pleasantly became engaged in planning a much-cherished visit to Southern Italy. He focused on the Amalfi Coast and decided to negotiate the place by tourist bus service.

The Amalfi Coast covers the relatively steep southern shore of the Sorrentine Peninsula, which separates the Gulf of Naples to the north from the Gulf of Salerno to the south. That travel to Southern Italy has its many natural features to unwittingly cause a simultaneous sense of immense excitement, an apprehension of immediate concern, a feeling of smallness, and an impression of awe as one negotiates the bending roads, encounters smaller vehicles, and sees smaller structures on their journey. The thrill of that journey is heightened by the steep shoreline roads getting narrower with bends and curves in immediate frequency and the variety of dimensions on the lap of rock-studded mountains. The other striking characteristic of that journey is the frequency of smaller paved roads with cobblestones, an increased encounter with both smaller vehicles and fairly large tourist buses, and a copious view of smaller constructions on the descending lap of mountains. As one glances through flowing slopes toward the sea with a crystal view of blue water thousands of feet below with stone-studded mountains and landscape graced by vineyards and groves of olive and citrus, that excitement rapidly turns into immense charm. That beauty and gripping experience are bound to have their unique impressions on any onlooker observing coastal mountains plunge into the sea in a magnificent vertical panorama. Tauseef was thrilled and overwhelmed and started silently thanking his friend for encouraging him to undertake the visit—even before reaching his destination.

The final destination was the hotel bearing the name Hotel Villa Eden. Tauseef did not have detailed information about the hotel. His expectation likewise was very modest, keeping in view the price he was willing to pay. When he was talking to the bus driver about his hotel, he was pleasantly surprised to learn that it was at a privileged location about half a mile from the Amalfi city center. With a manageable-sized backpack and a hand carry, Tauseef opted to walk to the hotel, following directions from the bus driver. That walk was about fifteen minutes, mostly negotiating through cobbled sidewalks, but was very enjoyable in the early afternoon of late August. That was made more captivating by the flowers and vines covering an overhead trellis of wayside structures and shops.

He knew it was a boutique hotel with limited facilities, but he was engulfed as he entered the hotel. As there was no one at the reception desk at that point in time, Tauseef looked around to get a feel of the place that would be his home for the next three nights. The terrace overlooking the bay saw the hotel and all adjacent constructions being built into the mountainside, offering a romantic view all day and evening. It was not difficult for him to envisage the sublime beauty at night because of rutted lighting. The vaulted ceilings and terra-cotta tiles of the floor made Tauseef very happy. He thanked himself for choosing a nice hotel, comfy and with all the traits of home.

As he was ruminating, a gorgeous lady softly said, "Hello."

Tauseef turned and unsteadily responded with a tottering "Hello." He was taken by the suddenness of undiluted Italian beauty. She introduced herself as Nanita Lorena and apologized for not being at the reception desk. Some sort of positive energy traversed between the two totally unknown individuals. They soon started chitchatting with each other while completing check-in formalities.

Nanita came to know that Tauseef was a first-time tourist with not much information pertaining to Amalfi Coast and introduced herself. "My grandfather established this boutique hotel with fourteen rooms. Over time, six more rooms were added with the carefully nursed bougainvillea covering the portico. Besides my father, two other persons manning the reception desk take care of our guests, in addition to the kitchen, cleaning, and laundry staff. One of those fellows on the desk is on leave, so I am helping manage the hotel. We run this hotel as a family business, always prioritizing the needs and expectations of our guests. We fondly hope that this service concept and attitude will bring guests back to us whenever they are here."

Over a welcome drink, she continued, saying, "The most popular place around is known as Positano. It is the most precipitously picturesque township with a lineup of brilliantly decorated cafés, well-appointed boutiques, and galleries with classic art works. In addition, it is endowed with the most pleasurable beach. Positano is the most sought-after tourist attraction, but the most important natural attribute it has is the view of vertiginous homes, hotels, and other constructions in the laps and gradients of surrounding hills and mountains, emblazoned by bright peach, pink, yellow, and terra-cotta colors."

Tauseef picked up his modest hand-carry items and slowly went to the elevator as Nanita attended to other guests. As he stepped into the elevator, he pushed the button for level 4. The door closed, and to his amazement, the elevator started going down instead of going up. That was a unique experience for Tauseef, realizing that like most constructions of the coast, including villas and inns, this hotel was also built possibly on a small flat surface of the mountain slopes to reach the only coastal land route above, stretching about forty kilometers. Adhering to what Nanita suggested earlier, he took the remaining part of that afternoon easy, sipping coffee on the terrace and taking a little rest in his room. Because of this and his unfamiliarity with the surroundings, he decided to have dinner in his small hotel. To his surprise, he met her again, this time supervising and helping in dinner service. Sitting in a corner table of that cozy dining room and observing Nanita and the other waiter interacting with guests, Tauseef really appreciated what she meant that afternoon by saying "family business."

Nanita took a little longer to approach the table of Tauseef. The spontaneity of her attendance and the affability of her approach, coupled with an unmitigated smile, predicated her query about choices for dinner. As Tauseef was haphazardly scanning the menu, Nanita did not waste any time. She could implicitly assess his predicament, which could either be a lack of familiarity or an attempt to impress her. She volunteered to help him. Tauseef readily consented with one rider—cautioning his inability to have any food item that had direct or indirect inputs based on pork and ham. She looked at the menu, as she did with most customers, and suggested *spaghetti alla norma*. For Tauseef's peace of mind, she went on explaining, "This dish originated in Sicily and is both healthy and popular. This spaghetti is usually made with grated ricotta *salata* cheese, roasted eggplants, and tomatoes flavored by herbs, including oregano, parsley, and a bit of basil."

She went to the kitchen, and the only other employee in the restaurant, the waiter, came to his table and placed a sliced baguette of warm sourdough bread and an accompanying bowl of deep green extra-virgin olive oil. During his earlier visit to Italy, he was exposed to some Italian traditions and practices; none had yet included dipping bread in olive oil. He was further surprised to see the waiter bring a bottle of balsamic vinegar and, through sleight of hand acquired over time, carefully pour a bit on the olive oil to create a floating W. He politely said, "Welcome, sir, and enjoy your bread."

Hungry after the long bus ride without any evening snack, Tauseef started munching the warm Italian bread pieces, alternating between butter and flourished olive oil. He continued observing the courteous interactions between the guests and the waiter, while Nanita was busy in the kitchen. His admiration for the small hotel swelled, observing the apparent quality of service considering the size and resources.

He was taken aback to see Nanita approach the table with two servings of spaghetti. She placed one plate in front of Tauseef and the other plate in front of the empty chair by his side. She went to the service counter of the bar, poured half a glass of red wine, and took off her half apron and scarf. She came back to the table, occupied the chair in front of the other plate, looked at Tauseef, and said, "Bon appetit!"

Tauseef was in a muddled mood. His responses were slow, lacking focus and action, Nanita noted in between gently swirling and sipping her wine. She was palpably in a jovial mood and wanted to talk. She initiated her soliloquy, saying, "After observing and talking to you during check-in time, I have a fair idea of the questions you have presently in mind. So instead of asking you, let me explain each of those possible thoughts. First, sharing a dinner table with guests, subject to comfortability, is a normal practice of mine. That is the way we bond with our guests. It is important for a business of our type and size. Second, the front desk staff currently on leave is my boyfriend. We are going to be engaged early next year. Third, as a staff working in the restaurant, we are the welcoming face. So a range of aprons, shirts, blouses, and accessories are relevant. As a female attendant, I also prefer to have a chiffon scarf, which is both fashionable and feminine. As per practice, we are to take off such accessories while dining with guests. Lastly—and as I am observing—you are wondering why I am playing with my wineglass, holding its stem. This is called swirling, an act done for ten to twenty seconds to slowly aerate the wine, releasing gently evaporated vapors from sides of the glass to enable the person to smell. That is the reason wineglasses are so designed. All connoisseurs of wine invariably indulge in it while tasting wine."

Tauseef was beguiled by Nanita's adroitness and ability to read the mind of a relatively unknown person and to have interesting and thrilling discourse. He relaxed himself after finishing his meal, smiled at her, and said, "Not only is Amalfi Coast beautiful, but its people are too, and so is the food. I could never think of meeting someone like you—gentle, considerate, understanding, friendly, supportive, helpful, and more importantly, with an open mind and intense poise. I do not know how to thank you for making a naive visitor like me at home, both in the hotel and Amalfi."

She smilingly responded, "You do not really need to thank me. It is too early for you to be at home with Amalfi as you have not experienced it as yet. So what I suggest is that you spend tomorrow strolling around the Amalfi city center and focus on the west toward Positano. Enjoy Amalfi at its best natural setting and sip coffee along with croissants. Please note that we will have tomorrow's dinner together. Because of staff leave, we will have to have that here and somewhat late, say, about tonight's time."

Tauseef returned to his room with a newfangled feeling and perception about goodness embedded in social dealings and affiliations. While wondering how a beautiful, young, and vibrant young lady like Nanita could so easily communicate with a totally unknown person like him, Tauseef was amused and started recollecting. In the process, he fell asleep.

As agreed, Tauseef met Nanita on the following evening in the hotel restaurant. She wanted to know about his daylong activities and what he liked most, so Tauseef went on talking. But his prompt nod to an offer of red wine surprised her very much. Tauseef clarified that while in the States, he had a few drinks but didn't like it. He said that he was opting for red wine as he had never tried it. He joked further that his decision was predicated on giving needed comfort and company for her. He assured Nanita that he would sip that slowly and would stop if he did not like it.

He had casual sips from his wineglass, more following swirling done by Nanita but not at the frequency of her sips. He was wondering why she did not ask him about what he would like to have for dinner. He started looking at his wristwatch as it was getting rather late. Nanita signaled the waiter, who promptly served a salad in a round glass bowl with a stem. Tauseef recalled that such bowls, manifestly of smaller size, were generally used in Bangladesh to serve fruit mélanges and ice cream.

As he was having a look of revelation, Nanita stated, "We serve salad like this as it is convenient to pick it up. Besides being transparent, giving a feeling of familiarity with what one is having, the shape helps the proper rotating of salad that many guests prefer to do."

She continued, saying, "This is made of vinegar, minced cloves of garlic, dried oregano, salt, some pepper, a little sugar, and extra-virgin olive oil as dressings, chopped romaine lettuce, fresh shredded mozzarella, roasted red peppers, thinly sliced pepperoncini peppers, pitted Kalamata olives, and thinly sliced small red onions. It is very popular locally besides being healthy. So let us start."

The ambiance for dinner between two individuals of totally different roots and social backgrounds could not be more amiable. Tauseef enjoyed the salad so thoughtfully worked out. The presentation was the icing on the cake.

In between cordial exchanges about Tauseef's day and his observations, Nanita changed the subject unexpectedly and began a discourse on his plan for the following day.

Tauseef flippantly observed, "I have not even thought of tomorrow. Forget about any plan." In spite of that, on his impulse, he felt the need to frame a more specific response as Nanita had been gracious enough to think about it and made the query. Tauseef said, "I do not have any plan. May it be that I will try to explore more intensely the surroundings of Positano."

This was followed by very unusual silence. Soon after they finished the starter, the waiter served the main course: two different dishes based on chicken. There was no need for Tauseef to make any query as Nanita narrated the premise of the order. She said, "First, tonight's dinner is on the house. So I exercised my right to make the choice. Second, as you were talking last night about your country—social traits, food habits with preference for curry preparation, etc.—I realized that chicken is a preferred item of meat, with fish being the popular other. So I opted for chicken. I, however, deliberately ordered two different preparations. Mine is roast chicken with rosemary. Yours is called Veneto chicken. My choice for that was predicated on your preference for rice, vegetable, and gravy, with small cuts of chicken pieces. This recipe is called Veneto chicken as it originated in Venice, your first place of visit outside Rome. I hope you will enjoy that. Now let us start eating."

Nanita's ability to read the mind of others and to comprehend various aspects of diverse homilies dazed Tauseef. He was at bay at how to thank her and what to say, so he concentrated on eating as testimony of his liking the choice made by her.

Nanita was enjoying Tauseef in a bemused situation. So while sipping wine in between munching portions of her main course, she said, "I could somehow guess that you did not have a plan as you came to the coast without much idea as to what it has to offer beyond the apparent attributes more commonly detailed in tourism publications. So I thought of a plan and, without consulting you, took some actions to operationalize that."

Surprises in life are not unusual, but they can either be hilarious and fulfilling or unnerving and worrisome, depending on their nature and frequency. In the case of Tauseef, he was stuck with the successive supportive initiatives and actions of Nanita, whom he knew barely for about twenty-eight hours. The worrying part related to fathoming the premise of the present relationship, with the reality that she was to be engaged soon and that he was married. All immediate thinking and concerns markedly clustered around values, cultures, and practices evolving around social systems that swayed his growing up.

Nanita, on the other hand, was quite oblivious but did not fail to properly interpret his facial reactions. She said, "I do not know how you would have handled our nascent affinity in your social setting, but I know for certain the insinuation of that at my end. Somehow I liked you when I first talked to you. I discovered an innocent person with an ingenuous mind who ventured to be in Amalfi without clarity as to his priority and interest. Also, we seldom have guests from Bangladesh. So I felt an urge to help you so that all through your life, you would fondly recall your visit to Amalfi."

Saying those words, Nanita initiated the induction of her thoughts for the next day. She premised her exposition by introducing the place she intended to take Tauseef. She started her narration with the following: "A journey to the South would remain incomplete for anyone without a visit to Capri Island one of the jewels of the star-studded crown of nature. The island of Capri is both a famous and equally popular tourist destination between the offshore area from Naples and towns along Amalfi Coast. It is famous for boutiques, beaches, and the Blue Grotto. Grottos in and around Capri Island are famous for their natural edifices and features. The one at Capri Island is the most breathtaking and famous one. Known as Blue Grotto, this sea cave rises above the water level with extremely incandescent turquoise lighting inside. The brightness of the transient turquoise reflection in the stirring water of the cave is beguiling to any pair of eyes. The journey to the Blue Grotto usually entails a boat ride from the coast of Capri Island, a shopping arcade with a pier. One normally boards a mid-sized boat to go near the site and then disembarks to one of the many floating rowboats to negotiate the approach. The tiny opening at water level is the only approach to enter the Blue Grotto. By dimension, it is just suitable for a small rowboat with two to three people [tourists] sprawling flat on the boat to avoid injury. The local boatman maneuvers delicately his boat with the help of a sturdy synthetic rope hinged in the boulders edging the opening of the cave. This is needed to ensure a safe entry. Any carelessness or slippage could as well be fatal. Because of the uniqueness of the opening and its correlation with the water level, the access is susceptible to high tide, a surge in water, and the velocity of the wind. In most of such conditions, entry is suspended. But once inside the Blue Grotto, the cave opens up, allowing the passengers to sit comfortably and enjoy the uniqueness of the bright blue water reflection inside. Nature is at its best in creating that natural turquoise reflection in the water, having no outside light. It is caused by the light emanating through a much larger opening just below the one that provides access inside. The larger opening below is not visible at all. To most observers, the source of blue light is likely to remain a conundrum.

"On any normal diurnal, there are several rowboats near the entry point of the Blue Grotto looking for tourists to be taken inside for a fee, so the availability of a rowboat is never a problem, even if we show up without confirmation. Considering this, I have a plan for tomorrow. I will spend the whole day taking you to the island of Capri and onward to the Blue Grotto."

Tauseef smiled a bit and said, "I have some elusive impression about the grotto from casual reading during my visit to Rome but did not venture to harbor any thought of visiting the island of Capri. It has always been beyond my comprehension because of unfamiliarity, time constraint, and the language barrier. I am so happy that you have thought about it and have planned for a visit. I am immensely thankful to you for all your consideration for a subtle dream of mine to come true."

Nanita was pleased with his response and said, "It is wonderful that you have some idea about the grotto. Because of that, you will be able to enjoy and absorb the beauty and uniqueness of it instead of just being awed by the splendor that nature unfolds. I have visited the Blue Grotto three times before. My feeling each time was more intense than the previous one. Some prior knowledge is always helpful."

Nanita then detailed the arrangements she made. "We have a young man who often works in our hotel on a need basis. I have contacted him, and he has agreed to work for two days. Also, I have borrowed my dad's car for tomorrow. First, we will drive to Marina Piccola port of Sorrento, park the car, and then take a ferryboat to Capri Island. It is preferable that one sits outside on the deck. If one is inside, the preferred position is on the left side to have a full and enchanting view of the gorgeous coast."

The visit to Capri was undertaken on the following day with precision to the details Nanita outlined the night before. It was a pleasant car drive along the coastline. Though the drive to Sorrento was stunning, with rugged mountains plunging into sea in a conspicuous vertical fashion, Tauseef's eyes were scouting the physical posture of Nanita but maintaining due propriety. Nanita was oblivious and continued talking ceaselessly on diverse issues. In addition, the journey entailed coffee in Marina Piccola and a deck-top ferryboat ride to Capri Island, boarding a mechanized boat for travel to the site of the Blue Grotto, embarking a small rowboat, and entering the Blue Grotto, lying physically very close to Nanita— enjoying a body smell that he had never experienced before.

Those few seconds had an eternal antiphon within Tauseef until both of them straightened themselves vertically once inside the Grotto. But it was just not something sporadic; this was an upshot of a rare feeling that was unknowingly harbored in his mind when he first saw her that morning in the hotel against the backdrop of a clear blue sky, bright morning sun, and dazzling blue water far below, visible through a large glass partition setting. When Tauseef first saw Nanita that morning waiting for him, wearing a flowing white silk gown embossed with a light yellow tulip supported by a stem with light green leaves dotted all over, he was not only impressed but also mesmerized. What astounded him was a most unexpected hug from her and an unusual outburst of talking loudly and in an incessant manner. That was not the Nanita he met. Instead of being bothered by that, he opted to relish the change. That social dictate of propriety that Tauseef was used to was withered away by the need to lie in the rowboat, and the resultant closeness had an impact on his thoughts and reactions. He was charmed by the body smell emanating from her because of their closeness.

As they repositioned themselves in the rowboat inside the grotto, Nanita started playing with the water, beguiled by exquisite turquoise lighting inside. That included the occasional flinging of water toward Tauseef. In doing so, she noticed that the toddler in the next boat was about to fall in the water while trying to get hold of his toy. She instantly reacted to position the boy safely and, in the process, plunged into the water traversed by many tiny boats. Tauseef was stunned. His sense of puzzlement turned to utter jolt and instant fret, seeing Nanita flapping her hands in an effort to delay immediate drowning. He instantly jumped out of the boat, grabbed Nanita, pulled her up, and got her on the boat with the help of boatmen surrounding them. On the boat, Nanita started shivering but had to lie by the side of the wet body of Tauseef, complying with mandatory requirement for getting out of the Blue Grotto through its small opening. In a semi-disoriented situation like that and more as a redress to tenacious shivering, Nanita clenched herself against his body.

The bright noon sun greeted them as they came out of the Blue Grotto. Tauseef, drawing the attention of the boatman by sign language, obtained an extension of their stay on the boat. That time and the bright sunrays helped Nanita stabilize a little while her respective clothing also desiccated partially. They boarded one of the mechanized boats after a while and returned to the pier. They kept on waiting on the pier to get dry fully before undertaking a "funicular" railway trip up the side of the mountain to the town of Capri.

Following the incident involving the near-drowning of Nanita inside the Blue Grotto, there were two marked behavioral changes on her part: she maintained perceptible silence as opposed to the continuous chatting since morning and was always physically very close to Tauseef—many times resting her head on his shoulder. While he had no clue for the first change, he rationalized the second one as a response to get the required sense of security against the backdrop of what the outcome could have been.

After an enthralling brief ride up and casual walk around, they took their seats in a convenient coffee shop overseeing the island. They had their quiet moments, Tauseef looking around, positioning his eyes far to the blue water underneath, and thanking Nanita silently for thinking about the trip and making it possible. He shrugged off the thought about the incident as something incidental to any escapade. Nanita, on the other hand, was very much engrossed with what could have happened to her and thanking Tauseef silently for all he did.

Against that milieu, Nanita, seeing the restaurant staff serving coffee, leisurely raised her head from his shoulder, repositioned herself on the chair, and reshuffled her dress; all that, she did as if to unveil her buoyancy after the grotto incident. That assessment by Tauseef was not erroneous as she soon resumed the continuous talking. She recommenced her colloquy by saying, "Seeing that boy tilting perilously, I just had no time to think as my own childhood trauma with water flashed instantly in my memory. I totally forgot that one of such incidents enduringly slashed any future option for me to learn to swim. I never tried it as I was growing up. I just can't think of what would have happened to me had you not retrieved me instantaneously. You have given me a new life. I am eternally thankful to you and will always cherish you as a dear friend from Bangladesh."

They had friendly verbal exchanges on what Nanita alluded to. Tauseef tried to downplay his role and response, and Nanita persistently maintained that what he did was something exceptional. The unfinished coffee provided the needed respite, with Nanita requesting a refill. As the refill was being made, in that solitary setting, Nanita made two observations on which Tauseef did not have to say much.

She commented, "When you talked to me earlier about your culture and faith as to things or events ordained, I not only disagreed but shrugged it off. I now realize that ordained matters are relevant. There was no reason for me to ask you to place your important documents in my pouch. Had I not said so and you did not act, most probably, your documents would have been all blemished by your sudden jump to rescue me."

Tauseef happily beamed and nodded. Her second observation was about the relationship matter that they had discussed casually before. In earlier discussions, Tauseef took a position where he maintained that in spite of love and commitment to someone very dear, one should not be blamed for succumbing to sporadic temptations so long as it was not a habit. Every situation and happening in life's setting has its unique magnetism, very much valid and germane at that particular moment. Judging that subsequently in normal milieu is not fair so long as those types of happenings are not repeated or affect normal life. Love relationships should have space to deal with unexpected events of uncommon nature in life. Many of life's activities and events are products of specific moments and very much influenced by supportive ambiance. At the height of feelings premised on certain but unpredictably erratic situations, the normal value indicators like good or bad, moral or immoral, just wane in the mind and thinking of an individual. While wrong things always remain so, there is not enough justification to carry on that indefinitely. The bond of a relationship should be dense enough to withstand and overcome such experiences.

After that discussion, Nanita stated that she was having a fresh thought on that issue since today's experience, though she had disagreed initially. Sipping the coffee, she resumed her oration by saying, "When I contacted our part-time staff to work, I told him that we need his presence for two days. Day one was meant for today, and the following day was for me to take rest and be relaxed as my fiancé, Ernesto Cataldi, would return to his job the day after tomorrow. I wanted to look fresh when he encounters me after his leave. I should be gorgeous and appealing. But now I have a different plan depending on your willingness to participate."

Saying those words, she paused for a moment, trying to read his initial reaction. He had no clue as to what she had in mind and gave a resultant blank look. Without wasting any time, Nanita said, "Look, you are married, and I am going to be engaged soon. There is, thus, no option for a relationship between us premised on what happened inside the Blue Grotto and what you did to give me a second life. But my feeling is that there is no impediment on our way to be really good friends and to enjoy tomorrow, the only day available, to our hearts' content, forgetting the past and being oblivious to future. Let us get lost for the day."

The idea was both unexpected and strange to Tauseef, but he did not waste time in communicating concurrence as he, unexpectedly though, was enamored by the proposition. He liked the idea of "getting lost." There was no further discussion on this during the remaining stay in Capri, the boat ride back to Marina Piccola, or the drive to the hotel from Sorrento. Tauseef was somewhat bemused but decided to relax while enjoying the passing shades of nature as Nanita was driving back. It was a welcome change for him. He could not fully appreciate nature's beauty while going to Capri partly because of excitement of the unknown and partly because of the relentless schmooze of Nanita dealing with history, features, culture, and specialty of Capri, even mentioning the use of the Blue Grotto as the personal swimming hole of the Roman emperor and as a marine temple. The only spontaneous variation from the recurring tenor of their earlier discourse was because of the impromptu decision to finish dinner in a traditional Italian restaurant near Amalfi.

The discussion started with Nanita repeating the features and likings of Italians with respect to their food types and habits. Tauseef took the opportunity to iterate specific features and tastes of Bangladeshi food. He very convincingly emphasized, "Even though it is not known widely, no two items of Bangladeshi food of the same cluster taste the same. Such specific identifiable taste is because of the intricate combination of spices and their use. For example, Bangladeshi people use different types, mixes, and combinations of spices even for preparing diverse types and sizes of fish. The same is applicable to preparation of different types of mashed items, commonly known as *bharta*. Partly because of this, Bangladeshi food chains in England are so popular, even though they are marketed as Indian restaurants."

As they reached the hotel, Tauseef got down while Nanita kept sitting in the car. Unlike other occasions, she neither said thank you nor good night. It so appeared to Tauseef that she perhaps was burdened by some inner coercions. He merrily returned to his room, engrossed by the constant urge to make out what Nanita meant by "get lost for the day." Neither a nice shower nor a hot cup of chamomile herbal tea could soothe his torrid nerves. He tried in vain to fall asleep. His thoughts traversed through the wildest imaginations and possibilities. Eventually, Tauseef concluded that he had played a rather passive role in his interactions in the company of Nanita the last two days. But tomorrow would be his day. He would take all initiatives to amaze her. He decided that when they met in the morning, he would hug her and hold hands in conducting her to the breakfast table.

Tauseef got up very early in the morning, finished all morning rituals meticulously, and decided to go to the lobby to receive her when she stepped in.

Nanita decided to be in the hotel earlier than usual to guide the staff about things to be done during the day. As she was engrossed in reading an incoming communication from a travel agent, she heard the sound of quiet footsteps. She raised her face and was astounded to see Ernesto standing before her a day earlier than scheduled. As they were hugging each other, he faced the reception desk, and she faced the lobby, Ernesto, enjoying the warmth of embrace, said, "I've missed you so much and wanted to give you a surprise. That motivated me to show up early."

Right at that moment, Tauseef, full of enthusiasm and wild thoughts, stepped out of the elevator. He was bewildered and shocked, seeing Nanita in an embrace, presumably with her boyfriend. He was frozen, ogling Nanita's stance.

Nanita, to keep Ernesto focused on the reception desk, started warmly inveigling and fondling him but could not avoid visibly shivering. As Ernesto was caressing her softly, uttering soothing words, teardrops started rolling down Nanita's face and falling on the upper portion of his long sleeves. Those teardrops, evidently meant for Tauseef, could not have any response.

Tauseef quietly went back to his room, packed his things, and checked out of the hotel quietly without having breakfast. He took slow steps toward the bus stop but could not impede his eyes getting moist. Unwittingly, two teardrops graced his cheek.

Culmination

While sitting in the bus on his return journey to Rome, Tauseef could not help but consider the convoluted turn of events. The most exciting night of his life was quelled by the most unexpected happening of the following morning, putting him on this unpromising seat of a bus. His despondency was why it was to happen, affecting the most thrilling visit and turning that into a gloomy one. His remorse was in his inability to say thank you to Nanita and in his deprivation of a most cherished experience he was slated to have. In the midst of associated dismay and gloom, Tauseef looked outside of the moving bus with picturesque scenes, incredible structures, and captivating settings disappearing in quick succession. An unlikely philosophical simulation suddenly triumphed on him: nothing in life is permanent. Things are bound to fade away. There is always a reason. Tauseef's cultural orientation on believing the premise of "ordained" eventuality came to his rescue. He consoled that whatever happened was perhaps for the good of both, instead lingering on a sense of frustration or guilt. His related comfort position was that perhaps Nanita would have a similar feeling based on what she told him yesterday about the significance of what he meant by being "ordained." He, thus, decided to relax, planning on an early arrival in Dhaka to give a surprise to his dear wife Chandni. With that thought in mind, he closed his eyes and went into involuntary slumber.

Tauseef had completed his assignment earlier than scheduled, beguiled his way to convince the agency's travel agent to get him a seat a day earlier, readily agreed to pay an additional sum for almost last-minute itinerary changes, and reached Dhaka a day earlier. All his related thinking centered on the incredulous facial expressions of Chandni seeing him return earlier than scheduled and his most unexpected intense kisses to her amazement. He was determined to make a calculative exertion to discover his conjugal relationship, a feeling and urge vitalized by his brief closeness with Nanita and the most bewildering frustration emanated.

The six-mile travel between the airport and his abode in a private yellow cab appeared to be too long. The varied nature of the scenario jumbled Tauseef's thinking. As he approached his apartment, Tauseef involuntarily slowed down, took smaller steps, kept on waiting near the entry door, and precipitously put his finger on the calling bell, beguiled by a host of expectations and uncertainties. The usual time elapsed, but there was no response. So he pushed the bell again. The door opened at the same time. The person on the other side was not his much-anticipated wife but their relatively new household help lady, Banu.

There was not much communication between Tauseef and Banu before his departure to Rome. The need to leave for Rome unexpectedly, related works, his focus and urge to excel in developing and delivering timely a quality product, and other related professional needs precluded much-immediate interactions. His early leaving for and late return from work, together with the care and attention of Chandni, left not much room for contacts between Tauseef and Banu. He had little impression about the new employee. As she unbolted the door, exhausted Tauseef was stunned to see a beautiful young lady. It was perhaps the first complete look of his to one who worked for him. He was taken aback.

Opening the door and seeing Tauseef standing there, Banu, with all surprise, exclaimed, saying, "Oh Ma [Oh Mum], Khalu apni [Uncle, it is you]! You are supposed to come tomorrow evening. Keeping that in mind, Khalamma [maternal aunt, meaning Chandni] rushed to Chittagong to see her ailing *chachi* [wife of paternal uncle], who suddenly fell ill. She is slated to return in the late afternoon tomorrow."

Tauseef, to the reverse of his mental and physical reflexes, said, "Would you continue to talk or allow me to get in?"

Banu was discomfited and stepped aside. As Tauseef entered the apartment and went to his room, Banu took possession of his luggage outside and bolted the doors again. Retiring in her own space momentarily, Banu felt abashed for facing Khalu in makeup and dressing that was neither normal nor becoming for one who worked as a household help. She was baffled, thinking what had bizarrely caused an inner urge this morning to be attired in a trendy manner, to comb hair in a chic fashion, and to titivate her face. But the fact was that Banu felt enthralled and quite gratified when she looked at herself in the dressing mirror just before the doorbell rang. Banu was certain that to show up before Khalu with that sort of getup was embarrassing and indecent. Her consolation was that she was unaware of Khalu's sudden arrival and that there was no time for her to change. In fact, she delayed opening the door, thinking it was someone else.

Tauseef, sitting in the bedroom, was still in a mystified mood, thinking about Banu and her freshly divulged draws. All thoughts and linked yearning concerning Chandni momentarily vanished. As Banu slowly stepped into the master bedroom to enquire what Tauseef would like to have besides tea, he just beamed, looking straight at her without any response. Banu kept on waiting for the answer and repeated the question. Instead of replying, Tauseef concentrated glaring at the physical features of Banu as could be gauged ostensibly. The feminine instinct of Banu could sense it discernibly and partly relished the feeling as the same master ignored her persona and presence in the immediate past.

In the tangling act of elation and being beguiled by precipitous reflexes caused by the locale they were in, the two differing individuals of divergent social settings had a most astonishing but similar toxic feeling. Tauseef quietly called Banu closer and passionately said, "Yes, I am hungry. I have not eaten much for the last few days, but the fact is that I am extremely exhausted and tired. Will you first soothe my somatic self by massaging my head and neck? And then prepare some food of your liking but quickly. In the meantime, I will call your Khalamma, informing her about my arrival."

Banu's immediate response was spontaneous. She did not have any second thought and complied promptly. That initial response had its likeness with many other tasks she was asked to perform in that house regularly. But something happened. Yearning that dominated her thoughts since that morning unwittingly overtook her standard sense of propriety. She started talking about herself and stirring Tauseef's hair by moving her fingers on his head in an effort to mitigate discomfort.

She said, "Khalu, it appears that you were not taking care of yourself at all since you left for a foreign country. Your hairs are so dry, and your skull is so rustic. I will tell Khalamma when she comes back. Meanwhile, allow me to go inside and bring some hair oil. I can't massage your head without that."

Banu's statement that she would tell Chandni about his hair and skull dryness unnerved Tauseef instantly. His immediate thought quickly concluded that if Chandni knew about Banu's massaging his head in the lone setting of the apartment, it would probably be the end of their otherwise happy, friendly living if not cause actual separation. Even before talking to him about this, Chandni would drag her thought to the culminating point with no scope left for exception. She would be certain about the ultimate sexual relationship between Tauseef and Banu, more propelled by the reality of their not having regular conjugal immersion. In having such thoughts, he recalled discussions with Nanita in the coffee place in Capri concerning relationships and possible fortuitous happenings shaking their foundations in spite of the sincerity of the feelings. Tauseef closed his eyes and was lost in a myriad of possibilities.

Banu returned inaudibly, put some hair oil in her palms, and softly started caressing Tauseef's hair and skull. In doing so, she physically moved very close to Tauseef. Such closeness caused Tauseef to sense Banu's body aroma and torridness, and that reminded him of the almost similar experience when he was holding Nanita in the rowboat. He recalled that subsequent unforeseen happenings had deprived him from the much-desired culmination of his inner craving. Tauseef was, thus, engulfed by the closeness of Banu while she moved her fingers, massaging his neck and shoulder joints. All perspicuous positive attributes of his persona that had shaped him as an ideal individual, intellectual, and husband were lost momentarily. Tauseef succumbed to compelling physical impulse and took possession of Banu's moving hand. He stood up and drew her very close to him, hugged her intensely, and resorted to caressing and kissing her. Banu was not surprised but started to shiver, even though she was enjoying every bit of Khalu's physical advances.

The saga that was premised on the simple massaging proposition eventually culminated in intense physical discourse in which both participated equally. The only difference was that while Tauseef's involvement had all the elements of aggressiveness, he thought Banu enjoyed it with sublime pleasure. She quietly left the bed without a word or even looking at him soon after he released her. Tauseef continued to lounge in his bed, enjoying every bit of his most unexpected sexual experience and realized for the first time what it meant in a complete life situation and how it bonded two individuals. His startling happiness found an unsought justification for his mother's getting pregnant so frequently as his father probably had no other openings in the setting of Apurba Neer for needed physical relaxation. He mollified his long-held anger against his late father and felt relaxed. There was another comforting realization for Tauseef. He was convinced that Banu, keeping in view what eventually happened, would not open her mouth when Chandni returned as she too was an equal participant.

As Banu was busy in the kitchen preparing food as per earlier indication, Tauseef leisurely picked up the telephone to talk to Chandni. He was very relaxed and overtly joyful in his communication with Chandni, never mentioning his missing her absence but more explaining the reason for his early return as a surprise. Chandni was happy to know about Tauseef's early arrival, but the instinct of a wife started harboring a pensive apprehension within. She was disturbed by the fact of his staying in the apartment with young Banu around. Her faith and confidence in Tauseef was strong, but she could not stop whining about the negative possibilities in the solitary setting. His very exuberant conversation without any mention of missing her caused the aggravation of her concern.

Tauseef felt more tranquil after making the call to Chandni but was equally amazed to note the very normal and casual comportment of Banu in having a follow-on conversation with him. She moved around and talked in a manner as if nothing had happened except bearing an impish smile adorning her lips and the reactive movement of her eyes. Tauseef was bemused but found comfort in the feeling that the noticeable trait of Banu would serve as a cover when Chandni came back from Chittagong.

The early hours of the night had a repeat performance of the noontime bustle. Tauseef, being swayed by Banu's boosting partaking, wanted her to stay in the bed. She, however, disagreed, retreated to her space, and went to sleep. Waking up late the following morning, Tauseef was once again reassured, seeing Banu as her usual self, attired in her daily sari and having the look as normally household helps were supposed to have.

Tauseef was having his breakfast leisurely as Chandni was expected in the late afternoon. While mincing *parata* (fried flatbread) and egg, he was engrossed in reminiscing his physical involvement with Banu. He was totally oblivious of its likely ramifications as he rested all negativities in the safe and normal conduct of Banu.

The tranquil setting was suddenly disturbed by the ring of the doorbell. As Banu opened the door, Chandni had a subterranean long cold look at her, gauged her physical bearing, and stepped in without any word of greeting or query. Seeing Chandni arriving earlier than scheduled, Tauseef started eating hurriedly, saying, "How come you are here? You were supposed to be coming late afternoon. Keeping that in view, I agreed to be in office to handle an important issue and am needed to go soonest."

Chandni had no strain in assessing the reality. Tauseef's welcoming statements were contrary to his previous practice of walking promptly to welcome her and hugging and conducting her to a chair for rest whenever she used to return from a travel. The gaffe was committed by Tauseef inadvertently, but the worst was that he was totally unmindful of it. He was more concerned in monitoring the moves and words of Banu. Chandni went to her bedroom and sat on the bed lugubriously. Tauseef came to tell her that he would be back in about two hours' time. That was the second solecism he committed in quick succession. The questions that distraught her were how his office came to know about his early arrival and how he could conclude that the issue he was to attend would be addressed to in two hours. The other one was the hurry to leave, more a telltale of nervousness. A somber thought about these two and what she could read in the facial expressions of Banu left no doubt in her mind that the apprehension she initially assumed had all the elements of reality.

Sitting alone with Banu, the only other person in the apartment, most of the time avoiding usual contact and babbling, Chandni had focused thinking. She argued with herself about the aptness of her current thought and allied bizarre conclusion. She was in deep thought about handling the situation. Chandni then concluded that if her trepidation was even remotely correct, she had a part of the blame in not being adept at what was expected from a wife. Premised on such thinking, she softly called Banu after a while and said, "Thank you very much for your services. We do not need you anymore. Please pack up and leave within the hour. As a compensation for the sudden notice, I am giving you two months' salary. It's in the envelope on the table on your way out. I would not like to have any more discussion on this matter. It's final."

Banu kept her eyes focused on the floor, picked up the envelope, and quietly left the room with an evoking smile. As Banu left, Chandni, lounging on the big bed alone, pressured herself to recondition her physical impulses to have the lascivious instinct very normal for any young lady. She neither had such a feeling nor had the yearning to address the problem besetting her conjugal life. She was feeling dejected and despondent, thinking that she never made a resolute exertion to wash out her experiences and negative physical riposte. She had taken her physical limitations as something she would have to live with throughout her life. Chandni felt slighted in thinking about her inability compared to Banu, a household help, even though she herself was significantly more attractive, smart, and relevant to Tauseef's life. Chandni started thinking positively and concluded that no one else except her could redress this problem. The main logic in her mind was predicated on the conviction that similar to many gears in life, any occurrence of edginess must have a threshold to overcome. Thinking all about such prospects and because of waking up early for the journey back to Dhaka, Chandni fell asleep unwittingly.

In that involuntary sleep, she had a very unusual dream of having an intense sensual encounter with Tauseef. She woke up impulsively with a feeling of vaginal lubrication for the first time in many years of her life. She did not leave her bed soon after waking up. She continued to slouch in her bed, reminiscing the kernel of her dream with the discernible feeling of wetness in the bubbly organ of her body. She only left the bed with a unique resolve to replicate in real life what she had dreamt and what she was feeling in her body.

After having a light snack with her tea, Chandni donned herself in a beautiful chiffon sari of light yellow pigment with a contrasted bright red sleeveless low-cut blouse without the usual bra, and put on mild makeup with a distinct "nude-colored" liquid lipstick with the resolution to reverse all her previous manacles and start a life akin to normalcy. She was all set to come out of angsts and inabilities that had dazed her feelings and life since her growing-up stage's outrageous encounters. She also recalled every word of counseling from Nani. It seemed that time was passing inordinately in a slow pace. Chandni continued to monitor time in the antique wall-hanging regulator pendulum clock, which Tauseef had brought from Italy during his previous visit, along with some makeup items, including the lipstick she used.

During that phase of looming expectation, the doorbell rang. Chandni opened the door, and as Tauseef, with a cursory glance, was bypassing her to go inside with his head down and with physical expressions of having symptoms of guilt and nervousness, she got hold of his swinging right hand, pulled him toward her, accosted and hugged him, and lost all sense of propriety in her invasions and acts. While drawing him toward the bedroom, she stripped off her sari, blouse, and petticoat, focused on taking off his shirt and trousers, and submitted herself on his bare chest.

Tauseef was beguiled, notwithstanding the hidden element of momentary surprise, and responded equally while caressing her in the process as well in bed. For the first time in their married life, they had a fulfilling physical encounter. It was repeated that afternoon in different forms of performances. That marked the beginning of a new day and new life for the couple, who had a lingering distraught feeling about their happiness and future. While the librettos were few and the feeling was intense, they enjoyed every move, every interchange, and every meddling with passion at its zenith. For the couple, it was a new beginning of married life with assurance and hope. Their time passed with exuberance, leaving the past behind. A fresh beginning was ushered. Neither Tauseef made any inquiry about the absence of Banu, nor did Chandni mention anything.

In the midst of boundless happiness, they decided to have their dinner for the evening outside and, as an apposite response, decided to go to the first local hotel where they met initially to discuss life but failed to make progress. Chandni picked up her clothing from the floor and attired herself decently with the addition of a bright red bra.

Days passed in the euphoria of newly felt exuberance. Based on earlier thoughts and current feelings, Chandni emphasized the need to plan their delayed sojourn to Apurba Neer to enable her to be a part of Biesh Moisher Bari. Conveying his concurrence, Tauseef stated that he was also thinking about it, but the constrain was in approaching authorities for leave after two successive long absences because of professional need. It was agreed that the later part of December would be more ideal as the holidays around the period would minimize the need for a longer leave request.

That conformity was soon outshined by an unexpected proposition articulated by Chandni. Without sheltering her feelings to unknown predicaments, Chandni said, "During the last few days, I have been thinking and developed an urge to do something meaningful to bolster the name and fame of Biesh Moisher Bari. I think I have the right to do something within our abilities, even though I have not, as yet, formally stepped into the house as the new daughter-in-law."

The mist that shrouded the articulated indication of Chandni baffled Tauseef, but he preferred to keep quiet. Perceiving Tauseef's apparent miens, Chandni continued, saying, "Since we do not need so many apartments that I accidentally own now, it is my suggestion that we off-load at least two of them and place the sale proceeds at the disposal of Brother Tanveer for some social development programs in Apurba Neer. Keeping that in view, I have already initiated preliminary actions and engaged a real estate agent. I earnestly urge that you do not disagree with my proposition. My suggestion has no other built-in intentions. It is very unalloyed and guileless. Neither our names nor our future involvement has any space in that stipulation. The envisaged identity of that stipulation will be centered on Biesh Moisher Bari and Brother Tanveer."

Tauseef's senses of contentment and gratification were overwhelming for any immediate oral response. He continued looking at Chandni with admiration for her thought and intention and was lost in the subterranean realization of having a person like her as a life partner. He was soon provoked for a response.

In his thoughtful and slow response, Tauseef stated, "I am in awe and do not have words to respond. What you proposed would be wonderful, but I think you should equally do something palpable for your *nana* and *nani*. That will be a befitting recompense for all that they did for you apart from material things. Let us think it through, and we will discuss the details tomorrow."

With those inspiring words, Tauseef closed the discussion and started cuddling Chandni. The apparent element of positivity in his tone and words enchanted her. She yielded herself in his heartfelt embrace, thinking of the rewarding outcome.

They discussed the proposition in detail and agreed on the following. The delayed visit to Apurba Neer would be slated for late December. Keeping a reasonable balance of funds for future activities and to honor the name of Chandni's *nana* and *nani*, a substantial amount of money would be placed at the disposal of Tanveer to be used for social development in Apurba Neer. A foundation would be established in the name of Biesh Moisher Bari to pursue that objective, and Tanveer would be sole executor. It was also the consensus that to start with, funds would be spent to upgrade the existing boys' middle school to a high school, with emphasis on math and science, and make it more attractive in terms of facilities as well as an excellent seat of learning by recruiting qualified teachers. A proposal will be mooted before the community to rename the school Kazi Azmat Ali High School, while simultaneously, a girls' school will be established with learning facilities up to class eight, with choices clearly articulated for future upgrading, including residential facilities. The girls' school will be named Hashi Banu Girls' School.

Based on such broad understanding, Tauseef devoted time and energy to articulate the related position and conveyed the same to Brother Tanveer. In that process, two other understandings were agreed to, one suggested by Chandni and the other proposed by Tauseef. She suggested that in his proposed communication to Tanveer, it should be abundantly clear that in planning and implementing the proposal, neither she nor Tauseef would be visible physically or notionally. He would be given all authority and power to undertake and support all social development–related initiatives involving the fund. What Tauseef had in mind was to suggest the timing and arrangements for implementing the immediate activities suggested, coinciding, however, with the proposed visit in late December.

Tauseef acted very fast and drafted the charter establishing the fund for social development, giving it the title of Biesh Moisher Bari Foundation (BMBF), designating Kazi Tanveer Ali as the sole executor, and emphasizing full authority to manage BMBF, commit its resources, and supervise all works funded. In a separate letter enclosing the draft charter of the proposed BMBF, Tauseef highlighted the need for prompt actions to complete related consultations with the community and the taking of actions so that all formalities are completed upfront. He specifically mentioned that it was the earnest aspiration of both of them that matters pertaining to the boys' school should be done in advance and that the foundation-laying ceremony for the girls' school should be programmed for the last Friday of December to ensure that the whole thing would be seen by the community as that of Biesh Moisher Bari, steered by Tanveer only. He also categorically requested that their names or involvement in this endeavor should not be mentioned at all in any related actions and deliberations. In concluding the letter, Tauseef stated, "It is our utmost hope that Biesh Moisher Bari and Tanveer, as the custodian of the house, should be in the forefront for all time to come."

It was also mentioned that Chandni and he were planning to be at the house on Saturday morning, following the Friday mentioned earlier, to participate in the merriment with the simultaneous induction of Chandni as the new daughter-in-law.

Tanveer was awed by the weight of the envelope that carried the letter from Tauseef. With hesitation swamping his immediate reaction, he slowly opened it and was confused by seeing different documents, with an accompanying bank draft of forty lakh (four million) taka. He read the letter. On finishing, he went to a sort of hibernation. After some time, he read and reread it again to digest its contents and to be assured of his understanding. He decided to return to Biesh Moisher Bari to inform Mother and the family.

The ever-vigilant Badsha Chacha observed the entire episode and quietly followed, positioning himself silently outside the abode as Tanveer went inside.

Qulsum was reading a Bangla magazine, while infant Malvina was asleep. She was shaken beyond comprehension seeing Tanveer back at home silently at such an odd hour with a heavy envelope in hand. Her immediate angst was soon defused, noting a happy facial expression. He went closer to her chair, and she inquired by gesture so as not to wake the baby about the reason for his return. With a shadowy smile, he handed over Tauseef's letter and whispered, "Read it carefully and try to understand the contents and their implications."

On finishing her reading, Qulsum promptly stood up, held the hand of Tanveer, and dragged him to the room of Mother. Sensing commotion in the room, Hashi Banu woke up and looked at Tanveer and Qulsum, trying to grasp the reason that prompted them to be in her space at this unusual time. She momentarily kept quiet as Qulsum hurriedly left the room. Tanveer repositioned the chair and sat silently when Qulsum returned in the company of Pori Khala and Badsha Chacha.

Observing all present, astounded, Mother opened her mouth, inquiring about such an unusual presence at the odd time. Tanveer, with all delight and contentment, detailed everything that Tauseef stipulated. The joy of everyone present was overwhelming.

Tanveer opened up by highlighting the implications inherent in Tauseef's stipulations, saying, "In suggesting all that is contained in the letter, Tauseef has diligently acted on his promise to Mother to maintain a link with his roots. Not only that, but also, by proposing the establishment of the foundation and the naming of the boys' and girls' schools after the names of our parents, he prudently proposed something that will bear the names of Biesh Moisher Bari, Hashi Banu, and Kazi Azmat Ali for all time to come."

As Tanveer finished his statement, Qulsum stepped in and said, "Not only that, but also, by keeping them aloof from these initiatives in all their manifestations, Tauseef and Chandni bestowed and showed extraordinary gestures to Biesh Moisher Bari and his elder brother. That ensured the continuous enhanced prominence of this house and Tanveer in the future social setting of Apurba Neer."

The contented setting experienced a happy jolt when Pori softly joined the deliberations, reflecting with full courtesy, "Hashi-bu often was unhappy with me for my love and understanding for dear Hira. I was certain that he will not get delinked from Biesh Moisher Bari but that his association and involvement might have different shades and sounds. I am thankful to Allahpak that he lived up to my hope and expectation. I have had always my conviction that he would not disappoint us in choosing a life partner. Betty Chandni's decision to put that big amount for the name and fame of Biesh Moisher Bari is something unique. I will say a few *rakat*s of *nafal namaz* tonight to express my gratitude to Allahpak."

Always less talkative, Badsha kept standing silently but his beaming physical responses were worth a thousand words.

Pori, alluding to the desired consent of her Hashi-bu, suggested the preparation of special food for the dinner. Hashi Banu nodded. Tanveer asked Badsha Chacha to join the dinner. All related actions were taken promptly. Events and activities concerning those were the talk of the community. That also included the highest attainment of educational pursuit by Tauseef and his imminent visit with a new wife. Everyone was ecstatic, and many of them participated voluntarily. Biesh Moisher Bari attained a new status and new distinctiveness.

Tauseef was kept informed and included in the family's plan to have a *jayafat* on Saturday, following the foundation-laying event for the girls' school, coinciding with the stepping in of Chandni to Biesh Moisher Bari for the first time. Tanveer communicated that the event of *jayafat* was being organized at the expressed desire of Mother to honor dear Chandni.

All needed arrangements were being undertaken, keeping the schedules outlined by Tauseef earlier, and subsequently endorsed by the family. While decisions had been articulated by Tanveer, in consultation with community elders, it was Badsha who labored hard to ensure their timely implementation. However, an unforeseen snag developed. That was because of Hashi Banu's expressed hesitation to lay the foundation stone of the girls' school in a public gathering among male attendees. As the event was drawing closer, her casual dithering was taking the shape of a firm position in spite of Tanveer's intermittent efforts. Everyone was worried.

Taking the opening of a post-dinner family discussion concerning *jayafat* arrangements, Qulsum made a decided effort to raise the unresolved issue of laying the foundation stone of the girls' school as fondly desired by Tauseef. She emphasized that any deviation from that would cause unhappiness, besides marring the grand event of *jayafat*. She then, keeping in view the family's focus on propriety, said, "Mother's hesitance to publicly lay the foundation stone has good reasons."

Taking note of her initial remark, Tanveer was puzzled and made an inquisitive exchange of eye contact with Qulsum. She resumed, saying, "But instead of resting the issue there, we need to address it to come to a more acceptable arrangement. Please do not misunderstand me. Amma [Mother], you stepped into this noble house many years back. The world around us and many social values have undergone visible changes. Ladies now work in fields and factories. Girls now go to schools. The female presence on streets demanding their security and right is a common phenomenon. Even then, I find the relevance of your position against the backdrop of Apurba Neer and the traditions of Biesh Moisher Bari. I propose that both Pori Khala and myself, along with some ladies from the neighborhood, will accompany you and be present in the event. In adhering to the modesty of this noble house, you can put on a burka [veil], and all of us will have *chador*s [akin to shawls] on the tops of our saris, respecting propriety. I think that arrangement, if acceptable to all, can pave the way for the total happiness that all of us are looking for."

Hashi Banu took some time, looked at ever-trusted Pori, and nodded with content. Tanveer was thrilled and volunteered to talk to the community elders to ensure the adequate presence of female folks in that event. Activities pertaining to the foundation ceremony for the new girls' school were completed on time with a structural map on display and some construction materials stacked on the site. Everywhere, happiness was overpowering the surroundings of Biesh Moisher Bari.

Then everyone of the family was surprised to receive a message to be in Hashi Banu's room. As Tanveer, Qulsum, Pori, and Badsha positioned themselves, soft-spoken and taciturn Hashi Banu opened up surprisingly, saying, "I am free today. I am not being haunted anymore by the burden of unforeseen trepidations. I am glad that Tauseef proved me so wrong. I am thankful to Pori for giving him the necessary shoulder that he needed and happy without reservation for Betty Qulsum, helping Tauseef in the pursuit of his chosen objectives of life, and unconditionally bless Tanveer for the understanding, compassion, and support he has extended to Tauseef always, before, and after Kazi Shaheeb's demise."

All present were taken by surprise when Hashi Banu, for the first time in all those years of her married life, addressed her husband by name. She grew up in a setting where pronouncing the name of one's husband was not only discouraged but also considered as an affront. She unknowingly came out of that, signifying a monumental change in her thinking. But her subsequent statement was even more extraordinary. "Life's experience has taught me that social and behavioral changes are inevitable and that there is no sense in resisting those. But that also imparted in me a feeling that perhaps each bend of such changes needs caution and guidance. After saying my *esher* [Muslim prayer at night], I will devote myself in performing a few *rakats* of *nafal namaz*, and thus, our family dinner should be served a bit later. In that prayer, I will pray for you all in my family and would specifically like to bless both Tauseef and Chandni with all my heart and genuineness. Please don't misconstrue that my changed mind has been influenced by the money Chandni paid, which has nothing to do with my present position. I was influenced by their intent and commitment."

Family members started leaving her room after exchanging looks with one another. Tanveer led the process but was taken aback when Mother called Badsha, saying, "Thanks for all your services. Keep that up and ensure that tomorrow's *jayafat* is an extraordinary one."

She also took the unusual step of asking him to join the dinner, an act she did for the first time.

Tanveer got up the following early morning and went to the site of cooking in the company of Badsha Chacha to monitor the progress as guests would be coming around early noontime. Suddenly, a boisterous cry from home shattered their nerves. An ominous thought immersed both. They started running to the house, only to face the most ominous reality of life: Hashi Banu in a static position, with ever-caring Pori crying while holding her.

Seeing them, she fretfully started saying, "Like all other days, Hashi-bu got up early morning, said her *fazar* [early morning Muslim prayer], and went for a nap before getting up to have a cup of tea as a precursor to her breakfast. I came with her tea and called her to wake up. As she was not responding, I touched her to face an inert body. I instantly realized the truth and called others. Our common finding was that she has left us eternally."

Shock and sadness were pervasive in the surroundings of Biesh Moisher Bari. What was supposed to be a day of immeasurable contentment and gratification soon turned into a day of dismay and disarray. The news spread in the community instantaneously, and people started flocking to Biesh Moisher Bari.

Tauseef planned with Chandni to leave Dhaka by road early in the morning so as to reach Apurba Neer before noontime with the fondest desire to physically participate in the *jayafat* after ensuring the tradition-laden ushering of Chandni as the new daughter-in-law of the noble house. As the vehicle carrying them approached Apurba Neer, Tauseef started excitedly showing various places and sites he used to frequent in his childhood. Nearing the abode, Tauseef's exuberance got a sudden shock as he found people slowly leaving the premise of Biesh Moisher Bari with heads down and despondent physical responses. He immediately sensed something ominous but refrained talking to Chandni. As the vehicle stopped near the open entry yard of Biesh Moisher Bari, Tauseef jumped out, leaving Chandni in the vehicle alone. As he reached the patio, he was dumbfounded, seeing the shrouded dead body of his beloved mother, with her face still visible for him and Chandni to have a last look.

His arrival was greeted by loud and incessant crying by those present to demonstrate the sense and extent of grief being suffered. Tauseef surrendered himself in the embrace of Tanveer and, after a while, bent on his knees to have a close look at his mother. Tanveer put his fatherly hand on Tauseef's shoulders and urged his getting up. He advised him to get Chandni out of the vehicle and bring her to the patio. Tauseef complied with him and escorted Chandni to the patio, bypassing scores of ladies reciting the Holy Quran with blazed *agarbatti* (incense) placed in glasses with rice at the bottom to keep them steady. Those *agarbatti*s were emitting mild scented smoke, considered auspicious in the given situation of grief and sorrow.

Chandni was feeling embarrassed for having her trendy makeup and dress in such a tragic setting. She took small steps and stood by the side of her dead mother-in-law. Sensing the uneasiness Chandni was sustaining, Qulsum closed her Quran, came forward, and stood by her side as a silent support.

Moments passed by without any word or action. On being winked at by Qulsum, Tanveer came out of that traumatic mind-set, came close, requested Pori Khala's presence, held Chandni's two hands with all emotions, and said, "Our dear mother has left us permanently, but she perhaps had some premonitions last evening. Last afternoon, Mother called all of us, including Pori Khala, and, among others, blessed you both with all earnestness. She was elated, knowing your acts and deeds, and accepted you as the dear daughter-in-law of this noble house. She performed a given number of *nafal namaz*, beseeching success and happiness for you both."

Saying those introductory words, Tanveer put Chandni's right and left hands on the respective hands of Qulsum and Pori Khala and said, "Qulsum, you are a good friend and well-wisher of Tauseef. Pori Khala, you are not Tauseef's mother but brought him up with all motherly care. So I implore you both to usher Chandni inside as the new daughter-in- law of Biesh Moisher Bari with the grace and dignity she deserves. We both, with the help of Badsha Chacha, will ensure proper pending arrangements for mother's timely burial."

As pre-burial rituals except *ja naza* (prayer prior to burial) were completed, both brothers came near Mother's body to have their final looks before the shroud covered her face. Tauseef was shaking with grief for not having seen his mother alive since before his wedding. He genuflected, thanking Mother silently for her prayers and blessings, and bent himself farther down to kiss her forehead. Uncontrolled teardrops swamped his cheeks, with a few drops gracing her forehead.

Changes omnipresent in fruition and breathing are dictates of nature that make life what it is all about—challenging, defying, indeterminate, bewildering, and frustrating, coupled with happiness when things entail positivity or await the tide as time elapses. However, an innate feature of living is to resist initially anything new or any trend of change. Comfort of known locus, fear of the unknown, and a sense of prestige and protection built around are some of the influencing factors. But in life, changes are inevitable. Divergent views may dominate innate decisions, but inevitability cannot be repelled. Changes creep in in spite of conscious efforts otherwise. Against that backdrop, Biesh Moisher Bari continued to remain relevant with all its tradition and glory, premised on new realization and fresh focus.

Edwards Brothers Inc.
Ann Arbor MI. USA
January 2, 2018